The Way from Here

Also by Jane Cockram

The House of Brides

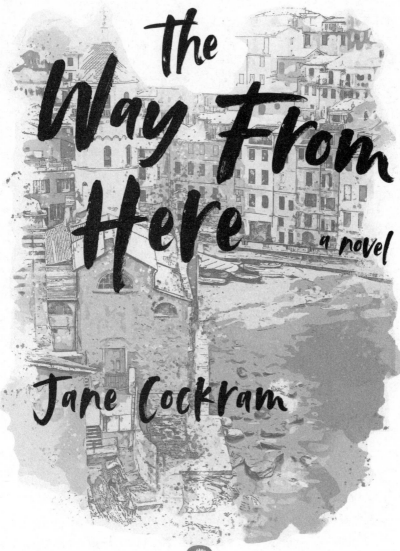

the Way From Here

a novel

Jane Cockram

HARPER

An Imprint of HarperCollinsPublishers

THE WAY FROM HERE. Copyright © 2022 by Jane Cockram. All rights reserved. Printed in the United States of America. No part of this book may be used or reproduced in any manner whatsoever without written permission except in the case of brief quotations embodied in critical articles and reviews. For information, address HarperCollins Publishers, 195 Broadway, New York, NY 10007.

HarperCollins books may be purchased for educational, business, or sales promotional use. For information, please email the Special Markets Department at SPsales@harpercollins.com.

FIRST EDITION

Designed by Leah Carlson-Stanisic
Illustration by Destiny/AdobeStock

Library of Congress Cataloging-in-Publication Data has been applied for.

ISBN 978-0-06-293932-6

22 23 24 25 26 LSC 10 9 8 7 6 5 4 3 2 1

For Wally

The Way from Here

part I

1

Letter One

Dearest Mills,

I must be dead. I can't think how I would have died. Thirty-nine years old and in rude health. An hour of yoga a day and finally kicked the cigarettes—a nasty little habit I picked up in France, but more on that later. It can only have been a horrific accident.

I'm turning forty this year. I always thought I would be fine with that. But as the date gets closer, I'm thinking about the past more than ever. Things that happened when I was nineteen are still as meaningful to me as they were in the moment that they first happened—and the future I looked forward to then hasn't turned out the way I expected. They say youth is wasted on the young, but it feels to me like not a moment is wasted—we carry our youth with us forever. How I felt when I was sixteen, who I loved when I was nineteen, what I regretted at twenty-one—none of this goes away. It's all me, it's all still here.

Mostly I've been thinking about the overseas trip I took the year I turned nineteen. It all comes back to that trip. Things happened on that trip I want you to know about. There have always been things I wanted to explain to you, but words between us have a way of getting tangled up and misconstrued. Of course, I hope you never have to read these letters. I hope we both lead long and fulfilling lives and one day, on the veranda at Matilda Downs, I will gather the courage to tell you my story in person.

But, just in case, these letters are my insurance policy. A promise to myself that one day this story will be told. Even as I write them, I worry about getting the words down right, so I have a crazy idea. Reading the words is not enough. I want you to walk in the hushed halls of the National Gallery of London, to breathe deeply in the salty island air of the Île de Clair and shelter in the green gardens of Pond Cottage. I'm going to ask you to visit these places and do something for me. And because I'm dead and it's my last request, you'll have to do it.

Nineteen ninety-eight. I had just finished school, and you were at university. I convinced Mum and Dad to let me go on a gap year, traveling and working. You were slogging away at your classes during the day and long nights at the little Italian restaurant. I'd just finished thirteen years of school, and I couldn't bear the thought of more study. I had no idea what I wanted to do with my life, but I had a feeling there would be clues for me out in the world, if I could just get out there and find them. You couldn't believe Mum and Dad were letting me go, and what's more, that they were paying for my airfare. I think they were just glad to see the back of me, after the accident. You never considered that, did you?

While I was away, Grandma Nellie sent me letters every week until she died. Newsy, filled with updates on her garden and bridge games, listing who among her many friends had called in to see her and, more importantly, who hadn't. Every now and then she included a check. Talcum powder money, she called it. That's not what I spent it on. As I'm sure you can imagine. Don't tell your mother, she would write, but I remember what it's like to be young and penniless in London.

When we were little, Nellie told us stories of growing up in Ireland with her seven sisters and two brothers, remember? And she told us about traveling to Australia on the steamship, the only woman on board with hundreds of returning soldiers. There were other stories she used to tell me, when you had grown out of listening: tales of wood sprites, fairy gardens, and changelings. One story stayed in my mind long after she told it, and even though every visit I begged to hear it again, Nellie refused to repeat it. It was of a magical house filled with impossible riches by a river where salmon jumped and splashed and children played in the gardens all summer long.

For you, Nellie was just Grandma, old and kind and good at baking scones. But in the letters she sent me when I was in London, she gave away a little about her past. Something in the synchronicity of our stories moved her to tell me about the time she spent in London as a nanny. The smell of the wisteria in hidden laneways, the terror of the blitz, and the feeling of freedom on her days off. If I wrote back with questions, she never answered them. But little by little, we were getting there. There was more she wanted to say.

The last letter she sent was in the summer, just after I turned nineteen. By the time I received it in London, she had died. It was thicker than her normal airmail letters, padded with the inclusion of a newspaper cutting about a painting of a horse. The painting had just been donated to the National Gallery and was available for viewing to the public for the first time. She had seen the painting when she was young, she thought, in a grand house in Devon where she had gone to escape the war. Go and see it, she urged.

It wasn't like her to ask me to do anything. She always let me follow my twisty path through life and took my side when Mum and Dad railed against my lack of direction. I didn't go straightaway. I waited until what would have been the morning after her funeral (back in Australia, I missed it, as you know). Some people light a candle in memory of their loved ones; I was going to visit a painting of a horse.

Things would have turned out differently if I hadn't visited on that day. I would never have met him at all. But because I went on that day and because I met him, I convinced myself that it was a sign from Nellie, rather than the dumb luck it really was. But I'm getting ahead of myself.

When I came back from Europe in 1998, you knew that I was different, that the trip had changed me. Mum asked me what happened and I lied to her; you knew better than to ask. I had my heart broken on that trip, and it never properly healed. It started that morning in the National Gallery, and it became something bigger than me, outside my realm of experience and understanding. You'll be able to work it out though, Mills. If something happens to me before I find the courage—or the money—to go back myself, I know you're the best person for the job. You're smart—and, well, you've got skin in the game, as they say, even if you don't know it yet.

Things have been tricky between us lately, Mills. I'm sorry about what happened at Timmy's party. I honestly didn't realize that your friends had only recently separated. Two to tango, yada yada. But I know it's not just that. I've let you down over the years. But we've had some fun, haven't we? I'm thinking of the time you split up from your boyfriend at university (the only one you had before Ian, can't remember his name, the yawn fest?) and we went out together for two whole days and nights. My favorite memory of you is on the dance floor about twenty-four hours in, arms spread out wide and your whole face lit up by the music, the feeling of freedom. After that night, you shut that vibrant being inside you away again, but I know she's in there. Waiting to be let out.

I'm sure you're still the same Camilla you were when we were kids—determined, smart, and caring. Remember when I broke my arm trying to scale a boab? You made a splint for me with a branch and your jumper and chatted to me all the way home, distracting me from the bone sticking out at my elbow. When we got back to the house, you burst into tears as soon as you saw Mum. You were strong until you didn't have to be. Well, you don't have to be strong anymore, Mills. I think something is going on with you and Ian. I wish you could tell me, I wish we could talk about things the way we used to. But maybe if you know more about my story, then you will go easier on yourself. Remember what my friend Leonard says about how the light gets in.

The preparations for my fortieth birthday party have started. I'm planning a party in the garden. Even though the nights are chilly, I'll have fire pits and fairy lights and people will keep warm by dancing. There's lots to do.

Saturday, 6th July. I hope you'll come to the party with Ian and the boys, or alone. Who knows? Maybe I'll talk to you about all this then. Maybe I'll admit my morbid plan to you, and we will laugh and drink champagne at night and in the morning we will dance barefoot under the canopy of the Moreton Bay fig. There's every chance I'll destroy these letters before you ever have a chance to read them.

But if something does *happen . . .*

Read these letters. Read them in order. I have numbered them, and I have written on the envelope the location where I would like them to be read. And because I know you may see this as yet another example of my grandiose ideas and hyperbolic nature, I am going to assign you a task. I know how you can never say no to a task. (Alphabetized bookshelves, wardrobe spreadsheets . . . hmmm?)

In the event of my death, there will be ashes—I've been clear all my life that I want to be cremated. No boxes in the ground for me. I would like you to scatter my ashes. Scatter. The word seems wrong here, random. Especially as I know precisely the four places I want you to take them. London, Île de Clair, and Devon. The fourth is Matilda Downs. These places made me who I am—good and bad.

So do this for me, Mills. It has to be you. Not just because I don't have anyone else I can ask, but because this might just fix things for us. I know you may never read these letters. I know they are more for me than for you. Midlife crisis etc. But just in case. I want you to know what I know and see what I've seen. I want you to do this favor for me, and I want to know that the daring girl inside you might have one last chance to break free.

There are six letters in all. This one and five more. Take them all with you and head to the National Gallery in London. I'd give you recommendations for a hotel, but I don't think you'd enjoy the flea-ridden hostel I stayed in when I first arrived. Maybe you could splash out a bit of the cash you have been sensibly saving all your life and book a nice room somewhere.

There's another letter for you to open inside the gallery.

Travel safe, Mills. I love you.

2

Camilla

Six letters. Camilla counted and recounted the envelopes, and still she came up with only five. Math had never been Susie's strong point, but neither was letter writing, and yet here she was, reading Susie's epistolary legacy. Susie's friend Nina had been vague on the phone, noncommittal: "It's all in the letters," she had said, and then they arrived, sealed and withholding their secrets. Susie's secrets.

The arrival of the letters had nothing on what followed them in the mail a few days later. Even though Camilla was expecting the ashes to be sent directly from the funeral home, it was still a shock when they arrived. More than a shock. A deep, visceral punch. The appearance of the solid cardboard box, filled with her sister's ashes, represented a line in Camilla's life—the time before Susie was dead and the time after it.

Susie's death was a surprise. The day before she was due to turn forty she had been climbing a ladder to string up lights for her birthday party. The ladder tipped, and she fell, hitting her head on the rocky edge of a flower bed. But the particulars of her death were not surprising, not to Camilla. The ladder—missing a rung and with no safety catch—had been rescued from a neighbor's rubbish pile. A ladder! For free! Susie would have seen it as treasure. Her housemates were working, and rather than waiting for them to come home and help, she had climbed the ladder and attempted to hang the lights on her own.

Susie had spent her whole life dancing with the vagaries of chance and luck. The tires on her car were bald and her health insurance unpaid, but she would always score a bargain last-minute deal on flights or meet someone who knew someone who could introduce her to someone. It was a series of hits and misses, and there had been no one there to rescue her on this final miss.

What was surprising was the discovery of these letters. The letters suggested forward planning, introspection, neither of which were attributes Camilla associated with her dear baby sister. It made the letters much harder to ignore. They were carefully labeled, numbered, and, from the one Camilla had read so far, utterly Susie: revelatory, intriguing, and a touch scatterbrained.

And Camilla's response to the letters was utterly Camilla. She had done exactly what was asked of her. She had gone to London.

That first morning, Camilla walked from her hotel in Earl's Court along the Cromwell Road, past the National History Museum and the Victoria and Albert Museum and Harrods, then cut around the front of Buckingham Palace on a carefully planned route to check as many landmarks off her spreadsheet as possible. By the time she got to St James Park, she was boiling, her list was a sweaty mess, and all the thoughts she had been trying to suppress were crowding back into her mind. She needed a rest, so she sat down on one of the few unoccupied park benches.

Why was it so *hot*?

Across the park, the line for the War Rooms snaked away from the entrance and down the street. Any ideas she had of taking a quick detour and popping in for a visit were dashed. She groaned and placed a question mark—in pencil, just in case—against the War Rooms on her spreadsheet before fanning her face with it. She needed a hat, but she didn't have a hat. Who brings a hat to London? Camilla had ashes. That's what she had. Ashes.

By instinct her hand went to her bag to check on them. Three bags of her sister's ashes. Before she left home, she had gritted her teeth and scooped out enough to half fill the bags, telling herself it was only sand and not really tiny little sprinkles of her sister. At one point during the grim task, she had felt nauseous and dry retched. Needed to take a break. It was the sort of job she would have had her husband Ian help her with, once upon a time.

While her hand was in her handbag, it found its way to her phone. A little look wouldn't hurt. Would it? Recent experience had told her it could, very much. She pushed that thought down and let her fingers wrap around the familiar shape. A quick touch of the screen to wake it up. She wanted the hit of a distraction, the soothing reassurance that someone out there was thinking of her.

Nothing.

She checked the weather app, needlessly. It only confirmed what she could see with her own eyes. A clear day, a gentle breeze. Another swipe to find her calendar. Clear. Nothing to distract her from the task at hand. No messages. No missed calls.

Her fingers tapped out the message before she could stop them. After twelve years of marriage it was instinctive. I've arrived, she wrote, it's hot here! Hello to the kids. I'll call when I get back to the hotel tonight. She hovered over the X key for a moment before quickly pressing send, ignoring the short sharp pain in her heart as the message winged its way to Ian without their customary sign-off. Even though she waited a few minutes, there was no sign of the ellipses. No return message.

Ian had been against the idea of this trip from the get-go—he was always against any of Susie's ideas—so Camilla had pushed the parcel of letters to the back of the linen press and tried to forget about it. It worked, for a couple of weeks. And then the guilt set in. Her sister had asked her to do this one last thing, and she was saying no. Camilla just couldn't say no to Susie. But this trip had been the final straw for Ian. There was no money for the things they wanted as a family—a swimming pool in the backyard, guitar lessons for Oliver—but somehow there was money for this. She thought he would come around; he hadn't.

Theirs had been a happy marriage. Aside from the usual niggles about her long working hours, family life was a peaceful harbor away from her stressful work life. She had never taken it for granted, knowing that the open seas were too much for her and the harbor was what she craved. The trouble was, Susie kept pulling her out into the rough.

As always when she felt unsettled, her fingers automatically moved to her mother's name in her contacts. She hovered her thumb over the call button. Normally she rang her mother every morning. To get an update on the farm, to tell her how the children were doing. To share a podcast recommendation, a recipe. Normally. But it had been two weeks since they last spoke. Sighing, she turned the screen off and tossed the phone back in her tote bag.

Exactly two weeks after Susie's death and a little over two weeks before this day, Camilla returned to the cupboard and retrieved the parcel. First, the envelope marked "Camilla Anderson— to be read FIRST in the event of my death," the one she had already read with her heart in her mouth and shoved into the cupboard with haste, left reeling by the contents. And then another four, all unopened. They had place names written on them: National Gallery, London. Île de Clair, France. Pond Cottage, Devon. Matilda Downs. She moved them to the desk in her study and marveled at how innocent they looked, far from being the grenade she was about to throw into her marriage.

There was no money to accompany the letters. Susie's life had been a series of odd jobs and casual employment: on weekends, she ran a small crêpe stand at the farmers' market near her home, selling her authentic buttery crêpes to loyal customers; during the week, she worked a couple of days as a receptionist for a holiday letting agency. In the last few years she had taken up pottery, and what began as a hobby had transformed into a small business. In one of their last phone calls, Susie proudly told Camilla that she was finally financially secure, that for the first time in her life she had money in the bank. A buffer, she had called it.

When Camilla saw the amount in the account after the accident, she nearly cried. A couple of hundred dollars represented the sum total of Susie's buffer. Susie couldn't have made the journey herself, even if she had wanted to. She must have known that Camilla had a savings account. In her own name, as all the financial planners advised, with direct debits coming out of her paycheck every month.

This final, grand request was pure Susie—dramatic, indulgent, and spontaneous. It was everything Camilla tried to avoid in her safe, suburban life. It was everything that Ian hated about Susie, and the final straw in the breakdown of Camilla's marriage. It was the catalyst for a huge fight with her mother. But the idea of it cracked a window in Camilla's grief and distracted her from the otherwise suffocating sadness of the Susie-shaped hole in her world. There was no way she wasn't going.

Pushing aside her doubts, she put the spreadsheet back in her bag and pulled out the first letter from her sister instead. Taking a deep sigh, she read it again.

3
Camilla

In most parts of Australia, the months December through to February are considered summer. At Matilda Downs, deep in the Kimberley, where Susie and Camilla had grown up, those months are subsumed by something larger: a prolonged wet season that can run from November to April without letting up. Despite this, Camilla still thought of the wet season as the summer. In particular, she thought of the months from December 1997 to January 1998 as the last summer of Susie, because that's the summer the tensions between Susie and the rest of the family boiled over once and for all.

It started out innocuously, as most disagreements with Susie did that summer. The atmosphere in the house was tense, the days after Christmas merging into one another. Four people in cramped quarters made worse by the claustrophobic conditions of the wet season. Even though the property was enormous—Matilda Downs was hundreds of thousands of acres of outback grazing land with wide-open plains, natural swimming holes, and roaming Brahman cattle—the house was small, perched on a high spot above the river, surrounded by a patch of green garden and protected by towering eucalyptus. It was hard to find space to be alone during the wet season.

It was only January; weeks of rain lay ahead. By the time the sisters left the Kimberley for university in March the gorges would be over-flowing, the air a little clearer and the roads almost passable again. But for now, it was humid, the clouds building up all day into spectacular afternoon rainstorms.

Camilla was lying on the floor. It was the coolest spot to be, and Camilla spent most of her free time lying in different areas of the house, moving constantly as the boards below her warmed up and became sticky. She was reading *Emma*, a book she loved and reread every summer. Despite numerous attempts to convince Susie to read it, she had never been successful. This was probably for the best, since Camilla often compared Susie to Emma, a comparison Susie had no reason to believe was not favorable.

Susie flopped down on the floor beside her sister.

"It's too hot," Camilla said, pushing Susie's sweaty body away. Susie ignored her and rested her legs over her sister's. Camilla had their mother's build, tall and elegant, while Susie took after their father. Squat. Muscular. Even the words weren't as kind.

"Can you take me for a drive?" Susie said, resting her head against Camilla's, using a needling voice that she knew Camilla found very hard to resist.

"No."

"Come on, I need to get my practice up. My test is in a few weeks."

"No. It's too wet." Camilla spoke sharply. She was just up to the picnic, a scene she liked to savor.

"It's always wet. I'll never get any practice if you're going to use that excuse." Susie sat up suddenly and looked out the window. "Anyway, it's stopped."

Camilla listened for a moment. Susie was right. The rain had stopped. The only sound was of their parents on the roof. During the wet season they took advantage of every break in the weather to get jobs done. The night before, a leak had developed above the kitchen, and they would be up there investigating. Sure enough, moments later the sound of a hammer against metal started to reverberate through the house.

Camilla did not want to go outside. If their parents saw them, they would draft the two girls into helping. She returned to her book. After another page, she grew aware of Susie staring at her.

"What?"

"It's just they say you should learn to drive in all conditions. What if I break my arm one day, and I need to drive to the hospital but it's raining? Will I just say, 'Oh! I can't drive to the hospital, it's raining'?"

"No." Camilla looked Susie in the eye, laughing. "You'll say, 'I can't drive to the hospital because I've broken my arm.' And then I'll have to come and pick you up and take you, because that's what happens with us."

Susie rolled onto her stomach. They were practically shouting over the hammering now.

"What if . . ."

Camilla threw her book down and groaned. "Stop. Okay. I can't read in this racket anyway. But you have to stay on the driveway."

"Fine!" Susie was already up, dancing on the spot. She held out a hand to help Camilla to her feet.

They snuck out the back door to avoid detection and headed to one of the outbuildings. There was an old jeep there, reserved for driving around the property. Camilla had learned to drive in it when she was a kid, but Susie never bothered. There was no need when Camilla was always around to drive her. But now Camilla was at university, and Susie would be leaving home soon. If she wanted to have any freedom, she would need to get her license.

Trouble was, Susie was a hopeless driver.

The jeep stalled three times before she got it out of the yard. Finally she got the delicate transferral between her foot and the clutch just so, and they lurched forward.

"Quick, put it into second!" Camilla shouted as they began to pick up speed.

"What?" Susie hovered her hand above the gearstick. "Which way is that?"

Camilla put her hand on top of Susie's, momentarily baffled at how her capable parents could have produced such an impractical child. She pushed it into gear. The jeep bounced and then mercifully switched

gears. They eased through the narrow gates and onto the long driveway to the end of the property. It was five kilometers to the main road,
and there was a big area at the end where they could turn around. One
lap, Camilla told herself, and I'm done.

The rain started to come down again. The road hadn't been graded
for months, and the ruts were deep; the jeep started to move of its
own accord, bouncing around between the bumps and sliding along
tracks.

Susie started to laugh.

"Susie, it's not funny." Camilla felt her toes curl up in her shoes,
grabbing at the floor beneath her feet. "Pull over. I'll drive."

"It's fine," Susie said. "It's fun!" The jeep hit a bump and flew up
in the air, landing with a thump. Camilla, not wearing a seat belt, flew
through the air and bumped her head on the ceiling. Susie saw Camilla's angry face and laughed some more.

"Susie, come on!" Camilla grabbed the armrest, hanging on until
her knuckles hurt. They coasted down the road a bit farther. There
were paddocks on either side of the driveway, mostly empty at this
time of the year. The only animal they kept this close to the house
was their mother's beloved horse, Pilgrim. The wipers on the old jeep
didn't work that well, and the sound of them screeching ineffectually
across the glass was audible even over the rain.

"I've got the hang of it now!" Susie shouted, looking over at Camilla
for confirmation. The jeep sped up as she moved through the gears.

"Watch where you're going," Camilla said, her teeth gritted. She
wasn't going to let Susie talk her into something against her better
judgment like this again. She was twenty-one now, officially an adult.

"There's nothing out here, remember, Mills?" Susie twisted the
steering wheel from side to side. "Nothing to hit for miles."

The car slipped again, and Camilla squealed. Susie took her eye
off the road and turned to Camilla. "It's okay, Mills, I've got it." She
reached over to squeeze Camilla's leg, and the steering wheel pulled
away from her remaining hand as the car jerked to the side, swerving
off the driveway.

For a few seconds, the two sisters stared at each other in silence.

Then the car plowed through the fence with a hideous sound of metal scraping on metal. Through the noise came the unmistakable scream of an animal, a thump. Darkness flashed past the windscreen, and the car plunged to a stop against a tree.

For a moment, Camilla had forgotten she was even in London. The daydreaming had been happening a lot since Susie's death. More and more, she found herself not just thinking about the past but feeling as if she was actually in it. Mostly she tried to avoid remembering the accident. The silence that followed. The long march back to the house. Waiting with their mother while their dad went out with the shotgun. At the sound of the shot, their mother had walked into her bedroom, shut the door, and not come out again until the morning.

Not long after, Susie had suggested she might go overseas. No one had argued with the idea.

It was the grief, stirring up all the memories. It was always a shock to find herself back in the present, a grown woman. Compartmentalizing had always been one of her strengths, but Susie's death—and the letter in her hands—had weakened the membranes. Her edges felt raw and exposed, as if her insides were on the outside.

Taking one last longing look at the queue for the Cabinet War Rooms, she rubbed out the question mark and replaced it with PM. Feeling satisfied with the new plan, she turned and walked in the opposite direction, the letter balled tightly in her fist. At the edge of the park she hailed a black taxi.

"Hot enough for you, love?" the taxi driver asked as she climbed in and he swerved out into the traffic. She nodded, holding on tight to the loop hanging from the ceiling, letter still clasped in the other hand.

"The National Gallery, please." The National Gallery. Her research told her it was the outcome of the coming together of several serendipitous events in 1823: an art bequest to the nation from a wealthy financier; the repayment of a war debt to England and the subsequent acquisition of a collection of Old Masters. And the home of a painting that was very important to both her sister *and* her grandmother.

It seemed there was so much she didn't know about the pair of them.

They had always been a pair, Nellie and Susie. That hadn't bothered Camilla because Camilla paired with their mother, Margaret. Margaret overlapped with Nellie and Susie overlapped with Camilla, in their very own familial Venn diagram. Their father Bill floated around the edges of the family like a mathematical exception.

"Should be a bit cooler in there on a day like today," the cabdriver said, interrupting her reverie. "I might join you." For a moment she paid attention to the streets unfolding around her, until they entered an enormous roundabout without slowing down. She closed her eyes, bracing for impact, as her body was flung from side to side around the curves. Then, just as quickly, the car stopped at a traffic light. Camilla opened her eyes, remembered to breathe.

"Are you in town for long?" the cabdriver asked.

"Not long, no. Just a few days." Camilla's voice was clipped.

"Only a few days, eh? Been to London before, have you? Just a fly-by-night visit this time, is it?"

"No, no, I've never been before." Camilla hadn't really been anywhere. "I've always been too busy working to travel. My sister was the traveler. That's why I'm here, you know. To scatter her ashes."

"Ooooh, that's a good one, I haven't heard that before." The driver slowed down as a cavalcade of shiny Range Rovers passed. "There goes Princess Anne."

Camilla leaned closer to the window. "Is it really?"

The taxi driver ignored her. "Ashes." A disbelieving shake of the head.

"I know. It's crazy." Camilla's voice stuck in her throat. The taxi driver watched her carefully in the rearview mirror as he slowed for yet another set of traffic lights. They must be nearly there now.

"Isn't it. Isn't it." His voice was somber, gravelly with resonance. "You must have been very close."

"Yes." Camilla looked down at her hands. "No . . . I thought we were." She was going to cry.

The driver shifted in his seat. Camilla continued anyway. "It turns out she wanted to tell me something, all this time, and I was oblivious. Oblivious! I didn't know anything." She let go of the letter a moment to retrieve a tissue from her handbag, catching sight of the meter as she did. The frightening amount stopped the tears in their tracks. "Are we nearly there?"

"It's all right, love. We're nearly there."

Camilla sat back. "Her name was Susie. Susanne. But we all called her Susie. She came to London in 1998, and she wasn't the same when she got back. Turns out she had her heart broken." Heartbreak. It sounded minor and pedestrian when she said it aloud. Not like the sort of thing that would necessitate the rapid mobilization of your nearest and dearest after your death. It was just like Susie to take a heartbreak and turn it into a life-changing catastrophic event. Camilla sighed. Susie was hard to explain.

The driver chuckled. "Haven't we all?"

"Something must have happened." She was trying to convince herself just as much as the driver. "It can't have just been a heartbreak. Susie wouldn't send me across the world for a heartbreak." She rested her head against the window. The cool glass felt good on her face. "She said I had skin in the game."

"Here we are!" There was a wary tone to his voice. "All right, then?"

"Oh, yes, right." It took her a moment to find her wallet in her cavernous travel bag. Finally, her fingers met the soft leather, and she paid the fare with some of the crisp pound notes inside it.

Camilla made her way across the busy square toward the gallery and looked up at the vast columns. Normally this sort of building would reassure her, with its sense of history and order; it had borne witness to plenty of events more momentous than the arrival of Camilla Anderson with her sister's ashes. But it still felt as if the stern facade was singling her out as she approached.

It had been a long time since nerves had overtaken her body like this. When she started teaching, she sometimes felt them at the start of a new school year. All those expectant faces looking up at her. Not anymore. First-day nerves were a thing of the past when you had been teaching as long as she had. She grabbed hold of the shoulder strap of her bag and tried to stop the shaking.

The main entrance hall of the gallery was cavernous and filled with people. Camilla climbed the vast steps leading up past dark columns and under domed ceilings, trying not to gape. Susie lived in a dilapidated Queenslander, drove an old Subaru station wagon; she reused, recycled, avoiding buying new things as much as possible. The National Gallery didn't feel like a Susie kind of place. Camilla was expecting everything to fall into place when she got there, but the grandeur of the setting left her even more confused.

She walked over an intricate tiled floor, recognizing it as the Anrep mosaic from her research. The depiction of Winston Churchill raising his hand in defiance was somehow comforting, and she took a deep breath before claiming her place on a bench seat alongside a younger woman and child in a stroller. London, for Camilla, was becoming a city of benches.

"It's lovely, isn't it?" the young woman remarked, peeling a banana. "It's my favorite thing here, and it's not even on a wall."

"The Anrep mosaic," Camilla murmured, scanning the floor until she felt she had given it sufficient attention to justify turning her attention to the letter in her bag. Still, she felt the eyes of the young woman on her as she opened the envelope. Apart from the letter, there was a photo. It was dark, blurry, and out of focus, a photo from the predigital era. A painting in a dark room. Something colonial, maybe. Pastoral. A horse?

"My favorite too," the young woman said, pointing to the photo with her banana peel.

"Oh." Camilla tilted the photo away. "Yes. It's lovely."

The woman started to speak again, but Camilla turned her body away to read the letter in peace. Thankfully, the woman got the message and began to feed her son chunks of the banana. The smell was nauseating. Camilla had never liked banana, a repulsion born from years in classrooms overtaken by the smell of the ripe fruit in students' backpacks.

Breathing through her nose, she began to read.

4

Susie, 1998

Susie always associated the death of her grandmother Nellie with meeting David for the first time. They were connected in her heart from the very first instant. Without Nellie, she wouldn't have met David. The heart knows, as Nellie would say, patting Susie's hand with her own, its papery-thin skin laced with veins.

When Susie was a girl, Nellie lived far away in a big city. The journey to Matilda Downs was long and arduous, so when Nellie came to visit, she would stay for weeks. The year Susie was eleven, the rains came early and Nellie stayed for the entire wet season. It was one of Susie's happiest memories, the time when Nellie came to visit and didn't go home. Camilla, thirteen that year, had her nose buried in books, but Susie preferred Nellie's stories at bedtime. Nellie would sit on Susie's little iron bed and rub Susie's back until her breath lengthened and deepened and she drifted off to sleep, listening to her grandmother's tales of other worlds and times.

Susie was alone in London when Nellie died. It was Camilla who rang with the news, half dazed with the shock and grief of it, her trepidation about telling Susie making her voice crack and stumble. The conversation was quick, after the details were given—she died in her sleep, her long battle with bone cancer finally taking her breath in the night—and once Camilla hung up the phone, Susie sat in silence, feeling more alone than she'd ever thought possible.

Nellie was her favorite person in the world, and now she was gone. There would be no one now to listen to her stories of woe, to help her out of scrapes. No one to forgive her, especially in the times when no one else would. Nellie was her harbor in a storm. Whenever she was in trouble, she stayed with Nellie, sleeping in her tiny second bedroom, in the same single bed with the candlewick bedspread that her mother had slept in, growing up.

The day after the accident with Pilgrim, Susie had phoned Nellie. After she listened to Susie tell the story, Nellie was quiet for a moment, thinking. Susie could just see her sitting by the little stove in her kitchen, weighing up the story. Finally, she spoke. "You made a mistake, Susie, but you're not on your own there. Your mother has her own demons. She will come to forgive you eventually. Come and stay with me as soon as the rain eases." And Susie had gone, and after a couple of days with Nellie, the world had looked brighter. Now where would she go for comfort? Without Nellie in the world, she might have to finally grow up.

By the time the gallery opened the morning after Nellie's funeral, Susie had been sitting outside for hours listening to her Discman. The coolness of the gallery was welcome after the oppressive heat of the morning, and Susie took her time wandering. The perspiration on her neck cooled to a chill, reminding her of something else Nellie used to say: "Horses sweat, men perspire, women *glow*." Everything over the course of those few hot London days came back to Nellie.

Eventually, after a few hours of wandering through the galleries, she came across the painting her grandmother had sent her to see. It was large, much bigger than Susie was expecting. There was no house in Susie's frame of reference with a wall big enough to hold such a painting. What sort of people had Nellie been mixing with during the war?

There was a leather bench some distance back from the painting, away from the crowds. Susie took the last remaining space, nestled between an old man who seemed to be sleeping and a young man who also seemed to be—no, wait—was definitely asleep. She paused and let her eyes run over the younger man, momentarily distracted by his looks and the ease of him. It wasn't normal, to sleep in a gallery, was it?

Susie tried to summon memories of Nellie, but between the spaced-out tones of Massive Attack on her Discman and the close proximity of the sleeping men, her mind wasn't cooperating. Even as she pictured Nellie playing old Irish songs on the piano or leaning over her front gate on a warm summer evening, her mind kept coming back to the young man beside her.

She opened one eye to check that he was still there.

Yes.

Meeting men in London hadn't been a problem for Susie so far. At least once a week, she would have a drink after work with one of the pub's customers. Chloe, who worked alongside her at the pub, had a raft of friends and was happy to make introductions for her new Australian friend. It was, as her father would say, like shooting fish in a barrel. But this was different. Broad daylight, no alcohol involved, an art gallery. Susie was out of her depth.

They sat for a while longer, an incidental trio. Hitting play on her Discman for the second time, she looked at the painting in front of her. It was definitely the one from the newspaper article. She pulled the newspaper cutting out of her bag, where she had tucked it between the pages of her book. *Sophie's World.* She had read only the first few pages, but so far it had started a few conversations with men on the Tube. Jeremy. Lewis. They both turned out not to have read much of it either, but the dates had been fun. Leaving the book on the seat next to her (just in case the sleeping guy was a reader), she unfolded the cutting, held it up in front of her. Bingo. Perfect match. A big painting of a horse.

Camilla and their mother shared a love of horses. In the Kimberley, that wasn't so rare. But Susie wasn't interested. She never had been. Camilla and Margaret were drawn to the horses in a way that united them. They could ride out together for days, unrolling their swags and sleeping under the stars, as easily as they could murmur in the ears of the older workhorses. Soft, encouraging whispers. Horses were how they steadied themselves, how they celebrated, and how they came together.

It was just another way that Susie felt on the outside. "You'll find your thing," Nellie would say down the line, when Camilla and Margaret left for another of their rides. "Everyone has something." But as Susie got older, she felt less certain she was going to find it and more certain that if she did, it wouldn't be anywhere near Matilda Downs. She didn't think it was going to be in this gallery either. Unless her thing turned out to be the good-looking guy beside her.

From the sideways angle, he looked slightly older. Lovely olive skin, slight crinkles at the corners of his eyes even in repose. The usual guy outfit. Jeans, even though it was warm; a T-shirt so worn out and faded that she could imagine the softness against her own skin. Trainers. Adidas. They were all anyone wore. Susie had spent her first paycheck from the pub on a pair of cherry-red Gazelles. She edged her feet toward him slightly, and his eyes snapped open.

His mouth started to move, but no sound came out. The music! She reached down to press stop as his arm came toward her. Was he about to take her hand, right there in the gallery? She was looking pretty good, she thought, for someone coming out of a long London winter, but her hair was a little wispy from the walking, and she wasn't wearing any makeup. Their hands reached the Discman at the same time, his cool against hers before he smiled apologetically and pulled it away. He pointed at the stop button and shrugged. Susie slid the headphones off her head, trying to flatten any flyaway hair in the process.

Nellie wouldn't begrudge her a quick flirt. After Nellie's lover died in the war, she would twist her Claddagh ring and say she'd had her great love and she needn't worry with all that anymore, but she was still a hopeless romantic, always relishing hearing about Susie's misadventures in love. Apart from the one particular misadventure that had tested the boundaries of their grandmother-to-granddaughter relationship—but they had agreed never to discuss *that* incident again.

"Sorry!" he said, holding up both palms. "I thought maybe . . ." He stopped, his cheeks a little red.

"It's okay." Susie smiled and looked him directly in the eye. He broke the eye contact first, but not in a way that made Susie think she had disarmed him. More like—and Susie wasn't sure about this, having never encountered it previously—disinterest? She was mulling this over when he surprised her by speaking again.

"What do you think?"

Susie swallowed. She wanted to say something smart here. The art-world equivalent of reading *Sophie's World*. "I think he looks scared."

"Scared?" The guy turned his body toward her, his knees getting close to Susie's. "Interesting. Most people see this painting as an expression of freedom, a horse without its owner. See"—he leaned even closer, still looking at the painting—"no bridle, no saddle. No master."

Susie nodded. She could see that. But she could also see the raised forelegs, the shadow of worry in the horse's eyes. If she closed her own eyes, she knew the memory of Pilgrim would come back. The crash of metal. The high-pitched squeal. Human or animal, she still wasn't sure.

"You know the artist used to hang horses up so he could learn to draw every part of their anatomy. Sometimes he even cut them up."

Susie shuddered. The guy registered the repulsion on her face. "He was trying to learn more about the world around him and hoped to share what he learned with others," he added. "That's not such a bad thing, is it?"

"My grandmother suggested I come here. She knew I appreciate fine art." Her eyes watered a little at the lie. The closest they got to fine art at Matilda Downs was repainting the garden fence each dry season.

Even though they were talking quietly, the old man on the other side of Susie opened his eyes and glared at them.

"I come from an artistic family as well," the younger man said, gesturing for Susie to move a little closer to him and away from the older man, who was now sighing heavily at their continued conversation. "Makes it hard to have a normal life." He put his hand out at an awkward angle. "David," he said.

Susie shook it. "Susie."

"We have some other pieces by the artist at home," David said, talking very quietly now. "Not so grand as this one, but some of the lesser-known pieces. Sketches. I sometimes come here when I want to be near them but I can't bear another of my mother's lectures. She wanted me to be an artist, you see."

"We don't have a lot of art at home," Susie conceded, thinking of the lone piece of art at Matilda Downs, an amateur watercolor left behind by the previous owner. "So I don't know why my grandmother wanted me to come here."

David took the clipping from Susie's lap. "I think I know why your grandmother sent you here." He folded it up and tucked it back between the pages of her book, tapping the cover in recognition. Susie's heart started to beat a little faster.

"Why?"

Finally he turned to look at her properly. "You're far from home, right?"

Susie nodded, feeling the full heat of his scrutiny. Something flickered in his eyes, a moment of recognition. Susie felt it too. The feeling that they were meant to meet, the connection immediate and preordained.

"If I had a daughter—" He paused, swallowed. Maybe even blushed a little.

"I don't, by the way." A blush. "If I had a daughter—or granddaughter—and I was sending her out into the world, I would want her to seek out art. I would tell her to come with questions but also to listen. And I would not want her to read the little signs. Not to start with."

"The little signs? I make all my decisions based on little signs," Susie said, surprised. Coincidence. Astrology. The direction of the wind. So far it had worked well for her.

"I mean the actual little signs on the wall."

"Oh. Right. Anyway, my grandmother knows I'm not mad on horses. I mean, I can imagine her sending my sister here. But me?" She let the question hang in the air as the image of Pilgrim up on his hind legs came back into her mind. The fear in his eyes. She swallowed hard to make it go away.

"Or she wants you to feel like the horse does in this painting, experience life without a master. She imagines you heading off into the world, strong, independent, and with intent."

"And scared."

David looked at her carefully, like he was trying to work something out. A cloud passed over his face. "Why not? It's good to be a little afraid." His words were unconvincing. He smoothed his hands down the front of his trousers and stood up.

Susie cursed herself for the brief show of vulnerability. She had broken the spell, and now he was going. "David," she said, carefully packing her belongings into her backpack as if she had been planning on leaving all along. "Would you like to go for a drink?"

5

Letter Two

Dearest Mills,

If you have followed instructions—do I even need to write that?—you will be sitting in the National Gallery now. I'm picturing you at the entrance to the gallery, maybe sitting on one of the benches at the top of the steps, having walked over the Anrep mosaic without even noticing it.

It's quite a powerful feeling to think that even though I'm dead, I'm still able to make you do my bidding. Ha! Just joking, Mills, you know I am.

The thought that something has happened to me and someone (I'm thinking Nina, I will tell her where to find them) has given these letters to you and, after all of that, you, Camilla Anderson, who hates to leave her comfort zone, is now standing in the National Gallery in London, because I asked . . . While I'm marveling at the wonder of that, Mills; you take a minute to soak it all in. Don't *ask for a map just yet. Just wait and watch and imagine me there, nineteen years old and full of wonder.*

Massive Attack was playing on my Discman as I walked into the front hall, head craned to take in the glorious architraves, nearly tripping over my own feet as I climbed the stairs without looking down. On that first visit, I meandered through the galleries, stopping when something really grabbed me. Even though I wanted to find the painting Nellie had sent me to see, I took my time, marveling at the storytelling of the Hogarths, the light and dark of the Caravaggios. Finally I came across it, enormous against the end wall, a small crowd gathered around it. A spidery thread of gratitude connected me back to Nellie, a sharp feeling of her presence beside me as I pushed through wafts of strangers' perfumes to get as close as possible. And then I stepped back again, for it was a painting to be appreciated at a distance.

Now, I know that approach won't suit you. I know you will go straight to the information desk and ask for directions in your most polite teacher voice. You'll nod to show you understand as they're being given. Perhaps you'll even sketch out your route on the map they will give you. There's no way you will stop and be distracted by the voluptuous figures of the Botticelli or the silvery Turner landscapes. You will do what you're told and head straight up the stairs and through the rooms with the bluish walls, and you will see it. And there's nothing wrong with that. We're different. And that's okay.

Why did Nellie want me to see this painting? I wondered too. What did she think I would gain from seeing it, years after she thought she had seen it in her youth? I think she was gearing up to tell me something about her past, and maybe she thought if I saw the painting I might start to ask the right questions. Kind of like what I'm doing to you, now.

I might never have asked the questions had it not been for some fortuitous timing. A collision of all the magic of coincidence. Fate. Kismet. All the good things.

Because that was where I met David.

God! I'm right back there! While I've been writing this, the sun has set and the room has gone cold and I. Haven't. Even. Noticed. You never mentioned the strange creep of nostalgia that grows stronger as you near forty—or didn't you feel this way? I suppose it's hard to feel nostalgic for long study sessions in the university library and getting the exact teaching role you wanted right out of college. Nostalgia is laced with sadness and regrets. The could-haves and should-haves. Do you have any of those, Mills?

Meeting David was like finding a piece of myself. Growing up, I felt so different from you and Mum—your can-do, stiff-upper-lip mentalities and your pragmatic outlook on the world. My skin always felt thinner, my nerves sensitive to all the good and bad in the world. David let me show the softer side of myself, let me open myself up to newness. I didn't know on the first day in the gallery what he would come to mean to me.

I wanted you to come here and feel what I felt at the start of my adventure. Hope. Excitement. Possibility. I felt as if the top of my head had been pulled off and light was pouring in. It was amazing. It was so, so good before it all turned bad. But there's no way I can ask you to sprinkle ashes in the National Gallery. For one thing, they'll get swept away by nightfall, and for another, there's always someone watching in there.

Head out into the parks—I don't mind which—and think of me there, lying in the sun with David, drinking wine and talking, talking, talking, my head exploding and my heart full, and then leave a little piece of me there.

And when you've done that, I want you to take me to France. To the Île de Clair, to be exact. That's where it gets serious.

Safe travels.

All my love,
Susie

6

Camilla

Ha! Camilla flapped the letter in outrage. She *had* noticed the floor. She had *admired* the special floor. The Anrep mosaic was on her list of notable things to see while she was at the gallery. It was on the spreadsheet, on the London tab, along with the Tower of London, a show in the West End, Buckingham Palace. The Churchill War Rooms. She had designated two nights and two days for London, and she had already used up one night (fallen asleep on her hotel bed before dinner and not woken until the early hours of that morning) and was halfway through day two already. If she didn't have the spreadsheet, she wouldn't get through everything she needed to see.

Her hands shook as she pushed the paper back into the envelope, tearing the seams, finally tossing it aside in frustration. France! She knew it was coming; she had seen the other envelopes—London, France, Devon, home; but she'd expected more than a quick visit to a gallery, a cursory nod to an equine portrait. She wanted closure, goddammit! It all seemed so arbitrary and profligate and so unlike Susie. Susie, who always offset her flights and deliberated over nonessential travel, had sent her to see a picture in London with a sweet accompanying story about lost love.

Camilla knew the painting wouldn't have the same effect on her.

She just wasn't the sort of person to be moved by art. Sometimes, deep down, she admitted to herself that she didn't even really *get* music. But that wasn't the sort of thing you could say out loud. It wasn't acceptable not to be moved by art. Especially not in her job. She had to pretend a lot. Every year she pretended as she opened the school art show. She pretended as she allocated more money to the music program and encouraged broad career choices. Stick with science, she wanted to shout. Math will never let you down! And now she was being directed by her dead sister to appreciate art.

But here she was, in the fifth-most-visited art museum in the world (she had googled it; it went without saying she had never been to the four in the top spots either), and she would do what she was told. While she waited in the queue at the information desk to get her map, Camilla looked around at all the people, cherishing the feeling of anonymity. She let go of a deep breath, and another one, feeling some of the stored-up tension leaving her body. Finally, when she was feeling almost light-headed, it was her turn.

"Hello, I'm looking for this painting." She pushed the photo across the desk toward the attendant, her accent bouncing off the hard surfaces. He looked down at the photo, his eyebrows raised. No response.

"I think it's up on the right?" she asked. Her hand twitched toward the pile of maps stacked on the counter. She knew she would be able to work it out for herself in moments but Susie's letter had left her feeling self-conscious and second-guessing all her instinctive behaviors.

"No, it's not."

"Pardon?" She snatched up a map just in case.

"It's not." Was that a smirk on his face? Sometimes Camilla rubbed people the wrong way right from the first moment.

"Oh—well, has it moved?" She attempted to smile, but the man shuddered a little as if frightened.

"You could say that." He tapped his fingers on the desk. "I'm afraid it's not on display at the moment."

"What?" Camilla gripped the counter, her knuckles white, the map forgotten.

"It's been loaned to another gallery." The man looked panicked, registering the rising hysteria in her voice. He spoke quickly, eyes darting around. "We have lots of other rather good paintings here. If you take the stairs up and head through the Barry Rooms, you can see the British portraits. My favorite painting in the whole gallery is by Joseph Wright of Derby—that's worth a look." Camilla looked at him blankly. "Or you can keep walking through to gallery 34 and see where the painting normally is, if that's any comfort to you?"

She gulped. "I came from Australia."

"Yes, we have lots of Australians here. Americans. All sorts. And we also have plenty of paintings." He looked meaningfully at the people queueing behind Camilla.

She tapped the photo on the desk again.

"This one." She pushed it across the desk.

"Yes, I understand." He was struggling to hide his frustration now. "From time to time some of our more important pieces go on tour, and this is one of those times. Now, if you don't mind?"

Camilla stepped back. Bloody Susie! Typical! Sending her halfway across the world to see a painting that was no longer on display! She marched up the stairs and found Gallery 34.

Just as the man had promised, there was a large expanse of wall where the painting had hung. Bare, apart from a small card. "Not on display," it read. Camilla wanted to tear the card off the wall and rip it into tiny pieces. She would have, if it weren't for the rather small woman with an earpiece in the corner of the room, standing with her hands clasped together. The guard looked agile, as if she could cross the room in an instant. Camilla decided not to risk it. Instead she sat down on a bench to think about her next move.

She had done everything she could for Susie. She'd fought all the battles first, growing up, so that Susie wouldn't need to. Ear piercings, school trips, pocket money. She'd taught her to dance. She'd taught her to smoke!

She had driven her to the airport when she set off for Europe in 1998, and then picked her up again on a cold, wintry morning, months before she was meant to return. As they drove through the deserted predawn streets, Camilla had pretended not to notice how wan Susie was beneath her tan, the dark circles under her bloodshot eyes, her nails bitten down to fleshy stumps. Susie had smiled and said she was jet-lagged, and Camilla had believed her. This trip was meant to explain everything.

But all she had gotten was a horse painting. Or, to be more accurate, an empty patch of wall where a horse painting had once hung.

Camilla groaned. There was no way she was telling Ian about this. The worst part of it was that Susie had her pegged. Everything Susie had written in the letters so far was true—apart from the bit about the painting being there and all. She must have known that this would mean nothing to Camilla.

You couldn't just order up an emotional response. If Susie intended for this painting to make Camilla understand how she felt as a young adult, poised on the edge of a life-changing adventure and momentous meeting, it hadn't worked. For starters, the painting was on tour. But Camilla suspected that even if the painting had been there, the result, or lack of result, would have been the same.

She thought about what she knew so far: her grandmother had sent Susie to this spot to see a horse painting. The January Susie left for overseas, there had been the accident with their mother's beloved horse Pilgrim. Then Nellie had died before Susie could ever ask her about the painting.

And then there was David. The name meant nothing to Camilla. Try as she might, she couldn't summon up any memory of a conversation with Susie about any David. And why would Nellie have predicted that Susie might meet him in the gallery? There was every chance that this trip would turn out to be the wild-goose chase Ian had predicted—a series of letters without substance, dragging Camilla from pillar to post, amplifying her grief rather than assuaging it.

At best, she was a glorified courier; at worst, a fool. She had been naive to assume that Susie had changed, that death would have made her less obtuse. Susie might have set her off on this journey, but Camilla would have to take charge, especially if the next letter turned out to be as much of a dead end as the first couple.

Anyway! Camilla forced herself to look on the bright side. She was here, and she had a task. Susie thought she wouldn't be able to scatter the ashes inside, but Camilla had a surprise for her. She placed her bag on the bench and opened it, leaving the letter on top while she took the little linen sack out. The attendant moved positions to the other end of the gallery, talking to an older woman as they both looked at a map. No one was paying any attention to Camilla. She could blend in, in a crowd like this.

She stood up, moving closer to where the painting had once hung, pretending to look at the empty space. She loosened the ties and pushed her fingers and thumb into the grainy ash. It was hard to get a good grip on the stuff, but she pinched up enough to scatter on the floor beneath the empty wall. She was close enough to the adjacent painting to see the intricacies of the gilt frame and to follow the lines of the brushstrokes, and she wasn't sure if the feeling of relief that came as the ashes fell through her fingers was satisfaction at a job well done or the moment she finally came to appreciate art.

Epiphany or not, lunch was in order. Camilla didn't need to check the spreadsheet to know that lunch that day was booked for NOPI. She had cooked from the cookbook endlessly after Ian gave it to her for Christmas; today she would be able to compare her efforts against the originals and see how she'd fared. After lunch she would queue up for the Cabinet War Rooms. Visit Harrods. The Tower of London. A show tonight. And then Buckingham Palace tomorrow before leaving for France. No more art.

She felt a tap on her shoulder.

It was the guard, a reproachful look on her face. Camilla felt other eyes on her as well.

The ashes! Heat rose in her cheeks.

"Excuse me, miss." The woman spoke in a hushed voice, even though all around them people were chattering at normal volume. Camilla looked around for the backup guards, the ones who would march her up to a back office somewhere to review footage of her tipping ashes over the hallowed floors of the National Gallery, but there was no one apart from an older couple who were watching with great interest.

"You can't leave your bag unattended," the guard said, pointing to

Camilla's bag open on the bench, meters away. Camilla waited for her to continue, but the guard just patted her kindly on the arm and moved back to her position.

Camilla opened her mouth in surprise, then nodded. She knew from her experience in the schoolyard that in these types of situations, the less said the better. Keeping one eye on the little pile of ashes, she moved across to collect her bag.

The letter was gone.

7

Susie, 1998

On their third date, David and Susie played tennis at a garden hidden away in the backstreets of Kensington. There had been the drink at the pub after the chance meeting at the gallery (Susie counted this as a date), and then the very next night he had introduced her to chicken tikka masala at a small Indian restaurant (second date). On what was *meant* to be their third date—a trip to the Tate—David hadn't shown up. When he phoned to apologize, Susie played it cool and pretended she had the plans mixed up as well. Her strategy worked; David proposed a game of tennis the next evening and arrived right on time, picnic basket and racquets in hand.

Susie had a good feeling about David, and she had Nellie to thank for all of it. It felt as if Nellie was looking down on her, taking care of things just like she always had. As Susie reflected on the serendipity of it all, David rose on the tips of his toes and launched his racquet through the air to deliver a serve that whizzed past Susie's ear. Her racquet was idle at her side.

"Oh!" she exclaimed. "We're starting?"

Sadly, Nellie hadn't also somehow arranged to improve Susie's tennis skills. She hadn't quite worked out how to tell David she was a god-awful tennis player. But she had wangled a tennis racquet from

Chloe and she was wearing a white denim skirt and a white polo shirt combination that even Chloe conceded looked quite tennis-y. She shifted her weight from side to side while she waited for the next serve, trying to get her grip on the racquet right while David switched sides without even glancing in her direction.

Another ball flew past.

"Will we do best out of three?" she asked as David raised his arm up once again.

He lowered the ball. "As in best out of three games? Or serves? Because if it's serves, then we're already done."

They had been playing for only around thirty seconds. Even Susie realized that it would be bad form to call the game off so early on. Not to mention a waste of a perfectly themed outfit. And she so desperately wanted to impress this guy. So far, two and a half dates and no physical contact. She could not work David out, and she loved it.

"Sure, games!"

"Thirty love." David wiped his brow as he lined up yet again. "You're killing me!" And then he winked. A wink! Susie felt her spirits lift, and this time as the ball came toward her, she took a step back and made contact with her racquet. The shot sailed over the fence and landed on the pristine grass beyond.

"Bit rusty," she said, looking at the strings on her racquet as if they were somehow to blame. Her cheeks were starting to burn a little.

"Forty love."

Susie crouched down on her haunches and waited. This time David landed the ball squarely in front of her, the type of serve you might offer up to a child. Susie rushed toward it, and her feet got tangled up. She hit the ball directly into the net.

"Game," she whispered to herself, because even though her skills were poor, she knew how to score. She had often been relegated to the umpire's chair during school matches.

"Better luck next time," David said, coming around the net. "Do you want to have a break?"

"Is it that obvious?" Susie smiled. "Maybe just a quick sit in the garden." There was a picnic blanket set up under the oak tree, and a basket. The sight of a bottle of white wine sticking out the top gave Susie hope that the date was not dead in the water. Perhaps after a few drinks, her game might improve. It couldn't get any worse.

"Shall we?" David held open the gate and Susie scooted past, terrified he might change his mind and subject her to more projectile balls.

"How do you know about this place?" Susie asked, once they had settled on the blanket and she had a glass of wine in her hand. It was a balancing act, with the short skirt and the full drink, but David didn't seem to notice as he sprawled out next to her. Close. But not close enough. A slight breeze lifted the leaves on the trees above, leaving a gentle pattern as the sun filtered through them onto the grass below.

"My parents live just over there." He tilted his wineglass in the direction of a row of stately looking white-stucco town houses, each with a magnificent front garden and front doors painted in various bold shades. It was hard to determine exactly which one he meant, but it didn't matter. Any house in the street told the same story.

"Did you grow up here?" Susie asked.

"Yes, my parents have lived here since they were married. Before that, it was a family house. It belonged to an aunt. No one in my family buys houses or furniture, they just circulate them around like library books."

Susie thought of the homestead at Matilda Downs. Her parents had bought it on a whim, furniture and all, from an old widower. Matilda Downs was too much for one person. It was too much even for the four of them. There were years when the bank threatened to foreclose, but they always held on, through drought, floods, and fire. It seemed an unimaginable luxury just to have a house handed to you.

"I grew up on a farm in the Australian outback—miles away from anything, anyone. I loved it when I was a kid but as soon as I was a teenager, I was desperate to get out of there."

"Oh, we have a farm too. In Devon."

"Do your parents live here or in Devon?" If they were here, perhaps David would introduce her. That would be a sure sign he was interested.

"They move around a little." He glanced up at the houses. "Things are a little tricky between us at the moment."

"Right," Susie said, inching a little closer. David reached behind him and grabbed the picnic basket, putting it between them. He rummaged for a moment and then produced a breadstick. "Baguette? Cheese? I have some ham as well."

"I'm okay with wine for the moment, thanks," Susie said, hoping the basket would make a swift disappearance. "What sort of tricky?"

"Oh, the usual." David cut the baguette with a special bread knife on a board he had pulled from the basket as well. It looked more appetizing than the soggy packet sandwiches Susie had been living on, but she couldn't change her mind now.

"Things were tricky between my mother and me at the start of the year," Susie started, trying to build a bridge. "There was an accident at home. With my mum's favorite horse." It was still hard to talk about without choking up, and she snuck a glance at David to see if he was listening. He was.

"Is that why you came to London?" he asked. He didn't move the basket, though.

Susie nodded, letting the tears well in her eyes a little. It wasn't too hard; she got teary at the thought of any animal being hurt, regardless of whether it was as beloved as Pilgrim.

"How are things with your mum now?"

"I don't know. She hasn't written to me at all. My grandmother was sending me updates, but she . . ." Now she really had to hold back the tears.

"She what?" David's voice was gentle.

"She passed away last week."

"Oh."

"We were very close."

"And still no word from your mum?"

"No." Camilla had phoned. And then her dad called a few days later, with details of the funeral. "My mum was an only child. Her mother fell pregnant during the war. She moved out to Australia, all on her own, and my mum was born there. It was just the two of them until Dad came along."

"How did they end up in the outback?"

"Mum was a journalist before she met my father. The women's magazine she worked for sent her on assignment to the outback to interview a group of bachelor farmers."

"I can guess what happened next."

"Sounds romantic, I know. It's not." Susie thought of the isolation her parents endured year after year, the constant backbreaking work they did to keep the property running, the letters from the bank that gathered on the kitchen dresser, unopened. Once again, she counted her lucky stars that she had broken free. London. David, maybe. A new life. It dawned on her that Nellie might have felt the same way, moving from Belfast.

"You know, from what my grandmother has told me, I can imagine her here." She looked around again. "This is the London she described. She was a nanny for a very fancy family, apparently."

"Yes, this is certainly the London of dreams." David sighed. Susie realized she had perhaps been waffling on a little too much about her family. Talking about your mother—and your grandmother!—was hardly conducive to romance.

"Let's talk about something else," she said, stretching her legs out.

"I was there at the gallery that day because of my mother," David said. They were sticking with the mother theme, then.

He reached over and pushed the basket out of the way, refilling the glasses at the same time. He brushed her leg with his arm on the way through. Was it on purpose? It was hard to tell. "We had a tremendous fight that day, my mother and I. I went there because that painting reminds me of her. It helps me to remember what her life was like before me, and why sometimes she just doesn't get me at all."

"Oh?" Susie rolled onto her front, but it was harder to drink wine in that position so she rolled back again.

"I've always felt like I don't quite fit in with all of this." He waved an arm around the garden.

"You seem pretty comfortable to me." David couldn't have looked more at ease if he had tried. An air of grace surrounded him at all times, and he seemed just as at home lying on the grass in his faded blue polo shirt as he had fast asleep in the National Gallery.

"I lost my job last week."

"Oh." Susie took a large sip of wine. "So that's why you were in the gallery in the middle of the day."

David raised his eyebrows and took a swig as well. "I went to my mother's looking for sympathy." He shook his head. "Wrong move."

"Was she angry?" Susie asked.

"Angry? Ha!" He kicked off his runners. "She was ecstatic." Susie averted her eyes as he peeled off his socks as well. She had a thing about feet. Didn't like them. Hated them, in fact. No one liked feet. It was hardly unusual. It was too soon for her to see David's feet without the inevitable wave of repulsion that would follow. She looked away, focusing instead on his face. It was a nice face to focus on.

"What happened?"

"With what? My mother?"

"Yes, that. But what happened with your job?" David had told her he was a teacher the first day they met. Art. He worked at a small school in Devon. It sounded like the Enid Blyton books Camilla had always forced on her as a child, frustrated that Sweet Valley High were the only books Susie wanted to read.

"Oh, yes. The usual thing." He rubbed at his chin, thinking. It looked as if it was the first time someone had actually asked him for the details.

"The school I went to was staffed by teachers so old, it seemed like death was the usual thing. I can't actually think of one who was fired. Plenty who should have been, though."

"Differences of opinions, methods. It happens."

"What will you do now?"

"Mum wants me to take some time off teaching."

"Sounds like a terrible fight. The worst." She struggled to keep the sarcasm out of her voice, especially with the creeping effect of the wine. She shuffled over a little toward David, who remained resolutely on the other side of the blanket. There might as well have been an ocean between them.

He rolled a tennis ball across the blanket in her direction. "Why didn't you say you don't like tennis?"

Susie swatted the tennis ball back toward him, regretting it immediately. The action felt too familial, too childish. The age gap yawned wider between them.

"You mean *can't* play tennis?" Desperate to recover the intimacy of moments before, Susie leaned toward him as if she meant to grab the ball back, angling her head so her face was open to his. Their eyes finally connected, a brief moment of friction and a pause, a silence that felt loaded with anticipation. A breeze moved through the garden and a shadow fell over the blanket, making David look away. Something— panic?—flashed through his eyes, and his body stiffened.

Susie turned her head to look behind her just as David spoke. "Mother," he said. "I didn't think you were in town."

8

"Just as you didn't mention you would be in the neighborhood."

David's mother barely moved as she spoke, her body slightly angled toward them, her eyes set on something in the near distance. "Forgive me if I don't clamber down to the grass with you—I've just had my bath. And please, don't stand on my account," she added to the motionless pair. They both quickly leaped to their feet, one of the wineglasses tipping in the process. Susie tried to ignore the trickle of wine heading toward her prized red trainers.

"Mother, this is—"

"Isabel." Her lips pursed as she said the name.

"No . . ." David shifted from one foot to the other. His face was turning red in front of her eyes.

"Susie, actually. Susanne." She stuck out her hand, just as she had been taught, but the older woman didn't take it, her nose wrinkling slightly, whether from distaste at her name or her presence, Susie couldn't tell.

"This is my mother, the . . ." David ran his hands through his hair, looking between the two women. It was as if he had regressed twenty years and was a scared child. Susie wasn't sure whether to feel sorry for him or to make a getaway while she could.

"Please, call me Lucinda." David's mother continued to ignore the hand Susie held out in front of her so Susie dropped it back by her side. "A spot of tennis, I see?"

"Sadly, not my day," Susie began, in an attempt to break the ice and compliment her son. "David thrashed me."

"He *thrashed* you?" Her eyebrows rose.

David coughed. "I've had a lot of lessons."

"This is much more my pace." Susie pointed at the blanket, where the remains of the picnic were slowly being submerged in spilled wine. "Would you like a glass of wine?"

"No." Lucinda looked away.

It was hard not to stare at Lucinda. She was wearing a floor-length white linen dress that would have overwhelmed her skinny frame had she not cinched it at the waist with a Japanese obi. The look was made more dramatic by the silk scarf wrapped around her head, the bright red lipstick, and the golden hoops at her ears. Everything about her seemed calculated to attract the most possible amount of attention; even her posture, two feet firmly planted and one hand on her hip, cried *Look at me!* Susie found it easy to oblige.

"I was going to call in after . . ." David's voice trailed off as Lucinda turned her razor-sharp eye beam on him.

"Your father and I have dinner plans," Lucinda said firmly. "If I'm not mistaken, Susanne, you are quite a bit younger than David. How did you two meet?" She shot a meaningful look that Susie couldn't decipher in David's direction. "You're not English either." A flash of distaste crossed her face and just as quickly was replaced with a smile and a tilt of her head. There was a slight feathering around her mouth where the lipstick bled a little. Susie found if she focused on that imperfection, she felt less intimidated.

"We met at the gallery," she began. "We were looking at the same painting."

"A gallery." Lucinda smiled harder. "Representation, David? I told you Nigel would be happy to take a look at some of your work."

"The National Gallery, Mother." Was it just the afternoon sun, or was he sweating? Susie's face was starting to hurt from the smiling.

"We were looking at a painting," Susie interrupted. "Of a horse. It's—"

"Oh yes, I'm familiar with those sorts of things," Lucinda said. "I just don't know why David is wasting his time in galleries when he has so much work of his own to do."

"I thought you lost your job?" Something was going on between David and his mother, and Susie didn't understand. There was a strange energy, a current that pulsed between friction and actual dislike, made even more unsettling by the smile permanently plastered on Lucinda's face. On all of their faces.

"He lost his job as a teacher, thank God. *That* was a sorry little situation that I'm sure he has filled you in on. And now it's time for his proper work. The art he has been neglecting while he toiled away at that minor school, peddling A-level art history and coaching games."

Susie leaped down and picked up the wine bottle and her glass. "Top up, anyone?" She waved the bottle around and sploshed some in her glass, swallowing a big gulp quickly and trying to ignore the slightly sick feeling in her stomach. David was looking at her; she could feel his eyes on her, but she couldn't bring herself to meet them. Not yet. Not while her feelings were all over the place.

"Susie."

She had to look at him now.

"Yes?"

"I'll have some more wine, please." While she was pouring it into David's glass, their eyes met. David smiled, and Susie felt better. It was okay. Perhaps he wasn't quite so intimidated by Lucinda as he seemed.

"Susie and I are just friends," he was saying. Susie's hand slipped, and the bottle knocked the glass, leaving a chip in the rim.

"Sorry!" she said, snatching it away and replacing it with her own glass. "I'll take the cracked one."

Lucinda's head snapped around. "Are they the Lalique?"

"Not from your set," David said. "These are from Pond Cottage."

Lucinda eyed the glassware suspiciously. She didn't believe him, clearly. "Well, you're one down now."

"It's just a glass." David shrugged, immediately diffusing the situation. "I thought you had dinner plans," he said pointedly.

Lucinda looked up toward the houses. Susie was still trying to work out exactly which one was David's family home. They were all equally impressive, but she particularly liked the one with the shiny black door and the festooning wisteria. Any would do, though. All were a world away from the sagging veranda and rusted-out roof of Matilda Downs. She bet the families inside these houses never had to mend fences or dig out trenches in the wet season.

"Your father takes his time to get ready."

David softened. "How is he?"

"The same." Lucinda reached a hand out to her son. "Please. Promise me you'll think about going."

Susie stood very still. Where was David going? Things were just warming up between them. It was okay for things to move slowly when she thought she had all the time in the world, but now it seemed that David did need to be somewhere. Somewhere he hadn't mentioned. Come on, Lucinda, she urged silently, don't clam up now. Give me a clue. Keep your hand on his arm, keep him talking.

And then—hallelujah! David turned to her and explained.

"Mum wants me to go to France for the summer." He gently removed Lucinda's hand, patting it as he did. "We have a cottage there, on the Île de Clair. She wants me to work on my painting."

"Oh!" Susie said. "France?" The name sparked a yearning in her. It was one of the few subjects she had been good at in school. Not the written assessments, mind you, but the language itself, listening and speaking it, had come surprisingly easy for her after years of struggling with school. Paris was high on her list of places to visit while she was away. "France sounds lovely."

David looked at Susie. "You do mean in general, right? This isn't an invitation. Let me make that very clear." His face was rigid, unkind.

A beat. The sound of a gate closing across the road. A car door. Susie felt a dampness creep down her back. Then, just at the moment it became unbearable, he smiled. A long, slow smile that moved across his face and transformed his features; a smile that had worked for him before. The air between them pulsed with an energy Susie couldn't recognize.

"David! Don't be cruel!" Lucinda swatted at him. Susie had almost forgotten Lucinda was there. She swallowed. If she opened her mouth, she felt sure her voice would betray her. "Susannah was being polite. The Île de Clair has nothing to interest a beautiful young woman like Susannah."

"Susanne. Susie," Susie stammered. "Not Susannah." She watched David carefully. Had he been joking? "It's okay. I know he's teasing."

Teasing.

Two could play *that* game. But no one could play it as well as she did. She smiled innocently at David and then at Lucinda and tried not to let her excitement show. David had invited her to France. She was sure of it.

9

Camilla

The Île de Clair.

Camilla still remembered the first time she heard those words. It was 1998, Melbourne was in the grip of a cold, long winter, and it had been barely a fortnight since their grandmother Nellie died. The phone rang in her share house in the middle of the night and Camilla, knowing straightaway it would be her sister, had shivered down the hallway to answer it. Despite the hour, she'd been thrilled to hear from Susie. Phone calls were few and far between, and they hadn't spoken since the distressing call during which Camilla broke the news about Nellie.

"Mills?!" Susie was shouting.

Camilla pulled the phone with her into the kitchen and shut the door on the cord. "Yes, Susie, I'm here," she whispered. The linoleum in the kitchen was icy underfoot. She shifted her feet to minimize contact.

"I can't hear you, Mills!" Something like a foghorn sounded in the background.

"Where are you?" Camilla said, a little louder.

"I'm at the ferry terminal," Susie shouted again. "Hang on!" There was a shuffling sound and some whispering, and the line became clearer. "Can you hear me?"

"That's better."

"I asked Christian to close the door."

"Christian?"

"The terminal manager—he's letting me use his phone."

Camilla rolled her eyes. No phone boxes for Susie, not when there was a terminal manager around at whom she could bat her eyelashes in exchange for a phone call.

"Why are you hanging out with a terminal manager?" Camilla asked. She wasn't wearing a watch, but the darkness outside the kitchen window told her it was still nowhere near dawn. She needed her sleep for her teaching rounds later that morning. Closing her eyes, she rested her forehead on the wall. She couldn't hang up, not while Susie was grieving the loss of their grandmother, far away and alone.

"I'm not hanging out with Christian, I'm just using his phone. I'm going to France!"

"France?" Camilla eyes popped open. This wasn't the phone call she was expecting.

"France!" Susie squealed with excitement. Camilla felt a sharp stab of jealousy, and not just because her sister seemed to be coping better with Nellie's death than she was. London she could take or leave, but she had always wanted to go to France. It was against the natural order of things, Susie getting to go first. *After my degree is finished,* she promised herself, *I'll go then.*

"What about your job?"

"I'll find one in France."

"You'll need a visa." Camilla twisted the phone cord around her fingers, watching the skin turn white from the pressure.

"Got one," Susie chirped. "Not for working, but I'll sort something out."

"You don't speak French."

"I speak *un peu*," Susie countered. "First prize in the Alliance Française, 1996, don't forget."

"It was hardly a tough field."

"*Mon dieu*, Mills," Susie exclaimed. "Mind your manners! I speak enough to get by."

"Where will you stay in Paris?" Camilla knew she was asking a lot of questions, but details had never been Susie's strong point.

"Oh, Mills, I'm not going to Paris!" An announcement in the background, permeating even the walls of Christian's office. "I'm going to a little island off the coast of Brittany. The Île de Clair."

"The Île de what?"

"Clair—like Claire Mason from school, but without the E."

A feeling of dread settled in Camilla's stomach. Susie had been well set up in London: a job at the pub, a room above it, and new friends. Camilla had liked the sound of Chloe, the English girl Susie made friends with through the pub. This change in plans could only mean one thing.

"It's a guy, isn't it?"

"Mills!" Susie laughed. "It's France! I don't need a reason to go to France."

"I'm right, aren't I?" In the dim kitchen, Camilla could see the stacks of notebooks she had left on the table, ready for some early-morning study. It had been almost midnight when she went to bed, and her alarm clock was set for six. She still had months of classes in front of her before she could even think about taking a weekend off to go somewhere, and even then, she would find it hard to swap her weekend shifts at the café. It was hard not to feel a little bitter.

"Oh, Mills. Nothing has happened yet." Susie sighed. "But there's something really special about him. Hang on, Christian is saying something." Silence. Camilla waited. "My ferry is about to go," Susie said when she finally came back on the line. "Listen, Mills, don't tell Mum and Dad yet. I don't want them to worry."

"You don't want them to flip out, you mean?"

Susie ignored her. "I'll ring them from the Île de Clair when I get settled. Gotta go, Mills, love you!" And she hung up, leaving Camilla wide awake and alone in the dark kitchen.

Camilla had remembered that phone call as she passed through the ferry terminal earlier, imagining her sister making the same journey twenty years earlier. Was Christian still the manager, or had he moved up the ranks to a more important terminal? She had seen a number of middle-aged men in the uniforms of the ferry company, and for some reason the idea that Christian may have been one of them made her feel sad. Another piece of Susie's human flotsam.

Did Camilla have regrets about not getting involved then? Ian had always told her she facilitated Susie's movement through the world. In later years, and as his commitment to therapy deepened, he started to say that Camilla was Susie's enabler. Would Susie's life have been different if more people had said no to her? Camilla could have told her to stay in London, to stick at her job. But she doubted it would have made any difference in the long run.

The buildings of St Aldo retreated in the distance as the ferry pulled away from the mainland, the ocean growing slightly choppier as they moved into open waters. Camilla had slept badly in her tiny hotel room in the port town, but now, sitting on the deck and breathing the sea air deep into her lungs, even the lost letter didn't seem so bad. After all, she had the gist of it. David. Nellie. A painting. She always felt better by the ocean, which was ironic, given that she had grown up in one of the most landlocked places in Australia.

The English Channel. The Île de Clair. France. Camilla never made that trip overseas when she finished university. The last school she did a placement with offered her a job, and she took it. After that, she met Ian, did her master's, had children. The grand European trip was put on hold, to be taken when the children were grown up.

Overseas travel had been limited to a yoga retreat in Bali five years before—with Susie. After five days of breathing in other people's body odor and listening to scratching in the walls at night, Camilla had flown home early. Susie stayed, returning home two months later than planned with a new boyfriend in tow. Camilla hadn't met that one. Or the guy Susie met in India. Nina had told her that Derek was very upset about Susie's death. Camilla didn't even know who Derek was.

And now, another man to add to Susie's back catalogue.

David.

As there were no further clues to his identity, Camilla prepared herself by rereading the limited information she had been able to find about the island. The Île de Clair was the smallest island in a much more populous archipelago; where the others had their own websites, their own Wikipedia pages, and even their own tourist boards, the Île de Clair had none. Most of the details Camilla found were either historical—the islands had played host to everyone from the Celts to Julius Caesar over the years—or ancient mythology cloaked in romantic language, stories of water sprites and changelings mixed with prosaic tales of the derring-do of lighthouse keepers and Breton lifeguards. Over a thousand shipwrecks were scattered around the surrounding seabeds.

Tourists, it seemed, were not encouraged. Which was odd, because when Camilla dug deeper, she found a number of idyllic-looking sandstone cottages available for holiday letting, as well as a youth hostel and a stunning boutique hotel right on the sand. When Camilla saw the rates for the hotel, she swallowed hard before making the booking. She had even paid extra for a water view.

Around her, the ferry was filled with holidaymakers: women dressed in colorful sundresses and children in bright shorts and T-shirts. Camilla had read somewhere that it was best to roll clothes for a suitcase, so she had picked lots of gray and black jersey items from her wardrobe, trousers and tops that wouldn't crush. But among the other passengers she felt dowdy and invisible. They didn't even notice her as they unpacked their generous and well-planned meals. Golden baguettes, thick slices of *saucisson*, and, without fail, an enormous wedge of cheese. Some families had shiny green apples, others baskets of juicy red strawberries. Camilla nibbled furtively at the packet of potato chips bought in haste at the ferry terminal.

She heard shouts of excitement and looked up to see the craggy coastline of the island in the distance. They were maybe halfway through the journey, equidistant between the main bulk of France and the island. It had been a moral battle last night not to rip the remaining envelopes open and devour them in one go. But she was practically there now, wasn't she?

The envelope was in her hand before she even made a conscious decision to retrieve it. *For Camilla Anderson. To be read on the Île de*

Clair, France. The directions gave her pause, and at that moment a wave splashed up against the ferry. The boat shuddered and stalled before pushing on through; large drops of seawater landed on the envelope, smudging the ink that Susie always insisted on using.

"Bugger!" Camilla shook off the envelope and pulled out its contents. There was a letter and some photos. She put the letter aside—safely this time, in her pocket. She would look at the photos now and read the letter later, on the island. That way she was still technically following instructions.

The first photo was a close-up of Susie, her face taking up almost the whole frame, her yellow swimsuit familiar, only a hint of the background peeping over her left shoulder: a brilliant blue sky, the brushy dark green branches of a conifer of some kind. At the bottom corner, a blush of pink cliff. And then, just Susie's face—a lightly freckled, happy young face looking lovingly at the camera—or whoever was holding it. Camilla allowed herself a tiny burst of sadness before turning the photo over. Susie had scrawled some love hearts in pink marker on the back and written "Île de Clair, 1998."

The door behind her opened and slammed. Camilla jumped, scrambling to keep hold of the photos, her hands shaking as she flicked to the next one. Same swimsuit, same summer sky. But this time Susie had her arms around a boy. A young man. David. Both Susie's arms were looped around his neck, like a monkey's, as if she were afraid he would move away, out of the shot. She was always like that, physical. Constantly touching. It could be claustrophobic to be around her sometimes.

David was gorgeous. Dark hair, tanned, lines around his eyes as he squinted into the distance. Only Susie was looking at the camera. Susie had also annotated this one. Same pen. Same writing. More hearts this time. "Susie & Henri, IDC, 1998."

Henri?

Camilla had never heard of Henri. She fetched out her spreadsheet and quickly scrawled "Henri?" just under the "David" she had written the day before. A cloud passed over, casting a shadow over the paper, and for a moment the spreadsheet was easier to read. She double-checked the booking confirmation from the hotel, as well as the tickets for her return ferry in a couple of days' time.

After a moment, she had the unmistakable feeling of someone reading over her shoulder, and she realized that the shadow was made by a human form. She turned her head, but the woman was facing away from her.

Ten minutes or so later the ferry shifted gear and paused for a moment at the entry to a small protected harbor. The horn sounded right above Camilla's head and she jumped, the bundle of photos and her spreadsheet flying out of her hands and onto the damp deck. Rushing to pick them up as the ferry lurched into the dock, she fell forward onto her hands and knees, watching helplessly as the photos spread across the wet deck.

"Ici et la." A young French man in a bright red spray jacket passed her the photos. Camilla snatched the photos back and then, as his face turned from earnest to dismayed, realized she had been abrupt.

"Désolé, désolé!" She frantically rubbed the photos on her jeans, the pink ink blooming across the fabric. "Merci!"

The last photo was soggy, but the image was still clear. It was of four people: Susie, Henri, another man, and another young woman. Camilla turned it over, hoping to see the same annotations as on the others. But the ink was smudged.

There was a rush of air as someone pushed past her, knocking her in the legs with their luggage.

"Sorry," Camilla said as she turned, instinctively apologizing though she'd done nothing wrong. It was the woman from before. From behind, she reminded Camilla of her mother—her height and her upright posture—and with a pang, Camilla realized she hadn't spoken to her mother in days.

The passengers waited for the ferryman to tie up and set down the gangplank. In no rush, Camilla waited for everyone to pass by before she gathered her belongings and made her way from the boat. Pausing at the top of the gangplank, she was momentarily taken aback by the beauty of the island. She had seen photos online, of course; she had even copied some and pasted them onto her spreadsheet for visual reference later. But nothing could have prepared her for the dramatic panorama that greeted her that morning.

At either end of the beach the sand rose into pink rocky cliffs, the morning sun reflecting off the water in shimmering spikes. Small sailboats bobbed in the harbor, and tiny specks of people were scattered along the waterfront. The whole island looked and felt enchanting, as if it had been conjured up in the imagination of a Hollywood set designer.

Perhaps this was why the locals tried to keep this place to themselves. While the international jet set headed to Ibiza and Saint-Tropez, the Île de Clair hid itself away amongst treacherous waters and rocky outcrops. Only once you got close could you see the azure waters, the white sand, and the lush green land beyond. Its name was known only to locals—and her sister. How had Susie ended up here? She hoped her sister's secrets were easier to uncover than those of the Île de Clair.

10

Susie, 1998

It was late morning when Susie arrived on the Île de Clair for the first time. She was a little shaken by the whole misunderstanding with Christian in the terminal office—how was she to know the phone call wasn't technically *free?*—and the resulting rush to get to her ferry, but the episode was quickly forgotten as she got her first glimpse of the Île de Clair.

As they sailed into the harbor, she let the sea air fill her lungs and took a moment to contemplate the events of the last few days, the quitting of her job and the leaving of her stable, affordable accommodation chief among her ruminations. She told herself it was normal to have misgivings about coming to France without telling David; that it was totally fine that there had been no physical contact between the two of them, no real reason to think he was interested.

She couldn't anticipate how David was going to react to her arrival. She could only focus on what she knew for sure: first, there was an unmistakable connection between herself and David; second, the smile in the garden had been a definite invitation for Susie to come to the Île; and third, Nellie had always told her that the good ones took *time*. Time was the one commodity Susie had in abundance. She closed her eyes and sent a silent thank-you to her grandmother for inadvertently leading her here before opening them again to drink up every little aspect of the view unfolding in front of her.

Drenched in sunshine, the harbor was in the narrow middle of the island, protected from the worst of the treacherous winds by rocky promontories at both ends and a tract of hilly farmland behind. A small chapel sat at the top of one of those hills, overlooking green copses hiding clusters of houses. Narrow paths snaked inland from the azure coves toward unknown destinations. Back down at the harbor, tourists meandered along the cobbled streets and stone cottages in search of café au lait and postcards. Farther around the bay, fishermen worked on their boats, clearing out their catches and calling to each other.

For a moment Susie was still, taking it all in. Then, as the ferry bumped against the jetty and people around began to jostle and move off the boat, her skin started to tingle at the prospect of the adventures in front of her. The Île de Clair. She whispered the name to herself, certain that this was the place where she would find love.

But first she had to find David. Her Lonely Planet guide told her there was a small hostel in the town square. It was only a couple of kilometers inland and an easy walk by the look of it, but she considered it her absolute last resort. She hadn't come all this way—a train to Plymouth, a ferry to Paimpol, and then another ferry here to the island—or spent all this money to stay in a hostel. Chloe had picked up bedbugs the last time she was in France, and Susie wasn't about to make the same mistake.

The Lonely Planet didn't have much else to say about the island. The hostel, a campground, two bistros, and an authentic crêperie, all open only in the summer. Lucky for Susie, it was summer. One word had bounced between all the French passengers on the ferry: *la plage*. The beach. The beach was enough for Susie.

Susie and David had met one more time before he left for France. She'd tried to extract the exact location of his cottage, but the only details she managed were the name of the island and that David's family owned a small stone cottage by the water.

Her heart sank as she scanned the surrounding area. She could see at least a dozen small stone cottages on the water. Her rucksack was heavy, and her feet were hot inside her Gazelles. She climbed down onto the sand and let her rucksack drop next to her. Lowering herself to the warm sand, she kicked off her shoes. It felt good to be breathing in the fresh, salty air. She closed her eyes and let the sun warm her whole body. She was here. She couldn't quite believe it.

By her calculations, David would have been here for a couple of days already. It took Susie a bit longer to arrange her visa, and anyway, it would be best for him to settle in before she surprised him. In her experience, guys liked it better when you were independent, so she'd told him she was planning to travel through Europe for the summer. Italy, France, she had said with a shrug of her shoulders. Greece. And then her travels would bring her to the Île de Clair—just passing through, she would say breezily, when she found him.

But she hadn't counted on how off the beaten track this island was. Her plan was starting to look a little transparent in the bright island sunshine.

Still, she had seen the way David looked at her when he thought she wasn't paying attention. He was definitely interested. He just needed a little shove in the right direction. And she would give him that . . . as soon as she found him. She tried to think about what Camilla would do in this situation despite the fact that Camilla, of course, would never find herself in this situation. Nevertheless, it would be something very logical, like consulting a phone book or asking at a post office.

Neither idea appealed. They both seemed too try-ish. In Susie's experience, if you sat tight and kept the faith, the universe would provide. In the meantime, the sun was shining and she was on a beach. In France. She could always work on her suntan for the moment, or until David materialized. There were a number of cafés along the curve of the shoreline; it was only a matter of time before he felt thirsty.

Susie watched a family with two small children playing in the water. There were two girls, almost identical in age. One was jumping over the waves at their highest point, screaming with delight as she sailed over the top. The other girl was waiting right until the last minute and getting caught in the spray every time. She looked as if she might cry. Every time her sister tried to take her hand and lead her to deeper water, she shook her head in terror. A man in a tiny black swimsuit seemed to be supervising them, but he was more interested in two young women sunbathing nearby.

Susie tucked the sleeves of her T-shirt into her bra straps and rolled up her shorts. She considered trying to wriggle into her swimsuit on the beach, but it was right at the bottom of her rucksack. There would be plenty of time for swimming. She had given her notice at the pub and hadn't booked any return tickets. A masterstroke, she realized now, looking around at the sun-drenched paradise she had stumbled upon.

She brushed the sand off her denim shorts and wandered down to the shoreline. From there, she could keep an eye on both the girls and the houses along the water. They really did all look the same. Some had windows framed in white, some in light green, but they all had pitched roofs, windows hidden high in the gables. There were no distinguishing features, no sign of David.

A shout from the water jolted Susie's attention back to the little girls. They had both swum out deeper, and the more fearful girl was panicking, pulling at her sister and dragging them both under. Without thinking, Susie ran into the water. It was brisker than it looked, but Susie didn't stop. By the time she got to the girls, they had both swallowed a lot of water and grabbed on to her gratefully. They weighed practically nothing, and Susie had them back on the sand in no time.

The father met them at the water's edge, his cigarette still dangling from his mouth, talking in rapid French.

Susie looked at him blankly. "I am Australian," she said, quickly. "I don't speak French." She could imagine Camilla's smugness. Not even twenty-four hours in France, and her knowledge of the language was letting her down.

"The girls are okay," the man said, in English this time, looking over his shoulder to make sure the two women hadn't disappeared. "Elodie will look after her younger sister, won't you?" He tapped one of the girls on the head, the one who had been crying with fear. "Estelle, Elodie will take care of you." The doubtful look on Estelle's face matched up with what Susie was thinking. Elodie, despite being older, wasn't much use.

The man took a drag on the cigarette in his mouth without touching it. "Australienne?"

"Oui." A little burst of pride.

"What are you doing on the Île de Clair? There are not many Australians here. Only the English." He took the cigarette out of his mouth and flicked the ash on the sand.

"I'm staying with a friend. David Rowe?" She pointed at the cottages in the distance, hoping the man might give some indication of which one was the Rowe cottage.

"Oh, yes. The famous Rowes." He bent down, put his cigarette out in the sand, and then walked off.

"Have you seen David?" she called after him, but he didn't look back.

Returning to her belongings, she tied her runners to the front of her rucksack, her denim shorts crispy with salt water and rasping between her legs as she headed up to the row of shops along the harbor.

If the Rowes were as famous as the French man suggested, then it shouldn't be too hard to find them, right?

11

Camilla

Camilla gathered her belongings, double-checked her handbag. Everything was in order, if a little soggy.

The timetable on the wall showed that there wasn't a return ferry until the morning. Her original plan had been to stay two days. The lack of information about the island had made her think there wasn't much to the place, but now, looking across the blue water to the white sand and the fairy-tale harbor, she felt, first, that two days wouldn't be enough, and second, that the oversight was deliberate. The Île de Clair was a secret for a reason.

Once her feet were on dry land, Camilla took a moment to look around. The day was still young, and the island basked in gentle sunshine, bathing the soft pink rock of the shoreline in a pearlescent glow. Crowds were starting to gather on the white-sand beaches, a brave few already splashing in the waves.

It didn't take long for Camilla to spot La Belle Hotel. It was only meters from the sand, the terrace rimmed with flowering rosebushes, its name plastered across the face in bright blue letters. Her initial reaction to the name had been bemusement, but now she could see that no other name would have done.

The bell over the door heralded her entry into the reception. "Mrs.

Cooper?" a voice came from the terrace. The French doors were thrown open, the tables filled with people enjoying lunch. A woman, her face in shadow.

"Mrs. Cooper?" she repeated, as she came closer.

"Oh! That's me!" In a romantic gesture after her wedding, Camilla had changed her name to Cooper on her passport, but she kept her maiden name for all other purposes, including work. After all these years, the name still sounded foreign to her. Perhaps she would change her passport back, now that there was no longer any need for romantic gestures toward Ian.

"Are you sure?" The woman looked at her suspiciously.

"Yes! I'm Camilla Cooper."

"I'm Valerie." The woman ducked under the counter and turned her attention to the computer monitor, her kohl-rimmed eyes darting across the screen. She wore her long blond hair piled in a vertiginous mass on her head. Camilla patted her own neat ponytail and tried to stand up taller.

"Ça va, Valerie?" Camilla asked. It was all she had left of her schoolgirl French. "C'est une bonne jour."

Valerie didn't even look up. "It's okay. I am very fluent in English. I have been running this hotel for years. Although we do get mostly Europeans. Not usually so many Australians, no." Valerie tried her best to look sad about it. "You have booked for two nights, *non?* That's not long when you have come so far." She glanced up at Camilla, who shifted uncomfortably.

"It's just a quick visit. I'm here on family . . . business."

"Which is it? Family? Or business? It is not the same thing." She would make a good teacher, Camilla thought. Or customs official.

"Family matters."

Valerie nodded and tapped away at her keyboard. "Passport?"

Camilla handed it over, feeling a pang of anxiety as it left her hands. "Are you very busy?" she asked, distracting herself with small talk.

"Yes, we are fully booked." Valerie pressed a final key with a flourish. "We are always fully booked in the summer." She handed Camilla a beautiful antique bronze key, recently polished and gleaming.

Despite the task ahead of her, Camilla was starting to relax. It almost felt as if she was on holiday, the type of holiday she had never dared treat herself to in the past. Even the three flights of stairs up to her room barely slowed her down. The Île de Clair was bliss, she thought as she flopped on the large, pillowy bed, not caring if she messed up the sheets. She could see why Susie would want her ashes scattered here. Camilla wanted *her* ashes scattered here!

The hotel staff had left a dish piled high with amazing-looking fruit. Ignoring the delicate gold cutlery, Camilla took a greedy bite of the peach, letting the juices run down her chin. It was so good. She took another bite and another, eating it standing up, her body soaking up every bit of goodness. When the peach was done, she plucked oversize grapes from the bunch, one by one. Once she was sufficiently fortified, she wiped her hands on the starched white napkin and grabbed the third envelope, taking it with her to the balcony.

Her hands still slightly tacky, she pulled the letter from the envelope, unfolding it as she watched a small boy paddling in the still evening water. The son called out to his father who then joined him in the shallows. Something landed on her lap and she looked down. Another, smaller envelope had been concealed inside the letter she was holding.

But this one wasn't addressed to her.

It was addressed to someone called Henri.

Taking a deep breath, she put the letter to Henri—and the question of who, in fact, Henri was—aside for the moment and read the letter in her hand.

12

Susie, 1998

Susie checked the scrawled map in her hand. This was it. The only thing that set it apart from the numerous other similar cottages she had passed along the way was that David would be inside this one. She hoped.

After a few hours waiting for the universe to provide, Susie had started to feel hungry and a little sunburned. She started by asking a few people along the beachside path if they knew the Rowe family, David in particular, but either the language barrier or the fact they were also all tourists like herself meant she was met with only blank faces.

In the end, she tried the man working at the ice cream stand. He hadn't known, but gestured for her to follow him across the road to another kiosk, where he had a long and complicated discussion with an old woman. After a lot of head shaking and pointing and extended periods of them both simply staring at Susie, they managed to produce both pencil and paper and prepare the map she was now holding. It didn't fill her with confidence, but here she was.

On this side, the path side, a low fence set the cottage apart. The garden beyond was filled with mimosas and camellias. A small white front door needed a lick of paint, but the hydrangea bush next to it was well tended, lush and green and bursting with pink blooms. The fishing net propped just so next to the door appeared to be for show only, the metal of its pole rusted and dry.

On the walk over, she had caught glimpses of the treacherous waters on the northern side of the island, but from the front step of David's cottage, only a tiny triangle of azure water was visible through the trees. The contrasts of the island were slowly revealing themselves: peaceful coves hidden away from the roughest open water; lush over-grown gardens opening onto wild rocky coastline. It reminded her of home; the jewel-like swimming holes hidden away in inhospitable bushland, paradise awaiting those who took the time to look for it.

When she did finally knock, the sound echoed through the house, and a small gray bird flew out from the bush beside her. There was no response. Stepping back, she looked at the upstairs windows. The blinds were drawn. She checked her watch. Past noon. She had been up for so long, she hadn't considered that David might still be sleeping.

After a few more minutes with no response, Susie decided to follow the stone exterior wall of the cottage around to the back of the house. The cottage was three stories tall, with a row of dormer windows tucked under the eaves on the top floor. Made from honey-colored stone, it was roofed in dark slate tiles, a chimney at each point. In con-trast to the orderly garden, the white wooden windows looked as if they had endured a hard winter.

David was in the back garden, most of which was a terrace. Paints and papers lay strewn across a table, weighed down by ocean pebbles, a wine bottle. He sat looking out to the view, bare-chested and strum-ming a guitar, a half-empty coffee cup forgotten at his feet. Susie didn't recognize the tune, but it was slow, moody, and just clunky enough that he might have written it himself. The next time he paused, she coughed and said "Nice tune."

He turned his head, and it was a few moments before he spoke. Long enough that Susie started to feel a little uncomfortable in the hot sun, conscious of her still-damp clothing and bedraggled hair.

"I went for a swim," she offered when it was clear that David was lost for words. His half-nakedness was distracting; she tried not to look.

"How was the water?" The question would be a natural one, normally; in these circumstances, there were others he could be asking.

"Lovely." It was Susie's greatest wish that they carry on like this, skipping all the awkward conversations about why and how she came to be here and proceeding directly to the fun and romantic part of the summer. Could it be that easy?

"It's perfect here," she said. There was a low wall at the edge of the terrace, and she moved over to look at the view. The tide was out, and a small fishing boat perched on the pebbled beach. Silence from David. A familiar tree with pendulous yellow flowers at the shady end of the terrace caught her eye.

"Laburnum," she said as she walked over to it.

"Yes. It's my mother's favorite tree. We have one in London as well. They make her feel at home, she says." He was speaking in a strange monotone, as if he'd just woken up from a deep sleep. Or as if a random woman had turned up in his garden. Either was an option.

"You're meant to remove those seedpods, you know." Susie went up closer to inspect the pods. Her mother was diligent in their removal, and Susie had never had the chance to properly inspect them.

"Old wives' tale," David scoffed.

"Is it?" Susie trained her eye on the view, watched the fishing boats bobbing out in the deeper water.

"You're too old to believe in fairy tales."

This wasn't looking good. Susie thought she might throw up.

David fiddled with one of the pegs on the end of his guitar. Finally, he spoke. "I'm just a little unclear why you're here. Especially when I told you not to come."

"I told you I planned to travel in Europe over the summer. I'm sure I mentioned France." She had. After Lucinda left the tennis court on the night of their last date, Susie had said, explicitly, "I'll see you in France." David had laughed. She could see now he had laughed because he thought she was joking.

"France is a big country. The Île de Clair is an unlikely place for you to end up. I thought Paris. Provence. Maybe Cannes? Nice?" His voice trailed off. Tight rounds of color were forming on his cheeks.

Susie hoped they were sunburn, even though they were more likely connected to the anger in his voice.

"It was in my Lonely Planet and it sounded good and I knew you were here, so I thought I'd call in on my way past." Her heart was beating fast now. She was waffling. David was different here, more distant. She was used to the pendulum of his attraction swinging back and forth, but here it had swung away and didn't seem to be coming back. He was making her nervous. She slipped off her rucksack and grabbed the Lonely Planet from the very top. The page for the Île de Clair was folded over. "Do you have a phone? I tried to call the hostel from the ferry terminal, but there was no answer."

"There's one in the house," David said. Susie tried to remember the David of London. Carefree, friendly. Interested? She hadn't imagined it, had she? A thought occurred to her. Slowly she turned her head to look back at the house. There was only one beach towel slung over the back of a chair, one coffee cup, but the house was dark compared to the bright sunny terrace. Anyone could be inside.

"Are you alone?" she whispered.

David didn't answer. He whipped the Lonely Planet out of her hands and read aloud. "The Île de Clair, one of the smallest islands off the coast of Brittany, has little to set it apart from the larger and more populous islands along this coast. Its stunning coastline and numerous beaches are hard to beat, but Île de Ré and Bréhat have more to offer the casual tourist. If you do stumble off the ferry by accident on the Île de Clair, don't miss Maria's authentic crêpes in the village. A passable hostel is nearby."

"See? Hard to beat." Susie tried to make light of the situation. David had yet to smile.

"Hardly a rave, though, is it? I expect there's a larger section about Paris?" A smile finally started to twitch at the corner of his mouth. Susie crossed her fingers behind her back.

"It said Paris is overrated, actually." She snatched the book back before he had a chance to check. "Where is the phone?"

"You won't get into the hostel," he said, lowering himself back into his chair. "It's always fully booked at this time of year."

"Oh, well, I'll stay in the hotel." Susie had seen a hotel at the end of the dock as she got off the ferry. She had enough money for one night there, maybe two if she didn't eat. That might just be enough time to win David over.

He laughed. "You've got that kind of money?"

Susie didn't have an answer for that.

"I made it very clear that you shouldn't come here." The lightness had gone out of his voice. Susie realized he was serious. Very serious. She had totally misread the situation. In the past, she had never understood what people meant by saying they were so embarrassed they wanted the ground to swallow them up. Now she did. She wanted the entire island to upend itself and deposit her in the deepest reaches of the ocean floor, somewhere far away and far below the Rowe cottage. She wanted not only to obliterate herself from the Île de Clair but also from the memory of the people who lived there. She squeezed her eyes shut and tried to calculate the least humiliating path of retreat.

"What are you doing?" David's voice was softer. He had moved closer to her.

Susie opened one eye. "I'm working out my next move," she said. He was definitely closer. Heat radiated from his body, creating an aura that made him seem more alive than he had in London. More dangerous. Was he glad she had defied him?

It was hard to think straight. David was so close. Her next move was proving elusive. She knew she should be thinking about ferries and trains and hostels, but all she wanted to do was stay. In the few short hours since she had arrived, the Île de Clair had seduced her. The place hummed with an energy that had already seeped into her body, making her feel languid, porous. There was something—or someone—waiting for her on the island. She was sure of it.

David was watching her, waiting.

"I'd really like to stay," she said, the words coming out in a rush. "I'll be no trouble, and I'll keep out of your way."

David was silent. He watched a boat clip across the small bay in front of the terrace. If Susie knew him better, she might have been able to interpret his silence, but the short time she had spent with David had left her bereft of any insight into his psyche. If she was honest with herself, that was part of the attraction.

"Okay," he said finally.

Despite her concerns, Susie started to smile. "Thank you, David, you . . ."

He held up his hand. "There will be ground rules."

"I'm ready to hear them." She placed the Lonely Planet down on the table, out of David's reach. Apart from the incriminating review of the island, she had also made some notes in the back. Possibly her and David's name entwined in a pink heart. Juvenile, she knew, but the train ride had been long and the carriage overheated. She would rip the pages out at the first opportunity.

"One." David held up one finger. "Separate rooms." Susie nodded, unfazed. She was no stranger to crawling corridors when required.

"Two. I'm here to work. You'll need to find something to do with your days, but we can eat together in the evenings." He stopped and looked around, as if the garden surroundings would remind him of anything he had forgotten. "Actually, I think that's it. There aren't many rules on the Île de Clair." He looked up from under his eyelashes and smiled.

Susie smiled back to conceal the effect he was having on her. He couldn't sense her elevated heart rate, right? She was going to act normal, play it cool, wait for the pendulum to swing back again. "I'll get a job!" she said brightly, "You won't even know I'm here."

He took a sip of coffee and grimaced. "What are you like at making coffee?"

13

Letter Three

Welcome to the gorgeous Île de Clair.

Isn't it heaven?

I thought it was heaven as well when I first arrived. I spoke to you, remember, from the ferry terminal. There was a nice man there, Christopher or something, who let me use his phone. Didn't end well, from memory.

I sailed into the harbor on a sunny morning in late July and was dazzled by the beauty of the place. We didn't see a lot of beaches growing up, did we? Once I saw the sheltered harbor of the Île, I was an immediate convert to island life. Every day we explored the is-land, following hidden tracks down to private beaches, sandy coves, and twinkly rock pools. We jumped from high rocks into the deepest water, climbed the stony ramparts, and picked our way across rocky beaches. If the weather is right, dive under the water, Mills—there's no other feeling like it. The Île de Clair is an idyll in the truest sense *of the word: an extremely happy or picturesque situation that is ultimately unsustainable.*

I didn't really have a plan when I arrived on the island. Nowhere to stay, nowhere to work. After all the train and ferry tickets to get there, I didn't have a lot of money either. It should have been scary or overwhelming but it wasn't. I felt good as soon as I arrived, like I knew things were going to be okay. Well.

It's funny to think back and remember that now. All my early memories of the island are now clouded by what happened later.

But on that first day, my priority was finding David. We had met up a few times in London, including one notable tennis match (I know), and he had mentioned he was coming to his family cottage on the Île de Clair for the summer to work on his art. A stone cottage on the water, he said. Trouble was, when I arrived, all the cottages were either stone or on the water or both. Take a look around you: I'm right, aren't I?

To start off with, the locals viewed me with suspicion. Even though I got the impression that they didn't love David's family, they were even more wary of strangers, especially English-speaking ones. Eventually the man who ran the ice cream stand by the water felt sorry for me and pointed out the Rowe family cottage.

Did I tell you that David didn't know I was coming? He got over his initial shock pretty quickly, and we became friends. Yes, friends.

Because apart from David, I met two other special people on the island.

Henri and Isabel.

There is a small chapel, up on the hill. It has a view of the whole island—from up there you can see how the island is really two islands, connected by a bridge. The bridge was built by Vauban in the time of Louis XIV (I looked it up for you, Mills, I know how you like your history), and it connects the inland village with the smaller township by the port, where you would have arrived by ferry. You can also see David's cottage from up there. If you look down the hill toward the sheltered cove, you will see a white house with stone windows. Beyond that is a house surrounded by low stone walls and *looking out to sea. That's David's cottage, where I stayed while I was here.*

But it's the chapel that's important to me. I met a boy there. Henri. He was so gorgeous. If David opened up the world for me, then Henri opened up my heart. I spent the rest of my life trying to find someone who made me feel how Henri did in those short few weeks.

Side note: You might have thought I was interested in David at first. Well, snap, so did I. But things got a little tricky on that front (more on that later), and well, turned out Henri was the guy for me. More or less. Until he wasn't. Again, more on that later.

We had so much fun. They were the best weeks of my life. Day by day I was getting closer to David—we spent so much time together, and I loved the way he saw the world. He was so engaging— positive, charming, funny—and he challenged me to think more creatively. I thought he brought out the best in me.

And then Henri. He was so gorgeous, so French. It wasn't just that, though. He had a tenderness about him that I had never before encountered. When I spoke, he looked deep into my eyes and listened. If I spoke glibly, he would put a hand on me, as if reminding me to return to myself. He was such a true soul, and for a brief moment in time, he loved me.

For the first time in my life, I felt as if I fit in somewhere. We spent a blissful few weeks swimming, fishing, sailing. We drank cheap wine and ate oysters from the rocks and bread and cheese.

If you can scatter some ashes in the grounds of the chapel where Henri and I met, I'll be eternally grateful. Take a moment to enjoy the view and imagine me there, heart full and body buzzing, looking out over the island and imagining how my life would turn out.

And then see if you can find Henri—I don't know if he's still on the island. He's a hard man to pin down and seems to exist entirely outside of social media. But if he's there, you'll be able to find him. Just ask any woman on the island, and I'm sure she could point you in his direction.

Show him the photos of us, and he will remember me.

I've cheated a little here and included a letter for you to give to Henri. Wait while he reads it. He may have something for you. I hope he has something for you.

And then, to Devon.

But don't forget: Henri.

Safe travels,

All my love,
Susie

14

Camilla

Camilla should have felt calm. She was on the Île de Clair! It was beautiful! Idyllic.

But a tightness gripped her chest, and she was short of breath. She had forgotten this feeling only Susie could give her, the sense that everything was great—and then, *Bam!* Was this what a panic attack felt like? Camilla gripped the arms of the chair, forced herself to breathe deeply, slowly.

This feeling was why Ian hadn't wanted her to come. He had dealt with the fallout of her relationship with Susie so many times in the past. He knew the destruction Susie could cause in one afternoon, let alone a few weeks.

One disastrous Christmas, when the boys were smaller, Susie came to stay. They had a barbecue on Christmas Eve and some champagne. All was going well. And then, sometime after they went to bed, Susie disappeared. At dawn, when Timmy and Oliver jumped out of bed to empty their stockings, she was nowhere to be found. She arrived back with pupils like pinpricks and stinking of booze just as Ian was carving the turkey. Somewhere on her travels she had procured a Christmas snow dome, a village scene painted in red and gold and green, and she persisted in shaking it all afternoon, long after the boys had lost interest.

That evening, when Susie was finally asleep on the couch, Camilla threw the snow dome in the rubbish bin. It reminded her too much of the way Susie made her feel; her world calm and picturesque, until her sister came along and shook it up.

These letters were like the snow dome all over again.

There were so many names, so many men. Reading a letter from Susie was just like having a conversation with her in real life—topics were deserted and never returned to, allusions were made but not explained. Susie could be just as infuriating posthumously as she had been alive.

Camilla switched her attention back to the view in front of her. The weather looked like it would hold, so there was no need to switch the plan around. Time to get moving again. She sighed and pushed her feet back into their shoes, ignoring her swollen feet, the rubbing at her heels, her right little toe. She hobbled down to the hotel reception, where the front desk was attended, once again, by Valerie. A hard worker. Camilla appreciated that.

"Valerie, hello. I would like to hire a car."

Valerie tilted her head on one side, her eyes wide. "There are no cars on the Île de Clair."

"Oh." Normally Camilla was so observant. She could spot a new haircut on a student in assembly, movement among friendship groups, teacher friction. Even though Valerie had no reason to lie, Camilla looked out the window for confirmation. A family walked past, then a man on a bicycle. But no cars. She hadn't been able to find a hire company online, but she had written TBC on the spreadsheet and assumed she would sort it out when she arrived.

"We have bikes out front here." Valerie pointed to a lineup of blue bikes, all adorned with wicker baskets.

"How much?"

"They are free!" Valerie proclaimed. "To hotel guests," she quickly added, scanning the lobby for non–hotel guests who might take advantage of the situation.

"Oh. Right. Well, do you have a map then?"

"You don't need a map on this island, Mrs. Cooper. It is more fun to ride around. Explore!" A man cleared his throat behind Camilla.

"Camilla."

"Quoi?"

"My name is Camilla."

Valerie looked at her blankly.

"Never mind. I need directions."

"Okay! I will give you directions for wherever you would like to go." Valerie took a piece of paper out of a wire basket and the pencil out of her chignon. Her hair fell in well-behaved Brigitte Bardot waves around her face. Camilla sighed at the injustice of it, but Valerie continued on unawares. "Where would you like to go?"

"The chapel. It's on a hill."

"You can just follow the path, Mrs. . . . . Cooper. There are signs. See?"

Camilla turned around and walked over to the window. Valerie was right. The chapel was visible from the hotel. A path led up from the curved promenade, and even though it was hidden at times between trees and nestled among houses, at the very top it became apparent again. The man waiting behind her took his chance and pushed up to the desk. To her credit, Valerie ignored him.

"You just follow the sign for the chapel, Mrs. Cooper. It is very hard to get lost on this island." Was it Camilla's imagination, or was Valerie deliberately talking slowly?

"You can call me Camilla," she repeated, emulating Valerie's drawn-out vowels.

"Valerie."

The man at the desk sighed audibly.

"So, I just walk up the hill?"

"If you do not want to cycle, yes, you can walk. You will not get lost. There are not many places to go on this island, and the chapel is one of the most popular. Are you a pilgrim?"

"A pilgrim? No!" Camilla laughed at the absurdity of the idea. Pilgrims were something from the Middle Ages, *The Canterbury Tales*.

There were no pilgrims in the modern world, were there? She touched her dark clothes self-consciously, tried to fluff her hair. It dropped straight back down again. Fluffy hair would be much more secular.

"We get a lot of pilgrims on the Île de Clair," Valerie said, her face etched with sincerity. She had little to no awareness of the man in front of her, tapping his credit card repeatedly on the counter. "Sometimes, to be a pilgrim is not a religious thing."

Color crept across Camilla's face. She could feel the heat of its slow march.

"Okay! Thanks! I'll head off now." Her stomach growled. "Is my reservation for dinner confirmed?" She looked at her watch. "Six p.m.?"

Valerie sniffed. "You will be eating with the children at that time. Perhaps you would be better to have a tray in your room." She scratched something out in her reservation book.

"What are you doing?"

"I'm canceling your reservation. There is a card in your room; you can phone down with your order. At six p.m." She smirked.

"I don't mind eating with the children," Camilla said. She was used to children; her own as well as all the students at the school. The thought of sitting on her own in the room a minute longer than she had to—well. She'd prefer to be among the hustle, where she could pretend she was here on holiday like the rest of them.

"There is a restaurant on the square in the village. There are signs for the village, as well. But . . . you may be too early for it, too." Valerie shrugged. It looked for a minute as if she would keep talking.

"Please, I will eat here." Camilla reached over the desk and picked up the pencil, holding it out to Valerie. After a moment, Valerie accepted it and wrote MRS. COOPER in giant letters right at the top of the booking sheet.

"Six o'clock," Camilla urged. "Please."

The man behind said something in French, loudly. Valerie looked up and laughed, nodding. For a moment, they had a conversation without her, but definitely *about* her.

"Okay. That is done." Valerie put the pencil back in the jar with a flourish. "Your key?"

"What?"

"It is hotel policy to leave the keys behind at the front desk. Too many guests have lost them in the sand." She gestured at the board behind her, filled with similar large brass keys.

"I don't lose things," Camilla said huffily, pushing away thoughts of the second letter lost in the gallery. The idea of leaving her key behind filled her with anxiety. Anyone could reach over and grab it.

Valerie shrugged. "It's hotel policy."

Camilla relented and took the key from her pocket. She watched as Valerie put it back on the peg, not feeling any better about it. Her passport and her room key, both out of her control.

"Next!"

Camilla didn't move. She had one more question for Valerie. She had to do something about her clothes, her shoes. What seemed like a sensible traveling wardrobe in Melbourne—one pair of black trousers; one pair of jeans; three T-shirts, two black, one gray; a cardigan; a cotton sweater; a black dress; one pair of black loafers; a scarf and necklace to add color—was suddenly grossly austere and, well, just *hot*.

"And is there somewhere, I could, somewhere I might . . ." Camilla waved her hand in front of her clothing, unable to describe what she needed. She suspected it would take more than new clothes. "Fenêtres?" she asked hopefully.

"Vêtements?" Valerie suggested, trying not to smile. "Clothes?"

"Yes!" Camilla exhaled, finally feeling understood. "Oui! Clothes!"

Valerie smiled. "Across the street, there is a small boutique."

"Right! Bye!"

The bell rang behind her as she went out the door. The man at the desk began to speak in rapid-fire French, and Valerie replied in similar tones. A cyclist rushed past, narrowly missing her and furiously ringing his bell. She decided not to get a bike. Walking would be fine.

She ducked into the boutique and grabbed the first thing she could see, a buttercup-yellow wrap dress with a soft tie at the waist. As she slipped it over her head, every inch of her skin tingled at the feel of the light, cool fabric. The reflection in the mirror pleased her—without the dark clothing, she looked younger. The color of the dress suited her, the deep neckline exposing her smooth skin. Normally her fringe gave her gravitas, but with her new clothes it took on a bohemian edge. The shop had given her a string bag for her old clothes, and if she turned her focus away from her feet—unfortunately, the shop didn't sell shoes—she could almost pass for French.

Camilla left the shop with a spring in her step and, ignoring her rumbling stomach, pushed on in the direction of the chapel. The walk was a gentle incline and not too taxing. She paused every now and again to peer over the quaint little gates, red, blue, sea-green, all opening into overgrown gardens and sudden vistas of bright blue. Camilla had read about the microclimate created by the nearby Gulf Stream, and now she saw evidence of it everywhere. Lanky eucalyptus mingled with stocky palm trees. Geraniums. Agapanthus. Hydrangeas.

A bell rang behind her, and Camilla moved to the left of the path. At the last minute, she remembered where she was and jumped to the right instead. The tire hit her leg first, and then the pedals. Next came the full impact of the bike and its passenger. The cyclist muttered in French. The word was foreign, but the meaning was universal.

Camilla stood up to get a look at the rider, even though her leg was smarting. He was wearing a uniform, and his cap was embroidered with the word GENDARME. She remembered enough French to know that meant police.

"Allô!" The gendarme pulled off the path and dusted himself off, smiling the whole time. When he turned to pick up his bike, he still had long twigs and leaves and other organic matter clinging to his backside. Camilla resisted the urge to brush him off.

"Hello!" Camilla shouted back.

"English?" He was still smiling.

"Yes! Please!"

"Holidays?" the policeman asked. His eyes traveled to her leg. Camilla reached down to touch it, and her hand came away bloody.

"Oh! I'm bleeding!" Her handbag—with her first-aid kit in it—was back at the hotel; there was nothing in her new jaunty string bag that could help her. The gendarme continued to smile at her. Without comment, he reached into his jacket and retrieved a handkerchief, perfectly ironed into a square.

"Oh, I couldn't!" Camilla said, taking it anyway. Stop talking in exclamations, she told herself.

The policeman pointed to the chapel up on the hill. Camilla nodded. He said something in French and pointed at her leg. It was just a surface graze, the gravel and blood making it look worse than it was. Still, she winced as she splashed some of her water on it and then applied pressure with the handkerchief.

The policeman watched. After she had patted the wound ineptly for a few moments, she offered the handkerchief back to the gendarme, carefully folded to conceal the markings of blood. To her surprise, he took it. She thought of the processes at her school when there was a blood injury: plastic gloves, antiseptic swabs, sterile tweezers, ice, elevation.

"Merci," she said, putting her hand to her head in a feeble salute.

The gendarme smiled and asked something about papers. Did he want to write something down for her? Give her directions? She felt a sudden affection for the Île de Clair and all the kind people on it. Tears pricked at the corner of her eyes. The only paper she had was the letter from Susie. Perhaps he could write on the back of it. She passed it to him.

He turned it over and over again, looking for something and not finding it.

"Non!" He suddenly shouted. "The papers!" Inspiration crossed his face. "The passport!"

Camilla snatched the letter back. "I don't have my passport with me!"

The smile came back onto the gendarme's face just as quickly as it had disappeared. "I will ask Valerie. Bien. Bien." And then he hopped on his bike and cycled off.

Flustered, Camilla continued on up the hill. It was only a little bit farther, but by the time she reached the top, her breathing was all over the place and her leg was stinging. Still, the view was incredible. Ignoring Susie's instructions to take a moment and imagine her there,

Camilla decided to sprinkle the ashes as quickly as possible. If Susie didn't want this process to be transactional, she could have asked someone else. The gendarme could reappear at any moment.

She found a geranium bush by the stony fence. It was far enough from the chapel building to avoid the threat of deconsecrating but close enough to feel she was still following instructions in the unlikely case of an audit. Unceremoniously, Camilla undid the string and dumped the contents on the straggly bush. Some of the ashes danced off in the gentle breeze; the rest clung to the leaves momentarily until they dropped down to the ground, resting on the soil.

For a moment, Camilla considered the physicality of what the ashes represented. Every part of her sister—her golden skin, her perpetually knotty hair, her funny little toes—was reduced to tiny flakes of grainy ash. It was better not to think about it. She pulled out Susie's letter again.

Take a moment to enjoy the view and imagine me there, heart full and body buzzing, looking out over the island and imagining how my life would turn out.

She tried to imagine Susie standing there as a nineteen-year-old, in love and on the adventure of a lifetime. She really did. But her eyes kept jumping ahead to the next passage in the letter. Henri. The question of Susie's last night on the island. *Just ask any woman on the island, and I'm sure she could point you in his direction.*

Valerie.

15

Susie, 1998

"Make yourself at home. You can have the green bedroom, up on the third floor." David pointed to a window nestled in the eaves.

He turned and walked inside. Susie hadn't been lying earlier. It was perfect. The island was beautiful, the cottage picturesque. But there was something about the remoteness of the location that put her on edge. For the first time, she realized how little she knew about David. She felt grateful she had called Camilla to tell her where she was going. Even though it had been a buzzkill, it meant that someone in the world knew where she was.

Not that she was scared of David or anything like that. It was just, well, there had been a number of dates, and now here they were in actual paradise, and still not so much as a hand being held. That in itself was a little weird. There was only so long you could blame his reticence on English reserve. As soon as the sun went down that evening, Susie intended to ramp things up a bit. Until then, she would play his game.

Not wanting to be away from him for long, Susie took her bag up the narrow stairs, pausing on the first landing to count the doors— three, all closed—before heading to the third floor. There were just two doors on this level. Behind the first one she tried was a tiny bathroom, behind the second, a twin bedroom, its striped curtains closed against the summer sun. Flinging them open, she turned to take in the white-painted furniture, the green foliage on the wallpaper. A small lamp sat between the beds and floral eiderdowns were folded at their base. It was warm and a little musty, but it was in David's cottage, and for that she was very grateful.

"What next?" Susie called out as she came down the stairs. The day was marvelous, the sky a brilliant blue. She wanted to explore the island, have a proper swim. Blow out the cobwebs from hours of travel.

David was over by the kitchen sink, rinsing out wineglasses and turning them upside down on the rack. "Are you hungry?" David called out over his shoulder.

"What are you making?" She wandered through the downstairs room, taking it all in. It looked as if walls had been knocked out once upon a time, and the room completely opened up. One side was taken up by a kitchen with rough-hewn stone counters and linen curtains hanging underneath. The kitchen was separated from the rest of the area by a whitewashed staircase rising to the floors above.

"I'm not making anything," David said. "I hadn't planned on visitors today." He held up the dry heel of a baguette to make his point. "I'll take you to try the crêpes recommended by your guidebook, if you like?"

"Sure. Sounds good." Susie let her hand rest on the base of the stairs before moving across to the other side of the room. Here, an enormous stone fireplace held the ashes of its last inferno. Susie inhaled deeply, the smoky scent reminding her of the paddock bonfires at home. "The house is beautiful." She flopped on to one of the three oversize sofas surrounding the fireplace, hardly knowing where to look next. The walls on either side of the fireplace were lined with bookshelves, broken up only by tiny porthole windows looking into the garden.

"You play chess?" She had put her feet up on the coffee table, narrowly missing what looked to be a game in motion. Not that she knew much about chess.

"Ha. Not since last summer." He came over and sat on the sofa perpendicular to Susie's. She pretended not to notice. "This game"—he pointed at the board—"ended in a fight. Dad likes to trounce me a couple of times while he's here. You could say my chess game is on a par with your tennis."

If David was closer, Susie might have given him a friendly punch on the arm, got the ball rolling on physical contact, but as it was, she had to make do with a "Hey!"

She took her feet off the coffee table and moved a chess piece absentmindedly. A queen? A rook? She had no idea. "Do you come here often?"

If David caught her meaning, he didn't show it. Instead he straightened a pile of books on the table and launched into a brief history of the Rowe family.

"We come every year. We used to leave London as soon as school finished. Now it's a bit much for my parents, but they try to get here for my birthday at least."

"Which is?"

"Tenth August."

Susie inhaled sharply. "Leo," she said, once she'd composed herself.

"Yes, yes, I think I am." He looked at her blankly.

"I'm a Cancer." It wasn't the most auspicious match. Thankfully, David didn't seem to understand the implications.

"And did you get this house from your aunt as well?" Susie asked, changing the subject quickly. The room had the richly layered air of a house that was lived in; books left splayed open on the table, interspersed by pillar candles at varying levels of height, burned down over many evenings. A silk shawl was draped over a lampshade in the corner, a pair of binoculars looped on the curtain rail.

David snorted. "Not quite."

"But almost?"

"The house has been in the family for nearly fifty years. My mother's parents bought it after the war. They were looking for somewhere my mother could recover from a bout of pneumonia. As a child, we divided our summer holidays between this and Pond Cottage in Devon. My parents were older than the parents of my friends and very protective, so I looked forward to it every year. I learned to fish at

Pond Cottage, and on the island I learned to swim and run free. It was a chance to have a normal childhood, far away from the rules and regulations of home."

"Pond Cottage?"

"It's exactly as it sounds."

"Oh well, at least you didn't have to wait until school finished this year." It was a clunky attempt to bring the conversation back to the mystery of David's recent firing, and it fell on deaf ears.

"The Île is very quiet. There are no cars, and most of the year there's hardly any residents. The locals still see us as interlopers, but over the years we have managed to make some friends. There's not too many people our age, though."

Susie raised her eyebrows.

"I mean, there's not too many people my age *or* your age. It tends to be young families and older couples. It will be good to have some company." He coughed, looked away.

"And what will we *do* here?"

David looked at her carefully, thinking something over.

"Swim at the beach. Go fishing. Play music. Paint. Drink wine. It's a quiet place. Don't make that face—Lonely Planet *did* warn you."

Susie hadn't realized she was pulling a face. "Are there any . . . you know, clubs? Pubs?"

David laughed. "Clubs? No. If that's what you're after, you're in the wrong place." Susie must not have looked convinced. "You'll be fine."

"I'm starting to think I should have stayed in London."

"Just think, if not for that rave review in the guidebook . . ." He stood up, stretched. Reached behind the cushion for a faded T-shirt that he somehow knew was there. "Come on, let's go."

The sun was still shining brightly, and the little paths outside the cottage were busier with people passing through to the numerous beaches nearby. One couple, overloaded with an umbrella, two folding chairs, and a basket, turned down a path directly opposite the cottage.

David pointed after them. "That's one of the best swimming coves on the island, down there. We call it Rupert's Regret."

"And who is Rupert?" Susie asked as they passed another couple, this time carrying their shopping in burlap totes. They didn't look up.

"Rupert is my father. It's an old family joke. My dad always says, 'You never regret a swim.'"

Susie looked at him, half smiling. "I guess it's one of those things."

"You must have names for things in your family? All families have their own shorthand."

Susie thought for a minute as the path came up along a towering hedgerow. "Not really. I get called Susie instead of Susanne. Camilla gets Mills instead of Camilla."

"That's not the kind of thing I mean. Nicknames are a whole different kettle of fish."

Susie was on a roll, though. "Mum is Margaret, and never anything else, but my grandmother Eleanor is—"

David held up a hand. "I get the picture." The path forked, and he paused. He gestured toward the right side, just as a family with two little children came through. Their buckets and spades knocked into Susie's legs, and the mother cheerfully apologized.

"Holidaymakers," David said with a note of disdain once they were out of earshot.

"What are we, then?" Susie asked.

"We're locals. Île de Clair, through and through."

Susie wasn't so sure.

When they got to the crêperie, David exchanged a few sentences in French with the stern older-looking woman behind the counter. The conversation ended with both the woman and David looking at Susie. Susie smiled, but David steered her away without introducing the two women.

"That's Marie. Marie is friends with Yvette, and Yvette keeps in touch with my parents."

Susie didn't know who Yvette was, but she didn't know anyone, so it hardly differentiated her from the rest of the local population. After a few moments it became clear that David wasn't about to volunteer the information of his own accord. "Who is Yvette?" she asked.

"Yvette is the local midwife, Henri's aunt. You'll meet Henri soon enough. I suspect you'll like him." He paused and then looked at Susie intently, scanning her whole body in a way that made her feel naked. She shifted in her seat, and Yvette was promptly forgotten. "Yes. Henri," David said again, in a way that made her feel a little confused.

"Do you think your parents would mind that I'm here?" Her voice wobbled a little. David had the ability to make her feel helter-skelter just by looking at her.

"No!" David laughed. "I just don't want them to get the wrong impression," he said, and patted her on the hand.

When Marie waved at them to say their crêpes were ready, David went to fetch them. Susie stayed put at the table, thinking about what he had just said. She was starting to worry that David's parents weren't the only ones who needed to think about impressions, wrong or otherwise. Turning up on the island like this couldn't have made her intentions any clearer, but so far getting David to recognize this had been like butting her head against a brick wall.

"Merci, Marie," David said over his shoulder as he carried the plates back to the table. Each plate contained just one golden crêpe, the sugary scent diverting Susie's attention momentarily, making her mouth water. "She's short-staffed this summer. Her daughter has gone to the mainland to study something. My French wasn't quite good enough to understand what. I got taxidermy, but that seems rather left field."

Susie didn't wait for David to finish. She cut off a piece of the golden crêpe and put it in her mouth. The sweetness of the sugar and the lemon tang had her reaching for more before she had even finished her mouthful.

"They're good, aren't they?" David said.

"Amazing." There was no time for more words. She had to eat every last mouthful while it was hot and perfect.

"I've been coming here since I was a baby. Marie has been here since my mother was a child. She's like family to us." He turned and smiled at Marie. She continued to ignore him.

"She seems to really like you," Susie said.

"Oh, she's just like that. She won't even talk to my mother."

"So why aren't they here now?"

"My parents?"

"Yes. It's summer, and you're here. Surely they want to be here too."

"They only come out for my birthday. For a week or two. They're quite elderly now, and it's not the easiest place to get to."

Susie thought about the trip David's parents would have to make, if it was anything like the one she had made to get to the island. London to Plymouth. The ferry at Plymouth to Roscoff. Roscoff to Paimpol. And then the small ferry to Île de Clair.

"It's the same journey, though, whether they make it for a week or a month."

"You're right."

"Maybe it's just an excuse."

"Maybe it is. It's not just the distance—once they're here, the lack of cars makes it pretty tricky for them. It's always been family tradition to meet here for my birthday, and they won't give that up easily. They're people who like tradition." He kept looking up toward the front door, where Marie was serving an endless stream of customers. They were lucky to have gotten a seat. The rest of the café was full, and the tables that spilled out on to the village square were also full.

Susie was done, but David continued to push the crêpe around his plate. When Marie came over to take their plates, David ordered another cup of coffee, and she glared at him. Susie recognized the feeling from working the tea room at Matilda Downs during the high season, when the people just kept coming and the orders started to overwhelm the staff.

Susie had an idea. She stood up, grabbed a pile of dirty plates from the table next to them, and followed Marie back to the counter, where there was already a line of customers waiting to order.

"Marie?" Susie asked, putting the dishes on the crowded counter. Marie looked up, annoyed at the interruption. "Could I . . . could I possibly help?" For a moment, it looked as if Marie might not understand. Susie mimed the action of washing a dish and pointed to herself. She could feel David's eyes on her back.

Finally, after what seemed like an eternity, Marie reached for an apron from the counter behind her and passed it to Susie. Their eyes connected for a moment, and Susie felt something pass between them. A warning? It was gone before she could put a name to it. A man pushed past Susie to the counter, and the moment was lost. She turned back to face the room, ready to start work.

16

Camilla

Camilla's bags were in the foyer when she returned to the hotel. She didn't need any sort of sixth sense to tell her that wasn't a good sign.

Valerie was waiting behind the desk, her arms crossed, expression hostile. It took a moment for Camilla to work it out, and then she almost laughed. Camilla had thought her an ally, but it was Valerie who had sent the gendarme after her! Was there some archaic law against scattering ashes or visiting chapels on foot that Camilla had inadvertently broken? Or was it something to do with Susie?

Fragments of the letters were coming back to Camilla. *So good before it turned bad.* It was starting to feel possible that there were other reasons than lack of money that made it impossible for Susie to return to the Île de Clair. What was it she had written? She couldn't come because she didn't have the money—or the courage. It was difficult to understand why a person would need courage to visit a place like this. But Camilla had been on the island less than a few hours, and already she was being followed by the police.

Camilla! Who had never had so much as a parking ticket in her life. Once she had knocked a car door with hers in the supermarket carpark, but she had left a note and paid for the repair. In Camilla's experience, the police were helpful, protective. She had never had a reason to fear them. Yet another life experience courtesy of Susie that she could have done without.

Camilla forced a bright smile onto her face as she crossed to the front desk, though she felt wobbly and strangely vulnerable in this beautiful bright setting. Wordlessly, Valerie pushed her passport across the top of the counter. Not sure what was happening, Camilla took it anyway, putting it safely in her pocket and out of Valerie's reach. She hadn't felt comfortable with the European hotel custom of holding on to passports. There was a perfectly good safe in her room, a much better spot for it.

Then she saw that the photos of Susie and her friends were also on the desk.

"Where did you get those?" Camilla reached over the desk to snatch them, but Valerie was too quick. She put her hand down firmly on them and moved them out of reach. Camilla felt blood rushing under her skin. She knew exactly where Valerie had gotten them. From between the pages of her book, where she had tucked them for safekeeping.

"Where did *you* get them?" Valerie asked, her English more heavily accented.

"What were you doing in my room?"

Valerie shrugged. "It's a hotel. I go in the guests' rooms."

Something was not right. Valerie's nonchalance, rather than intimidating Camilla, had the opposite effect of emboldening her further. She grew taller, inhabited by a sureness she hadn't felt in weeks. Valerie had been caught doing something wrong, and Camilla knew exactly what to do in that situation.

She repeated herself, slowly and quietly. "What were you doing in my room?"

"I was refreshing your fruit plate. It was nearly empty." Valerie raised her eyebrows in silent judgment.

"I was hungry! I've barely eaten all day," Camilla snapped. "It was *my* fruit!"

"You can't stay here," Valerie said. "I've packed your bags and placed them by the door."

An older woman, dressed for a day at the beach, had come into the lobby. She was inspecting the luggage as if it were part of a bric-a-brac sale. Camilla waved her away. "I can see that," she said. "I've paid my bill and I have a reservation. I'm going back to my room."

Valerie looked around at the wall of keys behind her and made an apologetic face. It wasn't convincing.

"This is extortion." Camilla felt something twist in her chest, a burning. It was a familiar feeling. She knew she should take a step back, concentrate on her breathing, find some fresh air, but she needed to deal with Valerie first.

"I'm not leaving until you give me my photos." Her voice came out as a whine, her throat constricting as she spoke.

Valerie had the decency to look a touch uncomfortable. A flush came into her cheeks. "I don't know what you want with us," she hissed. "Why are you here?"

"Why did *you* put the gendarme onto me?"

Valerie stepped back. "Shhh!" The older woman moved closer, her day at the beach forgotten for the moment. "I did not put the police onto you!"

"Then why were you looking through my book?"

Valerie looked sheepish. "I like reading. We don't have a bookstore on the Île de Clair. I have to wait for the guests to leave their unwanted books behind."

She pointed at a bookshelf behind the desk. Camilla hadn't noticed it before. It was filled with dozens of books in a variety of languages, mostly paperback thrillers with cracked spines and water-bloated pages, evidence of days spent at the beach.

Valerie shrugged again. "I thought yours looked good."

"It is, actually," Camilla admitted. "I'll give it to you, if you like, when I'm done."

Valerie smiled. "I like those ones the best. The thrillers. I like trying to work it out before the end. I like trying to find the red herrings."

Camilla clutched at the opportunity. She would give Valerie the book if there was a chance that could get her back on her side. "I'll give it to you now, if you're that interested." She took a couple of steps back and unzipped her suitcase. The book was right on top. "Here we go."

Back at the desk, Valerie took it in both hands. Camilla reached down and grabbed the photos. "Ha!" she cried triumphantly. She tucked the photos in her pocket. "Ha!"

Valerie's face was ashen. "I'm sorry," she whispered. "I couldn't help myself. I don't normally take things from guest's rooms. I have never done it before."

"Why me, then? Why my photos?" And then a more important question came to Camilla, the one she really needed to ask.

She put her hands down on the counter and bent toward Valerie. Up close, Valerie's perfume was discernible: a delicate, smoky sandalwood fragrance that made Camilla's department-store perfume feel matronly. "Do you know a boy—a man—called Henri?"

Valerie's face was blank. The name didn't register at all. "I am sorry. I will have to ask you to leave." She pointed at the suitcase still splayed across the front of the doorway, where yet another hotel guest was stepping over it. The conversation was over. She turned to retreat to the small office behind the counter.

"I don't understand. Is it something to do with the gendarme?"

Valerie paused for a minute, and then turned around. "It is nothing to do with Gerard. It is to do with you. We went to your room to freshen it up. I found the book and the photos."

"What about the photos?"

Valerie took a deep breath, and for the first time, Camilla noticed the deep lines across her forehead. The slightest cracks in the veneer. A warning that something wasn't right. It still didn't prepare Camilla for what Valerie said next.

"The photo of Susie and the others. I took it."

17

Susie, 1998

When David came down the stairs the next morning, Susie was already up, head bowed over a Scrabble board, playing a game for one. She and David had played the night before, after a simple supper of chicken and a grilled peach salad and before David had given her a demure good-night kiss on the top of her head. Despite the two bottles of white wine they had drunk, Susie was unable to notch up either a win on the Scrabble board or any indication of interest from David.

Instead, he had asked her a lot of questions about her childhood and what had brought her to London in the first place. They talked about her plans for the future. His interest would have been encouraging if it hadn't felt quite so anthropological.

The game had ended with Susie's score firmly in double digits and David's resembling a phone number. The kiss on the top of her head seemed like an indication that she had failed at some sort of test, and she was determined to show him there was more to her than he thought. She had seen Camilla play Scrabble against herself for relaxation—it couldn't be that difficult.

It was harder than she expected. Letters never really made sense to Susie the way they did to her sister. Crossword puzzles, word searches—Camilla spent her holidays completing whole books of the things, while Susie would be stuck on the first word search. She thought she had done a good job of the board; *yacht* running into a triple word score was a nice touch, she thought, even if she had tipped out the whole bag of letters to assemble it. Luckily Susie was an early riser, and David, it seemed, was not. It was ten o'clock when he stumbled in.

He looked good in the mornings, his hair mussed up and eyes bleary. Susie resisted the urge to rush and make him coffee or cut up a peach, instead leaving him to wander through the house on a sort of a morning round. First, the terrace, where he ran his hands through his hair and watched the horizon for a long time. Second, he filled a tin watering can and splashed some water on the pots of herbs by the doors. Lastly, he came in and placed his hands on her shoulders, looking over the top of her at the board. Susie's skin fizzed where he touched it.

"That's not how you spell broccoli." He took one hand away and touched the teapot. "You've been up for a while."

"Sorry, it's probably cold." Susie cleared the tiles back into the pouch before David could make any more observations about her wordcraft.

"That's okay, I'll make another." He shuffled off into the kitchen. "You're going to have to work on your Scrabble game before my parents arrive." His words stung. Only the suggestion that he might let her stick around took away some of the pain. He spoke again, but she couldn't hear the words over the whistle of the kettle.

Then she felt him race back past, running up the stairs. He emerged moments later fully dressed and holding an assortment of Susie's clothes. He tossed them over the stair rail. "Come on, put them on. I can't believe the time."

"What's the rush?"

"I'll tell you on the way."

Susie ducked into the downstairs bathroom to pull on her clothes. David waited outside the front door.

"I haven't done my teeth," Susie said when she came out.

"No time," he said, smiling. He was practically jogging as they headed down the path. Susie assumed they were heading to the village where they had eaten the crêpes the previous day. When they came to the point where three paths converged—one to the village, one to the port, and one back up to David's—Susie immediately turned onto the one to the left, to the village, but David grabbed her arm.

"This way!" Laughing, he pulled her toward the harbor path.

"Where are we going? I have to start work at noon—I can't be too long," Susie called after him, skipping for a moment to catch up.

"You start today?" David asked as she came alongside him.

"Yep. Someone has to earn the francs around here." It struck her that she hadn't seen David do any painting since she arrived. "How is your work going?"

"Slowly. I always think I'm going to get straight to work when I get here, but I forget it takes me a few days to acclimatize, settle into the rhythm of life here. The moment always comes, though. I just have to wait for it." He looked around at the blue skies, the gentle arc of the trees above them, the chip of turquoise water at the edge of the path. "I've got a good feeling about today, though. My muse is coming!"

Susie admired his faith in the creative process, but she couldn't help thinking of her parents, slogging away on the property day after day without a break. In their world, there was no acclimatizing; you simply knuckled down and got the work done. Not for the first time, she felt a great gulf between David's experience in the world and her own—and not for the first time, she thought she would far prefer to live life like David and his family. Houses scattered about the place, no money worries, and time to spend strumming guitars and working on your Scrabble game.

"Are you working on a particular project? Your mum said something about representation—do you have pieces that are ready?"

David stopped for a moment, snapped a leaf from the tree above. He rubbed it between his fingers until it split open and spilled its viscous green insides. "I can't have you on my case about this as well."

"Easy, David." She took the leaf from his hand and smelled it. It was lemony, fresh, alive. "I just want to know more about you."

They started walking again. David checked his watch as the harbor came into view. "Sorry," he said, after a few minutes walking in silence. "I'm quite sensitive about it."

"That's okay. I shouldn't have been so intrusive. I don't really know any artists."

David picked up his pace again. "It's a project about the island, a series of watercolors. I'm trying to show how everyday life here is entwined with the mysteries and ancient legends of the island. Perhaps I'll bring them together in a published journal—a sketchbook, I suppose you would call it—or hold an exhibition eventually. I want it to be a snapshot of a unique way of life. There's not many places like it in the world." He was slightly out of breath, but the passion in his voice was evident.

"That sounds fabulous," Susie said. Truthfully, she was just relieved it was a concept she could understand and not some abstract exploration of time and space or existentialism. She could deal with a few paintings of sailboats and farmers. Her breathing was becoming labored as well, and the morning sun was warm. "Seriously, what's the rush? I think there'll be enough croissants for everyone."

They came around the last bend in the path, and it opened up in front of them, revealing the full brilliant curve of the harbor below. Already the beach was filling up, and the shoreline was dotted with striped umbrellas. The water was calm, sparkling. Susie wished she had worn her swimsuit.

"Damn!" David cursed, breaking into a jog. "It's here already."

Susie reluctantly started to run as well. "What's here?" she called out.

"The ferry! It's here." He turned back, still running, his face ecstatic. "It's here, she's here."

A heavy feeling settled in Susie's chest as the meaning of David's distance became clear.

"Who's here?" The voice didn't sound like Susie's; certainly it had little connection with the deep sense of dread she felt.

"My muse! I told you she was coming."

18

Susie had thought the upcoming arrival of David's muse was meta-phorical. She didn't realize that the muse was coming in on a ferry, a ferry that, by the time Susie and David raced down the jetty, had al-ready docked, its passengers dispersed among the many delights of the island. All except for the muse, who sat implacable on top of a suitcase, smoking a cigarette and calmly gazing out to sea.

"Isabel!" David called as their feet thundered on the wooden boards.

Isabel turned around, then put out her cigarette and gave a shy half-wave. David pulled her to her feet, wrapping his arms around her and burying his face in her neck. She caught her sun hat in one hand and laughed with her chin thrown up in the air, delighted to be reunited with David. Susie waited, the impeccable Isabel making her aware she hadn't showered or even washed her hair since her swim the day before.

Finally the pair of them remembered Susie's presence. David stepped out of the embrace, keeping his arm around Isabel.

"Susie, this is Isabel. Isabel, Susie."

Isabel moved forward, her nose crinkling slightly as she kissed Susie on one cheek and then the other. Isabel, on the other hand, smelled fresh. A familiar, floral scent. Freesia? She tucked her long blond hair behind her ears, exposing a pair of golden hoops in each one, and smiled apologetically.

"I hope you don't mind me crashing the party," she said, putting her arm through Susie's. "Do you think we should find some breakfast?"

David picked up her suitcase. "Great idea, Iz," he said, slotting in on the other side of Isabel and putting a proprietary hand on the small of her back. There was an ease—a familiarity—about the gesture, and it gave Susie a wavy sensation in her stomach. She blamed it on hunger, even though her appetite had completely disappeared in the last few minutes. Had David touched her like that? She thought back to him placing his hands on her shoulders, kissing her on top of the head— taking her to play *tennis!*—and it all seemed so fraternal compared to the way he moved his body toward Isabel's.

There was a good chance she might cry. David was watching her warily. It was the humiliation that was threatening to undo her; she wouldn't let him see it.

"Are you a friend of David's?" Susie asked when she felt like she could talk without letting a sob escape.

Isabel and David looked at each other with goofy smiles on their faces and the pure excitement of a long-held plan brought to fruition. They laced their hands together and spoke at the same time. "We . . . ah . . . Isabel . . ."

Susie waited for them to sort it out.

"Isabel is, yes, a friend."

"You look a little more than friends to me." It was meant to sound like a joke, but judging by the look on David's face, Susie's delivery could have been better.

"We're still working things out," he said. "Isabel might share the room with you."

"Oh." A tiny spark of hope.

"David!" Isabel leaned her body into his, pushing him with her shoulder. She looked at Susie. "He's joking, I hope. David?"

"I wasn't sure what you'd be comfortable with." David coughed and stepped aside to let an old man pass with his fishing rod.

"I'll be more comfortable sharing a bed with you than some girl I've just met." She tossed her hair at Susie, who got another burst of freesia. "No offense, Susie."

"None taken," Susie muttered, looking down at the water through the gaps between the boards. She wished she could dive off the edge and hide under the waves until her embarrassment subsided. David hadn't mentioned Isabel, she was sure of it. It was cruel. But then, she had turned up without being invited. At its best, it was a series of crossed wires; at its worst, well, it didn't bear thinking about. She exhaled, considering her options.

"I'm starving, David." Susie had initially taken Isabel as a sophisticated woman of the world, but when she spoke, her youth became more obvious. Without her hat, you could see that there was still a light smattering of pimples around her hairline, and she had the shiny white teeth of a person who had not yet drunk enough red wine or coffee to tarnish them.

"Is it too early to drink?" David looked at his watch, only half joking.

"Is she even old enough to drink?"

Isabel laughed, thinking it was a joke. She grabbed David, pointing at the hotel at the end of the pier. "Maybe we can try there?" Her hand stayed on David's bare arm. Long tanned fingers. Nails bitten down, Susie noticed.

"Are you okay?" Isabel said. Susie hadn't realized she was staring.

"I'm okay." Susie nodded. She needed some time. "I think I need a swim before work. I'll catch up with you later." Without turning back to see their reaction, she rushed off down the jetty. She didn't have her swimsuit or a towel, which would make swimming tricky—as much as she wanted to dive under the deep blue water and forget the last few minutes, she equally didn't want to look like a fool, swimming in her clothing. The first imperative was to get as far away from them as possible.

She thought she was successful until David caught up with her. "Susie!"

"What?"

"I'm sorry I didn't tell you she was coming." He looked down at the ground. The sun was starting to really warm up.

"That's fine. I didn't tell you I was coming either."

"True." Isabel loitered to the side, just within hearing distance. "She's a great girl, you'll really like her."

"How long is she staying?"

"A couple of weeks, maybe. I don't know."

Susie let out a sigh.

David rubbed at his face. "Look, you'll like her."

"Okay." She turned and began to walk off. David grabbed her arm.

"It's going to be fun, Susie, I promise."

"Right." Susie stormed up the hill, so breathless with anger and humiliation that she only half noticed the view: the small cluster of buildings by the ferry point and the busy beach; the larger village, set inland to protect it from winter storms. A flotilla of sailboats flocked past the long curl of land stretching out from the uninhabited section of the island, the children on board earning their sailing stripes. Sheep dotted the rest of the landscape.

She knew the chapel was up this way, but she was still surprised when she stumbled upon it. It was a marker on the island; from most places you could look up and see the small but solid building, the white walls contrasting with the terra-cotta roof. The door was open and there was no one around, so she slipped inside, the cool air drying the perspiration on her body to an icy glaze almost immediately. A lone candle flickered silently at the altar. A fire hazard! Susie looked around. Seeing no one, she marched toward it and, holding back her long hair, blew it out.

"Hey!" The voice startled her. She stood bolt upright, twisting her body to see where it had come from. Whoever had spoken was tucked into the very back row, in a pew hidden behind a small setback at the entrance.

"Hello . . . um, *bonjour*," Susie said. "Sorry, was that your candle?"

A man stood up, his face still concealed. A priest?

"Désolé!" Susie muttered. Sensing a rebuke in the offing, she headed for the door, head down. The man moved quickly to intercept her, placing his hands on both of her arms.

Susie tried to shake him off, and his face moved into the light. Her eyes traveled from his bare tanned feet up his muscly legs and then over his linen shorts and shirt to his inquiring face. He was young. Not a priest, by the looks of it.

"Sorry!" she tried again in English, finally wriggling out of his arms.

"That candle was for my mother." His voice was softer now.

"The candle?" Susie stopped. "Sorry. I just thought it was a fire hazard. Hot day, you know."

It seemed silly, now she said it out loud. The candle was tiny and the chapel was cold. A faint smile moved across the young man's face.

"Fire?" he asked incredulously. "It's just a small candle."

Susie nodded. "You can't be too careful in the heat." She put out her hand. "I'm Susie."

He took his hand in hers and shook it. "Hello, Susie, I am Henri."

17

Camilla

"I knew it was fishy when two Australians turned up in one day," Valerie said. Camilla had just told her that Susie was her sister. She could practically see the cogs turning in Valerie's head as she digested the information.

"Two Australians?" This piqued Camilla's interest. The Île de Clair was an out-of-the way place, not on the usual tourist circuit.

"I think so. You and someone else." A cloud of doubt passed over Valerie's face, and Camilla suspected the other traveler might not be Australian at all.

Valerie dragged Camilla's luggage into the back office. "Follow me." She opened the door to the street and walked straight out. Camilla did what she was told, hoping that Valerie might be taking her to find Henri. It would be churlish to mention her sore and swollen feet, especially as it seemed she had just been granted a reprieve from her eviction from La Belle Hotel.

"I have lived on this island my whole life," Valerie said as Camilla shuffled behind her up the hill. "It's not a bad place to grow up, a little quiet perhaps, but there were always the summer visitors to spice things up. Like your people."

"My people?"

"The tourists. They buy the houses along the front and push the prices up. Now the locals can barely afford to live here. We are all squished in the middle like tiny sardines."

From the path, Camilla could see clusters of houses spread out across the landscape. They looked idyllic to her. Some were smaller than others, yes, but they all seemed to be surrounded by green fields and sheltered gardens.

"The Rowes were the first, though. My parents remember them coming."

"The Rowes?"

"The Rowes. David Rowe. In the photo. They were the first."

"Ah. David *Rowe*. The Rowe family cottage. Of course."

Valerie looked at her as if trying to work something out. "They tried, in the beginning, but people took against them from the start. They bought one of the most historic houses on the island and ripped out some of the walls inside, painted the walls white, and brought their pillows and the like." Camilla had never heard the word *pillows* spoken with such venom.

Valerie paused for a moment and looked down at Camilla's feet. "What size are your feet?"

"Ten."

Valerie looked again and didn't say anything. Camilla was self-conscious about the size of her feet and grateful for her diplomacy. "How did you come to run the hotel?" she asked. "Is it a family business?"

"A family business? No." Valerie gave a rueful laugh. "The hotel is owned by a German company who have a lot of little hotels that are made to seem like they are owned by people like me. People like me cannot afford a place like that."

Camilla regretted her insensitivity. From what she had seen, Valerie was embedded in the fabric of the hotel, and Camilla doubted that anything that went on there escaped her attention. She said nothing, and after a moment Valerie continued.

"I went to college in Paris for a little while, but I always knew I would come back. This island is in your blood, you know? I worked in the hostel for a while, in the village, and after a few years I got a job at the hotel. Then it was sold to the Germans, and they kept me, for the local knowledge. It is a good job." She looked pointedly at Camilla. "This way." They had passed the small row of restaurants and houses on the waterfront and were now climbing the same path Camilla had taken earlier.

"And is that where you met Susie? At the hostel?"

"No. Susie was not staying at the hostel. She was staying with David." She paused. "No. There was one night she did. At the end. Yes."

"So you knew her? Apart from taking the photos?"

Valerie slowed for a minute and turned to look at Camilla. For a second, with the breeze in her blond hair and her blue eyes rimmed in kohl, Camilla got a glimpse of what she must have looked like as a young woman. Glamorous. Susie would have been drawn to Valerie, Camilla thought; she was always drawn to the shiny people. Like a magpie.

"Yes. I did. But it was a long time ago."

"Do you remember her?"

"She was a sweet girl." Valerie sighed. "You said you were here on family matters. Is it something to do with Susie?"

"I'm sprinkling Susie's ashes." Camilla wrapped her arms around herself. Despite the warmth, she still got a chill every time she had to face the fact of her sister's death.

"Susie is dead?" Valerie stopped in her tracks.

"A month ago." The break was a good chance to catch her breath. "There was an accident."

"An accident?" Even with the accent, Camilla could detect suspicion in her voice.

"She fell from a ladder."

Valerie nodded as if that made sense to her. Camilla envied her calm. "And she asked to be brought here?" Valerie waved her hand to indicate the Île de Clair. Her face was thoughtful.

"Yes. The chapel, to be exact."

Valerie didn't offer her sympathy, and for a while they walked in silence. Camilla's shoes were loud on the gravel path, Valerie light on her feet. It wasn't a comfortable silence. Even though she could only see the back of Valerie's head, Camilla was sure Valerie was deep in thought about what she had just learned. So she was surprised that when Valerie spoke again, it was in the form of tour guide.

"The island is around twelve square kilometers. It is actually two small islands connected by a bridge. You can walk around most of it in a few hours." She looked at Camilla's red face before starting to walk again. "Or maybe a little more."

"And you walk everywhere?" They were following the exact same path Camilla had taken to the chapel earlier.

"We have bikes. And some tractors."

Valerie's legs under her navy hotel uniform were tanned and strong. Camilla remembered having legs like that once.

"It must be hard in the winter?" It was hard on a sunny summer afternoon to imagine the Île de Clair covered in frost.

"It is quite, but I am used to it. But we visit one another, take a trip. We paint, look after our buildings and gardens, and prepare for the next summer. From April to October, we are busy again."

"I know what you mean. I'm a teacher, you see. I like the way the years repeat themselves. The same sports days, the same school holidays, the same lessons. The only thing that changes is the children." And me, thought Camilla. Lately even she had started to feel hemmed in by the endless cycle of term times.

Valerie wasn't listening.

"It is because of Henri, isn't it?"

"You know Henri?" In all the fuss with the photos, Valerie had not answered her earlier question.

Valerie looked over her shoulder and raised her eyebrows. Susie was right, then. Any woman on the island would know Henri.

"I suppose it is because of Henri." It was disingenuous to suggest otherwise. There was another option, though. "Or maybe David."

"No." Valerie's voice was firm. "Not David." Camilla waited for her to explain why she was so certain, but instead Valerie asked, "Where will you put them?"

"The ashes?"

"Yes." They passed the spot where the gendarme had crashed into Camilla. Here the path curved alongside a low wall. The trees behind it opened up to reveal a wide stretch of sand, a gentle wave running into the shore. In contrast to the beach near the hotel, this one was nearly empty. Valerie waved at a mother and two small children who were building sand castles and then abruptly turned into a small opening, beckoning to Camilla to follow. Houses were dotted among the surrounding hills.

A line from Susie's letter flashed into her mind. *If you look down the hill toward the sheltered cove, you will see a white house with stone windows. Beyond that is a house surrounded by low stone walls and looking out to sea.*

Camilla looked around. There was a white house with stone windows across the way, and a cottage surrounded by low stone walls. She didn't quite have her bearings, but they had just passed through the narrowest part of the island. David's house. It had to be.

"I put them at the chapel already," she said, distracted now.

Valerie didn't notice. "So that's why you wanted to go to the chapel. I thought you were just being a, you know, tourist."

"Yes." Camilla lifted her hair and pulled at her dress to let some cool air onto her skin.

"The chapel." Valerie looked thoughtful.

"She met Henri there," Camilla snapped.

"Ah."

Valerie opened the gate, and they stepped into the concealed garden. It was overgrown and lush, the mimosa bushes drooped low with blooming flowers and the agapanthus below draped decadently against each other and over the lawn. Some came to higher than Camilla's waist; even the grass brushed at her ankles.

"Whose house is this?" Camilla couldn't bring herself to walk through the gate. "Is this the Rowe family cottage?" She wasn't ready to meet David yet. Susie hadn't said anything about David in the second letter. She needed to speak to Henri first. Her palms started to sweat.

"It's my house. Come in, sit down. I'll bring out some wine."

Valerie lived in David's house?

"Is anyone else . . . is anyone else home?" Camilla edged into the garden. There was still time to bolt. But bolt where? She was on an island, for heaven's sake. And the hotel where she was staying was run by the tiny woman in front of her. She couldn't exactly hide.

Valerie looked out across the garden, where a sliver of the ocean was still visible. "He won't be home for a little while yet."

A little while. They had a little while. Camilla would have one glass of wine and find out what Valerie knew about Henri, and she would be gone before David got back.

Wine. Yes, wine was the answer. Camilla needed a drink, especially after the walk up the hill. Water, perhaps, would be a better idea but wine might just take the edge off. Could Valerie see how nervous she felt?

She sat down on a rickety outdoor chair, an old wooden thing painted a delicate shade of lilac, its paneled seat even more uncomfortable than it looked. She sat half on, half off, ready to bolt at any moment.

Despite Valerie's declaration that the locals lived like sardines, the cottage looked spacious. The windows rose up three stories, the top row sitting high up in the eaves. Through the windows on the ground floor she could see glimpses of blue—the sea was on the other side of the house! This was definitely David's cottage, the house where Susie stayed while she was here.

In the quiet of the garden Camilla was sure she could feel Susie's presence. Despite the beauty of the setting, she could feel something else. Someone else. There were layers of secrets to be peeled back, and she suspected they would expose something darker than she had anticipated—perhaps even darker than Susie had intended to reveal. Valerie was right about Camilla not needing a map on the island, and it wasn't because all the paths and tracks were circuitous and intuitive. It was because Camilla's gut was telling her she was in the right place.

And for the first time in a long time, she was listening to it.

20

Susie, 1998

The next day, when Susie finished helping out Marie, Henri was waiting.

"How did you know I was here?" Susie asked, blushing as she fumbled to untie her apron, untuck her T-shirt.

"Marie told Yvette." Henri smiled at Marie, who uncharacteristically smiled right back. "She said a young Australian girl kept turning up and clearing plates without being asked."

"I asked!" Susie said, whipping around to check if Marie agreed with her. "She said yes." Susie nodded, imitating Marie, but still not entirely sure if Marie *had* said yes after all.

Marie and Henri laughed. Susie felt the same pulse of happiness she had felt in the chapel the evening before. There was something about Henri. It was different from David. Where she could talk with David for hours and find they had the same unconventional opinions about topics big and small, with Henri, the connection was physical. It was like they were circling each other with the exact same intent, drawn together by invisible fibers. It was intoxicating, the prospect of being so physically in tune with someone.

"I wanted to show you something," Henri said.

The crêperie was closed for the afternoon. Marie would open up again for a few hours in the evening as the tourists straggled in from the beaches, but her husband, Gerard, helped out then. Susie was done.

"Is that okay?" Susie asked. Marie held up her hand for her to wait and disappeared. She returned a minute or two later with a couple of grubby notes. Susie didn't mind; it felt good to be earning money again. She and David had been splitting everything two ways so far, and now Isabel had arrived, it would get more complicated.

When Susie returned from the chapel the previous evening, Isabel and David had been lying on the floor by the fireplace, David strumming his guitar. Susie had snuck up the stairs to bed unseen. All night she heard the murmur of their voices until, sometime near dawn, they had come upstairs. They paused on the landing outside David's room, and after a brief conversation, his bedroom door had softly closed behind them.

Susie tossed and turned until it was time to get up. The thought of Henri had gotten her through the long night, and she felt her chances of seeing him again that day were good. The island was not big, and Henri had escorted her back to the cottage the evening before. He knew where she lived.

She was right.

"Thank you!" she called out to Marie as Henri dragged her out the door. "Merci!" The skin on her wrist tingled where Henri's hand touched it, and he didn't take it away once they were out the door. Instead he moved his hand down her arm and took her hand in his, squeezing it softly.

"Marie asked me to tell you to come back tomorrow," he said as the door closed behind them. The village square was quiet in the late afternoon, the tourists at the beach and the locals resting. "I was tempted not to, though."

"Why?" she asked as Henri brought her to a stop beside two bikes.

"I thought I could take you out on my boat."

Susie looked down the hill to the small marina where the tourists moored their yachts and larger boats. Henri followed her gaze. "Don't get any ideas. My boat is a fishing boat. I'll put you to work." Reluctantly she let go of his hand as he swung his leg over one of the bicycles. "Hop on." He pointed to the rust-colored bike next to his.

"It's not mine."

"I know. It's Yvette's. She won't mind."

"Yvette?" It was the second time he had mentioned her.

"Yes." Henri looked over his shoulder as the clock tower struck three. "My aunt. Come on, the tide will be in if we don't hurry."

"Where are we going?"

"For a swim."

Susie had learned to pull her swimsuit on under her clothes every day. There were just too many swimming spots to explore around the island, and she didn't want to miss out again.

They cycled up through the town and out of the village square. It took a lot of concentration to make sure her tires didn't get stuck in the narrow cobblestones, and for a while they rode together in silence. Once they left the village, the path opened up slightly, curving up and around the coves and beaches that Susie was starting to get to know. Henri slowed down a little so Susie could pull up beside him as they passed by paddocks and open fields on one side and aquamarine water on the other.

"It's so beautiful," Susie said. "Have you always lived here?"

"I grew up on a vineyard in Burgundy. My mother died a few months ago." He paused for a moment, and Susie remembered the candle. "I didn't like being there without her. I was not . . . happy. My father used to send me here to spend the summers with my aunt, and this time, I think I will stay." He swung his arm out to show a fork in the road ahead, and Susie had to hit the brakes to make the turn.

"Your English is very good," she said, once back on track. "I can barely speak any French, even though we studied it at school. I thought I might get better here, but so far everyone speaks English."

Henri didn't answer. After a moment they passed into a darker, narrower track, covered overhead by interlinking tree branches.

Susie pushed on, trying to make it look as if she was finding the ride easy, but in truth she hadn't ridden a bike for years. They usually rusted out after the first rainy season.

Henri jumped off his bike while the wheels were still moving and pushed it into some undergrowth. Ahead of them was a small bluff, at the point of which was a tiny stone building. Beyond it was a natural swimming hole created by the tides. Henri was right, though; the tide was moving fast. Before long the swimming hole would be submerged under much deeper water. For the moment, it looked like paradise.

Susie held her breath as Henri pulled off his T-shirt. His back was brown and muscular, narrowing only where it met the frayed waistband of his shorts. Seizing the opportunity to take off her clothes while his back was turned, she whipped her T-shirt over her head and stepped out of her shorts at the same time. Her toe caught in the elastic and she tripped, falling with her head stuck inside her top.

Henri turned and caught her, his large hands almost encircling her waist as she fell. She waited while he untangled the T-shirt from her ponytail. Every centimeter of her skin was charged with feeling. She hadn't ever felt like this before. She hadn't ever been this close to someone who looked like Henri. She had to force herself to stop staring.

"You're not one of David's girls, are you?" Henri asked quietly. He hadn't taken his hands away yet, but there was still space between them.

"David's girls?" Susie didn't want to talk about David at this moment.

"He always has one girl or another here." Henri squeezed his thumb slightly on her hip bone. "Marie said you were different."

Susie sent a silent thank-you to Marie. "David is a friend," she said, feeling faint. If Henri didn't kiss her soon, she might collapse. "I've never even met him before this summer."

"Well, good. That family does whatever it wants. You need to be careful with them." Henri kissed her on the lips, and his warning was forgotten.

21

Camilla

Something thudded next to Camilla's feet: a pair of old canvas sneakers, the laces removed and the backs pushed down. With relief, she kicked off her loafers and pushed her feet into the cool canvas.

"Thank you," she said, despite her nerves. Valerie placed the bottle of wine on the table and offered Camilla a choice between the two sun hats she was holding.

"What's the English saying? You have caught the sun. We have to be careful."

She was right. Camilla's cheeks were burning. She was not at all prepared for the sun. Her ankles stuck out at the bottom of her dress, beacons of white skin. The sun felt good on them but not so good on her face. She accepted one of the hats and placed it on her head while Valerie poured the wine.

"Especially at our age." Camilla took a sip of wine. It was good— cold, fresh, and dry. She took another sip, enjoying how it took the edge off her frazzled nerves but also hoping to finish it and be on her way to finding Henri as soon as possible.

"I am guessing you are a little older than Susie."

Camilla nodded. Every year now she would grow older, and Susie's age would remain unchanged.

"We were so young, that summer when we all met for the first time. So young." Valerie shook her head at the memory and looked out to sea through the small gap in the hedge. The water was still and unchanging.

"How did you all meet?"

"I knew Henri a little already. I was working at the small hostel on the square that summer." Camilla nodded, even though she hadn't made it to the square yet. "It was my first summer working there—I had just returned from studying and working in Paris."

"Lucky you."

Valerie made the small *pffft* noise particular to the French language. "Yes, very lucky. Now I am back here, where I started. They all came that summer. Poor Isabel. Henri, to stay with his aunt. Susie. David."

Hands shaking, Camilla reached down to her handbag and retrieved the photos she had slipped inside earlier. Valerie sipped her wine and fiddled with a strand of hair at her jaw, waiting as Camilla laid the photos out like a croupier, the subtle flick of the paper on the table loud in the quiet garden.

Valerie placed a finger on the third photo, tapping on the face of the second young man.

"David. And this is Isabel." She clicked her tongue. "Susie, you know. And Henri." Her finger lingered on Henri's face. *Isabel. Henri.* Camilla waited for Valerie to elaborate.

Valerie poured some more wine in the glasses. "Olives. Would you like some olives? It's not right to drink without food, is it?" She leaped up and went back to the house again, leaving Camilla to look at the photo again.

Henri had the benefit of youth, a gentle suntan, and a full head of hair, while David's was slightly receding. Slightly older and slightly too tanned, David was nothing compared to the louche glamour of the young Henri beside him in the photo, but he was still a good-looking man. Camilla thought back to the phone call all those years ago in the middle of the night. She was sure that David was the one who'd lured her sister to the island—but why had her affections shifted so quickly to Henri? They all looked so happy in the photo.

A pungent smell wafted from the table. Valerie had returned with the promised bowl of olives, but she'd also brought a baguette and a wedge of cheese, oozy and ripe and the source of the smell, Camilla guessed. Her hunger surged. She tore off a great hunk of bread and smeared it with cheese. Shock and nerves had always fueled her appetite.

Valerie watched her chewing, her own delicate piece of bread and scraping of cheese untouched on the plate.

"Was there a falling-out?" Camilla asked when she had swallowed just enough of her mouthful to talk. By the look on Valerie's face and the crumbs flying through the air, she hadn't swallowed quite enough.

Valerie shifted in her chair. "A falling-out?"

Camilla wasn't convinced. Up until that moment, Valerie's English had been perfect. "Did something happen?"

"You will have to ask Henri." Valerie picked up an olive and nibbled on it. She threw the pip into the garden.

"Do you and David still see Henri? How do you think they will take the news about her death?" Camilla asked.

Valerie looked blank. "David? I don't know."

Grief. It affected everyone in different ways. "How old is Henri now?" she said aloud. "Forty or so?"

"I suppose so." Valerie took a sip of her wine, looking away.

"How old are you?" Camilla blurted out, curiosity getting the better of her.

"I am fifty." Valerie whispered the number.

"You look good." Camilla pulled the hat down lower over her face, suddenly feeling a little self-conscious, even though she was eight years younger. She also felt a little tipsy. No water all day. Not much food to speak of. She should be careful.

"Thank you."

Camilla picked up the photo again. "They all look so young in this photo. What do you know about this one? Isabel?"

"I don't know," Valerie said quietly. "Let's wait for my husband."

"Your husband?" The wine was buzzing in Camilla's bloodstream. She felt woozy. She had to go. She stood up. "I don't want to see David yet." She was still trying to work out where he fit in all of this.

"David?" Confusion in Valerie's voice. And then, softly, "Ah, here he is." Camilla turned to see the outline of a man behind her. It took a moment for her eyes to adjust. He was tall, with olive skin. Pale linen shorts, a denim shirt, and canvas plimsolls with the backs pushed down. Camilla barely heard Valerie's next words over the crashing sound in her ears.

"Camilla, this is my husband, Henri. Henri, this is Camilla."

22

Susie

David and Isabel were sitting out on the terrace when Susie and Henri got back from their swim. Isabel's feet were in David's lap, and he was absentmindedly stroking them while she read something aloud to him from the CD album notes she had in her hand. They had propped a speaker in the open kitchen window, and unfamiliar music played from it, an otherworldly mystical soundscape different from the folk music Susie and David had listened to on repeat since their arrival.

Susie held tight to Henri's hand and pulled him out of the shadows.

"Isabel, David—this is Henri." Henri held a bottle of wine up in greeting, and Isabel jumped up, clapping. She raced into the kitchen to grab more glasses, already right at home. Only twenty-four hours earlier this would have infuriated Susie, but now she was floating on a cloud of Henri-inspired happiness and could only think what the cottage must look like from Henri's perspective—a happy, chilled commune vibe. They took their places in two of the remaining chairs and sat back, the wooden slats pressing into their sun-kissed bodies.

"My favorite!" Isabel said as she took the bottle from Henri.

It was the cheapest bottle they could find in the market. Henri had been ashamed to buy it, but they were on a budget; he couldn't afford to be snobbish now that he was a long way from his family vineyard.

Susie was starting to learn that Isabel was one of those people who was enthusiastic about everything, even a bottle of wine she couldn't possibly have heard of before. Rather than being annoying, it was actually quite endearing. The way she poured the wine into their glasses—all the way to the top—was also very endearing.

"À votre santé," Henri said, raising his glass to each of them in turn.

"How did you two meet?" Isabel asked, taking a big gulp of her wine. She twisted her earring while she waited for the answer.

"We met at the chapel," Susie said, realizing it sounded a little weird.

"Oh, are you religious?" Even the thought of a visit to a church animated Isabel. "I wouldn't have thought it by looking at you! Do you pray every day?"

"I wasn't there—," Susie began, but Henri placed his hand on hers before she could finish. "I was there to pray to my mother," he said. "I like to light a candle and think of her some evenings. Susie was there. She is a spiritual person." He rubbed her thumb between his fingers, and she buzzed at the combination of his touch and being described as spiritual.

David still hadn't said anything.

"And then we went to the beach this afternoon, for a swim. Rupert's Regret, I think, David?"

Henri looked at her quizzically. "Rupert's . . . ?"

David pointed through the cottage. "She's talking about the beach opposite."

"*La plage* Pepin. We swam there today." For a second, the two men locked eyes. The older one spoke first. "How is Yvette?"

"She is good." Henri sipped his wine, one foot resting on his knee. He had a proprietary air about him, as if he, rather than David, owned the house.

"Yvette is the midwife on the island," David explained. "She was the one who delivered me, all those years ago."

"Wow. She must be very old," Isabel said. David kicked her foot gently.

"She is not that old, actually, not yet sixty," Henri said. "Anyway, she is a young soul."

"I was born in August 1968," David said helpfully. "I'm about to turn thirty." Susie and Isabel shared a moment of eye contact.

"You didn't tell me you were born on the island, David." Isabel spoke with an injured air. All those hours talking the night before, and they hadn't covered this territory.

"I consider myself a local."

"And how did you meet Isabel, David?" Henri asked. "She is a lot younger than you, *non?*"

Isabel giggled, reached forward, and grabbed her cigarettes from the table. "We went to school together," she said and took a deep drag of her cigarette. She eyeballed Henri, almost wanting him to challenge her. He waited until it was almost uncomfortable and then laughed, reached over, and clapped David on the shoulder.

David seemed to visibly relax. He laughed too, took another big sip of the wine, and sat back and took in the scene around him: the sun about to set behind the laburnum tree, the lapping of the sea at the garden wall mixing with the gentle techno beat, the four of them sipping wine in the dappled evening light. "Good," he said, "this is good. It's going to be a good summer."

Only Susie was confused by what had just happened. But it seemed gauche, somehow immature, to ask for clarification.

Susie screamed as Henri flew past her down the hill, the air shifting as he passed. David and Isabel were following, but they were prone to stopping from time to time to take a moment on the side of the track. David was always finding vistas he wanted to capture later, snapping flowers from their stems to sketch at home. Not Susie and Henri. For them, it was a race. From the moment they left the cottage until the first splash of briny salt water, they competed to be the first to dive under the cool, clear waves.

And it looked like Susie was going to lose today.

She raced after him, camera banging against her chest and her legs pumping furiously as the path rose up the hill. She came to a fork in the road. There was no sign of Henri. Both directions led to beaches; they split their time evenly between the two. One was sheltered, favored by families. The other was more exposed to the wind. On a good day, it was glorious, the larger waves perfect for bodysurfing. But was it a good day? Which beach was best in which weather was a curious alchemy she left up to the locals to decide.

"Wait!" she called. "Henri!" Her shouts disappeared down the empty lane, the low-hanging trees absorbing all sound. She couldn't hear David and Isabel either. A lizard wandered across the path in front of her, in search of sun like everyone else on the Île de Clair. It moved quietly over the stone, the only sound the thudding of her heartbeat.

"Henri?" Her voice was less certain now. She didn't like the sound of it.

Something cracked behind her, and she turned. There was no one. It was the middle of the afternoon, and the people of the island were resting. The shutters of the houses they passed along the way were closed against the warm afternoon sun; tractors and fishing boats sat empty until the cool relief of the afternoon.

Her bike jerked forward. Two hands landed on her handlebars.

"Boo!" Henri whispered. Susie jumped. The words sounded foreign and somehow sinister in his accent. She pulled her bike back, frightened. Angry. "Don't!" she said, unable to find any other words through her anger. "You frightened me!"

Henri laughed. "But it's the broad daylight," he said, and somehow managed to pull the bike toward him, Susie and all. Susie offered no resistance. She craved his physical presence and couldn't help being drawn into his orbit.

"Close your eyes," he said, rubbing his hands together and opening his palms under her nose. Susie inhaled deeply, used to this by now. Before he left home to stay with his aunt, Henri had worked on his family vineyard in Burgundy, and he let his nose lead him through the world.

"What is it?" she asked.

"You tell me."

The smell was familiar. Most of the time, Susie had no chance of identifying Henri's finds, but this one was different. Floral, but slightly soapy. It reminded her of home.

"Rosemary!" she shouted, opening her eyes.

He rewarded her with a kiss and placed the herb in her shirt pocket. His mouth tasted slightly of the cigarettes he was always smoking. Susie told him she hated the smell of the cigarettes, but in truth she was growing to like the way he smelled. It was just another layer in the composition of Henri: cigarettes and rosemary and something earthier Susie didn't recognize.

"Come on, lovebirds!" Another whoosh of air as David cycled past, his bike veering dangerously close to them, Isabel close behind, giggling. It was easier, as the days went on, to forget the age difference. At eighteen, Isabel wasn't that much younger than Susie. At one time, Susie had been prepared to overlook David's age in her own pursuit of him, yes. But still, Susie felt there was something off about the relationship between Isabel and David. She was trying to get past it.

Thank God for Henri. If it wasn't for Henri, she might have left the island when Isabel arrived. If it wasn't for Henri, she might have missed out on this incredible week. She didn't want to think about leaving. David's parents would be arriving soon, and he still hadn't decided whether it would be okay for Susie to stay on. In the meantime, she was going to be as nice as pie. Even to Isabel.

She rested her head on Henri's shoulder just for a moment. He put his arm around her and squeezed her shoulder reassuringly. He knew what she thought of the David and Isabel situation, even if it didn't bother him.

The four of them had quickly become a unit: David, Henri, Isabel, and Susie. The last week had been idyllic, and in between Susie's shifts at the crêperie, they had done little else apart from swimming and sunbathing and scouting for hidden locations.

The sketchbook had become their raison d'être: the reason they clambered down cliffs and set out at first light. David was convinced he was creating something of importance to the island. Sometimes Susie watched him as he painted, his tongue poking out slightly in concentration, his head bowed over the work. There was an intensity to his movements that showed up in some of the pictures, an emotional depth that gave the tranquil subject matter resonance.

Susie wasn't sure if it was creative satisfaction or something to do with the Île de Clair itself, but as the days passed and the pages filled up, David seemed to physically grow as well. As he cycled farther away from Susie and Henri, his back in the distance looked strong, his shoulders held back as he pushed up the hill.

Susie and Henri got back on their bikes and chased after them, taking the westerly fork in the path: the quiet cove. They all arrived at the rocky beach at roughly the same time. They had it to themselves, apart from one young girl drying herself after a swim. They piled their bikes up under one of the pine trees, Henri rushing to be the first in the ocean, David and Isabel collapsing onto a hastily arranged blanket in the sun.

"Come on, guys," Susie said, "how about a photo?" She had a few shots left on her roll of film, and she was determined to get a nice shot of her and Henri. Once she got home, she would want proof that this summer ever happened—that Henri ever happened.

If she went home. More and more over the last week she had toyed with the idea of staying. She could find more work on the island, maybe rent a little place for herself once David left at the end of the summer. There was a small hostel in town; she could stay there. She hadn't told anyone her thoughts yet.

"There is no one here to take it. Why don't I take one of you?" Henri asked.

"Okay. And then the four of us." And then she could suggest one of just her and Henri without it looking stalkerish. "We could get that girl over there to take it."

She smiled, her eyes slightly squinting in the sun. As soon as the shutter clicked, she reached for Henri. Casual. Keep it casual, she told herself.

"And one with you," she said, feeling his warm bare flesh against hers as she came in close for a photo. "David, can you take it?" David reluctantly got up from the blanket and took the camera.

Henri didn't protest as Susie pulled him even closer for the photo. She resisted the urge to turn and make sure he was looking at the camera. The shutter clicked again. Relief flooded through her. She had a photo. And it hadn't been weird. She didn't think, anyway. Henri kissed her on the forehead and was about to move away, but Susie put her arm out to stop him.

"I'll just ask this girl to take one of all of us."

The lone swimmer was leaving; she smiled at them on her way to the track. Up close, the girl was older than she looked from a distance, the fine lines around her eyes giving her away.

"Susie, don't . . ." David held the camera back.

"David, don't be weird."

"Would you mind taking a photo for us?" Susie asked, grabbing the camera from his hands and passing it to the woman before she had a chance to decline.

The swimmer accepted it and smiled at Susie. After a moment she said, "Hi, Henri." Henri looked down at his feet. Then to the others, "I'm Valerie, by the way."

David let out a sharp breath, somewhere between a sigh and a profanity.

"Come on, guys, hop in the photo," Susie said, grabbing Henri's hand in case he made a break for it. "Thanks, Valerie."

"Susie . . ." David's voice held a warning.

"What? Come on, just one picture of the four of us."

"Come on, David." Isabel jumped up and joined the others. Susie held Henri's hand tight. She could feel his gaze traveling to the beckoning sea. They didn't have long. Valerie was waiting, camera half raised. When they were all in a row, arms around each other, she took the photo.

The lens clicked. And something clicked in Susie's brain. She had taken a lot of photos since arriving on the island, and David hadn't been in any of them. He had taken one of Susie under the plane trees in the village and one of Susie up at the chapel with the view behind her. David was always behind the camera, Susie in front of it.

"Hang on," she said to David, still holding Henri's hand and feeling time moving against her. "Have you been avoiding photos this whole time?"

David looked uncomfortable.

"Have you?"

"I don't know what you're going to do with them."

"It's fine, David." Isabel threw her arm around David, whispered something to him. "She's not going to do anything with them."

Valerie was still holding the camera. Henri shook his hand out of Susie's and lit a cigarette. He walked off and stood down at the water's edge. Valerie handed the camera back and slowly wandered off.

"What do you think I'm going to do with them?" Susie asked, the glow from moments before fading quickly. "Don't you trust me?"

"I trust you," David said. Isabel hovered around for a moment and then walked down to join Henri. Susie couldn't help but watch as her figure retreated down the beach. Red bikini. Long hair down her back. She swallowed the jealousy she felt as Isabel accepted the cigarette from Henri and took a long, practiced drag.

"But?" The breeze tickled Susie's bare skin. It rose in dimples, the fair hair standing on end.

"What if someone gets hold of it?"

"Gets hold of it? The KGB?"

"I'm a private person, Susie."

Henri and Isabel shared the cigarette until it was down to nothing. Henri pressed it down into the sand. The gesture grated on Susie. It was the first wave of distaste she had felt for him. She pushed it away.

"But what about your paintings?" Susie said. Henri was saying something to Isabel. She shook her head. He kicked the side of his foot in the water, sending a gentle spray in her direction. Isabel tossed her head back and laughed.

Something shifted in David's face. He pulled his T-shirt over his head. His skin was already a deep tan, just like Susie's. Susie had gotten her mother's coloring, but her father's body shape. Even on the most overcast days her father was careful with sunscreen and hats, while her mother luxuriated in the sun's rays. David had not so much as sat under an umbrella the whole time they were on the island, and had not once ended up even slightly red. Just like Susie.

"Listen, Susie. The photos. It's just not a good look, you know, if the photo was to get out." He focused on a spot far out at sea.

"Okay." Susie wasn't sure what she was agreeing to. Something didn't feel right.

"Maybe you can give me the photo of the four of us. When it's developed."

Henri came racing out of the water. Isabel stayed out beyond the waves.

"Come on," Henri called, beckoning to them both. "It's good! Fresh!"

He came closer. Susie felt the coldness from his body even before he wrapped his arms around her. He kissed her on the shoulder. "Come on, less talking. More swimming!"

Susie looked back at David, and he nodded. Conversation over. She tried to smile. It almost worked. She let herself be dragged back down to the water, because Henri said it was good, and she trusted Henri.

23

Camilla

Camilla and Henri stared at each other. Life on Île de Clair was presumably free of interruptions by people turning up unannounced in your garden, especially middle-aged women who happened to be wearing your shoes.

"You're back early," Valerie said weakly before talking to Henri in French. Within seconds she was back inside the cottage, pausing to shout something out the window and then reappearing again with another bottle of wine, a glass, and a corkscrew and dragging a kitchen chair.

"Here," she said to Camilla. "This one is better."

Camilla felt a rush of gratitude for Valerie's kindness. She wished Susie had mentioned Valerie in the letters. She had no way of knowing how Valerie fit into the story. Could the relationship between Valerie and Henri be behind Susie's heartbreak? Had Camilla been sent all this way to settle an old lover's score? She felt like she had been unleashed inside a pinball machine, her sense of surety and direction completely taken away. She was at the mercy of Susie—and these strangers.

"I have to go inside now," Valerie said.

Henri hadn't spoken again. He sat down and opened the wine. The cork came out effortlessly, and he splashed a couple of inches in the glass. Camilla watched as he held the golden liquid up to the light, tilting it here and there and then just as suddenly tipping it into his mouth and drinking the bulk of it down in one satisfied slurp. He smacked his lips in appreciation.

"Nice?" Camilla asked.

Henri noticed her empty glass and poured a splash into it. "Very. It's from my family vineyard in northern Burgundy. You try."

Camilla started to take a sip.

"No, first this." He took the glass from her and swirled the wine in it, the liquid coming dangerously close to spilling. He held it up to her nose. "Then smell."

Camilla felt her cheeks beginning to burn. If there was one thing she liked less than trying new things, it was trying new things in front of other people. Particularly strangers. Particularly strangers who looked like Henri. She hadn't noticed other men for years, but he was something else. Perhaps it was the island air making her crazy, but her senses felt alive, prickling at the slightest stimulation.

She took the glass back and did what she was told.

"What can you smell?"

"Wine?" she said.

Henri was not impressed. He held his own refilled glass up to his face, his nose practically inside, and inhaled, a deep animalistic sound. "Lemon? Pear?"

Camilla tried again. "Yes, pear, for sure." She took a big sip.

"How does it feel in your mouth?"

She tried to talk, but the wine went down the wrong way, and she started to splutter. Henri watched her with great interest.

Camilla felt a pang of envy of his ability to live in the moment. He was so self-contained, happy to sit in his garden and drink wine and not ask who she was, what she was doing. It felt destructive to upset that equilibrium. But Susie had said to show him the photos. They were on the table, slightly hidden under the plate of cheese. She moved the plate aside so they were visible.

"I'm Susie's sister," Camilla blurted out, pushing the photos toward him.

"Who?" Henri looked perplexed, his dark eyes searching Camilla's for answers.

"Susie Anderson."

The name meant nothing to him; his face was blank. He tugged at his collar and scratched his chin with callused, yellow-nailed fingers. Up close, you could see the creeping march of age—his skin weathered, a darkness under his eyes. A stale smoky odor. Camilla waited for a spark of connection. Otherwise, it was just too—well, too sad. To think that Susie had pinned all her hopes on this man, and he didn't even remember her.

She tapped the photo impatiently, and he looked at it.

"Ah! Susie!" he said, finally. A long moment passed. "She was very attractive." He looked over her shoulder toward the house, swallowing visibly. Camilla understood: she would feel anxious if someone turned up at her house and wanted to talk about a romantic entanglement from her past. Or Ian's. Even if either of those scenarios was very unlikely.

"Susie is—was—my sister." At the past tense, a slight flicker of guilt passed across Henri's face. Despite the language difference, he obviously discerned the nuance. "She died a month ago." It didn't feel like a month. It felt like time had never felt before. Trickling past for hours, and then in an instant a whole afternoon could be lost staring at a wall.

"Ah, Susie." A deep exhale. The same words he had already spoken, this time filled with lament. Whatever Henri had forgotten, there was plenty he remembered. He sat back in his chair, visibly more relaxed.

"How did you meet Susie?"

"I met her one summer. It was 1998, the year my mother died. My father sent me here to stay with my aunt after some trouble at home." He waved his hand in the air. "I never left again. I fell in love that summer"—he paused; Valerie had still not come out from the house— "with the island. The peace. I was able to stay and help my uncle on his fishing boat, and I never went back to the vineyard."

"What was Susie doing here?"

"She was on holiday. With David. And Isabel. Poor Isabel." He paused again. "We spent the whole time together, when we could. Valerie and I, we still had to work. Susie worked too, a little. In the crêperie. But the others, they did what tourists do. When we could, we joined them. We swam, we caught fish. We looked at the stars. We never do those things anymore.

"The crêperie. It's still here, in the square. Marie, the owner, she might remember Susie." He clapped his hands together. "You could try her."

"Susie specifically told me to find you."

Henri looked sheepish. "Susie and I, we had a nice time. She loved the island. She was a great girl." He didn't even stumble over the past tense; for him, Susie had always been in the past. In Henri's mind, Susie had been gone for years, the young girl dead and forgotten as soon as she left the island. Camilla envied his scar tissue; her wound was fresh and raw.

"But?"

He shrugged and picked at his fingernail. "She was just a girl. I was just a boy."

"I think you were more than a boy to her."

Henri looked at the photo again. The one just of Susie. Her fresh face, big smile, eyes filled with love. The window to the kitchen was still open; he spoke quietly. "You are right. She was . . ." He blushed. A teenager again.

"She loved you."

Another shrug. He filled his glass again and went to do the same for Camilla. She put her hand over her glass.

"And?"

"And what? We had a holiday fling. A—what do you call it—summer romance?" He drained his glass, not meeting her eyes. When he'd finished, she watched him carefully. There was something in his eyes that hadn't been there earlier. A glint of something hard.

Camilla stood up and grabbed her bag from the back of the chair. She snatched the photo out of his hands, wincing as it ripped at the corner.

"Don't be mad, *chérie!*" Henri called to her retreating back.

Camilla was almost out the gate, but something was niggling at her. Something in the way Henri had examined the photo.

She turned back. Henri was leaning back in his chair, and in that short time had finished his glass and lit a small brown cigarette. He was taking long, languid inhales, but Camilla could see that his hand was trembling.

"Why poor Isabel?"

"Isabel?" he asked, sitting up. Valerie's face appeared at the window. Even through the glass, Camilla could discern a change in her demeanor, a shadow across her face that hadn't been there before.

"The other girl in the photo. Why did you say 'poor Isabel'? Valerie said it too."

Henri didn't say anything for a moment. There was silence in the garden. A bike crunched along the stones of the path beyond. Valerie came out of the kitchen and placed a hand on Henri's shoulder.

"You don't know about Isabel?" Henri finally said. And then he looked over Camilla's shoulder, at the same moment that she sensed someone behind her. She turned to see what he was looking at.

The gendarme was coming in the gate. He seemed flushed, hot from the ride up the hill. He spoke quickly, in French. Henri shook his head slightly and then tilted it in Camilla's direction. The gendarme turned slowly, and a shadow of realization crossed his face, just before he turned deathly white.

"What about Isabel?" Camilla looked between Henri and the gendarme, waiting for the answer to her question. Something passed silently between the two men, and she knew she wouldn't get any more out of Henri for the moment.

"Camilla, I need to speak with my friend Gerard." Henri took another cigarette from his pack and held it loosely between two fingers. When Camilla didn't move, he rubbed the skin between his eyebrows. "I will come and see you later."

"Unless Valerie decides to kick me out again. Then I'll probably be camping on a beach somewhere." Her voice sounded hysterical, even to her own ears.

The gendarme spoke quickly in French. All Camilla heard were a lot of *non*s.

"What's he saying?"

"He is saying you can't camp without a permit."

"I don't want to camp! I want to go back to the hotel and the bed that I have already paid for."

"Valerie!" Henri's voice was loud and clear; it bounced off the stone wall and around the garden. Valerie emerged from the house holding a book—Camilla's book!—her fingers marking the page. They spoke quickly in French, and then Valerie nodded once and returned inside.

"She said to go back to the hotel. Your room is okay for tonight." Camilla nodded, resisting the urge to thank Valerie for letting her have her room back. "She said you will miss your dinner reservation if you don't hurry." He looked up at the setting sun and smirked. "That must be a joke for you."

Camilla ignored the comment. "And you will come and see me later on tonight?" She wasn't going to let him dodge her questions.

"Oui," he said simply. It wasn't convincing, but it was hard to argue with.

Remembering the letter she had for him in her bag, for a moment Camilla considered giving it to him. He had shifted his attention to Gerard, and something about the way he had so quickly dismissed her was infuriating. She put her hand on the letter in her basket. She would not give it to Henri just yet.

She would read it herself.

24

Letter Four

For Henri—of Île de Clair fame

Yes, that's right, Mills, a change of pace.
Deliver this one for me.

xox

Hello Henri,

I wonder if you remember me.

I wonder if you will ever receive this letter.

My grandmother Nellie once told me that the cruelest part of life is the unknowing—the people you meet who become important to you and then fade away, the secrets people take with them, the words left unsaid. When I left the Île de Clair, I thought I would return. I didn't know that my last night on the island was the end of the story for me and you.

We never got a chance to talk about what happened that night. I blamed you, of course I did, but as I get older I can see how silly it was of me to expect any more from you. We were so young! You tried to talk to me about it, the night at the fair, and I brushed you off. If we'd just talked about it properly, maybe things would have turned out differently.

I was young and scared—I didn't have the perspective to understand that what we had was as good as it gets. Instead I was cavalier with the fragile bond that connected us that summer. And what you did that night blew it apart. I thought I would never forgive you, but I guess it's true what they say about age mellowing people . . .

If you're reading this, you will have met my sister, Camilla. Isn't she beautiful? She won't know what to make of all this—please try and make her feel welcome. By all means, encourage her to jump from the bridge. She could do with some exhilaration in her life.

Camilla has always been the quieter of the two of us, the more sensible. Growing up with Camilla always made me feel like I was a little bit wrong, like I didn't fit properly in my family. Of course we talked about that, you and I. You knew what it was like to be sent away from family.

I'm sending her to you so you can explain what happened on the island. Despite everything, I trust you. You made me feel safe and strong and alive. I was too young to know I loved you, and I was too afraid to say it. I don't mind saying it now, and I don't mind if you didn't love me back.

I think you did, though.

And luckily for me, it's too late for you to disagree.

One last thing.

As I was leaving the island, I gave your uncle the sketchbook. I wanted you to have the painting of us, the one David painted, of us jumping off the bridge. It summed up everything about how I felt about you.

I took the sketchbook in the heat of the moment, desperate to claim something of the island for myself. But mostly I wanted to take something meaningful from that family after all they had taken from me. It wasn't mine to take, though. It was David's life-work, and if you still have it, I am going to ask Camilla to return it to him.

You were always in my heart, Henri, broken and bruised as it was.

I love you,
Susie

25

Susie, 1998

"Wait!" David was furiously sketching, shifting his gaze between the sketchbook and the pair of them poised on the bridge. "I'll just get the outline right."

Susie looked at Henri, partly for reassurance and partly because if she looked down at the tidal waters below, she would lose her nerve. The bridge hadn't looked high from the path, but standing on the other side of the iron railing, the distance down to the water was daunting. Why had she agreed to this? Henri squeezed her hand, and she remembered why: one, because she would do anything Henri asked her to do; and two, because 1998 was her year of saying yes to everything. Jumping off bridges included.

"You can do it," Henri whispered to her. "It's not so high. The children do it all the time." He was right, they did. Susie heard their screams of joy every time she cycled along this path. It was no different from the gorges she had jumped into as a child, climbing up the rocks until she found the very highest outcrop, her father nodding his encouragement from the water below. She knew the fear would soon be replaced by the rush as she leaped into the air, the short sharp shock of the water, the bliss of endorphins charging through her system.

But these waters were unfamiliar, and she was putting her trust in Henri, not her father. She smiled weakly and with her free hand checked the ties on her bikini. The water surged beneath, darker blue than the nearby coves.

"David, come on!" The breeze was cool up on the bridge. The hairs on Susie's arms stood up, soldiers on hills of goose bumps.

"Nearly ready," he called back.

Henri leaned over and kissed Susie on the lips. "Let's do it." He was close enough to whisper. Susie nodded. "On the count of three," he said. And on three they jumped, holding hands all the way down and not letting go.

"David wants you to come and do a picture with me." Isabel rolled her eyes and turned her back to the shore so only Susie could see her face, and not David. "Again."

"You and *me*?" Susie wasn't sure how David felt about the fact that she and Isabel had been spending a lot of time together. Sometimes, and this was just a feeling she had, nothing concrete, she got the impression David was jealous of the closeness between them.

Because despite the rocky start, the two girls were getting on well. Isabel was easy to be around. She was certain about her opinions on everything, and she didn't let David change her mind. If he laughed at one of her CDs or sniffed at her taste in drinks, she simply smiled and carried on dancing or sipping. Susie found herself modeling her behavior a tiny bit on what she thought Isabel might do in the same situation.

"It's your lucky day." Isabel poked her tongue out and adjusted her bikini top where a tiny sliver of white skin was exposed. It was another glorious day on the Île de Clair. Susie had a rare day off, but Henri and Valerie were working—Henri with his uncle, Valerie at the hostel.

"What's he going to do with them all?"

Once Isabel arrived on the island, David's creative side came to life, and there was barely a day he didn't cycle off for hours on his own to paint different vignettes of island life. He carried his watercolor kit with him at all times—one of the bikes from the cottage had a specially engineered rack for the case to sit on. It was wooden, bulky, and had belonged to his grandfather, and watching David trying to cycle with it and keep his balance was entertainment in itself.

"Sell them to pay for our baguettes, I suppose."

"Do you think they're good enough to sell?" Susie's art education pretty much started and finished at what she had learned from David, so she lacked confidence in her conviction, but she was starting to think he was creating something special.

"I think the ones of me are nice." Isabel bumped her elbow playfully into Susie's forearm. "Don't you think?"

"Yes, he's made the best of a tricky subject," Susie said, even though she agreed: David's portraits of Isabel were the best. There was one in particular of her on the terrace at the cottage, eyes down and strumming the guitar under the dappled light of the laburnum tree. It captured the languid feel of the long island days and the melancholy, otherworldly feeling of summer twilights.

"Well, now it's your turn," Isabel said. "Let's see what he does with you."

They walked up the beach to meet David, Susie's hair dripping down her back, Isabel's dry and perfect. Isabel didn't really like to get her hair wet. It was one of her very few shortcomings.

"What would Grandfather think of that?" Susie asked as they reached David. His precious wooden painting kit was half submerged in the sand.

"Art in the wild." He winked and pulled two brightly striped beach towels parallel to each other. "Remember the Monet?"

"He's talking about *The Beach at Trouville*. The one with the sand in it?" Isabel explained, throwing herself down on the right-hand towel. "Just here, okay?" She lay back and flopped one arm over her face. She had a small mole under her bicep that Susie hadn't seen before.

David ignored her for a moment. "Susie, you sit this way," he said, grabbing her by the shoulder and pushing her down. She stretched out her legs in front and felt David's gaze on her feet. Part of the reason that she was so peculiar about other people's feet was because her own were so gnarly. Along with her olive skin and her stubborn nature, her mother had also handed down her unusual toes. Just like her mother's,

Susie's pointer toe was longer than her big toe and curled outward, twisting on top of her middle toe. She buried them under the sand self-consciously and reached for her hat and glasses.

"No. No hats or glasses, please." David held out his hand to take them away. "Just natural. I want it to be timeless. Not some golden-age Riviera pastiche."

"David, I love my glasses."

"I'll take good care of them." He jammed them in his pocket, along-side a corkscrew and a paintbrush. "Isabel, can you take those brace-lets off?" Isabel's left arm was piled with silver bracelets and bangles; they made noises when she walked.

"No. You said you wanted it to be natural?" Her voice was muffled as she reclined back into the sand.

"Isabel, can you please sit up? I don't want you lying around like a package holiday tourist."

"People lie down on beaches, David." Isabel sat up, wiping the sand from her hands as she did.

"I'm thinking I'll paint the others in later. Can you leave a space between the two of you for Valerie? I'll put Henri to the side."

"Of course you will," Isabel whispered to Susie. "Bet he gives him a double chin and a bald patch as well."

Susie tried to keep a straight face. David was sensitive about his art, but he was also strangely competitive with Henri. More than once she had seen David watching the younger man, but she knew better now than to think it had anything to do with her. David was obsessed with Isabel—obsessed—and apart from when he was working on his paint-ings, he hardly ever let her out of his sight.

"All right, girls, I'm going to step back and do this from a distance. Make it look as if you're chatting. Having fun." He stepped backward, losing himself in the appraisal of the scene.

"We have nothing to chat about," Isabel moaned, flopping back on the sand. "Nothing at all."

"Sit up!" David shouted across the sand.

Isabel pretended she hadn't heard him.

"Let's talk about David," Susie said, when it was clear from the shouting that David couldn't hear them talking at normal volumes. "That gives us plenty of material."

Isabel sighed.

Susie carried on regardless. "Where did you two meet?" Since the first day, Susie had chosen to avoid the subject. Their circumvention of the topic had made her uneasy, but her curiosity had finally triumphed over her discomfort.

Isabel rolled onto her stomach so she could see Susie better. From down the beach they heard David shout his disapproval. "Like I said, we were at school together." A small smile played at the corner of her lips. Susie felt her stomach twist a little.

"That's clearly a lie. You're what, eighteen?" Isabel nodded. "The same age as me. Pretty much. I just turned nineteen. And David is nearly thirty. It doesn't make sense." Isabel waited. And then, suddenly, it did make sense.

"Oh," she said, letting the revelation unfurl in her mind. "Oh," again, as the certainty of it joined together all the loose ends. "He was a teacher," Susie said, thinking aloud now. "And that's why he was fired."

David shouted again and started to move toward them. Isabel made a quick mea culpa face before rolling onto her back, giving Susie a few moments to process. The vision Susie had of their happy little group distorted and swam and became just a little murkier.

"He was my A-level art history teacher." Isabel sat up straighter, her eyes lit up. Was it possible that just the thought of David could physically transform her? Susie definitely felt a buzz when she thought about Henri, but was it visible to the onlooker? She didn't know.

"I'll tell you a little about David," Isabel said, watching him as he worked. "He is—was—the best teacher. He was the one teacher everyone in the school loved—his classes were oversubscribed, and his annual art trip to Venice was legendary. Three nights in the city, staying in a tiny pension David organized, and walking the streets and galleries for eighteen hours a day. There was not one person who went on that trip who didn't come back changed, their appreciation for art cemented forever."

Susie nodded, remembering him in the gallery.

"I was put in his class, and to start with, I wasn't convinced. He seemed a little too Dead Poets, a little too earnest for me. I sat in the back row and waited to be impressed. David wasn't used to that; he was used to students with stars in their eyes. And I think that's why he took a special interest in me."

"Right," Susie said dryly. She cast her eye down Isabel's bronzed body, clad only in her bikini. She could imagine Isabel at school, one of the shiny smart girls with a million friends and even more accomplishments.

"He spent a lot of time with me, helping me to work through my assignments. One weekend we caught the train to London together to see a Van Gogh exhibition. I didn't realize it was just me and him until we got to the station. Even then, it felt normal. Okay. It was during the Venice trip that things started to happen."

"What did the other kids think? Your friends?"

"It didn't seem like such a big deal. We didn't even try to keep it a secret, really." Susie raised her eyebrows. "I know," Isabel conceded, "obviously it was. But to start with, I told a few friends and nothing happened, and David told one close colleague and nothing happened, and well, I guess we got complacent."

"What happens now? I mean, you're eighteen . . ." Susie hesitated, not sure what she felt.

"He asked me to come out here during the summer, and I felt like I couldn't say no, not after what happened."

"You didn't want to come?" David clearly loved Isabel. Susie had thought Isabel felt the same.

"It was different when we were at school. More fun. Now he just seems, well, older. He wants to work on his sketchbook all the time. Things seem more serious." Isabel's voice wobbled a little.

"I thought you were having fun?"

Isabel shifted her weight onto one arm, scratched at a little bit of skin that was peeling on her shoulder.

"I *am* having fun. I *do* really like him. It's just, I'm eighteen and we're shacked up in his cottage like we're an old married couple. I mean, this could be it for me. David and Isabel, together forever. It freaks me out sometimes." She smiled at Susie. "What about you, Susie? Would you settle down with Henri now? For good?"

The idea had occurred to Susie a few times in the previous weeks, but she had quickly batted it away. First, she was too young. Second, it was a holiday romance, wasn't it?

"I'm meant to go to uni. Back in Australia. I'm going to study arts."

Isabel sensed her hesitation. "But?"

David looked up from his sketchbook and watched them carefully. Susie envied him his complete immersion in the task. She hadn't found her thing yet—the thing she could lose herself in, the way David lost himself in his painting.

"But I like it over here."

Isabel dug her feet into the sand. Her toes popped out farther down, ten tiny pearls. "What about your study?"

"I just don't know if I'm going to find what I'm looking for in a university lecture hall. I see the way David is when he talks about art, and I imagine how great he must be at his job. I want to find the thing I'm good at."

"David is a *brilliant* teacher," Isabel agreed, her fingers resting lightly on Susie's for a moment. "Brilliant." Her eyes danced, and Susie felt a weird gnawing sensation in her stomach. She changed the subject. "What are *you* going to do?"

"I'm going to take a year off," Isabel said, stretching her toes, even though they hadn't been told they could move. The minutes were ticking by, and sitting still wasn't as easy as it had been.

"And do what?" Susie crossed her fingers surreptitiously. Maybe there was a plan she could latch on to.

"I was thinking about joining an amateur dramatic society . . . Laugh," she said suddenly. "David is looking worried. We must look too serious." They both tilted their heads to the side and simulated laughter for a minute. "I think David's keen on the idea. He likes the thought of me following in his mother's footsteps."

"Oh? Was she an actress?"

Isabel dipped her head so David couldn't read her lips. "Lucinda Rowe? The famous stage actress?"

"Oh," Susie said. "I had no idea." The name didn't mean anything to her, but the reverential tone with which Isabel uttered it gave her pause. "I met her," she said, finally.

Isabel twisted her body. "What was she like?"

"Intimidating, I guess. I didn't know she was famous, but she had an aura about her, like she was used to being the center of attention."

Isabel nodded. "I'd love to meet her. She's coming, you know. Soon. For David's birthday."

"She might be able to give you some career advice." Susie couldn't imagine the woman she met in the garden being particularly generous with her time or expertise, but Isabel looked so excited at the prospect of meeting Lucinda that she didn't want to be the one to burst the bubble. "Are you interested in theater or film?"

"It's not an either/or situation," Isabel said, pursing her lips slightly, "as far as I know."

"And what do your parents think?"

"My mum doesn't really understand. My father died last year." Isabel put her hand up. "Don't. Don't say anything. I don't like talking about it."

"What about David? How does he fit among these theatrical plans?"

"I don't make my plans based on what David wants. My mother always told me to work so I could look after myself. That's why she didn't worry about me coming here, on my own." Her voice was strained.

"What does she do?"

"She works for local government. Civic planning, I think. I'm not really sure."

"I thought she might be arty. You're kind of arty."

Isabel laughed. "It's the bracelets, isn't it?" She waved her arm around, making them jangle. "No. My mother's not arty. She just really, really likes deciding where bus shelters go."

Susie laughed. Isabel smiled a little. "I'm not joking. She really likes her work. But I don't want a job like that. I just want to travel for a bit, maybe do a few auditions."

David took a step back to look at what he was working on. Susie's neck pulsed with the strain of holding it in one position. It couldn't be much longer before he'd had enough. Surely.

"What sort of travel?" Susie hoped she didn't sound too needy, but the idea of traveling with Isabel had sparked her interest.

"The rest of France. Italy. Maybe Greece. Want to join me?"

"Yes. Absolutely. Yes!" Susie grabbed Isabel's hand just as David reappeared.

"Well done, guys, thanks!" He looked down at their hands. "That's nice. Would have been a nice touch earlier. I think it's coming together, though." He flopped down on the sand and grabbed his backpack. "I'm starting to think maybe I could pull it together as an exhibition first, do the book later?"

Susie was touched by his earnestness. The book *was* starting to come together. That morning she had woken early and found David on the terrace, carefully clipping and rearranging his paintings in the sketchbook, singing softly to himself as he worked. She had crept back to bed without disturbing him. "An exhibition would be good," she agreed. "Here on the island?"

"Maybe." He looked thoughtful as he pulled out a faded T-shirt and wiped the lenses of Susie's sunglasses before handing them back over. "It's just a thought. Beer?" He reached in and grabbed three beers from his bag, using the corkscrew in his pocket to flip the lids off. Isabel shook her head, but Susie took one gratefully. It was barely cold, but she drank it down quickly.

"Thanks," she said after a while.

David opened his and leaned on Isabel's back, using her as a prop. In return, she lowered her head on his shoulder, eyes closed. They looked happy. It wasn't her place to make judgments on how they met. They were both adults now; that was all that mattered.

26

Susie, 1998

Days passed. Each was mostly the same as the one that came before it. Their bodies grew lean from the cycling, the swimming, the hiking, their skin tanned from the constant sun. Some days Susie worked; on others she was free to roam the island with Isabel or David, and even Henri, when he came in from helping his uncle. All the while she was aware of the vague deadline in the near future when David's parents were coming.

It was a Saturday afternoon, and Susie had the day off from the crêperie. She had been bent down under the trees for most of the afternoon, clearing out garden beds and pulling weeds. Her back already hurt. She was developing blisters on her hand where the trowel was rubbing. And David still wanted to wash down the outdoor furniture, trim the creeping clematis on the house, and paint the front gate before they went for a swim.

Isabel was nowhere to be seen. She had gone out to buy clams for a spaghetti vongole from the farmers' market in the village, but she had been gone for so long now it was possible she was out gathering them by hand.

David disappeared inside and came back with a jug of water. They sat down under the shade of the laburnum tree for a minute.

"Thanks for helping out with this," David said as he poured the water into tall glasses. He had cut up chunks of lemon, and the pith stuck to the edge of the glass.

"I like gardening. I used to do it a lot with my mother. She loves it. I told you that on the first day."

"You also told me I need to get rid of the seedpods." He pointed at the laburnum tree nearby.

"Well, you didn't listen to me on that."

"My mother never bothered."

"Maybe she lived on the edge more than mine."

"I've been thinking." David took a seat in one of the chairs.

"Mmmm?" Susie placed her glass down on the table. The pith was getting stuck in her throat. She stretched her neck one way and then the other.

"That maybe you should stay until my parents get here." She left her neck on one side, afraid any sudden movement might change his mind. "They'll be here on Monday."

"Monday?" Susie choked, forgetting about sudden movements entirely. "The Monday in two days, Monday?"

David nodded.

"Hence the gardening," Susie said.

"Hence the gardening."

"Will they notice?"

"I think they'll notice that I have two young women staying at the cottage, yes."

"I mean the garden—will they notice the work we've put in?"

"They'll notice if we don't put the work in."

"Ah," Susie said. There were a thousand questions she wanted to ask about Lucinda and Rupert, especially after Isabel's revelation. "Tell me about them."

"You really don't know about them?"

"Nope."

"Not a subscriber to *Tatler*, then?"

"Don't even know what it is."

"Come with me." They walked into the cottage, and Susie followed David up the stairs.

Normally, Susie continued to the third floor where her cozy attic bedroom was nestled in the eaves. The second floor felt off-limits to Susie—David had a bedroom there, and there was another room that Susie assumed belonged to David's parents.

She was right.

On the second floor, David threw open the door to the other room. Susie gasped. The walls were painted in a rich burgundy, and almost every inch of them was covered in old playbills. It took only a cursory glance around to see that one name was common to all the posters: Lucinda Rowe.

"Mum's shrine to herself," David smiled sardonically. "Excessive self-obsession is fine if no one knows it's here." The air was thick with stale perfume, reminiscent of tobacco, a masculine scent at odds with the feminine room.

"She was in all of these plays?" Susie walked around the perimeter of the room. A large bed draped in white linens dominated the room, but it was the posters that drew most of the attention.

"Yes—and in most of them she had a leading role."

"There must be at least thirty plays here."

"I've never counted them, but I'm sure my mother could tell you the exact number."

Susie took a moment to take it all in. "Does she still act?"

"No. She gave it up when I was born. There's a poster somewhere for the last play she was in." He moved over to the dressing table. "Here it is. *A Man for All Seasons*. She was Anne Boleyn."

Susie came closer. The perfume smell increased near the dressing table. She picked up one large bottle, removed the gold lid. Yes, that was the source of the smell. She dabbed some on her wrists and regretted it immediately. It was instant headache material.

"And she gave it up after that?"

David sat down on the bed. Susie slid down the wall until she was sitting cross-legged on the floor opposite. He reached back and opened the bedside cabinet. There was a fully stocked drinks cabinet within as well as a motley assortment of medications. "My mother's pharmacy. She's a big believer in self-medication. Drink?" he asked, holding up a bottle at random. Susie looked at the options and shook her head. David poured a splash of clear alcohol into a dusty tumbler.

"I'll tell you about my mother. She was born into a very wealthy family in London. Her mother, Pearl Mayhew, was a nurse in the first world war, and *her* mother, Emily, was one of the original suffragettes. These were not women who sat still and let life happen to them, even though they had the resources to do so. My mother was born in 1932, but her mother was busy and she was immediately put in the care of an Irish nanny. Her brother Laurence was much older. By all reports they never saw their parents." He stopped talking and waited for a reaction from Susie.

"And they didn't want her to become an actor?"

"What? No! They were quite liberal. They were happy for her to do something. Anything. They didn't want her to waste her life away, especially when she married so early."

"Your dad?"

"Yes, my father. He grew up in similar circumstances, and the families were friends. Lucinda and Rupert were always destined to end up together, but it was a surprise when they fell in love as teenagers. They never fought once when I was growing up. My mother was determined she would raise me in a happy home."

"Was hers not a happy home growing up?"

"It was very happy until she was a teenager. During the war, Laurence went off to fight, and her parents sent her away to the countryside with her nanny. She was very close to her nanny, but when they came back to London after the war, her parents sent the nanny away. My mother was thirteen years old, but she was heartbroken. It's why I never had a nanny growing up—my mother insisted on raising me herself."

There was pride in his voice, which Susie didn't understand. "Maybe she just wanted to be a regular mother?"

David was thoughtful. "Maybe."

"What about your father?"

"Rupert was an actor as well, but he was never as successful as my mother. He tried other things over the years, directing and casting. He had a little bit of success later in life, but to be honest, they didn't need the money. He was the sort of person who could get away with not doing much. Work was not everything to him. Not even close."

"Neither of them worked when you were growing up?"

This didn't seem to have occurred to David before. "Not really, no. My uncle Laurence died in the war, and the entire Mayhew fortune fell to my mother. They didn't need the money."

"Why did you become a teacher, then? Sounds like you could have enjoyed a life of leisure." Something was stirring in Susie's brain, scratching around at the edges. The strong perfume, probably perfect for the cavernous surrounds of a theater, was heavy and nauseating. A headache started to thrum in her temples.

"I really liked school. It sounds crazy. I know you're meant to hate school—especially the type of uptight establishments where my parents sent me—but I loved the order, the routine, the systems. I loved the tribal elements, the houses and the colors and the songs and the points." His eyes were practically misting over. "I was so sad when I came to the sixth form and realized it would soon be over. That's when I decided to become a teacher."

"Your parents must have been happy."

"Ha! They thought it was the pits. They wanted me to do something creative, like them."

"My sister is a teacher," Susie said. She couldn't remember if she had told him this before, but she felt sure she had.

"I know, I know. Obviously, I don't feel that way. And they had gotten used to the idea until I was fired and the old arguments resurfaced."

The door slammed downstairs. Isabel.

"David? Susie?"

Susie went and propped herself by the window. Isabel was standing on the terrace, empty-handed, looking around for them. For all her worldliness, sometimes Isabel lacked basic initiative. Susie opened the window and called to her.

"Where are the clams?"

"Long story. What are you doing up there?" Isabel asked. "David won't like it."

"David's here with me."

Confusion crossed Isabel's face. "I'll come up."

Susie went and stood by the door. Isabel entered the room and jumped on the bed next to them.

"What's happening?" she asked, and then seemed to clock her surroundings. "Wow—this room is cool! David—why haven't you taken me in here before?"

David looked at Susie and raised his eyebrows. She laughed.

"It's my parents' room, not mine. My mother is very protective of her inner sanctum."

"I'm just going to go and finish up in the garden," Susie said. "David here has just been telling me his poor-little-rich-boy childhood, but it's time for me to go back and pull some more weeds."

David groaned, and Isabel laughed and moved closer to David. She rested her head on his chest. "Ooh, tell me more," she said. "Sounds like a rough upbringing."

David moved an arm to encircle her, laughing as well. "Okay, I get it." He raised his other hand in defeat, eyes only for Isabel. It was time for Susie to make herself scarce. She headed toward the door and was almost out of the room when David spoke again. "I think it's because my mother always made such a big fuss about how she raised me all on her own, while she was raised by the famous Nellie. Her own parents were never there, whereas, she, Lucinda Rowe, the famous stage actress, gave up a career in the theater to raise her own child."

"David," Susie said, stopping in her tracks. "Did you say your mother's nanny was called Nellie? The one who left her suddenly after the war?"

He looked up, his hand still resting on Isabel's head. "I did. I never heard the end of it, growing up. Her name was definitely Nellie."

27

Camilla

Camilla knew she shouldn't have read the letter addressed to Henri. And really, it hadn't made things any clearer. If she was totally honest with herself, she was more in the dark than ever. The one thing she was totally sure about was that she wasn't going to jump off any bridges, even if Henri asked her to. *Especially* if Henri asked her to.

Thinking about Henri made her feel very guilty about reading the letter. It was clear from her writing just how much Susie loved him. Ian always said that Susie wore her heart on her sleeve, and Camilla agreed with him. Now she thought he was wrong. Whatever Susie had shown to the world was just a pale approximation of the depth of feeling that coursed below the surface.

Mostly though, the letter to Henri gave the questions circling in her head momentum. What happened that last night, and why did Susie blame Henri for it? Why was she mentioning David in a letter to her ex? Camilla thought it was weird for her to include that information. She needed to see Henri again, give him this letter and watch for his reaction. If he tried to conceal Susie's request for the sketchbook, she would . . . she would . . . well, she hadn't worked out what she would do yet, and she hoped it wouldn't come to that.

She sat down on one of the low walls on the path outside Valerie's house, took the crumbled—and, she realized, defunct—spreadsheet from her bag, and turned it over, starting on the fresh, unmarked side. She drew a circle with her name in it and then one with Susie's name, then connected them with a line. She drew a circle for Henri and Isabel and David, and joined them up with Susie's name as well. She paused for a moment, thinking. Then she added Nellie's name and drew a line from Nellie to Susie and herself.

Underneath, with a small bullet point next to each one, she wrote the following questions.

- What happened to Susie on the IDC?
- What did Henri do?
- How does David fit in with all of this?
- And what does it have to do with me?

Just looking at it spelled out like that made her feel more in control. It gave her an idea. She found the first three letters in her bag and, taking her pen to the letters, underlined certain passages.

In the first letter, Susie had made it clear that telling this story was her dying wish, and that doing so would "fix" any problems between Mills and herself. She played up the significance of meeting David in the gallery, only to write him off as an afterthought by the third letter. It was flip, even for Susie.

The second letter paid lots of attention to the art and the gallery, but by the second and third letter, she seemed to have forgotten about it completely. Was that significant, or just another example of Susie going on a tangent? Hard to tell.

By the third letter, Susie seemed to be indicating that there was something darker at play, and crucially she introduced the names Henri and Isabel. Camilla was tempted to read all the letters in one go. After all, that's what Susie would do. When they were given books to read as children, Susie always turned to the last page first. If she didn't like the look of the ending, she wouldn't read the book. Was that what Camilla needed to do here?

Because at the moment she was lost.

She recapped her pen and sat for a moment thinking. Aside from her dinner reservation at six o'clock, she wasn't in a hurry. All she could do was wait for Henri. It wasn't in her nature to rely on the whims of other people, but in this matter, she really had very little choice. Henri hadn't given her a chance to ask about Susie's last night on the island; he hadn't answered her question about Isabel.

Poor Isabel. Why did everyone keep saying that? Isabel was on the island with Susie, and something had happened to her. In the letters, Susie was blaming Henri for whatever happened on the island, but a suspicion was growing in Camilla's mind.

She thought back to the Christmas with the snow dome, allowing her mind to explore all the shadows of that memory.

The morning after, Boxing Day, Susie had woken up and asked where the snow dome was. Camilla eventually admitted she had thrown it out, and Susie raced outside and rifled through the outdoor bin, not stopping until she found it. By this stage the boys had stumbled out of bed, following the noise outside.

"I paid good money for this," Susie shouted, her eyes still bleary from the night before. "And you just chucked it out. It all comes so easy for you, doesn't it, Mills? You don't even consider how long I had to save to buy this present for your boys."

"I'm sorry, Susie. I thought you found it somewhere." Camilla tried to keep her voice light, her body slightly shielding the boys. Ian, thankfully, was nowhere to be seen.

"Found it? You mean stole it, don't you?"

Camilla shook her head. "No, I'm sorry. I just thought it was one of those joke presents . . ."

"A joke present from your joke sister. Well, do you think it's funny now?" And then just as Ian came out of the house, carrying yet another rubbish bag full of Christmas wrapping and food scraps, Susie smashed the snow dome on the brick path, a piece of glass flicking up and cutting Timmy's bare leg. The sight of blood changed the mood immediately.

"I'm sorry, Mills, I'm sorry." Susie started to cry, wiping her tears off on the back of her hand and leaning against the warm garden wall. Ian took the boys inside, but not before giving Camilla a look. A look that said *This is the final straw.*

Camilla shook her head. There is no way her sister would have hurt her friend Isabel. Besides, she never behaved like that around other people. Susie had been going through a rough time that Christmas. It was egregious of Camilla to throw her sister's gift away, and Susie had every right to react angrily.

Perhaps Ian had been right when he'd suggested this trip would be too much for her. Camilla walked slowly, dragging her feet, relishing setting her own pace after the earlier mission with Valerie. She came to a fork in the road. A small sign indicated the village to one side, the port to the other.

She wondered if she had time to go to the village. It was just after five, and she could look for the crêperie, maybe find Marie. As Henri had said, she might be able to help her. Camilla could still taste the warm, buttery crêpes Susie made on her old iron pans, chatting as she flicked them effortlessly onto plates and folded them in one deft movement. Camilla had never thought about where she learned that skill, who had taught it to her. Perhaps Marie had been more than a boss to Susie. Perhaps she had become a friend, a mentor. But Susie hadn't said anything about Marie, hadn't mentioned her in the letters. Was there a reason for that?

If she went straight back to the hotel, she could get some rest before her dinner reservation. Have a hot shower. Ring Ian and hear her children's voices. She took the path to the village; she wasn't here to rest. As much as she might be tempted to pretend it was a holiday, that she was no different from the many holidaymakers on the island, that wasn't true. She was here because her sister wanted to tell her something she hadn't had the courage to tell her when she was alive. It was never going to be easy.

The village came into view. There were lights strung up in the plane trees, and tourists milled in the cobblestone streets, looking at menus and calling to friends they had made on the beach. As Camilla passed

under the awning of a little bistro, she finally saw the small wooden
sign for the crêperie. It was a tiny little shopfront, the brown paint
of the windows peeling away. Even from a distance, she could see
that it was closed. The shop was in darkness, the outline of chairs
stacked within. She would come back tomorrow, adjust her itinerary
accordingly.

Back to the hotel, then, to wait.

She walked quickly. Evening was coming in, and despite the crowds
in the village, the path back to the hotel was deserted. As soon as she
left the cobbled streets of the village, she was alone and conscious of
every noise about her. Even the sound of her own breath was amplified
on the quiet path.

Finally the lights of the port town were visible. Camilla picked up
her pace even more. It felt silly to run, but she did, jogging the last
stretch of the path, clenching her toes to keep the old sneakers on her
feet. It was easier to dodge her thoughts as she ran, instead focusing
on her breath, the feeling of blood rushing through her stiff joints. Her
chest felt tight as she descended into the harbor town.

The hotel came into view. Climbing the stairs to the entrance, Camilla
let her breathing come back to normal, her nerves soothed a little by
the evening atmosphere of the hotel: the low lights, the coastal breeze
playing with the long linen curtains. On each step hurricane lanterns
glowed, lighting the way for weary travelers.

The reception area was full of people gathering at the end of the
day, some still in their beach attire, others dressed for aperitifs or dinner. At one end of the room a full-length window looked out over the
hotel garden. Camilla paused for a moment to take in the view. White-
and-blue-striped umbrellas were tied up for the night; a small group
of guests sat around a fire pit. Behind the stone wall a row of Cyprus
pines partly concealed the water beyond. Camilla pulled the photo of
Henri and Susie out of her bag again. Its background looked very similar to the view in front of her. Still, that didn't mean anything. The
whole island looked like that. She wasn't getting anywhere.

She thought back to Susie's phone call from the ferry terminal. Susie
had told her she was coming to the island, and then there was nothing

for weeks. At the time, Camilla had been hurt. Nellie had just died, and their whole family was grieving, working their way through sadness. Susie had been closest to Nellie, but they had all felt the pain of her death, particularly Camilla, at university far away from her parents and scrambling to stay on top of her studies.

And then, what was it, only weeks later? Susie arrived home, done with traveling, she said. She snapped at Camilla when she asked questions about her trip. She was ready to settle down, she said, start university. Trouble was, she never did. That was the beginning of the years when she wandered through life, through share houses and boyfriends and part-time jobs. She never settled down at all.

Something had happened to her on this island. Something to do with David and Henri and Valerie and Isabel. *Poor Isabel.* The last night. The wariness in Henri's eyes. The gendarme, hot and worried. Susie's face, pale and drawn in the car home from the airport.

Camilla's stomach rumbled again. She looked at her watch. There was time for a shower, maybe a phone call. She could do with a nap, but she knew she was better off staying awake a bit longer, knocking the jet lag on the head once and for all.

There was a man at the reception desk this time. Valerie must have alerted him to her arrival, because he had the key out and on the desk for her before she even reached the counter.

"Room sixteen," he said, pushing it toward her. He had lovely hands, his nails almond-shaped and pale pink. Camilla took the key and smiled in thanks. Words were beyond her at this point. She had turned away when he spoke again.

"Your friend is waiting on the sofa," he said, tilting his head in the direction of the small lounge opposite his desk.

"My friend?" Camilla turned to look, not expecting Henri so soon and certainly not before she'd had a chance to wash and eat her dinner. There was a large family gathered in front of the area, and she couldn't see past them.

"She has been waiting for some time."

"She?" A phone rang behind the desk, and the man shrugged, leaving her to skirt around the crowd and discover the identity of the visitor for herself.

She saw the hand first, clasped on one arm of the sofa. A large and sun-damaged hand, red earth trapped in its deep crevices. A small golden ring. She would recognize it anywhere.

"Mum?"

28

Susie, 1998

Even Isabel sensed that something crucial had just passed between David and Susie. She sat up and extricated herself from David's embrace. The bed was in shadow, but the late-afternoon sun formed a patch of warmth on the old oak boards where Susie stood.

"What?" she asked, looking from David to Susie in turn. "What does that mean?"

David had gone stiff. His face was pale.

"I don't know, Isabel," he said slowly and carefully. "Susie—what does it mean?"

"My grandmother was called Nellie." The words were spoken quietly.

"Lots of women were in those days," David said. For a moment he looked like he might sit up, and then he changed his mind. From a prone position, he could keep his eyes trained on the ceiling and not have to make eye contact. That suited Susie; she needed a minute to think things through as well.

Only Isabel was energized by the development. She pointed at David—"Your mother had a precious childhood nanny called Nellie"— and then at Susie—"and your grandmother worked in London and was called Nellie. Do you think they're the same person?" She clapped her hands together. "David, you have to ask your mother!"

"It's not happy families yet, Isabel," David muttered.

Susie walked to the window and pretended to concentrate on the view. Her mind was running at a million miles per hour.

"It *does* make sense," she said, deliberately slowing down the thoughts as they moved from her brain to her mouth. "Her letter said that the painting belonged to the family she used to work for, and, David, you said your family had some sketches by the same artist. Maybe she was a little confused and got the sketches and the painting mixed up. David, what are the sketches like?"

David was still looking up at the ceiling. He seemed to be weighing up his options.

"David?" Isabel cut in. "Is it the same artist?"

"I wasn't entirely truthful about the painting," he said finally. He picked some dirt out of his nails from the earlier gardening.

Susie felt her hopes drop. "Your family didn't own the sketches?"

"No," David said. "They didn't." The old house shifted in the heat. A beam cracked above them.

"Oh well," Susie said. "It would have been a bit of a coincidence, anyway. As you say, there were a lot of Nellies around in those days."

David sat up. He looked toward his mother's dressing table as if he were waiting for something. Finally he stood up and walked over to it. Moving a couple of Lucinda's publicity photos out of the way, he found what he was looking for. An old sepia photograph, framed in an ornate brass frame. He brought it over to Susie and handed it to her wordlessly.

"What is it?" she asked. It was a photo of a young child dressed in frilly bloomers, her cherubic face framed by pale curls. She was holding a small wooden pony and standing in front of a large painting of a horse. The horse from the National Gallery. "Is this your mother?"

"Yes."

"At the gallery?"

"At her family home in Devon."

"They owned that actual painting?" Susie tried to imagine a house with a painting like that in it. She couldn't.

"I'm lost," said Isabel. "What painting?"

Susie handed her the photo frame.

"I didn't want you to make assumptions about me," David said. "It's not the sort of thing you can mention, just offhand. 'Hey, my family used to own that enormous painting in front of us.' I didn't want you to judge me. I didn't know who you were." A flicker of something crossed his face; it was gone before Susie could pin it down.

"Nellie said the family she used to work for owned the painting," Susie said slowly, "Nellie must have been your mother's nanny."

David nodded. Isabel started jumping around the room in excitement. "I can't believe it," she was saying. "I can't believe it."

Now, more than ever, Susie wished she could pick up the phone and ring Nellie. She wanted to tell her she had met David, and she had seen the painting.

"There's something else," David said, coming alongside Susie now. He kicked off his shoes and placed his foot next to hers. "Take off your shoe," he said.

Susie refused to look down. "What? No! Yuck."

"What is it, David?" Isabel moved closer. "Go on, Susie."

Susie's heart started beating faster. She bent down and unlaced her Gazelles. The floorboards were warm on her feet.

"I noticed it on the beach the other day, but I didn't say anything because I've always been a little self-conscious about it, and I thought you might be as well."

Susie took a breath and looked down at her feet and David's, lined up on the floor next to each other. David's pointer toe was longer than the others, and it hooked around and over her middle toe.

Just like hers.

Part II

29

Margaret

"Mum?" Camilla moved toward Margaret and put her hand on her face. "Is that you?"

"Of course it's me, Camilla. You look like you've seen a ghost." Margaret swatted her hand away. She didn't believe in touching faces or sharing drinks. Even in exceptional circumstances. The long shadow of Nellie's fear of polio had never left her.

"What are you doing in France?" Camilla asked. The word *France* slurred in her mouth.

"Camilla, have you been drinking?" Margaret asked. Margaret was not a big drinker. A gin and tonic at sunset, a glass of wine with dinner. Camilla was usually the same. Thank God she had come. Things were as bad as she feared they would be.

"When in Rome . . . ," Camilla said. Margaret watched her carefully. "I'm just tired. It's been a big few days."

"Few days? You only just got here." Margaret didn't have any tolerance for hyperbole.

"Feels like forever." Camilla's face was flushed and there were beads of sweat on her forehead. Her hair disheveled and she was definitely out of breath.

"Come on, let's get you upstairs." Margaret stood up and hooked her arm through Camilla's. She felt her daughter sway a little and then lean into her. "I asked the man for the key to your room, but he wouldn't give it to me. There's no sense in us both having rooms. I can imagine this place is costing you a pretty penny."

"They're funny about keys here," Camilla said, leading her mother toward the stairwell. Margaret carried her small travel bag in one hand and kept ahold of her daughter with the other. She steered her away from the people gathering in the reception and toward the stairwell.

"I'm glad to see there are stairs. I hate elevators, don't you?" She just needed to keep talking. "Room sixteen, right?" They climbed up one flight of stairs and then another. "You do look nice in that dress, Mills. It's nice to see you in some color. I don't know why you always wear those dark colors. That yellow is lovely on you."

Camilla yawned.

"You might need a lie-down," Margaret scolded gently. "And then we can have something to eat later."

Camilla stopped at the top of the stairs. "I have a reservation at six—I'll see if they can add you on."

Margaret nodded and kept moving down the hallway. She had been a mother now for a long time, and she could see her daughter needed sleep right now. Not food—and definitely not more alcohol. She had gotten here just in time—in more ways than one.

The room was lit by gentle lamplight, the bed dressed in crisp linens. Margaret opened the door to the balcony, enjoying the smell of the sea breeze. It wasn't often she was by the ocean. Meanwhile Camilla flopped onto the downy bed, her shoes dropping to the ground one by one. She closed her eyes, and for a moment it looked like she might fall asleep. Then her eyes popped open again.

"Why are you here?"

"Why don't you just rest, and I'll make us a nice cup of tea?"

"Mum, why?"

"I came to look after you." Margaret found the electric jug, some cups and saucers. She still wasn't sure how much Camilla knew. "This is a big trip to make on your own, especially so soon after . . ." Her voice trailed off. Susie's death was not a topic she could tackle head-on yet. Especially as her grief was wrapped up in her guilt, the two so tightly embedded she could almost picture them inside her like two gnarly tree roots.

"Oh, Mum," Camilla said sleepily, "you didn't have to come. I would have been all right on my own. We have to go to dinner soon," she added, curling up farther on the bed.

Margaret had been Camilla's mother long enough to know this was her way of saying thanks. She ducked into the bathroom with the electric jug and took longer than she needed to fill the kettle, poking about in the complimentary toiletries so that Camilla might nod off to sleep. There was a conversation they needed to have, but it would be better after Camilla had rested. By the time Margaret came out of the bathroom, Camilla was on the bed with her eyes shut, breathing deeply.

Margaret gently moved a blanket over Camilla as her body softened into sleep and then climbed up next to her.

"Dinner," Camilla mumbled in her sleep.

Margaret patted her on the arm. "It's okay, we'll have something later."

"Henri . . . ," Camilla murmured as she rolled onto her side.

Henri? Margaret froze. It wasn't the name she was expecting to hear. Who was Henri?

"You just rest," she said, hoping her sleeping daughter couldn't hear the fear in her voice. "We can talk after."

Margaret watched Camilla on the bed in the twilight. As soon as Camilla told her the purpose of her trip, she had known. Seeing the itinerary confirmed it. It had been quite a scramble, getting things together in time to follow Camilla. In the end, she had explained everything to Bill. There was no other option. Money was tight—it always was—and an impromptu trip to Europe was not in the budget for that year. Or any year, for that matter. It hadn't bothered her before; she had seen enough of Europe. She was in no rush to go back.

Until Susie forced her hand. Her defiant daughter, stubborn and incendiary to the very end. Even as a baby she would fight her way out of her swaddling blankets, climb out of her cot. When she was at boarding school, Margaret lost track of the phone calls she had in the middle of the night to say Susie had gone missing.

She and Bill used to call Susie the Bolter—mostly affectionately, but there were times in Margaret's life when Susie really pushed her to the limits and exhausted the filaments of her love. And this, sticking her nose into other people's business like this, this really took the biscuit.

30

Susie

There was silence in the room for a moment, and then they all spoke over the top of each other.

"Do you think . . ."

"Is Nellie . . ."

"Are you two related?" This last was Isabel, who was struggling to keep up. Even Susie, who knew at least half the details, was lost.

Finally David spoke over the lot of them. "Okay, Susie, let's work out a few dates here. How old was Nellie?"

"She was born in 1916. What does that make her?"

"She must have been eighty-two when she died." David was quick. "And what year was your mother born?"

"Nineteen forty-six. New Year's Day. Nellie came out in the first wave of migrants on a decommissioned warship. She was one of the few single women on board. The way she told it, she had nowhere to go after she found out she was pregnant. She was fired from her job, and her parents didn't want her to come back to Belfast. She always said the father was a soldier who had died in the war." Susie was raking through her memories now. "Her first choice was New York, but the Australian government was running an assisted migration scheme, and it seemed like her only option. She talked a lot about that boat trip, but not much about before. She was more interested in telling fairy sto-ries of elves and goblins and babies being stolen in the night."

"David," Isabel interjected, "I bet your grandfather got her preg-nant, and she made up the story about the soldier. That's why they fired her! After all, how old would Lucinda have been in 1946?" Isabel seemed invigorated for the first time in days. Susie could imagine her now as a straight-A student, sitting at the front of the class and racing to get to the correct answer first.

"Thirteen." David, by contrast, was practically catatonic.

"Old enough to understand," Isabel mused.

"Not in 1946, though," Susie said. "The idea was probably so scan-dalous they didn't want her to know."

"And Nellie was thirty, practically an old maid in those days." David, at least, was keeping track of the numbers.

"Does your mother know anything about her father?" Isabel asked Susie. David was quiet.

"She always said it was someone Nellie met during the war as well—there were never any details." Susie remembered the wistful way her grandmother spoke about the time. It was always when Mar-garet wasn't around—she never brought it up around her daughter.

"What are you thinking?" Isabel asked.

"I thought you two could read each other's minds," David groaned from the bed. "I'm surprised you even have to ask."

"Here's what I think," said Isabel. Susie waited expectantly. David rolled over and faced the dressing table, his body stiff with the effort of making it appear as if he wasn't listening. "It was definitely your grandfather, David, who got Nellie pregnant."

"What year did you say your mother was born, Susie?"

"Nineteen forty-six."

"No," said David. "It still doesn't add up. My grandparents stayed in London and sent my mother away with her nanny for the whole war." His voice was muffled by the pillow.

"Where did they go?" Isabel nudged David.

"Devon," he muttered. "They were sent to the family house near

Tavistock. It's a beautiful old estate with famous gardens designed by Humphry Repton. Pond Cottage is in the grounds."

"So maybe your grandfather went down for a weekend." Isabel wasn't interested in gardens. "Either way, when they came back to London after the war, Lucinda's mother sent her away. Lucinda didn't have a chance to say goodbye. And that's how you both got your unusual toes. You have the same grandfather, and that makes you . . ."

"Cousins," David said quietly. Susie felt slightly sick at the thought that she had very nearly become romantically involved with him. Did the remorse in his voice suggest that he had, at least at some stage, some level of interest in her? For the first time she appreciated his faithfulness to Isabel, his reluctance to fall prey to her advances. They didn't know how lucky they had been.

"And then what happened?" David asked. He directed his attention back to Isabel, and a lightness crept over his face. Susie realized that there had never been any danger of anything happening between them. He had never looked at her like that.

"Nellie went on the boat to Australia. Banished by your family and rejected by her Irish family, she had no choice but to set sail for the colonies. She brought up the baby on her own. The baby who grew up to be Susie's mother."

Susie was starting to come around to the idea of Isabel as an actress. She was certainly a captivating storyteller.

No one noticed the afternoon gradually sliding into the gloaming hours of twilight. Across the island, fishermen were coming home with their catch, families trailing in from the beaches, waiters setting the tables for the evening diners. Soon the crepuscular creatures of the island would move out of the shadows. But here in the dim bedroom, Susie held her breath expectantly. She let it go to speak.

"Margaret."

"Margaret grew up in Australia, never knowing the truth about her father. But Nellie knew. And she sent her granddaughter to find her family."

31

Camilla

"You should have stayed in bed," Margaret was saying as they walked to find somewhere for dinner. She had let Camilla sleep through the six o'clock booking downstairs at the hotel, and when Camilla woke up, she felt groggy, disoriented, and a little cross. Still, it felt good to have her mother with her. She had a feeling that whatever Henri was going to tell her wasn't going to be pretty; having her mother there would be some sort of comfort.

"Mum, that is the first mistake of jet lag. You must get yourself in tune with the local time as soon as possible." Camilla didn't admit that she had done exactly the opposite her first night in London.

The temperature had dropped, and the breeze coming off the ocean was cool as they walked to the restaurant. It was cool enough to need a sweater, but Camilla was glad she hadn't brought one. She needed to be woken up; the nap had left her feeling spaced out and almost nauseous. No cars had seemed like a novelty twelve hours ago, but now Camilla would have given anything for her trusty Mazda. Her mother, on the other hand, showed no signs of slowing down. Camilla wouldn't complain first.

"Mills," her mother was saying, "why don't you check in on Ian? See how the kids are. You mustn't forget you have a family at home."

But this was precisely what Camilla was trying to do. The only way she could continue was if she blocked all thoughts of home from her mind; to forget about them eased the dull ache of missing them. If she forgot she had a family at home, she could pretend things were normal.

There was no chance of that with her mother around.

"Have a talk with the kids. It might make you feel better."

"Mum, I'm fine."

"Camilla, you're a mother. You mustn't forget that. Your first obligation is to your family, not to Susie."

"You sound just like Ian," Camilla snapped, and then immediately regretted it. She hadn't told her parents that she and Ian were "on a break." They were still dealing with Susie's death—they didn't need to have something else to worry about. Besides, they loved Ian. They would feel his loss as deeply as the loss of another child.

"Okay, Mum," she said, "I'll call him. Let's just decide where we're going, and then I'll ring."

"I saw some little bistros in the village earlier. Maybe we could try one of those."

"What were you doing in the village?" Camilla asked, pleased to be out of the hot seat for just a moment.

There was a beat. "I was at the police station."

Camilla stopped and turned toward her mother. The change in direction meant the wind now whipped her hair around her face. She pushed it back behind her ears, and within seconds it came free.

"The police station?"

"Yes."

"And why were you at the police station?"

Her mother's lips met in grim determination. For the first time, Camilla realized that her mother had her own agenda. She'd had the same feeling years earlier when her mother wanted her to drop out of teaching and change to journalism. There was something larger at play then, and there was something larger at play now.

"I had some questions I needed to ask."

"What sort of questions? Do you know what happened to Susie?"

Margaret didn't answer. Her body, if possible, became more upright. She tapped Camilla on the arm. *Keep moving. Don't make a scene.*

"The police have been following me around," Susie said. "One crashed into me on the path earlier."

She pointed to the scab on her leg, and her mother winced. "Doesn't look too bad."

"You can't compare everything to your run-in with the fence post, you know." Margaret had lacerated her leg on a fence post when Camilla was a teenager. The flesh opened down to the bone, and Margaret hadn't even cried. "Do you know why the police have been following me?"

"We'll talk at dinner," Margaret said. Camilla knew from experience there was no point arguing. A vein of stubbornness ran wide through all the women in the family.

They walked in silence for a bit. After a while, her mother stopped again. They could see the path opening out ahead of them, beyond that a reasonably crowded village square. The trees were laced with fairy lights, and they were just starting to sparkle in the dusk. She turned to face Camilla and put her hand on her arm. "Mills, do you think you should just read the other letters?" she asked, a gentle look on her face. "Don't you think you've had enough surprises?"

"What? No." Camilla didn't try to disguise the shock in her voice. Her mother was just as law-abiding as she was. Even in the middle of their thousand-acre property, miles from any law enforcement, every time she hopped in the car she automatically fastened her seat belt. "I'm doing what Susie asked."

Margaret nodded. The answer didn't surprise her. "Just don't forget that Susie's death was sudden. We don't know if she meant for us to find those letters, let alone to read them and follow them to the letter. They may just have been a form of catharsis for her, a way to order her thoughts. We mustn't let them take over."

"Me."

"What, darling?"

"She wanted *me* to find them, not us. I'm in charge here."

Margaret inhaled deeply. "All right, Mills. It's up to you. I'll walk on ahead and find a table. Maybe you can call Ian." She patted her on the arm. "And have a think about the letters."

Camilla felt a tightness in her chest as her mother wandered off. With her sweater draped around her shoulders and her elegant posture, her mother fit right in with the French crowd. She coughed to shift the tightness, but it wouldn't budge. It was the wine. It had happened before.

There was a park bench at the entrance to the square. She sat down at one end and listened to the busker. A barefoot young girl, she was dressed in a beautiful old kimono and sang a folk tune. Camilla's French wasn't strong enough to decode the words, but listening to the girl's voice was enough for her. She felt the breath come back into her body as the words floated over her.

The phone lay inert in her hand.

She loved Ian. She loved the boys.

At the thought of home, the feeling in her chest came back. Indigestion. Why had it taken her so long to realize? She rummaged in her bag for an antacid. She swallowed one and then another.

Now was a good time to call. The boys would be getting ready for school. Ian would be calmly making their lunch boxes, and the fridge would be stocked. She could picture the contents because they never changed. In fact, Ian had a standing grocery order, with the same things being delivered week in, week out. Low-fat milk, oats, chicken breasts, broccoli, bananas. If asked, Camilla could recite the whole order—but she never needed to.

Ian. Had. It. Covered.

She could feel Margaret's eyes on her from across the square as she pretended to make the call. She hoped her mother couldn't see the sweat breaking out on her hairline, the tremble in her hands. Deception had never been her strong point. She motioned for her mother to move on to the restaurant. Thankfully, Margaret took the hint and walked away.

After a reasonable amount of time, Camilla took the phone away from her ear and reached for the pile of letters in her handbag.

32

Susie

Even though the possible connection between them was exciting, it was equal parts tenuous, and David convinced them it would be best to wait until Lucinda and Rupert arrived on Monday before getting too carried away. His one concession was that Susie could tell Henri. Rather than wait for Henri to appear in the early evening, like he normally did, Susie asked David to take them to Henri's house right away. It was a stone cottage on the shoreline, partially hidden from the water by a disused water mill. Everyone on the Île de Clair lived in a picture-perfect house, and Henri's aunt was no exception.

Along the water's edge, fishermen were tending their nets and chatting among themselves. Every now and then someone whistled, and they would all come together to inspect the bounty. None of them paid any attention to Susie and David and Isabel as they approached. They were used to tourists at this time of year.

A small set of steps ran directly from the cottage door down to the water, and the three of them scurried across the ocean wall to end up on the doorstep. In a severe winter storm the angry ocean would slap at the cottage's foundations, but on a still summer's afternoon its location was perfect.

The top half of the front door consisted of nine equal-sized squares of glass, but the view inside was covered by a thin net curtain. A lamp shone within, the cottage dark despite the bright day outside. Isabel nudged the other two out of the way and tried to peer through the curtain.

This caught the fishermen's attention.

"Hey!" one of them called. The three of them turned around to see who had called out. "That's private property."

"We're looking for Henri," Isabel called back. Susie nodded her support.

"And who are you?" One man emerged from the pack, taking off his gloves and heading over to the stairs where they stood. As he came closer, they saw he was younger than the other men, though the weather had beaten the youth away from his face.

"I'm Isabel, and this is Susie," she said. "And David." David waved a hello from behind Susie.

"I know you," the man said, ignoring David. "You're Henri's friend."

"Yes, that's right. This is Susie," Isabel said, quickly grabbing Susie by the hand.

"Henri is still working," the man said, looking over his shoulder to where the others had returned to the job at hand. There were a finite number of oysters along this patch, and his workmates were moving quickly through the area. They could just make out Henri waving to them at the far edge of the group. He gestured something with his hands.

They did not hear the door open.

"Hello," a voice said from behind them. The woman inside held her body in the crack of the doorway, so they couldn't see into the house. Her face was round and warm but the look in her eyes was wary. "I am Yvette. Thank you, Philippe, I can look after this now."

Yvette smiled briefly at the man. It *was* Philippe. Henri's uncle, Yvette's husband. Henri had told Susie that his aunt had moved away from the vineyard when she was young, just like Henri. Yvette trained as a midwife, and the Île de Clair was her first posting. She fell in love almost immediately with the place and then Philippe, and never left. When Henri's father had needed somewhere to send his troubled teenager, he immediately thought of Yvette. How much trouble could he get into on an island?

"I'm Susie, I'm a . . . friend of David's, and this is Isabel. She's a friend of—"

"Susie's," David cut in. "They're staying with me for a couple of weeks."

"Have your parents arrived yet?" Yvette asked. Was there a smirk on her face?

"Monday."

"Your birthday," Yvette said.

"Same time every year."

"And why are these two gorgeous young girls staying with you? They should be staying at the youth hostel in town with the other young people. Valerie would look after them there."

"You have a nice spot to live," Susie said, when David didn't answer.

"It *was* a nice spot to live." Yvette shook her head.

"Oh, you're moving?" David leaned forward, suddenly involved. "Mother didn't mention it."

"Your mother does not know everything," Yvette said firmly. Isabel looked like she was trying not to laugh. It was probably the first time she had seen her teacher told off like a child. "The house has been sold to an English family. We have nowhere to go. Everywhere on the island is too expensive for us now. The locals are being forced out."

David put his hands up. "It's not us."

"You are part of the problem," Yvette said. "Where will our families live? Our children? If Henri decides to stay here, there are no prospects for him." Yvette scrutinized them both carefully. "And one of you has been spending extra time with my Henri?"

"Yes, that's Susie." Isabel pushed her forward. Meeting a boyfriend's aunt was a first for Susie, just as having a proper boyfriend was a first for her, so she wasn't sure what to say. She managed a little wave and a smile, hoping that conveyed the right message for now.

"Susie." Yvette stepped up closer. "You are working with Marie."

David finally spoke. "Yvette and Marie are old friends. Marie is married to Gerard, the gendarme. Gerard and Phillipe are brothers."

"I'm lost," Isabel muttered.

Yvette didn't clarify any of the details for her. "Marie says you are from Australia," she said to Susie.

"Yes."

"Why did you come to the Île de Clair? It is off the beaten track, no?"

"There was a rave review in her guidebook," David joked. Yvette didn't laugh.

"I'm a friend of David's. We met in London," Susie stammered. Henri had not warned her about his aunt.

"And you are just here for the summer?"

"She is just here for a couple of weeks, Yvette." David came to her rescue. "No wedding bells on the horizon just yet." Yvette didn't smile. Susie swallowed. Clearly Yvette had plans for Henri, and they didn't involve Susie.

The men were starting to come up from the rocks, saying their goodbyes for the day. Their baskets were full, and they looked happy with the day's work. Henri was at the back of the group.

Philippe arrived first. He put down his basket and asked Yvette a question. Yvette nodded and replied in French. Philippe smiled, looked at David and then the two girls, and raised his eyebrows.

Isabel interrupted their conversation, rattling off a handful of sentences in French. For a moment Yvette and Philippe looked shocked, and then they laughed heartily. Philippe took out a parcel wrapped in damp burlap and gave it to Isabel, squeezing her shoulder as he did so. She smiled and laughed. "Merci," she said, and something else that Susie couldn't understand. He picked up his basket to leave them to it.

"These young people are just asking me about property. They want to know if there are any other cheap cottages on the island they can buy with all their pounds."

David looked uncomfortable. "No, that's not . . ."

"I am kidding. Here is Henri now. I have been holding up these young people too long." Susie rushed over to Henri, and he wrapped his arms around her, his skin warm from the sun and smelling slightly of fish. Without caring who was watching, he kissed her on the mouth, whispering stories of the sea to her and making the moment their own. After a moment, they broke apart to find the others watching.

David was standing stone still, his cheeks flushed with color, his hands clenched at his side. He was glaring at Yvette. Had Susie missed something while she was wrapped in Henri's arms? The air seemed charged with emotion, as if something had just been said—or was about to be said. Yvette seemed about to walk away, but she changed her mind and came back to David. She kissed him on both cheeks.

"I never forget any of my babies, David," she said and put her hand on his brow. "Make sure you tell your mother I said that."

33

Letter Five

This one's for you again, Mills.

Time to leave the island and head to Devon.
Pond Cottage, to be exact.
Google Maps will be your friend here.

xox

Hello . . .

How was the Île de Clair?

It's not a hard place to fall in love with, is it? It's not a hard place in which to fall in love, either.

I hope you scattered my ashes at the chapel on the hill, but mostly I hope you found Henri.

Henri. I loved Henri, and he broke my heart. It's easier to look back now and realize that I was asking more of him than he would ever have been able to give. I was looking for everything that summer: love, purpose, direction, but mostly, a future. And Henri couldn't give me that.

His family helped me though, in the end.

We had a wonderful few weeks on the island, David, Isabel, Henri, Valerie, and I. It was going to be an endless summer. Isabel and I made plans to stay on the island with David as long as *he would allow us to, and then we would move on. Greece, Spain, Italy—we had a list of places we hoped to visit, and I had a guidebook to help us get there.*

You might have found out by now that our plans turned pear-shaped.

David and I thought we had uncovered a family secret—that our families were connected through Nellie. Not only did we think Nellie had worked for David's mother's family before she fell pregnant with our mother (good old Margaret, to think she kept this a secret from us all this time!), we also thought that the three of us in the younger generation—you, me, and David—were related. We were so excited! The way we figured it, David was a long-lost cousin of ours.

We didn't have long to develop that theory—or check it with Mum (not that I think she would have told me)—before David's mother Lucinda arrived. I think one of the island women alerted her to us—or me—being on the island. The Rowe family had a funny relationship with the people of the island, a strange push and pull of fealty and disdain—a puzzle I never managed to untangle.

Lucinda told us it was all nonsense. She had a way with words, that one, and she cut us down pretty quickly.

I believed Lucinda, to begin with. She had me convinced she was a good person. She wasn't. I trusted her, and I shouldn't have. She hurt Isabel and me that night. Lucinda said it was my fault, but it wasn't. I would never have hurt Isabel. But I should never have done what I did next. I had just turned nineteen! I didn't know any better.

I panicked and fled. When I left, Isabel was unconscious on the sofa. I still don't know what happened to her. I do know that if I had stayed, Lucinda would have blamed me for it. She warned me that I was out of my depth, that I didn't know what I was getting myself into. I went looking for Henri, and his family helped me.

When I got back to Australia, I wanted to tell you and Mum about David. I wanted to tell you about Henri, about my time on the Île de Clair. There were so many things I wanted to tell you, but I was afraid of Lucinda. I was afraid that Isabel might have been dead. It seemed safer to bury it deep and try to move on.

We both know how that turned out.

If Isabel is still alive, I want you to tell her I'm sorry. I'm sorry for leaving her.

I'm hoping David will know what happened to her. His address is on the envelope—Pond Cottage. I think that's the estate from Nellie's stories; a grand house in the woods, a small cottage by the river. I assume he ended up there—he told me that the Île de Clair and Pond Cottage were the two places he felt happiest, but I have a feeling the Île de Clair might have been forever tarnished for him, just like it was for me.

If you find him, give him the sketchbook.

Tell him I wanted to bring it myself, but I was too afraid. He will understand. He was there that night, and he was just as frightened as I was, I'm sure of it. If you find him, tell him that there was a stolen baby. It was him. Tell him that his mother didn't want to give him up, that she changed her mind, but it was too late.

How do I know this? Ask Mum.

Tell them all I'm sorry. David, Isabel, and most of all, Mum. Safe travels.

All my love,
Susie

PS. The ashes . . . there is a path that follows the stream at the bottom of the Pond Cottage garden. I saw it on Google Maps. Anywhere along there will do me nicely. It's not strictly somewhere that's close to my heart, but it's bloody nice. You'll see!

34

Camilla

How do I know this? Ask Mum.

The words repeated themselves in Camilla's head as she approached the bistro, where her mother was waiting outside. Camilla surveyed her carefully. Her mother looked the same: the carefully bobbed gray hair, the turned-up collar and pearl earrings. It all suggested the mother Camilla knew, loved, trusted. But now Camilla suspected that she didn't know everything about her mother.

There were so many things in that last letter.

Isabel and Susie had been hurt, and it sounded like Lucinda was to blame. Henri had helped Susie, and she had fled the island because she was afraid, not because she had hurt anyone. She had lived with the guilt of leaving Isabel behind all her life.

But that wasn't even all of it. Someone had stolen a baby, and her mother knew about it. Margaret's sudden arrival on the island began to feel more sinister than surprising.

Before Camilla had a chance to ask her anything, Margaret bustled her inside. She spoke in French to the waiter at the door. There was a long period where the waiter replied and her mother appeared to understand what he was saying, and then her mother spoke in French some more. The waiter laughed and touched Margaret on the arm, took a long look at Camilla, and kissed her on both cheeks.

Camilla was speechless. This behavior, coupled with what she had just read in the letter, was too much. Her mother's identity was shifting and transforming in real time. She was becoming a stranger, a stranger who spoke in French, flirted in French, and appeared to make jokes in French. Her mother! Her mother couldn't even make jokes in English.

The waiter led them to a cozy booth tucked alongside the bar. It was covered in the same wall paneling that covered the rest of the room. A narrow ledge packed thick with wine bottles ran along the top of the room.

They climbed into the booth, their legs touching under the table, the closeness intended for lovers, not mothers and daughters. Normally Camilla would find the proximity of her mother comforting, but at that moment it unnerved her. It was like sharing a table with a stranger.

"Wine?" her mother asked, raising an eyebrow slightly.

"I don't think so," Camilla said. "I've had enough for today, and I need to keep my wits about me."

Margaret didn't notice the tone of Camilla's voice. The waiter came back and fussed about and continued to converse with her mother in French long after the expected limit of her knowledge of the language might have expired. He eventually clapped his hands in agreement with something she said and walked away, only to return moments later with a chilled bottle of wine that he poured expertly and generously into both glasses.

Camilla started to protest, but it was too late; the wine was poured, and anyway it looked appealing. She reached for the glass and took a small sip. Then a bigger gulp. She waited to see if her mother would tell her why she was here.

"Cheers," her mother said and waved her glass in Camilla's general direction. Her mother had long limbs, and the glass nearly collided with the base of Camilla's upturned glass.

"Cheers," Camilla replied flatly, reaching for the bread basket and tearing off a price of baguette. She cut a thick slab of butter, placed it on top of the bread and without even bothering to spread it, popped the whole bundle in, where it stuck to the roof of her dry mouth.

Margaret pushed an envelope across the table. "This is yours," she said, blushing a little. Camilla recognized the crumpled envelope.

"You?" Camilla searched her mother's face for answers. "You took the letter in the gallery." Her voice was muffled by the mouthful of bread.

"I shouldn't have, I'm sorry. I wanted to know if I was doing the right thing by following you."

"And are you?" Camilla was trying to process a lot of things at once. Another thought. "Was that you on the ferry?"

Margaret nodded. "It was, and yes, I believe I'm doing the right thing. This is not a trip you should be making alone."

"You're full of surprises," Camilla said pointedly, desperately trying to swallow the bread. "When did you learn to speak French so well?"

If her mother noticed the sharpness in her voice, she wasn't letting on. "I learned here, on the Île de Clair." She paused to let this detail soak in.

"Here?" Camilla coughed. "When were you here?"

"I was here before you were born, years ago. I lived in London, you know, when I was younger."

"You what?" Camilla was suddenly glad of the wine in front of her. She took a big gulp and washed down the remainder of the bread. Her mouth still felt dry, her tongue claggy.

"I lived in London. I left home when I was eighteen, much the same as Susie did. I got some work as a model . . . What?" Camilla had spat her wine out and was now staring openmouthed at her mother. "I didn't last long, but I did some magazine work, and then I worked out that I preferred to be writing the words. I got a very low-paid job at a magazine and started out that way. You knew I was a journalist."

Camilla gaped. "For five minutes, until you met Dad. I didn't know you had an actual career in London."

"I think calling it a career is a little generous, Mills."

Camilla looked at her mother intently, as if her face might reveal the map of her life. She'd never thought much about her mother's life before she had children. Even when she and Susie used to rummage through the family albums at home, her mother jumped from pony-tailed schoolgirl to fresh-faced bride. There were no clues to this whole other life.

"How did you end up here? This place is hardly well known. It's still pretty sleepy now. I can't imagine what it must have been like in the seventies."

"Sixties," Margaret corrected. "Tail end." She twirled the stem of her wineglass. "I was here with . . . friends. Their names were Lucinda and Rupert Rowe."

"You were friends with Lucinda?" Camilla couldn't hide the aston-ishment in her voice. "But Susie . . ." She stopped, thought a moment. "Is that why Susie was here? To see your friend?"

Margaret was in no rush to answer. She took a contemplative sip of her wine and watched the waiters at work for a minute.

"I don't know. I can't think how she would have met them. But I think she was here because of me." She looked at her watch, twisted her Claddagh ring. "I need to tell you a few things. It might help us work out what Susie was up to."

Camilla inhaled, gathering courage for what she was about to say next. "The stolen baby," she said, watching closely for her mother's reaction.

Margaret's eyes opened wide.

"David," Camilla said quietly. She took a large gulp of the sparkling water, felt the tiny bubbles of gas evaporate on her tongue. Concentrat-ing on them was easier than trying to process the guilt moving across her mother's face, the reddening at the base of her throat.

After a moment, Margaret nodded. Camilla coughed, choking on the last of the water. Margaret waited for her to get her breath and then reached across the table, searching for her daughter's hand. "This is a hard story for me to tell. Can you promise me that you will try and understand my side?"

"Okay." Camilla felt a little wobbly. The bread and wine started to churn in her stomach. Her mother put her hand on hers and gave it a little squeeze, but Camilla moved her hand out of reach. Ordinarily she would find the gesture comforting, but there was something patronizing in it this time, as if her mother thought the touch might soften what she was about to say.

"It's probably best to start with Nellie."

"Granny Nellie? What does she have to do with it?"

"This all began with Nellie. You know she came from a big family, don't you? There were three boys and five girls—I couldn't even tell you all their names. Nellie didn't like to talk of them much, too painful to remember, I think. There wasn't enough money for the family to stay together. One of the brothers and one of the sisters went to New York before the war, but Nellie went to London. She was sent there by her mother, who had heard of a job going with a well-respected family. The Rowes were very wealthy. They lived in a big white house in Pembroke Gardens with a shiny black door. When Nellie arrived, it was 1932 and they were expecting a baby. Nellie took a small suitcase and arrived just in time for the birth of Lucinda."

"Nineteen thirty-two? Nellie would have been just sixteen."

"That was the way things were then."

"And she never saw her family again?"

"No. There was a reunion planned in the eighties, but Mum said she didn't have the money to get over there. I think it was an excuse. She made a decision to leave that life behind when she boarded the ship to Australia, and she never looked back."

Camilla believed that. Nellie didn't talk about her past much, not with her. Once, when Camilla had to interview an older relative for a school project, Nellie had pretended it was a bad line and hung up on her. But Nellie often took Susie in her arms at bedtime and whispered her stories. Camilla, with her head buried in a book, would pretend it didn't bother her to be left out.

"Nellie talked a lot about the house in Pembroke Gardens when I was growing up. I used to dream about it. The big white house with climbing roses, always filled with people and dancing and laughter. Cecil Beaton would come and take photos at their parties, and their antics made headlines. And Nellie became like a member of the family, with Lucinda at all times."

"And Lucinda was your friend? The one you came to the island with? Was she involved as well?"

"Slow down." Another sip of wine, a smile at the loitering waiter. "I'll get to that. Nellie was in charge of Lucinda. There was an older brother, Laurence, but by the time Nellie arrived he was practically grown and had no use for a nanny. Nellie and Lucinda were a duo, the way Mum told it; they were pretty much left to their own devices. And when the war started, it made sense to keep them together.

"Laurence was old enough to head to war, and Lucinda's parents were involved in the war effort. The Rowes had a family estate in Devon. Eventually it would come to Laurence, but in the meantime Lucinda's uncle lived there. Nellie sometimes spoke about the house; there were gardens along a river, and the entire property was nestled deep into a valley. They were safe, and the estate vegetable gardens were plentiful. The war was a happy time for her, even though it was hard for many people."

This would have been good detail for the school project, Camilla thought, childhood jealousy rising up out of nowhere. She loved history. *The Crown* was her favorite television show. She felt the sting of her grandmother's preference for her sister afresh, though she'd thought she was over it. Taking another sip of water to try and flush away the lump in her throat, she said, "And then the war ended, and they came back to London?"

"Not quite. Lucinda and Nellie came back, yes. But Laurence, Lucinda's brother, was killed in the war. Their home in London was a different place. Lucinda's parents were heartbroken, and so was Lucinda. She idolized Laurence—they all did. Particularly Nellie. They were a similar age, and the way she used to tell it, he was a great laugh."

The waiter came over and refreshed her mother's glass. When he was done, she waved him away.

"Not long after they got back to London, Nellie realized she was pregnant. She was nearly thirty years old, and Lucinda was thirteen by then. When Nellie went to Lucinda's mother for help, Lucinda's mother saw the opportunity to get rid of her. She reasoned, quite rightly, that she no longer needed a nanny. All of a sudden, Lucinda was their sole heir, and she needed to step up. A lot of pressure was placed on her to marry someone and start a family."

"But who was your father?" Camilla asked. When she was thinking of starting a family, she had asked her mother if there were any health issues in the family that she needed to be aware of. Margaret had assured her there weren't. Now Camilla suspected that she had no idea.

"Mum always said it was someone she met during the war. Later events caused me to believe that it was Laurence."

"And that's why Lucinda's mother was so keen to get rid of her?"

"I think so."

"But if there was a chance that Nellie's baby was Laurence's, don't you think the family would want to be involved?"

"It was a different time. I'm sure there was a great deal of shame surrounding the pregnancy." Her mother shifted in her seat. It was easy to forget that these were her parents they were talking about.

Camilla nodded, but it didn't quite add up. "Laurence was away at war, though—how would that have worked?"

"I don't know. Nellie took all her secrets with her to the grave."

"Unless she told Susie. The painting she sent me to see at the gallery was once owned by the Rowe family. I think that was a clue."

Margaret smiled wryly. "Maybe. I've resigned myself to the fact that I may never find out who my father was." She looked down at her hands. "I have this ring, though. I'm pretty certain it must have come from him originally." They were quiet for a moment, an ocean of calm in the increasingly busy restaurant.

"Did Nellie put you in touch with Lucinda when you came to London?"

"No." Margaret coughed. "Not at first. I don't think they left on good terms—Lucinda was cross with my mother for leaving her. They lost contact. Nellie hadn't been in touch with Lucinda for years, until . . ." Her mother's voice tailed off, her eyes slightly glazed.

"Until?" Camilla asked softly, afraid to break the spell.

"Until Nellie had to ask Lucinda for her help."

35

Susie, 1998

Isabel peeked into the large burlap sack that Philippe had given her. "Clams for the vongole. And oysters! I knew the universe would provide."

"Let's take them back to the cottage," David said. He hadn't spoken much since Yvette said goodbye. His face was dark, clouded with something Susie couldn't put her finger on.

Ignoring the other two, she moved closer to him. "Are you okay?"

"Fine," he snapped. "I just don't want to stand around all evening at some fisherman's cottage."

Luckily, Henri and Isabel were engaged in their own conversation about the oysters and didn't hear.

"Come on, let's go then." She put her arm through David's, but he shook it off and marched ahead. For a while, Susie tried to keep up, but when it became clear he wanted to be alone, she backed off and walked with the other two, enjoying their banter about the best way to shuck the oysters for their upcoming feast.

By the time the three of them made it back to the cottage—they made a detour to the village to buy some fresh baguettes to eat with their oysters—David had the cork out of a bottle of wine and was drinking steadily. When Susie went to pour out glasses for the rest of them, there was barely a dribble left.

"That was quick work."

David didn't say anything, so Susie left him to his wine on the terrace, joining the others in the kitchen to smear thick, salty butter on the bread. With the aid of a kitchen cloth and a sharp knife, Henri was showing Isabel how to prize the oysters open and reveal the opal goodness inside. Isabel oohed and ahhed, and between the three of them they managed to eat a number of the oysters before they even made it to the plate.

After they had eaten Isabel's spaghetti vongole—delicious, of course—and polished off two more bottles of wine, Henri told a story about a famous shipwreck near the island. He was rusty on the details, and even Susie could tell he was fudging the truth a little.

"A hundred people were killed?"

"Yes, maybe more. Only one child survived. A baby. It washed up onshore on an old tea chest."

"This might be good for your sketchbook, David," Susie said, attempting to draw him into the conversation.

"It's a load of rot," David said, his wineglass tipping a little with the forcefulness of his speech. "I've had enough of this island and its fairy stories."

"David," Isabel said, a warning in her voice. Susie sat very still. She hadn't seen this side of him before. Had Isabel?

"'Oh, Henri, tell me more! Oh, Henri, show me how to shuck oysters!'" David mimicked. Isabel sat back in her chair and stopped talking. The only sound was the ocean on the other side of the garden wall.

In a better mood, David was easily swayed by Isabel's entreaties. He happily traded fish for a chicken supper, swam in waters with fast-moving currents, or took the bike with the dodgy steering, all at the request of Isabel. But his patience had run out.

"Come on, David, that is a little harsh." Henri took a deep inhale on his cigarette, his nostrils flaring slightly.

"Is it?" David said, his eyes flashing a warning. Susie held her breath.

"She was just trying to help."

"Tell us another story, Henri. I'm sure you have more local gossip in your repertoire." David stared at him. A challenge. Something passed between the two men that Susie couldn't identify.

"I don't know what you mean." Another inhale.

"You know what I'm talking about." David held his jaw tight, waiting.

"You want me to tell that story?"

"Go ahead. I'm sure the girls would like to hear what you island folk say about us."

Henri nodded. "There is an old island story about David's parents." He coughed and swallowed visibly. In the distance an owl called out. "The story is, they stole a baby."

36
Margaret, 1968

Margaret paused for a moment to take in the grandeur of the house. White stucco columns and a shiny black front door, a perfectly manicured garden, trees bare and trimmed and ready for April growth. Pembroke Gardens. She had walked past it many times, peered over the fence into the garden and imagined her mother living in those rarefied surroundings. She had never rung the doorbell though, not until this moment.

Her finger had barely left the bell when the door opened.

Lucinda Rowe was tall and ghostly pale, with long blond hair and a blunt fringe ending just above her eyebrows. Her startling blue eyes locked on Margaret's and stayed there. Finally, she held out a bony hand.

Margaret took the hand and shook it. Lucinda looked relieved. "You must be Margaret," she said. "I'd know you anywhere. You look just like your mother." The blue filled with water. "I miss Nellie," she added.

"Yes, I'm Margaret," Margaret said. She wasn't so sure Lucinda had missed Nellie at all. After all, she could have written a letter or sent a postcard. She could have picked up the telephone. It wasn't the Stone Age.

Lucinda's gaze drifted to Margaret's midsection. It was concealed under layers of winter clothing—a woolen jumper, an oversize coat, and a scarf knitted by Nellie—but Margaret felt the full extent of Lucinda's penetrating stare. She wrapped her arms around herself.

"Mum said you might be able to help me," Margaret said eventually.

"Would you like to come into the sitting room?" Lucinda held Margaret's eye. "Rupert's not home. We thought you were coming yesterday." Her wan appearance concealed a steely demeanor.

"Rupert?" Margaret asked. The name caught in her throat.

"My husband."

The two of them entered a large light-filled room to the left of the entrance hall. A record player in the corner played a classical tune.

"Make yourself comfortable." Lucinda propped an extra cushion behind Margaret's back; at close quarters she smelled strongly of lavender and rosemary, like a summer garden even though it was winter. She disappeared and came back with tea and cakes and a small plate of delicately portioned fruit.

"You probably know that your mother—Nellie," she added helpfully, "was my nanny when I was small. She looked after me for years. Did she tell you about Devon in the war? We were so happy. So happy. The last days before it all turned to dust. And then we came back to London, and suddenly she disappeared."

"To Australia," Margaret volunteered.

"Yes, although I didn't know it at the time. She was simply here one morning, and by the afternoon was gone. She didn't say goodbye." Lucinda's lip began to tremble.

"Your parents didn't tell you she was going?" Her mother didn't like goodbyes at the best of times—but Margaret felt sure she would have made an exception for the woman in front of her. It was easy to imagine the child she would have been, waifish and sweet; it would have been hard to deny her anything.

"I begged my parents for Nellie's address, but they wouldn't give it to me. And then, just last week, out of the blue Nellie phoned me up to say she had a daughter, Margaret, and she was in London!" Lucinda clapped her hands together. "It's you!"

Margaret smiled uncertainly. There was something unsettling about Lucinda.

"Did my mother mention—ah, did she mention my situation?"

Lucinda ignored the question. "You know, there were stories. I heard the other housemaids talking. About your mother."

Margaret stiffened. "Oh?"

"They thought she might have been pregnant when she left! That's why she left so quickly, and it was all so hush hush." She bent forward toward Margaret. "They said it might have been my brother!" She placed a hand over her mouth and looked over her shoulder, as if someone might come along at any minute and chastise her for gossiping.

"I don't know about that." Margaret took a sip of tea, the cup trembling slightly in her hands. "Mum always said my father was someone she met during the war. A soldier who was killed."

Lucinda raised her eyebrows. She pointed at a framed picture on the wall of a young soldier. He was handsome, but Margaret couldn't see any resemblance. "Laurence," she said. "How old are you?"

"I'm twenty-two."

"Adds up. Your mother said you were working in London. Modeling, I hear?"

"I gave that up. I've been doing some writing. Magazines."

"Anything I would have read?"

Margaret glanced at the copies of *Country Life* and *The Lady* on the side table. "I don't think so. Do you have—ah—children, Mrs. Rowe?"

"No, I do not. I lost a baby a number of years ago, and I have been unable to conceive since."

"I'm sorry, Mrs. Rowe, but my mother said you might be able to help me." Margaret pressed her nails into her thumb pad.

The door to the sitting room opened before Lucinda had a chance to answer.

"Hello, I'm Rupert!" the newcomer said, not missing a beat. If he was surprised to see Margaret sitting on his sofa, he gave nothing away.

Lucinda sank back in her chair as he smiled at them both, and waved in her direction. "This is Margaret."

Instead of sitting on the spare sofa, he came and knelt down in front of Margaret. "Margaret," he said, taking her hands and putting them both in his. "Margaret, you amazing, amazing woman." Each time he said "amazing," he squeezed her hands. Margaret couldn't breathe.

"Rupert. Steady on. We haven't got to that part yet."

Rupert looked back toward Lucinda, a flush spreading over his face. He didn't retreat though, simply dropped down onto his bottom and sat curled up at Margaret's feet, as if he couldn't bear to be far from her fertile presence. "Carry on then, Lucinda." He let go of Margaret's hands but continued to watch her carefully, his eyes traveling along every part of her. Hairline. Jawline. Waistline.

"I'm Rupert, though! I think I said that. I'm married to Lucinda here." He nodded in her direction. "We are very happy. Very! And we have a lovely home! Have you met the cats?"

"No. I haven't met the cats. I don't need to meet the cats." Margaret didn't try to hide the hostility in her voice, the heaviness in her heart. She started the process of moving to standing. The recent changes to her body made it slow. "Look, my mum said you might be able to help me, but I'm not sure . . ."

Rupert leaped up and pushed Margaret back onto the sofa. He looked as shocked as Margaret felt, his mouth forming an O as he reached after her as she fell. "Oh! Sorry! It's a soft sofa, though." He patted it to demonstrate his point. "Don't go! We have so much to talk about."

He wouldn't meet her eye. She looked at Lucinda instead. There was such a mixture of concern and vulnerability on her face that Margaret decided to hear them out.

"Your mother phoned us, you see, and we rather have our hopes up. I'm not sure what Lucinda has told you." Rupert looked at Lucinda, "Shall I go on? Stop me, won't you, if I'm repeating what you've already spoken about." He reclaimed his position at Margaret's feet, even closer this time, now that he had decided she was a flight risk.

"I wasn't sure how much Nellie had told her," Lucinda said, filling up the cups with more tea. There was a third cup set aside for Rupert, and she let the teapot hover over it. He nodded, and she filled it as well. "But now I see it's next to nothing." Her hand shook slightly as she lowered the teapot to the tray.

"When we spoke, your mother mentioned that you had gotten yourself into a difficulty. I think she was hoping that I might put you in touch with the right people. But what she couldn't know is that we have been trying to have a baby of our own for years, and for one reason or another"—Lucinda looked at Rupert for an instant—"we haven't been able to."

They want to take my baby.

Margaret's heart had leaped into her throat, and she felt sure the rising bile in her mouth could not be totally attributed to her condition. Up until that moment she had been kidding herself that this unlikely pair might be able to click their fingers and make everything easier for her. Perhaps offer her a room so she could leave her dismal bedsit, or point her in the direction of a women's support center. She hadn't anticipated they might have their own ideas of what would be suitable for the baby. Her baby.

"Having a child is our dearest wish," Rupert said, and squeezed Margaret's knee.

"And you're, you're suggesting . . ." Rupert's hand on her knee was distracting, and it was hard to find the right words.

"*Your mother*," Lucinda emphasized, "would agree that Rupert and I will provide a stable and practical home for your unborn child. We will provide medical care for you and the baby up until the birth, as well as accommodation during the pregnancy. Once the child is born, you will be free to leave and continue on with your life as before." Lucinda smiled and made a gesture with her hands, suggesting a feat of magic. "And besides," she added, with a nod in the direction of Laurence's portrait, "this baby might be family."

Margaret felt hot and breathless. Her overcoat and scarf were her last line of defense; to take them off would leave her exposed. Beside her, Rupert choked on his tea and coughed.

"It will be easier for everyone—including the child—if there is no further communication between the two families after the birth. Sadly, that would also apply to my relationship with your mother." A single crocodile tear ran down Lucinda's cheek, the rest of her face twitching with suppressed excitement.

"And I just—" Margaret pulled at the scarf around her neck, but the movement only made it tighter. "I just give you the—ah, my baby?"

"Yes!" Rupert squeezed her leg again. He was so close that Margaret could see the beginnings of his five o'clock shadow. Her mouth went dry. She closed her eyes to block him out. To block it all out. A grandfather clock ticked loudly somewhere in the hallway, and closer still, she could hear a scratching noise. The cats.

"Is she all right?" Lucinda's voice was shrill, panicked. Rupert withdrew his hand and went to comfort his wife.

"I'm all right," Margaret said, even as her body swelled and lurched within itself. She had felt like this before when, as a child, she had taken too many turns on the spinning wheel at the playground. That had been self-inflicted, and strangely enjoyable. This time, the sensation was outside of her control. Her body slowly came to rights.

"I'm all right," she repeated. "It's all right." It was all right. The house was warm and clean. Rupert and Lucinda were clearly well off, and cared for each other. They were genuine in their desire to have a baby. Margaret had asked her mother for help, and this was what she had offered. It was all right.

"Margaret." Lucinda's voice again. "Margaret." Her eyes snapped open. "I know this might be a shock to you. I know you might have had a different idea of how things would turn out. It's not ideal, I understand that. But you're young. You have plenty of time to have more children. Meet someone. Get married. We don't have that option. The alternative for us is sad, and we're not ready to face the prospect of life without a family. The alternative for you is a life of hard scrabble. It's not easy to bring up a child on your own. You should know that."

She was right. Margaret couldn't imagine choosing a life like her mother's. She had plans to get as far away from the little suburban terrace house as possible, to travel the world. That wouldn't work with a baby strapped to her back.

"Do you think Mum would think this is a good idea?" Her voice trembled. If Nellie was there, she would tell her to sharpen up and stop acting like a baby. But she wasn't there, and Margaret had to make the decision on her own.

"Yes, she does," Rupert answered quickly. He moved from where he was standing behind Lucinda to a drinks trolley by the fireplace. The sound of liquid being poured. "Twelve o'clock somewhere," he said, and swallowed the amber drink in one go.

"Your mother said the hardest thing she ever did was raise you on her own. She doesn't want you to have the same burden in your young life. Your baby will be safe with us." Lucinda sat back as if the deal was done. "You do understand, this will be under the strictest confidence. The situation is delicate and we would need to behave as if the child was our natural progeny. I'm sure that will suit us both nicely."

"I'll have to have a think about it." Margaret stood up. Her voice was calm, even though every inch of her body was raging with the first pulses of an unfamiliar maternal instinct. Her childhood had been tough. They hadn't had a lot of money. But the best part about it was knowing how hard Nellie had fought to keep her.

37

Susie, 1998

They were silent for a long time. Finally, Susie gathered the courage to speak.

"Why didn't you mention it?"

"I didn't think it was true." The wind had gone out of David's sails.

"Why bring it up now?"

"It was something Yvette said." He gave a half laugh. "I wasn't sure if it was a warning or a threat." He shook his head. "They like us when they're taking our money. Do you know how much we paid for the new roof?"

Henri muttered something and stood up. He disappeared into the house.

"About your mother?"

David nodded, miserable. "Things just started to click after that. Stories don't come from nowhere. *You* haven't come from nowhere. The toe." They all looked at Susie's feet, thankfully clad in her trusty Gazelles.

"I don't have anything to do with this," Susie said helpfully. "I know who my parents are. I'm just not sure about my grandfather."

"It's all connected, Susie, don't you see? Where there's one secret, others follow."

Isabel stood up and went to perch on the side of David's chair. She wrapped her arm around him and rested her head on his shoulder. "David, maybe you're jumping to conclusions here."

"You don't know everything." His voice became more urgent.

"What do you mean?"

"Remember the day we met at the gallery?"

Susie nodded. The wine and the oysters were starting to swirl in her stomach, and everywhere she looked, she saw tiny dancing auras, like the beginnings of a migraine.

"And I said I had fought with my mother?"

Susie remembered every little thing about that first meeting. She had picked and unpicked it in her mind until it was an appealing montage of moments.

"About your art?"

"Ha. If only."

"What were you fighting about?"

David gave Isabel a nudge, and she returned to her own chair.

"We were fighting about the house in Devon. My cousin wants my mother to sell it, but she insists it is rightfully mine."

"And you?"

"It's already caused too much trouble. I'm happy to let it go as long as I can keep Pond Cottage."

"But if it is yours, then how can he sell it?"

"That's why we were fighting. There's something she's not telling me. We go around and around in circles and never get anywhere. My mother is not used to being told what to do, and she has taken umbrage at this cousin for even trying to do so. We don't need that big house. It's my mother's pride and sheer bloody stubbornness that's stopping her from moving with the times."

"Maybe she just wants the best for you, David," Isabel purred, stroking his foot with hers.

"That's what she says. That's what she's always said." David sighed. Susie found it hard to find any sympathy for him. If it was her, she would be so overjoyed with this house on the Île de Clair, she wouldn't care about anything else.

Henri came back with another bottle of wine. They sat in silence for a while, pondering what had been said over the evening. Isabel produced a pack of cards, and they played Canasta for a few rounds, but David kept messing up the scoring.

Finally Henri called it a night, claiming he had early work in the morning. He took himself off down the side of the cottage and disappeared into the darkness.

The sketchbook of David's paintings lay on the table between them. Susie grabbed it and flipped through the pages. She found the picture she was looking for; the painting David had done of Isabel and herself on the beach. In the dim light from the kitchen windows, it was perfect. Two young girls with their faces lifted to the sun, ready for the next step in the adventure of their lives.

"This one is good, David. It's my favorite."

David stood up and sniffed, "They're no good, Susie. You know it, and I know it. It's just a vanity project."

There was no point protesting, not when he was in this sort of mood. Anything Susie said would seem trite, placatory. The truth was, they *were* good. She just didn't know if a book of paintings could do all the things David expected of it.

Isabel and Susie started to clear the glasses, picking up a few playing cards that had blown away in the gentle evening breeze. Isabel snapped a flower from the laburnum and tucked it behind Susie's ear. Susie screamed and flicked it off, explaining about the tree. They both laughed, pleased to have a release from the evening's tension.

David stopped in the doorway, watching the scene in front of him. Finally, he spoke. "It's Saturday night. You girls should go out. There's a hostel in the village—you can stay there tonight. I just need some time on my own."

38

Margaret, 1968

A week later, Margaret agreed to meet with Lucinda and Rupert again. They asked her to come along to the National Gallery, and she did, meeting them straight after work. She could still remember what she wore: a smock dress in apricot rayon with buttons all down the back. She had turned it around and was wearing it back to front, the hemline short and her legs covered in white tights. It covered her bump; she still hadn't told her colleagues she was expecting a child.

Rupert took her coat at the gallery, and Lucinda nodded with approval as if Margaret was a prize mare, the legs and hindquarters appealing, the bloodstock suitable. They wandered through the galleries and talked about art. Margaret pretended she knew what they meant when they talked about Fauvists and Postimpressionism, but really all she knew was what she liked. And what she liked was quite different from the abstract pieces Rupert insisted on explaining to her.

Lucinda told her about a role she had coming up, a short run of a Tennessee Williams play at the Old Vic. Had Margaret heard about it? There had been quite a lot of buzz, she said. It was something different from everything she had done before, but really she was frightened, and she would be happy to give the part up if . . .

She left the sentence unfinished.

The thought of Margaret's child being raised by such sophisticated people and in such cultured circumstances was seductive, there was no doubt. A far cry from Margaret's past, and light-years beyond anything she might hope to provide for the child. Rupert took her arm as they went up the stairs, ordered her tea in the café nearby; his manners were impeccable. That evening, they repeated their offer to take on Margaret's child. They promised a world of education, travel, and opportunity beyond Margaret's realm of experience.

Gifts began arriving, things she didn't even know she needed but quickly came to like. Cashmere socks. A hot-water bottle in a quilted silk cover. An overflowing hamper from Fortnum & Mason. Classical records to play to the baby.

As spring turned to summer, the Rowes became even more present in her life; they were becoming friends. When Margaret began to show, they asked her to move in with them. Most of Margaret's clothes no longer fit her; all her belongings now fit in a small brown vinyl suitcase.

At Pembroke Gardens, life changed again. She was asked to stay inside as much as possible. Meals were brought to her room on a tray. Lucinda tried to keep her busy, running lines with her and asking her advice on nursery decor. Margaret's world got smaller and smaller with each day.

And with each retraction, her confidence diminished. She was told that phone calls to her mother were too expensive, that she must make do with letters. But even though she wrote to Nellie weekly, she received nothing in return. Lucinda passed up the role in *The Rose Tattoo*. She had too much to organize, she said. And besides, they would leave soon for the Île de Clair. It was the first time Margaret had heard the name.

From the tight confines of the attic bedroom at Pembroke Gardens, the Île de Clair sounded like heaven. An island off the coast of France, a cottage by the sea. The sounds of the ocean as she slept, and long, warm days. Just the thought of the sun and water unfurled something within her, and for the first time in months, she started to look forward to something.

But first, they said, there was the small matter of a meeting with the solicitor. It will be quick, they said; the solicitor had worked for the family for years, and was discreet. What family? Margaret had thought. During the long months at Pembroke Gardens there had been no sign of any other family, and no mention of relatives.

She pushed away these thoughts, just as she did the other feelings of foreboding that sprang up from time to time during those months of pregnancy. If she worried, she blamed it on hormones; if she had misgivings, she attributed them to homesickness. It was her penance, her price to pay for making a foolish mistake.

The adoption process was far simpler then. From what Margaret heard on the news, adoption was like jumping through hoops these days, with no guaranteed outcome. Perhaps if there had been a slight obstacle, a question of doubt, a concerned bystander—just one small voice of disquiet—things might have turned out differently.

The solicitor came to the house early in the morning, on the day they were due to leave for France. They didn't move into the sitting room, where the furniture had been covered with sheets and the curtains drawn. They stayed in the stuffy hall, and Mr. Carter mopped at his forehead with a handkerchief and fumbled with the lock on his small leather briefcase. When he finally opened it, there was only one document inside.

"Quickly," Lucinda had said, handing her a fountain pen. "We have a train to catch."

Margaret looked around at the faces—all nodding and smiling tight approvals—as she hovered the pen over the line.

She tried to read the document, but the words were swimming, and even as she chased them across the paper, they became disjointed, nonsensical. The hall clock marked out a steady and relentless beat, reminding her that it was time to leave. When she finally put pen to paper and signed her name, Lucinda breathed out audibly. She came and put her arm unnaturally around Margaret's shoulders for the briefest moment.

"There. That's done," she said, as if they had hung out a load of washing or completed some other daily domestic task. "Shall we go?"

And they had come here. An interminable journey with the three of them. Lucinda, Rupert, and Margaret. To the outside eye, they would have looked like a group of friends on holiday. One with slightly less smart luggage than the other two, but all the same, a nice-looking bunch of travelers.

As soon as the baby was born, they turned on her.

37

Margaret

When Margaret had finished, Camilla was quiet for a moment. "You didn't steal a baby?"

Margaret shook her head. At that moment the waiter reappeared, having skulked in the background waiting for an appropriate time to approach. Margaret appreciated his tact. This wasn't an easy conversation.

"I'll have the sole meunière. Please."

"I'll have the same," Camilla said, even though she wasn't hungry. The waiter took their orders to the kitchen. "You had a baby," she said, mostly to herself.

Margaret gave a half smile. "When you said you were going to the Île de Clair, I knew straightaway it was something to do with my baby."

Camilla was slowly joining the dots. "I have a brother."

"A half brother, but yes." Margaret placed her hands on the table, her palms entwined. "As I said, as soon as he was born, Lucinda and Rupert turned on me. It didn't help that I changed my mind at the last minute. The night before he was born, I had decided I wouldn't give him up. But Lucinda had thought of that. She had it all worked out."

"Mum." Camilla grabbed her bag from the ground next to the table.

"She met him. Susie met David. I have a photo of him." Her hands were fumbling so much, she couldn't get ahold of the envelope with the photos in it.

"Here." Finally she had them. She thrust them across the table. "Mum, she met him!"

Margaret took the photo in her hands. The photo shook as she inspected it. For the longest time she didn't say anything.

"She had this, all this time?" A combination of pain and confusion settled on her mother's face. "Why didn't she tell me? Why didn't you tell me?"

"I only just found out who he was." She took the letter from her bag and passed it across the table.

"'Time to leave the island'?" Margaret read aloud from the envelope. She raised her eyebrows and opened the envelope anyway. Camilla sucked on the inside of her cheeks, waiting nervously for her mother's reaction.

"Oh, Susie," Margaret said softly when she got to the end. She took great care refolding the letter.

Camilla couldn't wait any longer. "Do you think David's still here?"

"I went to the cottage this afternoon, to see," Margaret started, unable to take her eyes from the photograph. "It was a shock to see the place again, after all that happened there. He wasn't there, though."

"And then you asked at the police station," Camilla said, joining the dots.

"He said the Rowe family had moved on years ago. Nineteen ninety-eight, to be exact."

"Nineteen ninety-eight?"

Margaret nodded. "I don't think it's a coincidence, do you?"

A champagne cork popped across the room, jerking them out of their reverie.

"I can't believe I have a brother." Camilla shook her head. "Almost feels like we need to celebrate as well." After a moment, she added, "Why would Susie keep this a secret?"

Their meals arrived, the fish floating in the buttery sauce. As soon as the waiter left, Camilla pushed hers away.

Margaret picked up her knife and fork and at least acted like she was about to eat. "I have my suspicions." She paused with her cutlery poised in midair. "But I would like to find David first. And I'd like you to be with me." She put down the knife and fork and placed her hand on Camilla's. The sun was about to set, and the last rays shone through the window, catching the gold of her ring.

"Do you think David knows about you?"

"I don't know. If Susie worked it out, she would have told him. She never was good at keeping secrets."

"Until now."

"True."

"I want to find David too. I'm sure that's why Susie wanted me to come here. It all comes back to David. He must be in Devon. But first I need to talk to Henri again. I need to see if he has the sketchbook."

"Pond Cottage must be the Rowe family estate in Devon, where Mum was during the war." Margaret looked thoughtful. "It's not like you, to open the envelopes early," she added, a smile tugging at the corner of her mouth.

Camilla whipped the envelope back into her bag. "Maybe there's more to me than I've let on."

"Seriously, though, Mills, are you sure you want to do this? I can go on and meet David if you feel like it's too much for you."

"I'm here. I'm committed. I've got nowhere else I need to be."

"What does the school think about that?"

"They weren't rapt. I told them it was a family emergency. I've never taken time off like this before."

"What about your children?"

Camilla winced, and then disguised it by taking a sip of her drink. "Ian has it under control. He basically runs the show in term time anyway."

"Good old Ian."

A couple came into the restaurant at that moment, and Margaret nodded to them in greeting, just as she would at home.

"I'm glad you're here, Mum," Camilla said.

Margaret looked out the window, clearly searching for a way to change the subject. There was nothing but a lone seagull and an attractive but nondescript street sign. "I'm glad I'm here too, Mills. Even if I am a little nervous."

"It's normal to be nervous about meeting David." Camilla was happy to take on the reassuring role; it made her feel more like herself.

"Yes. It's not just that. I'm nervous about this place." There was something she wasn't saying. Camilla could tell by the tightness in her lips, her inability to meet Camilla's eye. "It's not just what happened to me here. I think something happened to Susie too."

"Do you think it had something to do with David?" Camilla asked quietly.

At that moment the door opened again, and this time a big family group walked in. A messy, multigenerational gang of grandparents, parents, teenagers, toddlers, and one very small baby. The family eventually settled at their table, the baby being passed from willing arms to willing arms as everyone found their place.

"That's how I always imagined it would be," Margaret said, watching carefully.

"We've had Christmases like that—when the children were small," Camilla offered, but Margaret knew she understood. The family across the room exuded comfort, familiarity, and ease. Christmas was Christmas. Any family could do it for one meal.

"Do I think it had something to do with David?" Margaret repeated the question. "When Susie got back from overseas, the wind was gone out of her. She had never been a delicate child, but when she got back from that trip, she was crushed, like her belief in the world—in goodness—was gone. I don't think it had anything to do with David." She paused, looked Camilla directly in the eye.

"I think it had to do with Lucinda."

40
Margaret, 1968

Margaret, Lucinda, and Rupert arrived on the island at the height of summer. "Hiding in plain sight," Lucinda said as they pushed through the crowds at the ferry docking point. "We'll say you're a friend." She looked approvingly at Margaret's linen smock. "We've done a good job with that—you can hardly tell."

Margaret's expectations were raised. She anticipated long days on the beach—if Lucinda could find a swimming costume to fit her—and afternoon naps. Relaxed meals in the garden, a sip of wine in the evenings. But once they got to the cottage, Lucinda and Rupert sat her down and outlined their requirements.

"It's best for you and the baby if you rest while you're here. We're not locking you in, of course"—and here Lucinda laughed nervously, as if the idea was preposterous and not almost exactly what they were about to do—"we're just asking you to keep a low profile. Take a walk in the evening, sit in the garden. We want you to do everything you can to keep the baby safe. There's no hospital out here. We can't afford to take any chances."

Margaret had agreed—what choice did she have? It didn't sound so bad, not after months of London life where the rooms were cold and food was scarce or inedible. She could rest on an island. And when they had shown her the room she would be in, she nearly cried with relief. Twin beds, made up in French linens and feather quilts. Just for her. A window out to sea. Lucinda brought in a small glass vase of honeysuckle, placed it on her bedside table. It was bliss.

And yet. After a few days, Margaret was stir-crazy. There was a small television set in the house, but reception was patchy, and the programming was in French. The books were too highbrow for her taste; Camus and Colette. She wanted something escapist, something to pass the time. The words in those books were like slugs, sticking in her brain as she tried to understand them. She asked for magazines, and Lucinda brought her *Paris Match*. The celebrities were unrecognizable, and the articles were in French.

Lucinda and Rupert didn't go out much either. On the days when they needed groceries, Rupert would take the bicycle and come back with wine, cheese, bread, and fruit. He would cook up elaborate meals in the tiny kitchen, and they would eat together. Rabbit stew. Coq au vin. Mussels in white wine. Lucinda and Rupert would share bottle after bottle of Chablis, pouring Margaret a glass of milk as if she was their child.

One evening, the bells of the chapel had sounded through the otherwise still air. Margaret watched as a procession of locals wandered out of the church, kissing their neighbors. Their laughter and chatter carried down the hill, and Margaret ached for companionship. She missed Nellie. She missed home. She couldn't think about the now unmistakable rounding in her belly, her time coming near. That was too much. She had to pretend it wasn't happening.

The next morning, she rose early and tiptoed down the stairs, past the closed door of Lucinda and Rupert's room. She grabbed a jacket from the coatrack, pulled it over her nightgown, and crept out the terrace door. Climbed the steps up to the chapel and pushed open the heavy wooden doors.

She had never been a religious person, but the chapel calmed her. She lit a candle and prayed in her own way for the baby inside her. She sat and thought about her life and her plans, and she told herself she wouldn't let this episode define her. She would get through it, and she would get on with her life.

41

Susie, 1998

By the time Isabel and Susie got to the village, they had convinced themselves a night in the hostel together would be fun. They had no interest in going out, not after the conversation with David. Besides, it was late. There was nowhere to go. All the shops and bars were shuttered.

Valerie lent them pajamas—well, one pair of pajamas; Susie had to make do with an old T-shirt—and found them toothbrushes. They squeezed into the one spare bunk bed. The next morning Susie went to work at the crêperie, keeping one eye on the door for David. When her shift was over, she and Isabel sat at a table outside the hostel. In the late afternoon, they helped Valerie sweep out the rooms and change the beds.

At five o'clock, they gave up on waiting for David and borrowed some bikes to cycle around the island. They went past the cottage, but there was no sign of him. They checked the beaches and the cafés, but he was nowhere to be seen. The day was fading into evening as they came back to the village, the swell of music reaching their ears as they approached.

It was Sunday evening; David's birthday was the next day. They were happy to give him time to digest things, but they didn't want to miss out on celebrating the milestone. Thirty! It was such a significant number. Older than either of the girls could ever imagine.

There were more people about than usual, groups gathered in the tiny front gardens of the village houses, outdoor tables filled with people drinking and laughing. Tents had popped up in the middle of the square, and fairy lights were strung up in the walkways between. It looked magical.

Valerie and Henri were sitting at a table outside the hostel. Henri reached into the rosemary behind him and snapped a leaf from the plant. Susie watched him, holding her breath. He held it between two fingers, telling Valerie about it, then brought his hand to her nose. She took a deep breath in and hovered longer than Susie thought was necessary.

Susie was still watching from her bicycle when she felt someone move up beside her. Isabel.

"It's nothing," she said, hugging Susie fiercely, holding her for a fraction longer than necessary. "Maybe David will come to the fair." Their eyes met, and they both laughed despite their worries. There was nothing less likely than David coming to the fair.

Henri looked up and saw Susie, waved the two girls over. He tucked the sprig of rosemary in his shirt pocket.

"This looks like fun," Susie said brightly, trying to squash her feelings of unease. "Shall we go and have a look?"

Aside from the tents with sideshow games, there were tables laden with produce and crafts. One stand was overflowing with brightly colored beads, another with leather goods. Someone had dragged out a wooden dresser, and it was crammed with earthy pottery for sale.

It was the smells that were making Susie's mouth water, though. The salty, buttery aroma of fresh popcorn, the sweet waft of waffle cones, and a savory undertone of sausage, onion, and freshly baked bread.

"I have to work." Valerie sighed and stood up, adjusting her apron and looking around at the fast-filling tables. She took a pencil from her apron pocket and twisted her long blond hair into a loose bun on top of her head, securing it with the pencil. She made it look effortless, the same way she made everything look effortless. Always first out to the rock when they swam out, always coaxing a cork from a wine bottle with ease, always tanned—no lines or burn or peeling skin. "It's the same every year."

"For you." Susie tried to keep the jealousy out of her voice.

A couple appeared at the door of the hostel, tapping their watches. Valerie went to see what they wanted. Henri took Susie's hand and kissed it. He still smelled of rosemary. Susie softened, the worry loosening its grip slightly.

"We will go," he said. Someone in the hostel put a CD player in the window, and the slow, languid tones of Portishead started to drift down, fighting with the piano accordion player at the other end of the tents. Susie took a deep breath, reminded herself where she was. It was better to try and forget everything for a few hours.

Valerie appeared holding four beers, her long fingers balancing them effortlessly. Henri's hand slipped out of Susie's as she reached forward to help.

"Cheers!" Isabel grabbed one and took a sip before anyone had a chance to respond. The rest of them clinked the bottles together and enjoyed the first crisp sip of beer. Valerie drank hers in a few quick gulps and then signaled that she needed to get back to work. Maybe it was the beer, maybe it was Valerie's exit, but Susie felt herself relax.

The day began to fade into a silky twilight. There were locals dotted in with the tourists, and Susie recognized some families from the beach, looking different with their shower-fresh air and sundresses, a day on the sand rinsed off.

"Another one?" Henri asked.

"Not for me," said Susie. "Come on!" She grabbed Henri's hand, and Isabel followed them, leaving her beer half finished on the table along with a handful of scrunched-up francs.

They ventured through the fair with empty stomachs and a gentle beer buzz. Henri bought crêpes for all of them from Marie, who had set up a stand outside her restaurant. It was the first time all summer he'd had money to spend, but he didn't explain himself, shaking his head softly when the girls offered to contribute. The sweet-and-sour hit of the sugar and lemon filled some deep craving within Susie, and the feeling of well-being she felt earlier increased.

The three of them walked in happy harmony. Susie bought a leather wrist strap for Henri and insisted he put it on. She bought a little salt dish for her mother, a pair of hand-painted earrings for Camilla. They bought another round of beers from a stand and sipped them slowly as they walked along the stalls. The fortune-teller's tent was the last in the row. Once brightly jewel-colored, it had faded, the colors only distinguishing themselves up close. Like everything, it was laced with fairy lights, and lines of glimmering prisms protected the entrance.

"Let's do it," said Isabel, looking at Susie with mischief in her eyes. "I've always wanted to."

"How much is it?" Susie asked, her hand moving instantly to the small pouch she wore slung across her body. She had spent most of her money on gifts.

"I'll shout," said Isabel. Money never seemed to be a problem for her. She pulled out her wallet and peeled a couple of notes off from the many inside.

"Don't," Henri said. He put his hand out and curled it around the money in Isabel's hand. For a moment the three of them didn't move. The crowd swelled around them, oblivious to the silent few among it.

Isabel looked coolly at Henri before using her other hand to remove his hand from hers. She gave Susie a look that Susie couldn't interpret before turning and entering the tent.

"What was that?" Susie asked, once she was sure Isabel was out of earshot. The power play between them had made her feel uncomfortable, unsure of where her loyalties would lie if it came down to choosing.

"This is for tourists. Don't waste your money." He waved in the direction of the tent.

"I am a tourist, Henri. A tourist, trying to have some fun."

Henri fiddled at the fastening on the leather wristband she had just given him. It was tight and had left an imprint on his wrist.

"So you will leave the island? Like a tourist? Summer is gone, and—poof!—you are too?"

"I don't know." Susie hadn't told him about the plans she had hatched with Isabel to take some time traveling around Europe. There had never been a right moment. And truthfully, she thought he must have realized that. "Isabel and I thought we might buy a rail card, see some more of France. Maybe Spain, Greece, Italy?"

"Is this true?" He looked hurt. "You are leaving?"

"Henri . . ." She took his hand, tried to get him to look at her. She didn't want to do this now, in the middle of the fair. Not when they had both been drinking, and there were people around. "I'm nineteen. I need to do things. I can't stay on this island for the rest of my life."

Henri snatched back his hand and returned to fiddling with the leather strap. "Why not? It's not good enough for you?" One of the local men walked past and clapped him on the back in greeting before seeing his face and shuffling off.

"I don't know. I can't settle down now. There's nothing here for me."

"Nothing here for you?" He almost spat out the words.

"What would I do? I can't work for Marie forever."

"No, of course not." A sneer.

"Maybe you could come with us? You don't want to stay here forever, do you? You're smart. You could do anything you want."

"I have everything I want here, Susie." In the distance the setting sun glanced off the water, and the whole town was cast in a pink twilight. "Or I thought I did." He looked at Susie. There was a hardness in his eyes, a glint that hadn't been present before. The pain from the realization was immediate, a brutal blow to Susie's heart, and she was responsible. She had hurt both of them.

"Maybe I could come back? When we're done traveling?"

"Don't bother." Henri snapped at the leather strap and flung it at her before walking away, disappearing into the crowd almost immediately. She wanted to race after him, but she couldn't leave Isabel behind. Besides, Isabel would know what to do. If she could just explain herself better to Henri, she was sure he would understand.

The minutes ticked by. The fair was starting to feel claustrophobic, the crowds, the music, even the smells, forceful and overwhelming. There was no sign of Henri, even though a small part of Susie thought he might come back and apologize, say it was all right. She picked up the leather strap from where it had landed on the dust and shook it off. She tried to fasten it to her own wrist so she could give it back to Henri later, but the fastening was broken. She slipped it in her pocket.

Suddenly the hanging prisms were pushed apart and Isabel ran out.

"Isabel?" But she pushed past Susie without looking at her. "Isabel, wait!"

Susie tried to grab her hand, but Isabel was too fast. She simply pushed Susie away and, ignoring the curious onlookers, disappeared into the crowd within seconds. Susie was about to follow her when she heard her name being called.

She turned. It was the woman from the tent. The fortune-teller.

Susie opened her mouth to make an excuse, pointing after Isabel, but the fortune-teller shook her head and beckoned. There was something resolute about her that made Susie obey. Wordlessly, she moved toward the tent.

On the inside, the tent was magical. Someone had taken a paint-brush to the canvas and covered it in giant mythical creatures, unlike anything Susie had seen before. The figures were round and amorphous and borrowed something from centaurs and unicorns but were also cherubic. Verdant leaves and vines danced between them. Flecks of gold paint flickered in the candlelight, and in the middle of it all was the fortune-teller, already stretched out on a pile of velvet cushions on the floor.

"How did you know my name?" Susie asked as she took in her surroundings.

The fortune-teller raised her eyebrows.

"Where is your crystal ball, then?" Susie joked, but the lilt in her voice gave away her nerves. First the argument with Henri, and then the sight of the usually implacable Isabel upset—it wouldn't take a clairvoyant to see she was rattled. Susie stood bent at the side of the tent, not willing to go any closer, even though this was the area where the ceiling was the lowest.

"My name is Mireille," the woman said, her voice gentle and smooth. "I am not that kind of fortune-teller. Your friend told me your name.

She has paid for you already." Mireille smiled and patted the cushions next to her. "Sit down, please." A mixture of perfume and mustiness wafted out of the pillows as they took her weight. Mireille shuffled over so that their knees were touching and took Susie's hands in hers.

"Now, Sous-cie," she said, making Susie's name sound European, "I am sensing . . . trauma. In your past." Susie's hands stiffened immediately. She tried to pull them away, but Mireille had a firm grip. She couldn't stop thinking about her fight with Henri and the fear on Isabel's face. Was that the trauma in her past that Mireille was referring to? It seemed too, well, recent, and to be honest, she wasn't ready to call it a trauma yet, because she was still sure she would be able to fix everything. Just as soon as she got out of the tent.

"I thought this was fortune-telling about, you know, the future," she mumbled. Mireille's face was slack with purpose, her eyelids twitching slightly and her head swaying almost imperceptibly.

For a number of minutes, the music of the piano accordion outside the tent canceled out the deep, steady breaths of Mireille, starting off jaunty and then moving into a maudlin refrain, the notes dragging and pitching. Mireille's hands started to twitch in Susie's. To start with, the movement was a shudder. Gradually it became faster, and then just as suddenly stopped.

"This is not good," Mireille whispered after a long silence. Susie felt a bubble of laughter rise in her throat. She tried to swallow it. "This is not good at all." Mireille's grip on her hands became tighter still.

"This is not good," Mireille repeated, as she abruptly let go of Susie's hands and opened her eyes. "I am wondering if it is even a good idea to say anything. After the last little girl . . ." She looked at the mural on the wall with great concentration. "I always talk to my animals in moments of doubt, and they tell me what to do.

"No. It's not right. No. Not me. It's not what I do." She cocked her head to listen. "Right. Yes. Right." She turned back to Susie. "It's not always bad to get a fortune like this," she began, "but chances are, in your case, it will be bad." She nodded sadly. "It looks like you will die young. Not very, very young like I have seen, but also not old."

"Okay," Susie said. She *was* going to die, eventually. "Is there any-thing about a French boy?"

"No. There is nothing else. This other thing is very strong, and it is clouding everything else for you." Mireille had the fortune-teller's equivalent of a bad bedside manner.

"Anything about love?" Susie asked again, hopefully. She didn't want Isabel to have wasted her money.

"No. There is not."

"Family? A new cousin?"

"No. There is nothing about love or cousins." Mireille rubbed the skin in the middle of her forehead. She looked drained as she waved for Susie to leave. "If there is someone waiting, please ask them to give me a moment."

She lay back on the pillows, her hand draped over her face. Susie knew just how she felt.

42

Margaret

Whenever Margaret was overexcited as a child, unable to settle to a task or drift off to sleep, Nellie would shake her head and say, "Margaret, you're wound up like a two-bob watch." Margaret used to say it to her children as well, shaking her head in much the same way. It was the perfect way to describe how she felt at that moment, walking back to the hotel after dinner. The memories were coming in thick and fast, and she couldn't stop talking. It was as if someone had turned on a highlights reel inside her mind.

"It was hot like this on the night David was born," she said as the path started its incline away from the village. In the intervening years, she had gotten used to thinking of him as David, even though she initially thought it wasn't enough of a name for the magnificent creature she had held only briefly in her arms. She wanted a romantic name like Orlando or Jasper—but what she wanted was of little concern to Lucinda. David was a family name, and it was set upon him at the very moment he was born.

"When is his birthday?" Margaret slowed for a moment so they could walk side by side.

"August tenth."

"That's in a couple of days. How old will he be?"

Margaret knew this. Even if she didn't have a calendar, she would know. Every year her body worked itself up into a frenzy around this time. She found it harder to sleep, harder to concentrate, for the few weeks leading up to August 10 every year. On August 11, things went back to normal.

"Fifty-one."

"Last year was a big one."

"I didn't miss it." Margaret had raised a glass that evening. She could hardly believe fifty years had passed. She had almost told Bill that night. Almost.

"Did you celebrate every year?"

"I don't know if 'celebrate' is the right word, Mills. Mum used to ring me on his birthday every year, even though she never mentioned him."

They walked in silence for a moment, and then Camilla said, "What were you saying about the night he was born?"

"It was a night just like this." Margaret let her feet fall into a rhythm beside her daughter's. Their long legs kept pace with each other. "We had been on the island for a few weeks by that stage. I told you, I wasn't able to do much. I practiced my French with Rupert, daydreamed about the future. I knew I was going to have a baby, but I hadn't really *thought* about it deeply. It's not the sort of thing you can understand until you've been through it. I don't think anything prepares you for it."

Camilla made a noise in assent. Margaret had tried to warn her about childbirth, but Camilla was more concerned about making plans for her return for work.

"It was just a deadline, a date when the baby would come. He was due to come in the first week of August, but he didn't arrive until the tenth. I always told myself he wanted the extra time with me." A cry caught in Margaret's throat.

"You're probably right," Camilla said kindly.

"We came to the island in July. Lucinda wanted to beat the summer crowds, she didn't want to see anyone on the boat. It was all arranged. We traveled separately on the ferry, and I wore a loose frock to disguise my pregnancy. Lucinda also wore a loose frock and made a large fuss about needing a seat, feeling faint. She was pregnant, she kept shouting to anyone who would listen. She really showed her acting chops on that journey. Meanwhile, I, eight months pregnant and feeling nauseous, stood the whole way. Carried my little case. I nibbled on crackers to keep my energy up, but by the time we got to the cottage, I was exhausted and slept for days. Lucinda at least had the decency to be a little ashamed of her behavior."

"She took care of you?"

"Ha! She made herself very scarce once we arrived. I hardly saw her. She took to her bed to 'rest' for the birth. Rupert looked after me, though. He brought me tea and toast in bed every morning and encouraged me to converse with him in French. He even found an old watercolor set for me to use in the garden so I could paint the view in the afternoons."

"I didn't know you could paint."

"I can't." Margaret clapped her hands together. "But it was something to do. The days got hotter, and I got bigger and bigger. My ankles puffed up, and by the end my face was like a blowfish. Big and round—yours was a bit like it with Timmy, I thought."

"Thanks," Camilla said dryly. Margaret was hoping she might laugh at the memory, but Camilla's mood was all over the shop.

They came to a path that ran down to one of the protected coves of the island. Margaret stopped. "Rupert took me for a swim down there on the night David was born. I had been asking the whole time. It was the one thing I wanted to do. Feel weightless. You saw the color of the water today, it's magic. I wanted to dive under it and feel free. I wanted to feel cool. Lucinda kept saying no. It was too risky, she said."

"Rupert disagreed?"

"I don't know if he disagreed, but he did it for me. I was restless that night and couldn't stop pacing. I think my body already knew the baby was coming, even though I didn't. It was late when Rupert tapped on my door. He handed me an old swimming costume, stretched out and faded from years of salt-water swimming. I put it on, and it just about fit me."

"Did you think that it was weird?"

"Not at all. Rupert was a kind man." She nearly said more but stopped herself. She pointed up the hill toward the other path. The one that went up to the cottage. "We came down the path in the moonlight. Rupert held my hand to make sure I didn't fall. He was worried about the baby, you see. We were both frightened of what Lucinda might do if she found out."

"Did she?" Camilla asked, quietly, as if Lucinda herself might appear at any point.

"We had a lovely swim. It was just as good as I had imagined. But then Rupert and I had a fight."

"A fight?"

"I told him I wanted to keep the baby." Camilla was very still. Listening. "He told me it was impossible, that the paperwork was signed. Lucinda would never give the baby up."

"Oh, Mum."

"I was sobbing. Hysterical. Rupert kept telling me to shush, but Lucinda came down to the beach and found us. She told Rupert he would regret ever taking me down there, and then she dragged me back to the cottage and locked me in the bedroom."

"Didn't anyone come to help? Someone must have heard something."

"People are very good on this island at noticing things but not saying anything. I think the shock of it all brought on the labor. David was born just before dawn." Margaret sighed deeply and started to walk again.

"You don't have to come with me, Mum," Camilla said.

Margaret didn't answer. She was still thinking about what she would do. She knew what she *wanted* to do, she just didn't know if it was the best thing for her to do. They walked along in silence.

"I don't know if I'm going to be able to sleep," Margaret said as the lights of the port-town buildings came into view. "Shall we walk on the beach for a minute?" Camilla looked tired, but Margaret didn't want to be alone. Not yet.

They kicked their shoes off in the sand and left them at the edge of the water, relishing the gentle waves on their weary feet.

"It's been a long day," Camilla said.

"I can't believe it's only been one day. It feels like a lifetime." Margaret let her feet sink deep down, enjoying the feeling of submitting to the heavy sand. "You know, I wanted to tell you girls everything, over the years. I wanted to tell your dad. But every time I thought about doing it, it was the wrong time. First, I didn't want to upset your childhoods, then you were away from home, and the time you spent back with us was too precious to ruin."

"Until it wasn't." They both knew that was shorthand for the summer of the accident.

"It was my fault, Mum," Camilla said. "I should have said no. I knew it was a bad idea."

"You were both young. I shouldn't have reacted the way I did."

"You loved that horse."

Camilla was right. Margaret had loved Pilgrim. She loved Pilgrim the way she loved all her horses, with a deep and certain surety that her love would be returned. Those animals never let her down.

Margaret remembered the day well. The rainy season. Margaret hadn't heard them go; she didn't know the plan. If she did, she would have told them the road was too wet. She had just brought Pilgrim into the home paddock, closer to the house, for a spell. Some sort of sixth sense brought her to the veranda just before the crash. She saw the moment of impact. The rusted-out white jeep careering into the gum tree. Pilgrim underneath the tree, bucking up in fright and landing on the wire fence.

Margaret started running. Camilla climbed out of the car, shouted out that they were fine, they were fine. Margaret turned her attention to Pilgrim. The horse was panicking wildly, becoming more and more enmeshed in the fence wire, until, with one last final bolt of energy, she bucked up and away, landing back down with a crack, the unmistakable sound of a bone snapping as she landed, her agonizing cries echoing around the empty landscape.

Bill came out soon after with his shotgun and shouted at them to go inside. Camilla ran inside, scared. Susie wouldn't come, so Margaret dragged her, holding her head so she couldn't look back. They were in the kitchen when they heard the gunshot. And Margaret had gone into her room to be alone.

"Susie was never the same after that," Camilla said quietly.

"No." Margaret's tone was flat. Not with indifference, but in the manner of someone who had worked something out a long time ago.

"And then she came here."

"Yes. It seems like it."

"And something happened here. Something to do with David and Lucinda and Henri and Valerie and Isabel and all these people that I've never heard of until this trip. I thought it had to do with David, and now I'm not so sure."

Margaret just nodded, letting Camilla speak.

"Ian thinks it was a crazy idea to come here." The light of a fishing boat bobbed in the distance. "I'm doing it for Susie. She said it would be good for me." Camilla looked older in the moonlight, the bags under her eyes somehow more pronounced. The trip was taking an emotional and physical toll.

"I'm just not so sure about that, Mills." Margaret looked at Camilla with concern. "Maybe she wanted you to have a break from all the seriousness in your life. All the schedules and timetables and appraisals and report writing . . ." Margaret tailed off. "But maybe she just wanted to get all this off her chest, and she never thought you would go through with it. I just hope you haven't spent all this money and put pressure on your family just because Susie asked you to do something. She doesn't always think out the consequences of her actions. What if David doesn't want to meet us? What if Susie did something awful all those years ago, and we end up cleaning up another of her messes?"

"It's possible," Camilla said slowly. "All of it is *possible*. That's the thing about life with Susie. *Anything* was possible. And this is my last chance to go along for the ride."

Margaret tried one last time. "But you don't *have* to do it."

"I'm just doing what I'm told." Camilla sounded like a teenager again. "Susie wants her ashes scattered here, and I'll do it because I am a *good sister*. Not because I am a martyr or a rule follower."

"You're right," said Margaret, in the same placating voice she had used when the girls were actually teenagers. "You are a good sister." Her heart filled with love for her older daughter. She tried not to think about the empty space next to her, where Susie might have stood had she found the courage to talk to her mother while she was alive.

"What about rule-follower?" Camilla looked at her mother with a smile, the cheeky one she'd rarely used since becoming an adult, a wife, a mother. Without warning, she ran up to where she had left her handbag on the sand. The last two sachets were at the top of the bag. Camilla held them up for her mother to see, and then tore them open. The contents scattered across the sand. Then she took out a handful of papers and tore them up. For a moment, it looked like she would throw them up in the air as well, but she changed her mind and raced the fragments up to the bin at the top of the beach stairs.

"What are you going to do now?" Margaret asked calmly when Camilla returned. She tried to ignore the gray dust of her daughter floating through the air between them.

"What are *we* going to do, do you mean? We," she said, loudly and firmly, "are going to find out what happened here."

They returned to the beach wall to put their shoes back on. Margaret had sensible sandals, but Camilla was wearing the most extraordinarily decrepit pair of sneakers. She had noticed them at the hotel earlier, but the time hadn't been right to question her. "Camilla, what on earth are those shoes?"

"They're Henri's," she said, without further explanation, pushing her feet in without wiping the sand off. "They really are very practical for island life."

Camilla stood up and put out her arms to pull Margaret up. Margaret waved her hand away. "I'm perfectly capable . . . ," she was saying.

"Henri."

"What, Mills?"

"We need to go and see Henri again."

43

Susie, 1998

Susie was looking for Isabel. She knew she shouldn't go back to the cottage until David was ready to see them, but she headed in that direction anyway. The last scraps of light hung softly, blurring the edges of things, darkness not yet completely obscuring them. When she got to the cottage, David was out front in the fading light, hunched over his sketchbook on the other side of the path, so consumed by what he was working on that he didn't even notice her pass by.

She stepped over the small gate so as not to make a noise opening it and followed the path around the edge of the cottage, a low-hanging branch almost taking out her eye on the way. One hand still covered her face as she came around the corner to see Isabel sitting at the outdoor table, the small ember at the end of her cigarette a beacon in the dusk.

"Are you okay?" Isabel asked. "What happened to your face?"

Susie dropped her hand down. "Oh, nothing. Are you?" She remembered the look on Isabel's face as she ran from the tent, not meeting Susie's eye or stopping. Even now, her voice sounded cloudy, choked. Had she been crying?

"That woman was crazy," Isabel said, the ember near her face again. Silence while she inhaled. "Don't you think?"

Susie thought back to Mireille. The memory already had a dream-like quality—as if it happened to someone else or was so far removed from reality that it couldn't possibly be real. "I liked her dress."

Isabel laughed, a honking sound that echoed off the stone walls around them. "I can't really see you in it, to be honest."

"Do you want to talk about it?" Susie asked.

"Not really." A clink of a cup on a saucer. Isabel was drinking tea. In the dark. Susie loved that about her.

"You know, she told me I was going to die young," Susie said. She stood up and walked over to the laburnum, breathing in the air around the tree. She was hoping for a scent from home, a memory of the delicate woodsy fragrance, but the jasmine nearby was too punchy, overwhelming everything else with its strong floral notes.

"You too?" Isabel stood up to join her under the tree, the bitterness in her voice unfamiliar. "It's just a silly fortune, right?"

Susie reached up and took down one of the pendulous seedpods hanging from the tree above her. "My mother has one of these trees at home. It doesn't do well in our garden. It's always looked a little sickly. She won't cut it down, even though it struggles through our warm winters."

"Don't you ever want to go back home?" Isabel asked quietly.

"No," Susie said firmly. "Don't get me wrong, I had a great child-hood. My family is *lovely*." She emphasized the word. "But I never quite fitted in. I wanted to leave as soon as I could. Do you?" Her voice wobbled slightly. She didn't want Isabel to go home. They had plans.

"No," Isabel said. She passed her cigarette to Susie.

Susie let go of the breath she was holding and inhaled, enjoying the feeling. The warm hit. She coughed slightly and then tried again. This time it was better.

"But if I could go back in time to when my father was alive, I would. I would do anything to go back and live those days at home with my dad again." Isabel rubbed her nose, sniffed.

"I get that," Susie said finally. "I just feel that my best days are in front of me. They have to be," she added softly to herself. She passed the cigarette to Isabel, who stubbed it out.

Isabel looked over her shoulder. "He's out there painting, you know."

"I'm going to go and find Henri." Susie placed the seedpod on the table, next to the tea tray. "Tell David he really should get rid of those. They can make you really sick."

"I will." Isabel hugged her. "It's going to be okay. We'll sort it out."

Susie felt the softness of Isabel's skin, the warmth of it through her summer dress. She still smelt like freesia, but laced with cigarette smoke, sun cream. Like summer.

"I don't want to go," Susie said, trying to hold back the sob that was rising in her throat.

The gate squeaked, loud in the still night air. Voices. Someone was with him. "He's fine now," Isabel said. "He just needed some time. He's going to ask his parents about it all when they come tomorrow. Come back after you've seen Henri." She squeezed Susie one last time, a hug that conveyed a multitude of feeling.

Susie didn't know who the other voice belonged to, but she didn't feel like seeing anyone else at that moment. David was coming along the side of the cottage, so she slipped through the open doors of the kitchen, grateful Isabel hadn't gotten around to turning on the lamps. She paused for just a second, taking in the low-beamed ceilings, the smoky aroma of old ashes in the grate mixed with the fresh jug of basil on the bench. The house had a warmth about it, but when it was empty like this, there was a sense of something missing. It was a house that needed people.

The front garden was thankfully empty. Susie crossed it in a moment and climbed over the gate, just as she had on the way in.

44

Camilla

The door opened almost immediately. It was as if Henri and Valerie were expecting them. Valerie simply nodded when she saw them and ushered them through the door, quickly shutting it behind them.

Inside, the lights were low. Henri sat at the dining table, the dregs of a bottle of red wine in his glass. He had aged a decade or more in the few hours since Camilla last saw him. Margaret had paused a moment on the threshold but was now walking about, her movements slow and trancelike. She touched the spines of some of the books, and Camilla swore she even smelled one of the curtains. Valerie stood behind Henri, her hands on his shoulders. The intimacy of the gesture made Camilla miss Ian. No one spoke.

She was marooned in the middle of the room. A central staircase rose up to the floors above, separating a large kitchen from the sitting area—which was even bigger, every wall lined with bookshelves, every bookshelf filled with books, trinkets, objets. Lamps dotted about the room cast a soft glow. Jazz music flowed softly from some invisible source.

Finally, Camilla cleared her throat and said, "I have something for you." She reached into her bag and retrieved the letter for Henri, her cheeks flushing at the sight of the torn envelope. "I . . . she . . . Susie was my sister, and I . . ." Henri nodded, and she handed it over. There didn't seem to be any point to trying to explain further.

"I will make the tea," Valerie said, looking between Camilla and Henri. She went into the kitchen and put a cast-iron kettle on the stove. Camilla felt a rush of gratitude toward her. A cup of tea was just what she needed.

Camilla went over and tapped her mother on the shoulder. Margaret turned, her face blank. It seemed to take a minute for her to recognize Camilla, and then she shook her head, smiled weakly, and followed her daughter to the table. Camilla watched her as she sat down, her hands instantly tracing out a groove in the woodwork as if she had only stepped away from the table moments before.

"Henri, this is my mother, Margaret. Susie's mother." Henri's mouth grew tighter. "Anyway. We will let you read the letter."

The room grew quiet again. The music finished, and no one moved to replace the jazz with something else. A cast-iron kettle clanged on the hob, the spark of the gas. Valerie rustled in the cutlery drawer, placed cups on the wooden counter. Henri's mouth moved slightly as he read, his brow furrowed from time to time, whether from Susie's handwriting or a word he didn't recognize in English. Every now and then he coughed, a dry, raspy cough that no one apart from Camilla seemed to notice.

Finally Henri sat back. He cast a look toward Valerie in the kitchen and refolded the letter. After a pause, he pushed the chair away from the table, the legs scraping on the tiles. The sound of his feet climbing the stairs receded, and then the floor creaked overhead. He was above them.

Camilla took the chair opposite the spot Henri had just vacated. Margaret came and sat next to her. They waited as Henri came back into the room and placed a leather-bound sketchbook on the table between them. He sat back down, his cheeks flushed from the trip upstairs or the contents of the letter, it was hard to tell. Camilla thought it might have been the latter. Henri caught her looking at him and gave her a little smile, and in that moment Camilla had an understanding of the power he must have held over Susie.

He pushed the book toward Camilla. "Susie gave it to my uncle to give to me before she left the island," he said, lighting up a cigarette that would eventually join the countless other butts already in the ashtray. Camilla coughed, but he took no notice of her subtle protest. "She asked me to keep it safe. It was just before the Rowes left the island for good."

She looked at him for permission, and he nodded for her to open it. The first page was blank, but after that the pages were filled with delicate watercolor renditions of the Île de Clair, annotated in fine ink script—observations about the scene or, in some cases, short passages of poetry. Camilla recognized some of the poems. Yeats, Cavafy, some Neruda. Exactly the poets she had been drawn to as a young adult.

Camilla sat back so her mother could see as well.

Valerie came back from the kitchen with a teapot and a stack of mismatched mugs. The smell of the peppermint tea leaves mixed with the cigarette smoke was strangely soothing.

Camilla turned the pages as Margaret watched. Each watercolor had been painted on loose parchment and fastidiously stuck in. On some pages there was just one large piece; on others there were up to five or six. Delicate studies of a stone wall were interspersed with sweeping vistas of the island, and throughout were small portraits of people on the island. Some had posed, and others were captured unawares.

"What do you mean, the last time they left the island for good?"

Valerie moved away from the table and opened the windows. A salt-laced breeze cleared the room almost instantly.

"Henri," Valerie said gently. "Tell them."

"Tell us what?" Camilla felt her stomach twist and turn. Did Margaret know what was coming? It didn't look like it. Her mother's face was as wiped out and expectant as Camilla imagined hers was.

"Okay. I will tell you what I know." He reached back across the table for the sketchbook. This time he brought their attention to a page near the back. It was a portrait of two girls on the beach. One in a yellow bikini, one in a red bikini. Both fair-haired and youthful, their heads turned to each other in rapt conversation.

"Susie," Camilla whispered.

"And Isabel." Henri tapped the picture of each one in turn. "I have not been so honest with you today. I am sorry."

Valerie poured the steaming tea into the mugs, and Camilla grabbed one, wrapping her hands around the warmth for comfort, feeling the burn of the water pushing through the clay.

"I would never forget Susie. I am sorry that I said I did. She was a lovely girl, and it was all so long ago. You gave me a shock after all these years, turning up like this. Even though I have been waiting for it." He shrugged.

"It was the summer of 1998. I had just finished school back home, and I had a big party to celebrate at home. Some of the very old vines got damaged, and my father was very angry. My mother had just died, and he didn't know what to do with me. He sent me to stay with my aunt Yvette and work with my uncle for the summer. Learn the value of money. That kind of thing."

Margaret took a sharp breath next to Camilla.

"What, Mum?"

"Yvette." Her voice was low and trembling, and she stopped tracing the lines in the table for the moment. "Yvette, the midwife?"

"Yes, she is my aunt. Was my aunt, I suppose. She passed away a few years ago, and Valerie and I took on the cottage."

"You took on the cottage? From Yvette?"

Margaret was getting bogged down in real estate, and Camilla wanted to get back to Susie. She tapped her mother on the arm to be quiet.

"I will come to that," Henri said. "The summer that year was incredible. I met David and Susie and Isabel and Valerie. I never wanted to leave. I never did leave."

"That's a lot of girls to meet in one summer." Camilla tried to catch Valerie's eye, but she was focusing intently on the leaves gathered in the bottom of her mug.

"Ah, yes. Yes. This is part of the problem." He coughed, flicked some dirt from the end of his nail. "I was seeing Susie, yes. She was just visiting for a short time, and we had some fun. Some good fun."

Camilla held up her hand. The way Henri was talking about her sister was at odds with how Susie had described their time together in her letter to him. She grabbed the sketchbook, flicking through in search of a certain page. Toward the end of the book, and only if you knew to look for it, a page was missing, only the serrated edge of the paper left close to the spine.

"What was here?" she asked, tapping the page.

Henri cast a glance at Valerie. She pursed her lips, but her eyes were wide; she had no idea what was going on.

"Was it the painting of you and Susie? Where is it now?" Margaret patted Camilla's hand, warning her of the hysteria in her voice.

"I don't know." Henri's knee started to bounce under the table, the cups rattling ever so slightly with the movement. Valerie put her hand on his leg, and it stopped just as suddenly as it had started. If Camilla hadn't been watching them so intently, she would have missed the look that passed between the two of them, a fleeting glance of agreement between long-term lovers. A shorthand, like the one she had once had with Ian, used when it was time to leave a party, discipline a child, pour another glass of wine.

Henri shifted slightly and reached for his back pocket. Camilla was surprised when he brought out a leather wallet, the seams frayed and open, the contents flattened from years of use. The three women watched as he opened it and took out a piece of paper. Once it must have been thick and white like the sheets within the sketchbook, but now it was folded and yellowed and thready in places.

Henri's hands shook as he opened it, the tenderness of his actions betraying his emotions. Margaret made a small noise once it was spread on the table in front of them. A painting, from behind, of a young man and woman jumping from the edge of a bridge. Beyond the figures, the deep blue of the ocean and the infinite sky; their hands held together as they leap toward them. Camilla recognized the Cavafy quote David had chosen to place underneath.

Ithaka gave you the marvelous journey. Without her you would not have set out.

"Susie—" Henri's voice wobbled as he placed a finger on the yellow-bikini-clad figure. Camilla wanted to slap the tobacco-stained hand away, but he moved it across. "And me," he added quietly.

Camilla took the paper from his shaking hands, running her fingers over the words. She could see the genuine emotion in Henri's face. It was clear he had once loved Susie in the way she had loved him, and Camilla wished, once again, that Susie was there with them.

"Why didn't you give it back to the Rowes? After all this time? It looks like it was important to David."

Henri's eyes glazed over, and he gave her a small smile. He looked down at his hands and muttered something.

"What?" Camilla was running out of patience.

"I hoped she might come back for it." The room was silent for a moment, the air thick with cigarette smoke and regret. On the other side of the table, Valerie shifted as if she had something to say. Henri noticed her discomfort.

"This was before Valerie." He looked around for a sympathetic pair of eyes and found none. "Susie and I, it was before Valerie. Nothing happened with Valerie and me until the day of the fair."

"The fair?"

Henri flicked through the sketchbook until he found the page he was looking for. It was painted from a distance, possibly from the wall outside the cottage. It showed the village square, filled with colorful tents and twinkling lights. Tiny pinpricks of color represented the townsfolk milling about.

"Isabel went to the fair with Susie that night. David stayed home— but he must have painted the evening from a distance. Susie and I had a fight at the fair, and I, well, I was angry. I thought it was all over between us. Valerie and I, we had a connection that I had tried hard to ignore while I was with Susie . . . but . . . after the fight, I ran into Valerie and I knew Susie was busy at the fair with Isabel, and we went for a walk . . ."

"And?"

"We went to a deserted cottage I knew, out near one of the fishing coves. I still don't know how she found us there."

"Susie?"

Henri nodded stiffly.

"Did you take Susie there as well sometimes?"

Henri nodded again.

"Well, there you go," Margaret said. "It's not rocket science, and Susie was a bright girl."

The past tense still gave Camilla pause, and it took her a moment to gather her thoughts. "Susie saw you?"

A bird called suddenly and deeply, right outside the window, and they all jumped. Wordlessly, Valerie got up and fetched a bottle of brandy from the sideboard. She splashed a bit in all of the cups, regardless of whether there was still tea inside. She pushed one toward Margaret, who had hardly spoken and seemed shell-shocked.

Henri nodded, breathing out slowly. "Susie ran off. Valerie didn't see her. I didn't tell her. You see, we were all very close that summer."

"Very close," said Margaret, her lip curling in distaste.

Henri at least had the good grace to look a little embarrassed. "It was after midnight by the time we left the beach. We walked past the cottage, and all the lights were on." He looked around as if he was still surprised to find himself living there, even after all the years. "I should have gone in."

"What happened then?" Camilla felt the story was starting to take shape. She was becoming Susie. She imagined running through the night, devastated after seeing Henri with Valerie. A fresh bolt of sadness flashed through her body. Yet another blow Susie had weathered on her own. Why hadn't she told Camilla about this when she got home? They could have made a Henri-shaped doll, stuck pins in it. Drunk cheap wine together and prank-called him in the middle of the night. All those things might have made it better.

"I don't know." Henri rubbed his face.

"You don't know?" Camilla was losing patience.

"I never saw any of them again."

45

Susie, 1998

There were no lights on in Henri's house. Susie knocked anyway. For a few minutes, no one came. And then a door opened in the hallway, and a light shone out. A second later, a figure in the hall. Yvette.

"Yes?" Her voice was wary when she saw who was at the door. She was still chewing, a napkin held in one hand.

"I'm looking for Henri." That was an understatement. Ever since he had stormed off at the fair, Susie had been counting the minutes until she could see him again. The fortune-teller was a frustrating diversion, the sight of Isabel upset was unnerving, but it was the fight with Henri that had really left her reeling.

"He is not here."

Yvette looked over her shoulder. The sound of a game show, recognizable in any language, carried down the hallway. Could she be lying? Susie tried to see past Yvette into the hallway.

"Henri is out. He has gone fishing with his uncle." Yvette pointed out to sea, the water gray and unwelcoming in the evening light. A slight breeze made ripples across the shallows, and out deeper it was even more rough. A fishing boat rocked in the choppy water. It looked familiar.

"Isn't that . . ." Susie turned back toward Valerie. She was certain that it was Henri's uncle's boat. The door slammed in her face, the net curtain still swinging as Susie peered through, calling out and knocking once more. There was no answer. A couple walked past, hand in hand. The woman looked at Susie sympathetically, and Susie smiled weakly back to show that she was okay.

Was she okay? The fight with Henri and the disturbance with the fortune-teller came at the end of a rough twenty-four hours. It felt like the endless, happy days of summer on the island were coming to a close. David's parents were due to arrive; who knew how they would react about Nellie? It had been a secret for so long. And then there were the other rumors about the stolen baby. What did her father always say when she got in trouble? *No smoke without fire, Susie girl*, that was it. There were spot fires all over this island.

She walked back to the village, wishing she had at some point along the way thought to grab a bike. It was slower on foot, and it had been a long, long day; she was getting tired of walking and her stomach was starting to rumble. There was no sign of Henri in the village, even though the fair was still in full swing. At the crêpe stand there was a full line, but Susie snuck past in the shadows. She didn't want to help, not now. The people crowded around the food tents, filling up on the salty, sweet carnival treats like they didn't know the summer would come to an end for them as well. Earlier that night Susie had been just like them.

There was one place that she knew would bring her comfort. The chapel. It was peaceful, with the added benefit of a bird's-eye view of the island, and she felt close to Henri there. If he and his uncle were fishing from one of the many outcrops or beaches around the island, the glow of their lantern would give them away. She crossed the village square once again, passing by groups of tourists, their English accents brazen in the night air. They would think her a local, she was sure of it. She walked a little taller, lifted her chin slightly, imagining what her life might be like if she did stay on the island. The idea kept her distracted all the way to the peak of the hill.

From the chapel, she looked out over the island. The view. It reminded her of her first days on the island, and when she met Henri. Standing up there on that first visit, she'd thought she had the measure of the place, that knowing the location of the paths and coves was the most important thing. It was harder to feel so certain in the darkness: the outline of land was merely a shadow, the rocks and cliffs dark monsters against the murky ocean. A cluster of lights was pinched at the edge of land—the port town—and a golden halo rose from the village. Solitary lights marked out farmers' homes, holiday houses, and coastal cottages. Everywhere else was darkness.

And then she saw it.

A flicker of light in the darkness. A candle or lantern.

It was coming from the old oyster farmer's cottage nestled in the rocks below. The structure—if you could call it that—was abandoned. The roof had been lost to nature a long time before, the glass in the windows blown out by a storm or time or a combination of the two. One night the four of them had headed there to dry out after an evening swim. They dragged driftwood and pine cones up the beach and created a fire right in the old fireplace, huddling in front of it where the oyster farmer's kitchen table might once have stood.

Susie held her breath and waited. Another tiny flash of light. It was either a small fire or a candle. But someone was in there. It had to be Henri. They had crept back there together some nights, just to be alone. Perhaps he was waiting for her.

It was quicker going back down the hill. Lights were on in the cottage, and garlic wafted out the open window. She resisted the urge to peer inside, imagining Isabel and David sitting down to a romantic dinner. David would have cooked the remaining contents of yesterday's burlap sack, and they would be at the dining table, a cold bottle of Chablis sweating between them, Isabel deftly reassuring David.

As she came around the bend to the little cove where the old oyster farmer's cottage was situated, an old fisherman was coming in from the beach. Susie smiled at him, trying not to look at the milky eye of the fish he was carrying. He was familiar. It didn't help that all the local men on the island seemed to wear the same beat-up uniform—corduroy trousers rolled at the ankles, a striped shirt so faded the stripes were no longer discernible—but Susie thought he might have been one of the men outside Yvette's cottage the day before.

He didn't smile back, but just looked at Susie, puzzled. She tried to smile again, but he shook his head and muttered something under his breath.

A sense of unease settled on Susie. A shiver, an adjustment in temperature, a cooling of the blood. She blamed it on the setting sun, a day out in the garden, sunburn, anything but what it was—a flaring of instincts. But she pushed on, undeterred by the look on the fisherman's face or the darkness creeping in across the water. She pushed aside the feeling that something wasn't right.

There was no cover on the last little bit of land heading out to the abandoned cottage. It sat alone on a tiny rocky promontory placed on a perilous outcrop. The waves, even on a still night like this one, crashed against the foundations. The moon was climbing higher in the sky as Susie clambered over the rocks. There was no one fishing.

Susie walked back through the rocky sand to the cottage, stopping as she got close enough to see the fire through a crack in the old walls. Two figures sat in front of it. Henri, yes. But the other one wasn't his uncle. A woman. Long blond hair down her back. Susie took another step closer. Henri leaned in, buried his head in the woman's neck. Her leg stretched out, barefoot, finding Henri's before he softly pushed her backward and her arms stretched up around his neck. A long female arm, a familiar hand.

Valerie?

Susie must have made a noise. A gasp. A cry. Something she couldn't control or feel. Henri glanced up and looked straight in her direction.

She turned around and ran from the cottage, stumbling out and over the rocks. Under the cover of the trees at the sand's edge she stopped to catch her breath, to see how long before he came after her. But one minute ticked past, and then another, and finally, after many minutes had passed, Susie realized he wasn't coming at all.

46
Margaret

"Can I ask something, Henri?" said Margaret.

"Of course. I may not be able to answer it." He looked around, anxious for a diversion, but the cups were full, the teapot still warm. In absence of any other options, he lit another cigarette.

"Enough. You know as well as I do that the locals know everything that happens on this island."

Henri opened his arms wide, his palms facing up. Outside, the wind shifted dramatically, and the window banged in its casement. Valerie jumped up to latch it.

"Was Lucinda here that summer?"

Henri thought for a moment. "Yes, she was. Not at the start, though."

"Was she there when my Susie was here?"

"No. No, I don't think she was. Yvette said . . ." He stopped in his tracks.

"Yvette said what?"

Margaret waited for the answer. She noticed that Camilla had not taken her eyes away from Henri either.

"Yvette said she didn't arrive until the day after," Henri said carefully.

"And why would Yvette bother to tell you that?"

"I don't know."

"Ah, but I think you do know, Henri." Margaret got up and walked around the room. It was like a time capsule. The sofas, still in the same position with blankets thrown over the threadbare patches. A cast-iron poker propped by the fire, exactly as it was over fifty summers earlier. "I'm going to tell you a little story about your aunt Yvette, and you see if any of it sounds familiar."

Valerie squeaked, but Henri just nodded, shifting his weight slightly in the chair.

"I was telling Camilla here earlier about the night I gave birth to my son, David, right here in this cottage. It was in one of the bedrooms on the third floor. I'll describe it to you, and see if I'm right?"

Henri visibly gulped.

"It's a lovely dormer room, yes? White-and-green ticking curtains. They were a lovely sage green when I was here, but I expect the sun has faded them to nothing over the years. Twin beds with turned posts? Am I right?"

Valerie began to nod but, seeing Henri's grim face, stopped halfway through and pretended to stretch her neck. Margaret noticed it all.

"I stayed in that room for almost a month in the summer of 1968. I was pregnant with my first child, and I had—willingly at that point, I might add—signed my unborn baby over to be adopted by Lucinda and Rupert Rowe. I was not a child, I knew what I was doing. But as the birth grew closer, I began to have my doubts. Lucinda had impressed me so much the first time I met her, and the second and the third. But by the time I came to live with them, I realized what a vain, nasty woman she was. She just did a very good job of hiding it. For that woman, all the world was her stage.

"She was getting older, and her beauty was fading fast. The younger actresses coming up through the ranks were making her bitter. Rupert's career, for the first time in their lives together, was starting to eclipse hers.

"At the same time, Rupert was growing more and more kind. He could see that the pregnancy was making me uncomfortable as I grew larger, and he found me a television set for my bedroom. There was barely any reception, but sometimes I would find a soap opera or a nature documentary. He taught me some French and told me about all the plants in the garden."

"What does this have to do with my aunt?" Henri asked wearily.

"On the night I went into labor, Rupert went to fetch your aunt. We had a fight, earlier that night." Margaret looked intently at Camilla. *Hold tight, don't say anything.* "I had decided I wanted to keep the baby and was very upset. Lucinda locked me in the bedroom. She didn't believe me, at first, when I said the labor had started. She thought it was a trick. By the time your aunt arrived, I was in agony."

"Did she know what was happening?"

"When she came in the door, I was so happy. Your aunt had a very kind face, Henri. She was so capable right away. She told Lucinda and Rupert to leave us alone. She turned the lights down very low and brought cool wet cloths and put them on my forehead. Then she sat by the bed, held my hand, and talked to me very quietly in French. By that stage Rupert had got my French to a reasonable level of understanding, but I didn't know what she was saying. It was like an incantation. She repeated it over and over and over. Relief flooded through my body, and I started to relax. When the pain wasn't ripping through it, that is."

"My aunt was a very religious woman." Henri's hands shook slightly as he raised his cigarette to his mouth.

Margaret could stop here, she knew she could. She could protect him from the truth about his aunt. Instead, she continued talking. "I told Yvette what was happening. I told her the whole story, and she listened without saying anything. I said I had changed my mind and wanted to keep the baby, and she squeezed my hand and smiled kindly at me. I thought she was on my side."

"You had signed the papers, *non?*" Henri asked.

"Do you have children, Valerie?"

Valerie jumped, surprised to be drawn into the conversation. "No." She snuck a quick look at Henri. "We, ah, we are not the family sort of people."

"Well, you do not know the rigors of childbirth. My labor was quick, yes, but agonizing. I shouted for them to take me to hospital. Yvette told me it was too late, there was no hospital. Which is why they had brought me here, of course. It was hot. The room was stuffy. I needed air, but the words wouldn't come out. I remember watching a bead of perspiration creep down Yvette's temple. It was the only indication that she was feeling what I was feeling. I knew the baby was close when Yvette moved me to a chair and brought in a pile of old towels, made the bed up in old patched sheets.

"David was born at three in the morning, the very dead of the night. At the last moment, Yvette brought Lucinda into the room. She was dressed in a nightgown, her hair damp with sweat. It looked as if she had labored alongside me.

"Yvette gripped my hand and told me to push. She used my name, called me Margaret. I don't know if it was deliberate, but it gave me strength. It made me feel human. It only took a couple of minutes after that, and David was in the world. There was a flash of silver, and Yvette cut the cord. Another push from me, and something else shuddered out, but I didn't feel any of it. Yvette washed David and wrapped him in a soft blanket. I couldn't stop staring. She gave him a quick squeeze and passed him over me to Lucinda. I can still hear Lucinda's voice. She cooed to that baby, made noises of love, promised him things I couldn't hear. I closed my eyes so I didn't have to see, but I could still hear her voice."

"Mum . . ." Camilla took her hand and squeezed it, but Margaret was back in 1968 in the dormer bedroom.

"I must have fallen asleep for a moment, because when I woke up, Yvette was bathing me with a washer and a bowl of warm soapy water. She wouldn't look me in the eye or answer my questions. Lucinda was gone. It was the darkest part of the night, just before dawn, and beyond our little room, the island was asleep."

"There was a pile of my clothes on the chair—washed and neatly folded and clearly put aside for this purpose. Someone had brought a sandwich and a cup of tea. It was ham and pickles. Rupert must have made it. Yvette got me up and helped me to get dressed, and Rupert was waiting at the bottom of the stairs."

"My aunt was just doing her job," Henri said quietly. "These other things have nothing to do with her."

"I was crying by that stage. Rupert took my hand, and I pulled it out. Tried to hit him. But Yvette held me back. She told me I had no choice. I had signed the papers. She said she would tell the police I was crazy, that she had never delivered my baby. I had broken into the house and disturbed a woman in childbirth."

"I went with Rupert then. He walked me down to the jetty near your aunt and uncle's house. He told me Yvette owed them a favor. You see, years before, when Yvette first came to the island, Lucinda had been pregnant with her first child. They planned to return to London for the birth, but Lucinda went into labor early. Yvette came to deliver the baby, but she was nervous and the baby was early. Mistakes were made—big mistakes—and the baby died. Lucinda nearly died as well. In their minds, Yvette owed them a baby. He was talking and talking at me, trying to justify their actions, and I was still faint from the childbirth. I could feel the blood trickling out into the pads Yvette had stuck in my knickers. At one point, I had to stop and vomit."

Henri looked a little nauseated himself.

"As I climbed into the boat, Rupert handed me a thick envelope. It was filled with money. Your uncle Philippe took me back to the mainland in his small fishing boat. I was crying so much, he gave me his handkerchief. The sun was just starting to rise as we left the island, but there was nothing abnormal about a fisherman going out at dawn."

"No, it's not possible. Yvette would never do such a thing." Valerie's face was pale.

"No?" Margaret took a long sip of her tea. She had forgotten there was brandy in it, and the combination with the peppermint tea was awful, but she needed the burn of the alcohol. That night was etched in her brain and had become part of the fabric of her body. After she gave birth to Camilla in 1976, she had shaken for two hours. The nurses said it was the shock, but Margaret knew it was her body remembering the fear from that night.

"Susie and Isabel went to see Yvette on the day they disappeared," Henri said quietly. "She told me they visited her earlier in the day."

"I thought as much." The brandy had calmed Margaret right down.

"And that summer Lucinda and Rupert handed the cottage over to Yvette. They never came back." Henri put his face in his hands.

"Yvette had already helped Lucinda and Rupert get rid of one young woman," Camilla said. "It's not too much of a stretch to think they might have asked her for help again." She was starting to connect the dots.

Margaret sat back, laced her fingers together in her lap. "Yvette was a canny woman," was all she said.

"Yvette is dead," Henri said.

"Yes," said Camilla. "Yvette is dead. But Lucinda's not." She looked to Margaret for affirmation. Margaret nodded.

"We're going to see Lucinda," said Camilla. She grabbed Margaret's hand, suddenly invigorated and in a rush. Then she snatched the sketchbook from the table. "And we're taking this with us."

47

Camilla

Camilla and Margaret and their luggage were hardly inconspicuous on the front step of the Pembroke Gardens house. Anyone passing by would wonder what they were doing, why they were here. Camilla was beyond caring what other people thought, so she was surprised when her mother took a hairbrush from her handbag and ran it through her hair. She wouldn't have thought of freshening up for Lucinda.

Margaret and Camilla had become attuned to each other's needs over the last forty-eight hours. Having her mother close by had been a great comfort, and probably part of the reason she had slept so well. For her part, Camilla had let her mother sleep until she saw the ferry approaching across the water in the distance. She had packed all of Margaret's belongings, apart from a fresh outfit for the day's travel, and had everything ready to go. The basket of fresh pastries and thermos of coffee Valerie had left outside the door in the night as her way of making amends was a bonus, and they enjoyed an early-morning feast once they were safely on the ferry.

Halfway between the Île de Clair and mainland France, Camilla withdrew the key to room 16 from her pocket. Brass, heavy, and difficult to replace, it sailed through the air and landed among the choppy waves with a satisfying splash. That was for Susie, she told her mother, but in truth it was for herself, a little. Tipping out the ashes, tearing up her spreadsheets, throwing away the key—it felt good to break a few rules.

Ferry, larger ferry, train. It was late in the afternoon by the time they got back to London. Camilla wanted to go to a hotel, have a shower, start afresh in the morning, but Margaret had insisted on keeping up the momentum. They needed to get to Lucinda as quickly as possible, she said.

Camilla nodded. It was time. Margaret fluffed her hair, straightened her collar. She took out her lipstick to apply yet another coat, but Camilla stopped her. If she applied any more makeup, she was in danger of frightening the woman—how old was Lucinda, anyway? Margaret put the lipstick away, touched her hair one last time, and put her hand up to the knocker.

"Margaret, is that you?"

The words were clearly enunciated, the voice strong and theatrical. It could only be one person. It still made them jump, though. That wasn't surprising, given how nervy they both were. What was surprising was that the woman speaking had on even more lipstick than her mother.

"Lucinda."

Lucinda paused in the gateway, framed in the afternoon sun. Margaret's words came back to Camilla.

All the world was her stage.

Her mother was right. How many times had Lucinda practiced this move? The angle of her body, the downward sweep of her hand. Even the shopping basket dangled just so from her shoulder, a bunch of celery positioned at the right angle. Then she smiled, revealing yellow teeth, grotesque against the pink lipstick. The effect was ruined, but Lucinda seemed none the wiser. She held the pose for a moment longer, still imagining adoring fans throwing roses at her feet.

Finally she came up the garden path. For someone so old, she moved well, and even the bag of shopping she was carrying didn't seem to slow her down. Each step, though, added a year to her age, and by the time she reached the porch, she looked every one of her eighty-seven years.

"It is you. I should have known you would come back."

"Won't you ask us in?" Margaret was all smiles. No one was deceived.

"No." Lucinda put down the basket of shopping. It tipped forward, and a tin of soup rolled out. An orange.

"Rupert not up to cooking?" Margaret asked.

"We always have a light supper when we've been out for lunch."

Camilla watched the two women eyeballing each other. Before that moment, she would have always backed her mother in a standoff, but she suspected that Margaret and Lucinda were evenly matched. It would have made for good entertainment if her heart weren't racing too fast for her to enjoy it.

"Claridge's? You and Rupert always liked it there."

"Darling, who said I was with Rupert?" Lucinda smiled again, and Camilla had to look away. The movement alerted Lucinda to her presence. "And who is this marvelous creature?" Camilla was forced to look back and smile.

"This is my daughter, Camilla." A flash of fear in Lucinda's eyes. It would have been easy to miss, but Camilla was looking for it.

Lucinda's eyes traveled over Camilla, and despite her dislike of the woman, Camilla felt herself straightening, wanting to look her best. "She's like you."

"Yes, this one is." Her mother put a protective arm on Camilla as she spoke. "My other daughter looks . . . looked like her father."

"Lovely." Lucinda looked like she was about to yawn, but she covered her mouth just in time. Her movements were languid, measured. In someone younger, they might have been sensual, but in someone so old, they suggested decrepitude.

"We need to talk, Lucinda. Is there somewhere we can go? I wouldn't want the neighbors to hear."

At the mention of the neighbors, Lucinda twitched. Although grand, the houses were at close quarters. Someone in the front garden of the house next door could easily hear the conversation, especially the way Lucinda projected.

"I'll get the key to the garden."

"Can't we just go inside?" Margaret asked. There was an edge to her voice.

Lucinda shook her head and disappeared into the house, taking her shopping with her. The minutes ticked by, and Camilla suspected she might not reappear. Margaret paced, and a siren blared from the main road at the end of the street, reminding them that they were in London. The area was so green and lovely, it was hard to connect it with the busy urban streets they had just traveled through in the taxi from the station.

When Lucinda finally reappeared, she had changed into a faded silk gown tied up to accentuate her waist. The lipstick had definitely been reapplied, and her hair brushed. She scuffed down the steps in velvet slippers, and Camilla reached out to help her down. Lucinda accepted the offer, holding on to Camilla's arm with her bony fingers and then leading the way across the quiet street into the garden beyond.

"This is beautiful," Camilla couldn't help but comment. A lush square of grass was surrounded on all sides by mulberries and magnolias, and many other trees she couldn't recognize. Margaret was silently taking it all in, walking around the perimeter until a spectacular magnolia in full bloom stopped her in her tracks. A man and woman were playing tennis on the court at the end of the garden, and they paused to inspect the newcomers. When they saw Lucinda, they raised a racquet in greeting and continued with their game, the consistent thwacks of the tennis ball familiar and soothing. Margaret twitched with every shot.

Lucinda gestured toward a wooden chair on one edge of the lawn and then took a seat herself. Great white urns filled with tumbling geraniums stood sentry at either end, and Margaret chose to stand by one of them. Camilla sat on the low stone wall that ran around the edge of the lawn.

"I don't suppose we ever took you in here, did we, Margaret? It's always been a special place for our family. We like to keep it that way. And besides, the other residents frown on too many guests. I'm too old to care about that sort of thing anymore."

"Yes, I suppose you're right." Margaret twisted the ring on her finger.

"Why are you here? David's not here."

"I'm not looking for David."

"Rubbish. I'm sure it's what you've always wanted. To take David. My son. Well, you're too late." She pulled a folded-up tissue from inside her gown even though the tears weren't materializing. "We had his best years. He was a divine boy. He was so worried about doing the wrong thing that he never put a foot out of line. I never worked again after he was born. I dedicated my life to him. And then, just like that, he was gone."

"Gone?" Margaret put her hand on her chest. One of the tennis players shouted "Out!" and play stopped for a moment. Camilla could hear her heart pounding.

"He moved to Devon. All my life I was afraid you would come back and try and take my boy away from me. But you're too late. You're miles too late. You can't take something from me that I no longer have."

"Camilla, show her the book."

Camilla retrieved the book from her bag. She had placed it in a plastic shopping bag to protect it from the spray of the ferry, and it took a moment to unwrap it and find the right page. Lucinda waited with her legs crossed, her patrician nose raised in the air, staring across the garden as if someone might leap out of the bushes and take her photograph at any moment.

"Here," Camilla said, passing it over. "This is a painting by David. The girl on the left is Susie—my sister—and the girl on her right is Isabel. Isabel was a special friend of David's. He invited them both to the Île de Clair to stay in your family's cottage."

Lucinda tilted her head to the side, as if she was absorbing new information.

"Really? When was this? We haven't been to the cottage for years." Lucinda turned some pages. "This is really marvelous work. I always knew that boy was something special."

"Nineteen ninety-eight. The last summer you were at the cottage. Something happened out there, and you never went back."

The rhythm of the tennis ball picked up. A long rally this time. The players were evenly matched.

Lucinda looked upward. "You're right. That's the year we handed the cottage on to caretakers. Rupert was just starting to fade, and the journey was becoming too much for him. Plus all the walking on the island. We might have kept on at it, but he had a fall in the garden that year, on the uneven path. He broke his ankle. It was a nightmare getting the proper medical attention, getting him off the island. We decided it was too dangerous."

"So you passed the cottage on to Yvette?"

Lucinda's mouth opened, then closed again quickly. "I'm not sure. It was someone from the island."

"You just handed over the most beautiful house on the island without looking back or even remembering who had taken it on. Come on, Lucinda. You owed Yvette a favor."

"We left it with a caretaker. I can't be expected to remember everyone who works for me." She waved her arm around the garden. "Next you will be asking me the name of the chap who mows the lawns in here."

"What happened to these girls, Lucinda?"

"Nothing happened to them. I took good care of them."

The play stopped again. No one spoke for a moment. Camilla watched a small patch of red creep up her mother's neck. She hadn't seen it many times in her life, but she recognized it. She took the sketchbook back and waited.

"Lucinda," Margaret began, moving her body so that she towered over the smaller woman. "I am giving you one last chance to tell me what you did to my daughter."

Lucinda laughed. "Margaret. Dear. I didn't do anything to your daughter." She opened her palms out wide, gesturing for the benefit of an invisible audience. The tennis players had finished their game and were raking the surface, taking great care with the nearest end of the court to where the women were sitting.

"Lucinda."

"I have to go and prepare Rupert's supper. He'll wonder where I am." She tried to stand, but Margaret put out her arm.

"Is everything all right, Mrs. Rowe?" The man on the tennis court was leaving through the side gate. Margaret adjusted her grasp on Lucinda to look like an embrace, her mouth twisted into a reluctant smile.

"Everything is fine, Simon. How are you, Kate?" Lucinda smiled at them and waved them on. "You can let me go now, Margaret, they're gone." Lucinda shook off her arm. "Nice acting. I don't think we'll see your name in lights any time soon."

"Fine by me," Margaret muttered. She had one last roll of the dice. "I know Yvette got rid of the girls for you. Just the same way you got rid of me."

That stopped her.

"Susannah was asking questions. Sticking her nose into my business." She stopped for a moment, took a breath. "You have no claim on my son. You never have. It was an agreement between myself and your mother. Nellie owed it to me. It was none of your business, and none of your damn daughter's business."

"Her name is *Susie*. What did you do to her?"

"I told you—I didn't do anything to her. The other one, she took the brunt of it. She was fine, though, just fine. I just needed to get rid of them."

"Why didn't you just ask them to leave?"

"They were talking, talking, talking. Asking questions. I saw my chance and I took it." Lucinda was wavering. Camilla seized her chance and went and sat by her.

"Yvette phoned me. She knew we were due to arrive on the island any day, and she called to let me know David had company. Not just any company either. A young girl who she thought may have been connected with you. Yvette reminded me that she had put her neck on the line for me all those years ago. She told me I needed to sort it out.

"I rushed to the island. I had to leave Rupert behind, as he had a show still running. He couldn't miss the last night. Normally we would take the train to Plymouth and meander over, but I caught a plane to Paris and hired a car to drive to St Aldo. I managed to get on the last ferry over the next evening. I was just in time."

"Just in time?"

"These two girls were running rings around my son. They were making him look like a fool. I did it for him. I don't know why he didn't understand that."

"How? You just said Susie was stubborn."

The gate opened, and the tennis player came back in. This time he walked straight up to the bench.

"Mrs. Rowe, let me take you home. I've just spoken to Rupert, and he wants his supper." The man looked sternly at Camilla and Margaret. He took Lucinda's elbow and helped her up. Lucinda's hands started to shake, and she made a great show of leaning on the young man.

"Oh, thank you, Simon. I'm ever so tired. These women are tiring me out."

Margaret stepped back and let her pass. Camilla slipped the sketchbook back into her bag. The last thing they needed was for Lucinda to claim ownership of it.

"Wait a minute," Margaret called out.

Simon looked at Lucinda for her consent. She nodded and they stopped.

Margaret crossed the lawn to where they were standing. She started to talk, quietly. For a second Camilla worried that she wouldn't be able to hear what her mother was saying. But at the right moment, the birds were quiet and the rest of London took a beat, and Camilla heard the words her mother had waited for fifty years to say to Lucinda.

"I *have* been to this garden before, Lucinda. I'll never forget the date. November eighteen, 1967. It was a cold night, but we stayed warm. The trees were bare, the ground was hard, but Rupert had a blanket. I've often wondered if you saw us."

Lucinda gasped, but Margaret kept walking. Camilla jumped up and followed her, keeping an eye on Lucinda and her reaction. The revelation came in blows. The old woman's shoulders dropped first, and then her knees, and then her whole body crumpled sideways.

Simon caught her just in time.

48

Susie, 1998

The lights were on at the cottage. Susie pushed open the gate and ran through. She needed to see Isabel, tell her what she'd seen. Henri with another woman. This was happening now—right this minute. It took precedence over any issues David was having with his past.

She burst through the open doors, scanning the room for Isabel. Despite everything, it still felt like home. Music was playing. Jazz. The table was set for dinner. Three places. Two candles and a bottle of red wine opened. A green salad in the middle of the table alongside a baguette. Three places! They were expecting her.

There were footsteps on the stairs behind her. She turned and saw David's familiar trainers coming down the stairs, followed seconds later by his body and then finally his head. The look on his face told her he was *not* expecting her.

"Susie," he hissed. "What are you doing here?"

"Where's Isabel? I need to talk to her." Isabel would know what to say, how to make her feel better.

"Susie, I'm not ready yet. You can't be here now." He flashed a look up the stairs. "Please." The note in his voice was unfamiliar, soft.

"Isabel?" She tried to push up the stairs, past David, but he caught her. His grip was firm.

"I saw Valerie with Henri." The tears were threatening to come any minute now.

David stopped. "What? What do you mean?" His face softened, and he put an arm around her. "Bloody hell. Valerie and Henri?" He shook his head. "Listen, Susie, I have to warn you . . ."

Another set of feet appeared behind David's. Female feet in delicate gold sandals. They were definitely not Isabel's feet. She wore the same pair of scuffed leather slides every day.

"What is all the shouting in aid of?" The rest of the woman appeared alongside him. Lucinda. She wore a long floral dress with sleeves that billowed out and covered her hands.

"Hello, Lucinda."

"Susannah, darling, I didn't know you were coming to the island. Do your family have a cottage here as well?"

"No, I, ah, I came to stay with David."

Lucinda looked between the pair of them, both shifting their feet nervously.

"What about the other little duckling, the lovely one I just met?"

David was lost for words. Lucinda walked over to him and placed her hand on his cheek. "Oh, I see. David, you *have* been a very naughty boy."

"It's not like that, Mother."

Susie looked at David, who shrugged.

"Well, Susannah."

"It's Susie," Susie said, quietly, through gritted teeth. "Or Susanne. Not Susannah."

Lucinda was unperturbed. "Susanne, then. The least we can do is feed you before you get on your way. Won't you join us for dinner? Can we start? I'm famished."

Lucinda swept across the floor, her golden clad feet now hidden under the length of her dress. She went to the drinks cabinet and took a bottle of champagne from the ice bucket. With her back to the room, she busied herself with pouring them all a drink.

"I thought you said she was coming tomorrow?" Susie hissed when

Lucinda had her back turned. David shook his head and threw his hands up, as if to say he had warned them.

Isabel appeared from the bathroom and mimed running toward the door. Susie was so relieved to see her. She went over and buried her face in Isabel's neck and told her what she had just seen. Isabel gasped and held her tighter.

Susie felt a tap on her shoulder and turned to see Lucinda holding out a glass for them both. She unwillingly moved out of the embrace and gave Lucinda a weak smile.

"Now, dear, repeat what you were saying about all those names earlier."

David, standing behind Lucinda, shook his head.

"Oh, nothing. Just some island gossip." Susie took a big sip of the champagne, but the bubbles caught in her throat, and she wasn't used to it. She had to stop herself from coughing it back out again.

"Don't waste it darling, it's vintage."

Susie grimaced and took another sip. She had been waiting for this moment, and now that it was here, she wasn't ready. She and David had no time to prepare what they were going to say, and she couldn't concentrate after what she had just seen. Her mind kept flashing back to the scene at the beach. The intimacy in the moment, the familiarity. The touches from Henri, the moves. She recognized them all. Another sip, bigger this time.

"Drink it all up, there's a good girl." Lucinda pulled out her chair and sat down. David brought a dish from the oven and placed it in the middle of the table. Susie stood behind a spare chair, unsure what to do.

"Sit down," Lucinda said. "I heard you say you saw Valerie and Henri together—isn't that right?"

Susie sat down. "Yes."

"I know of Henri—but who is this Valerie?"

"She's a local girl, Mother. They've both become good friends to us this summer."

"Sounds like you have quite the harem running, David. Your father *will* be impressed when he gets here."

"Better late than never," David muttered, and returned to the kitchen. He came back holding a bottle of wine. "Your favorite, Mother." He passed the bottle under her nose. "Châteauneuf-du-Pape."

"Lovely, David. Pour some for me. The young ladies will prefer to stay with the champagne, I'm sure."

"There you are, Mother." Susie and Isabel exchanged a look. It was unsettling to see the usually contrary David behaving so obsequiously.

"Now what were you saying about this Henri?" asked Lucinda after David was out of earshot. "I do like a little bit of island gossip." She leaned over to Susie and draped an arm on her shoulder. It felt bony and unnatural, and Susie stiffened underneath it.

"Susie and Henri are—were—an item," Isabel helpfully volunteered, seeing Susie was at a loss for words.

"Until I just came across him with Valerie in the old cottage down at the cove." Susie had found her voice.

"I know the one," Lucinda said tartly. "Very popular with the local men."

"Valerie or the old cottage?" Isabel joked. Susie tried to squeeze out a laugh. It sounded like a seal choking, and Isabel looked at her in alarm, probably wondering if she needed to medically intervene.

David took the lid off the casserole and spooned a large piece of chicken onto Susie's plate. Coq au vin. The smell of the sauce was rich, and her stomach turned. Lucinda passed her the salad. She spooned some onto her plate.

Susie took the last sip from her champagne glass and reached for the red wine, if only to prove a point. Lucinda intervened and topped up her champagne instead. Susie forced a smile of weak gratitude.

"Mother, you should eat something." David was oblivious. He put some bread on Lucinda's side plate. "There's nothing of you."

"You do like your girls big-boned, don't you, David?" Lucinda smiled and tore off a little piece of the bread. As she sat back in her chair, it was clear she wasn't planning on eating much.

Isabel opened her mouth in mock outrage and then took another piece of bread.

"Lucinda." Susie pushed back her chair as well, mirroring Lucinda's body language. "We have something to tell you."

Lucinda sat back and crossed her arms. Her eyes twinkled with anticipation. "Oh goody!" she said, tapping her fingers together. "I do like a little announcement."

David focused very intently on picking some candle wax from the tabletop.

"David and I have worked out a connection between our two families." Lucinda's eyebrows rose slightly. "My grandmother was Nellie Byrne, and we believe she used to work for your family, as a nanny."

"Nellie? Darling Nellie!" Lucinda clapped her hands together, the sleeves of her dress getting caught up and muffling the sound. "Why didn't you say?"

"We only just worked it out these past few days," David said, finally coming to her aid. Isabel stood up and started clearing plates.

"This is wonderful, wonderful, Susannah. You must stay as long as you like. Rupert would love to meet you. He feels as if he knows Nellie, after all my stories. How is she?"

Susie swallowed. "She died a few weeks ago. Just before I met David."

Lucinda looked crestfallen. "Oh. That *is* a shame. Life can be full of bitter twists, can't it? Just as you come into my life, I learn that Nellie has left it." She closed her eyes and sat very still for a moment.

"There was something else," Susie said, nervous about interrupting Lucinda's moment of quiet contemplation. Lucinda opened her eyes, which were filled with tears. Susie took a deep breath. "When Nellie left London to come to Australia, she was pregnant with my mother. We were wondering—I was hoping—you might know who the father was?"

Lucinda's mouth dropped open in shock. "Nellie?"

"You didn't know?"

"I was only a child! She left one day and didn't tell me why!"

Isabel topped up everyone's drink. Susie took a sip to steady herself. The champagne tasted flat now on her tongue, as if all the fizz had left the bottle.

"Did you ever ask your parents about it?" Isabel was back in earnest student mode. Susie shot her a grateful look.

"I asked them why she left," Lucinda said. "They said she took an assisted passage to Australia to start a new life. Lots of people were doing it after the war, especially of her class."

Her class. Susie felt her body shrink into her chair.

Isabel wouldn't give up, though. "You must have been quite old by then. What were you, a teenager?" She locked eyes on Lucinda.

"It was 1945, the end of the war. I was thirteen when she left. A lifetime ago! I haven't thought about Nellie in years. How lovely that you found us." She patted Susie on the hand and stood to leave the table.

"Do you remember her having a boyfriend? Any romances?"

Lucinda looked around as if the room might provide the answers. "It was so long ago. I hope you don't mind me saying this, Susie, but we weren't encouraged to get mixed up in the personal lives of the help."

Susie swallowed, her face feeling hot despite the cool evening breeze. She nodded and wished the ground would open up and swallow her. It made sense Lucinda wouldn't know anything about it. She was just a child!

Isabel spoke again. "We thought she might have been involved with your father."

Lucinda raised her eyebrows. David shifted in his chair. "Impossible. My father was a man of deep and abiding virtue. I remember Nellie leaving just after the war. We were in Devon the whole war—my parents' visits were few and far between. It would have been close to impossible. If anything . . ." She placed a hand on Susie's, her eyes downcast. "If anything, and I'm sorry to tell you this, it would have been one of the help. Nellie was very friendly with all the ground staff at the estate in Devon. Looking back, she was a little too friendly, even with the married men. If my mother and father had been around more, I'm sure they would have put a stop to it."

"Oh." Susie felt crushed. Then she remembered the toes. "David! Take off your shoes!" Susie kicked off her trainers and stood up. David, thankfully, obliged and came to stand beside her in his bare feet.

Side by the side, the similarities were unmistakable. The room was quiet for a moment, the silky jazz notes the only sound.

"That's something!" Lucinda agreed. "I've seen that before. It's really very common. I've been trying to tell David that all his life. Davie, remember the swimming carnival, when you got all peculiar about your feet? If only you'd known Susie then. Who wants to play cards? Hearts, anyone?"

They left the rest of the dishes on the table, Lucinda imploring them to clear up later. Susie was suddenly overwhelmed by a wave of tiredness, all the adrenaline of the last couple of days catching up with her. She wasn't any closer to finding out any details about her grandfather, and worse than that, Henri hadn't come. He had made his choice, and it wasn't her.

Lucinda directed Isabel to open another bottle of champagne, though it was the last thing any of them wanted. The rules to Hearts were complicated, and Susie couldn't keep track. The diamonds and hearts and clubs and spades blurred and shifted in her hands, and she struggled to even hold them up, let alone engage in the game.

David was the first to admit defeat. "Mother, if you don't mind, I think I'll take myself to bed. It's been a long day."

"David?" Susie stood up and tripped over her own feet. She wanted to talk to him alone, reassure herself that things were okay between them, even if they weren't related. The champagne glass on the coffee table tipped over, and wine bloomed across the table. Susie blotted up what she could with a napkin David gave her, but her hands weren't listening to her brain. Eventually she gave up and left the napkin to soak up the rest. "Can we talk for a minute?"

"Let's talk in the morning, Susie." He came over and kissed the top of her head, and Susie felt the warmth spread through her body. So what if she hadn't found a long-lost cousin? David was her friend.

"Good night, David."

"Good night, Mother."

David climbed slowly up the stairs. Near the top, he paused, and Susie thought he might turn around, but he just turned the landing light on and continued on his way.

Lucinda kicked up her sandals and gathered her knees up under her. "Just us girls now," she said. "Now we can get down to the nitty-gritty. Tell me more about this Henri and Valerie." Next to her, Isabel was nodding off, her feet tucked up under Susie's legs.

Susie started to tell Lucinda the story of how she and Henri had met.

Lucinda interrupted. "I have to say, when I met you in the gardens, I thought you were interested in my David."

Susie gave a weak laugh. "I was at first," she admitted sleepily, "but David was with Isabel here, and it was clear to everyone that they were in love. Plus we thought we might have been related." Lucinda patted her on the leg.

It was too much for Susie. All she could think about was the green bedroom at the top of the stairs. She just needed a quick sleep. And when she woke up, maybe Henri would be there, and he could explain everything. Maybe it was a mistake. She couldn't keep her eyes open.

She felt Lucinda lean over her. Lucinda smelled like the perfume from the bedroom upstairs. It smelled better on her. Spicy. Woody. Redolent with body heat. She was so close. Susie put an arm out to touch her, but found only air. Nothing. Nothing. She was so tired.

But Lucinda was still there. She was still talking, talking. Susie wished she would be quiet. She made a shush sound, turned her head away from the voice. "Shall we play another round? Susie?" The soft thwack of the cards being dealt on the table. And that was the last thing she heard before she drifted off to sleep.

49

Margaret

"That was some parting shot, Mum."

Margaret tried her best to look innocent. "She had it coming. She's had one over me for years. I've been saving it up for the right moment."

"Is it true?"

The rest of the carriage was quiet. Most of the passengers on the evening train from London to Plymouth were business travelers, anxious to get some shut-eye on the way home. Not Margaret and Camilla. They were still wired from their meeting with Lucinda, still buzzing that they had actually made the train on time.

The remains of their impromptu supper lay on the table between them: crisps in a variety of lurid flavors, and sickly sweet chocolate bars. A cup of tea from the machine had washed it all down.

Margaret nodded slowly. "I was only a girl. I didn't recognize the signs of a married man. I went to England when I finished school. I had saved some money from my modeling jobs at home so Mum couldn't stop me, even if she wanted to. I'm not sure what she thought of me going off on my own, especially when she had gone to such lengths to get me there to begin with, but I went."

They both made themselves as comfortable as possible in the cramped conditions. Margaret had taken the aisle for her long legs, but she still felt curled up like a pretzel. Camilla tried to make more space for her mother, but the middle-aged man next to her opened one eye until she stopped fidgeting.

"All my life, Mum talked about Eleven Pembroke Gardens as if it was a magical place in a fairy story. When I arrived in London, I lived in Earl's Court. Every day I would get my *A–Z* out and hit the streets, walking to go-sees and appointments. One day I had a showing on Kensington High Street, and I realized Pembroke Gardens was just nearby. I took a detour.

"It was a lovely part of London—I mean, you know, we've just been there. It's hard to beat. When I walked down the street for the first time, it was a lovely autumn day. The trees were just turning, and there was a surprising warmth to the air. The last burst of summer, just like you get in Melbourne.

"The house looked beautiful from the street. The shiny black door, the big brass knocker, the garden filled with the last jewels of summer. I sat on the wall opposite and watched and waited. I didn't have a reason to ring the doorbell. I just liked looking at it.

"It was a touchstone, a comforting tradition. I'd probably walked by half a dozen times when I met a man coming out of the gardens opposite. He was so handsome. A little bit older than me, but nothing scary. He was wearing tennis whites—I've always had a soft spot for tennis whites."

Camilla made a face.

"Don't look like that, Camilla. The heart wants what the heart wants. My heart wanted tennis whites."

"Doesn't sound like your heart was doing the talking to me, Mum."

The man next to them smirked.

"He was so lovely. The first time I ran into him, he saw I was looking at the house over the road, and he started talking to me."

Margaret could remember it as if it was yesterday. It was one of the little nuggets she kept stored up in her memory, returning to it every now and then when she wanted to be transported out of the life she'd ended up in. A bad rainy season, truculent toddlers, the day Pilgrim died. They were all times she escaped to Pembroke Gardens in her mind, revisiting her precious few memories of those days.

"A famous actress lives there, you know?" It was the first thing he said to her, pointing his racquet in the direction of the house. "If you wait here long enough, you'll see her."

Margaret had blushed, embarrassed to be caught out on her clandestine mission. "Oh! I just like the houses."

At the sound of her accent, he smiled. "Australian?"

"Yes."

"Lovely. I can't think what you would be doing here, then."

"I'm working. Hoping to travel a bit."

"Working?"

"I'm a journalist," she said. It was the first time she had admitted her aspirations out loud, but by then she was writing articles, having done her penance by responding to dozens of letters from readers seeking counsel in the magazine's advice column. From broken hearts to growing runner beans, her words of wisdom finally caught the eye and regard of the editor, who had rewarded her with proper assignments.

"I suspected as much," he said. "You have the air of a writer." He looked down at his feet. "I usually head to the pub over the road for a pint after tennis—would you like to join me?"

Margaret said no that time, but the next time she ran into him outside the gardens, she said yes. They sat in a darkened corner of the pub in a tiny little booth. Rupert brought their drinks from the bar and sat with his eye on the door. Keeping an eye out for his tennis partners, he said. They would give him stick if he had stood them up for drinks with a young woman.

That's what he called her, a young woman. He never asked her why she kept coming back—he was convinced enough of his own charms to expect that he was the reason. The truth was, she started coming for the address, but she came back for Rupert. She changed her routines, so she came in the evening, having worked out he played tennis at 5:00 p.m. for an hour.

"And what happened?" Margaret had forgotten she was telling the story aloud. She was remembering Rupert's voice, the way he leaned in across the table when he talked to her, touched her on the hand when he made a point. She didn't want to get to the end just yet.

"They closed the court for winter. Rupert told me he could no longer get away in the evenings. I remember the last time we met."

"November eighteenth."

"How did you know?"

"I heard you telling Lucinda. So you knew he was married?"

Margaret pretended she didn't hear. Selective hearing was one of the benefits of getting older.

"I hadn't told anyone about him. I was still going on dates with other men, meeting friends and work colleagues and anyone I could get my hands on, really. But Rupert was a special secret I saved for myself."

"You do love a secret." The train slowed for a station. The next minute, an announcement came over the loudspeaker. Something on the line. The man opposite snorted with weariness.

"We had some drinks in the pub. More than we usually did. I didn't want the evening to end, so I asked him if he could show me the garden. He hesitated for a moment, then asked me to wait exactly where I was, not to move. When he came back, he was carrying a blanket and a bottle of red wine. I said, Oh you must live nearby, and he said he lived down the road in a tiny apartment. The only benefit of the small space was its access to the communal garden."

"He was smooth. A smooth tennis-playing gentleman. I would never have picked it as your type." Camilla was smirking.

For a moment, Margaret was tempted to admit the true nature of her feelings. The fact that she had, for a brief moment, been in love with Rupert Rowe. That perhaps, if things had turned out differently, they might have raised David together. But the truth of it was, she couldn't think how to explain the connection they had. Describing it only diminished the essence of it. It wouldn't stand up to anyone else's examination. It was hers and hers alone.

"Oh yes, he was. He was my type." Easier to leave it at that. "We went to the garden, and at the end of the evening, he told me he would have to leave. He suggested that it would be better if I didn't pass by the house again. He was a good man. He tried to do the right thing. He really did."

"When did you work it out? Who he was?"

"Not until I was seated in his living room. It was too late. Lucinda was watching, and I couldn't back out. We didn't even get a chance to talk about it. It was one of the only things that got me through all these years—at least my boy was with his father."

And I wasn't.

The train got going again, and Margaret gripped the armrest. The agony of those early years, when she thought of them together without her, was still raw. It had taken all her self-restraint earlier that day not to follow Lucinda into the house and say goodbye to Rupert. Her heart hurt from the effort of holding herself back. She was glad now that she hadn't. It was best to leave her memory of Rupert as it was during the short months they had together. There was nothing to be gained by going back now. She closed her eyes, just for a minute. The pain in her chest was real; it reminded her that she had lived and loved before. It would always be there. Then she took a deep breath and forced herself back into the present moment.

"Camilla, before we get there, I want to talk to you about something."

The man next to Camilla sighed. It was just his luck to be seated next to two women who hadn't shut up the entire trip.

"Yes?" Camilla was looking out the window, semi-leaning across the man next to her.

"I think after this, after we see David, you should get on a flight home."

Ian had emailed Margaret the flight details for Camilla—he hadn't heard from her, he had said. Margaret didn't know the ins and outs of what was happening, but she had a good feeling that their marriage could be saved.

"Let's talk about this later, Mum. For now, I want to find David."

"No, Camilla. Listen to me." She grabbed her daughter's forearm. "You've worked too hard to give it all up. I don't want this family to take something else away from us. Promise me you will get on that flight tomorrow night and go home to your family. You've done your duty to Susie—now you need to look after yourself."

50

Camilla

A taxi—booked through an app specially downloaded by Camilla for the purpose—met the pair at the station when they arrived after midnight. The old historic house on the estate had been turned into a hotel and Pond Cottage was on its grounds. Even in the darkness, the setting was breathtaking. The driveway wound down the hill from the main road, the trees creating a dark tunnel, at the end of which the car emerged into a paved forecourt. A staff member took them to their room in a converted stable, where a tray had been left with supper: a ploughman's board with a wedge of cheese, some juicy pickles, and fresh, crusty bread. Camilla and Margaret had eaten in catatonic silence and then fallen into the huge, cloudlike beds.

In the morning the shutters opened to reveal a stunning morning: a dazzling blue sky above the valley, the scent of lavender from the garden floating through the open windows in the gentle breeze.

Margaret was already up and gone, but Camilla found her on the terrace of the main house with a pot of tea and a copy of *The Times*. She was wearing a freshly pressed white linen shirt and a pair of darker trousers. Empty breakfast dishes in front of her indicated she had already eaten. Nothing about her suggested any nerves about the day ahead.

"Sleep well?" Margaret asked, with the jauntiness of someone who had.

"Very." Camilla had lain in the dark for a few minutes, and just when she had started to panic about a restless night, sleep had stolen in and knocked her out cold.

"I thought as much. It's not like you to sleep this late."

Camilla panicked. "What time is it?" She had left her watch and her phone back in the room. Her watch was no good to her, anyway; she had given up on changing the time zones days ago.

"It's after nine." Margaret folded the newspaper and placed it on the table.

"You should have woken me up. We need to find David."

"Yes. Camilla. There's something I want to say to you about that."

"Hmm?" Camilla was inspecting the menu card. Scrambled eggs with fresh herbs from the garden? Or a bowl of fruit?

The waiter came to take her order, not batting an eyelid when she asked him to make the decision for her. Margaret, however, raised her eyebrows.

"What?" Camilla asked after he had gone.

"Not like you to leave a decision in someone else's hands."

"I don't know what I feel like," Camilla said. A calmness had washed over her in the serenity of the hotel grounds. It was an unusual feeling for her, and she wanted to stretch it out as much as possible. "What's happening in the world?" she said, pointing at her mother's newspaper.

"Camilla," her mother said firmly. "I don't want you to expect too much from this meeting. Obviously, things between David and Susie didn't go well. This might just be a very disappointing day." She poured some more tea in her cup. "You know, it's Friday morning. From what I gather, your flight leaves late tonight. You could still make it."

The food arrived. A plate of fluffy scrambled eggs, scattered with a selection of the most delicate baby herbs. All grown on the estate, the waiter declared proudly as he set down a variety of different dishes. The fruit was just as appetizing; melons and berries and sweet apples, all cut just so and served in a fine china bowl. For a moment, they sat in silence while Camilla savored every bite.

It was hard to equate the the turmoil of the morning ahead with the tranquility of the setting that lay in front of them. Climbing roses festooned the timber columns along the terrace, and the tables were filled. It was mostly couples, but one family with two small boys sat nearby. The boys were drinking hot chocolate and playing Uno. Camilla couldn't look at them without her heart filling with longing for her own boys.

"Something about this place is special." A butterfly hopped and skipped in an abundant patch of violets.

"It's beautiful," Camilla agreed as she scooped up the last of the melon.

"It's more than that." Margaret looked around. "I feel calm here. Since we arrived last night, I've felt a great peace. As if this place is somehow disconnected from the rest of the world."

"Me too," said Camilla, marveling at the fact they had both had the same response to the place. The hotel was beautiful; the elaborate stone frontage rose above them, the roofline turreted and concealing a mass of chimneys, and yet somehow it wasn't ominous. It nestled in the landscape, secluded in its private valley.

"I feel like whatever happens this morning, it's going to be okay. We are going to find some closure for Susie." Her mother was uncharacteristically reflective. "And me."

Camilla folded her napkin on the table and took her mother's hand. "Let's go." She pushed back her chair and stood up.

She had reverted back to her usual look; dark trousers, sensible shoes. The yellow dress had been right for the Île de Clair, but here she needed her uniform, armor against whatever they might find. It had worked for her in the past.

They walked to the edge of the terrace and looked out over the valley below. It was green and lush for as far as they could see, not a sign of another building or town. Camilla dashed back into the stable rooms to get her phone and the sketchbook. "The map on my phone says the house is just down there"—she pointed—"but I can't see it."

"I saw a path from the driveway this morning. Let's start there." They headed around to where the formal gardens met a towering forest of redwood trees. The river rushed below, and they could hear the murmurs of some keen anglers. "Best salmon fishing in the area," Margaret said as they descended down a walkway lined with rhododendrons. "I read it in the brochure."

"If we had any of the ashes left, we could have scattered them here. Susie and the salmon, for eternity."

"There are worse places." They allowed themselves a brief chuckle and continued along the path in warm companionship. Camilla was glad her mother had come; her presence had transformed the trip. She didn't know if she could have coped with all the twists and turns on her own. Plus, her mother had brought along her inside knowledge of Lucinda—Camilla doubted she would have been able to connect the pieces of the puzzle without her.

The path dipped and came to the river. A tiny wooden bridge ran over to a clearing on the other side, at the edge of which sat a cottage. A low wooden building, it had a loggia along one side, looking over a silvery pond. There was a car pulled up out front, incongruous in the bucolic setting. Still, it meant someone was home.

"Picturesque," Margaret whispered.

"Isn't it?" Camilla agreed.

"No, it's the style. Picturesque. I read it in the brochure as well."

"Was there anything in the brochure about poor, lost illegitimate children?"

"Camilla, that's not helpful." Margaret smiled at two fishermen who were very interested in their progress.

Camilla walked to the bridge. A small sign hung at the end: "Private Property."

"This is it, Mum."

"Yes, I suppose it is." Margaret held on to the railing. The bridge was slippery with moss; it lay low in the valley, where the sun would struggle to penetrate the thick canopy of trees shadowing the river.

As they crossed the clearing and approached the house, the door in the little architrave opened and a man stepped out, a tea towel and cup in his hands. Camilla reached for her mother's hand, but Margaret shook it off as she picked up the pace, moving quickly toward the man.

He looked like the man they had seen in photographs, his hair maybe slightly receded. His skin was tanned, and he had the look of someone who spent a lot of time outdoors. He waited for them to come closer before he spoke, and when he did, it was with the polite weariness of someone who has said the same words many times before.

"I'm sorry, this is private property. It's not open to guests of the hotel. If you just cross back over the bridge once more, you'll find that the public walking path continues along the river. The old dairy and war gardens are in that direction."

Margaret froze in place, staring openmouthed. "Actually, we're not guests of the hotel—well, we are—but we're not here . . ."

The man was looking at her, bewildered. Camilla put her arm out toward her mother, and Margaret grabbed on with both hands, as if she might fall if she didn't.

"We're here to see you," Margaret said, recovering. "My name is Margaret Anderson. I'm not sure if you will recognize that name."

A shout came from the river. A fish had been caught. None of them turned to look. Camilla waited. For the longest time, it seemed as if David might not say anything.

Finally he spoke. "Yes, I recognize that name." The polite weariness in his voice was gone, replaced with a nervous tremor.

"I believe you met my daughter, many years ago."

"Susie Anderson." He placed the cup and tea towel on the window ledge. "I won't forget her quickly."

51

Susie, 1998

It took a moment for Susie to work out where she was. She had been dreaming about Nellie. They were making scones in the kitchen back at Matilda Downs, and Nellie was talking about pigeons in a low, soothing voice, her kind face bobbing up and down as she pushed the rolling pin over the dough.

And then someone was rocking her back and forward, in time with the rolling pin. When she opened her eyes, she wasn't back home in the warm kitchen but in a dimly lit room with bookshelves on all sides and a fireplace at one end. Candles burned down to nubs sat on the coffee table, and a game of solitaire looked recently abandoned.

Her mind began to catch up. The cottage on the Île de Clair. The woman was wearing a nightgown, a dressing gown thrown over the top. Her hair was messy now, her mascara smudged.

There was someone else in the room. Someone on the sofa next to her. Isabel! She reached over to her and touched her arm. The movement took some effort, as if she was wading through mud to get to her friend. "What happened?" she tried to shout, but her mouth wasn't cooperating.

A hand tapped lightly on her cheek, getting more insistent each time. Susie swatted it away, trying to connect her thoughts, work out what was happening.

She was sad. Something had happened, but she couldn't remember. What was it?

The hand slapped harder now, and Susie pulled her attention to the figure standing in front of her. "Water," she croaked. She needed water. Her tongue was large and furry in her mouth, her head pounding. But the woman didn't listen. She was shaking Isabel now.

Isabel wasn't responding. Her eyes were closed, but flickering slightly. A silvery line of drool ran from her mouth. With gargantuan effort, Susie crawled across the sofa and leaned over her friend. "Isabel?" She shook her, but Isabel's body was limp. Unresponsive. A wave of nausea knocked her back for a moment, and she closed her eyes to steady herself. There was an acrid taste in her mouth. She felt as if she might be sick at any moment.

"What have you done?" Lucinda was still there, her eyes wild and accusatory. "What have you done to this girl?"

"What?" Susie kept shaking. "What?"

"Look at her! Something is wrong with her!"

"I know!" Heat rushed through Susie's body. She tried to stand up, but her legs weren't getting the message.

"Shhh! You will wake David." Lucinda sat on the coffee table in front of Isabel. There was a cup of tea and some foliage on the table. Seedpods. Susie's brain scrambled to catch up.

"It's too late, I'm awake." David appeared at the bottom of the stairs, pulling a T-shirt over his head. "What's going on?" His face softened when he saw Isabel. "What happened? Is she okay?"

"What? Oh what?" Susie was holding Isabel's wrist, desperately trying to find a pulse, but she could only hear her own heart.

"What did you do, Susie?" Lucinda asked quietly.

"What do you mean, what did she do?" David was looking between the three women, his face still bleary with sleep.

"I didn't do anything!" The words were slurred, unconvincing. Susie held a hand in front of Isabel's mouth to check if she was breathing. "I think she's still breathing."

"Do you know what this is?" Lucinda's voice was sharp.

Susie turned to look. She recognized it straightaway. "Laburnum," she said without thinking.

"What is it doing here, next to Isabel's tea?"

"I don't know!"

"But you know what laburnum is?"

"No!" Susie started to cry. Isabel. She grabbed her hand, squeezed it, desperate for a response. David finally pulled himself together. He sat Isabel up, put his fingers on her wrist.

"I thought you said yes." Lucinda picked a seedpod up and dangled it between two fingers. "Highly poisonous. Especially the seedpods. I always warned David away from the tree in the garden."

"David said it was an old wives' tale," Susie whimpered, looking at him for reassurance. He wouldn't look at her.

"But you knew all about it, didn't you?" Lucinda gestured to David's sketchbook, lying open on the table. One of his more detailed paintings was visible, a picture of Susie sitting under the laburnum, her yellow bikini picking up the yellow of the flowers. Underneath, David had annotated the picture, just as he had all the others. *Susie had a laburnum tree in her garden, growing up. Just like I did, she grew up with the stories about the poisonous seedpods. Just like me, she couldn't help but love the plant.*

"What are you saying?"

"Intense sleepiness. Slight frothing at the mouth. Vomiting. I'd say it's pretty obvious what's happened here."

"I didn't do anything!" Susie tried her legs again, and they finally got the message. She stood up and leaped out of Lucinda's way. A small trail of vomit covered the end of the sofa. "David! You know I wouldn't do this."

"Susie." Lucinda spoke softly. She was back onstage, the spotlight trained on her, the audience waiting for her grand finale, one of her famous monologues. She was Lady Macbeth, she was Blanche. "You followed my son to the Île de Clair when you barely knew him; you forced yourself into our house." Wordlessly, she passed a book to her son, pointing at a page in the rear. As it passed, Susie recognized it. Her guidebook. The love heart drawn in the back, with David's and her own name entwined; she had forgotten to tear the page out.

"You've been wearing my perfume." Lucinda pulled Susie's sweater from the sofa behind and tossed it toward her. Susie let it drop to the ground, but even as it passed, the scent was strong. Unmistakable.

"It was just a spray!" Susie wailed.

Lucinda held her hand up. "When Isabel turned up, you were thrown. You were jealous. You were in love with my son, and when you couldn't have him, you invented a story that the two of you were related."

"It's not true. I'm with Henri. I love Henri!"

Lucinda shook her head sadly. "Henri is with Valerie. Oh, darling, I've had stalkers before. Hundreds of them. I can spot them at ten paces, but poor David here is not as savvy."

Henri. That was what she was trying to remember. Henri and Valerie. The memory of the evening's events made her cry harder. She was hysterical now.

"David! It's not true. You know that!"

David didn't look convinced. "Susie, I . . . it doesn't look good. I mean, I don't even know you." He turned his attention to his mother, his voice shaky. "Mum, is she going to be okay?"

Lucinda placed her hand on David's shoulder, making soothing sounds as if he were a baby. After a moment, she turned back to Susie, who stood silently crying, trying to work out how to claw back time.

"Things don't look good for you, Susie. People will say you acted in a jealous rage. That you tried to poison your friend."

Isabel groaned, a deep, gasping sound. Susie ran to her. "Isabel!" She shook her, harder this time. "Isabel!" David and Lucinda watched her, not moving. "I'm going to get help." She propped Isabel up to help her breathe, but within seconds she was slumped over again. Susie tried to formulate a plan, but her mind was racing. There were no doctors on the island as far as she knew, but there was Yvette. Yvette was her only chance.

Before the others could stop her, she bolted out the door. She ran all the way to the cottage by the sea, the one she had visited only the day before with her friends. It seemed liked years ago. She remembered Isabel talking in French to Yvette and Philippe, her big wide smile, the way her golden earrings caught in the afternoon sun. Isabel. She had to save her.

52

Margaret

Margaret couldn't take her eyes off David. She was speaking and acting like a sensible adult, but really her body felt amorphous, as if she might suddenly look down and see her insides puddling on the ground. Every detail was a fresh revelation, at once recognizable and foreign at the same time. His hair—so like Rupert's. His eyes—like hers. He could pass for her daughters' brother, easily. He *was* her daughters' brother.

When he said, "Would you like a cup of tea?" her heart nearly burst. The simple words, the gesture of hospitality. He might just have easily turned a shotgun on them—by the look of the loggia behind, the cottage was well equipped for outdoor pursuits—but instead he offered tea. Margaret thanked her lucky stars.

"Thank you, that would be lovely. I can imagine this must be a shock, having us turn up like this. Out of the blue."

"Yes, well. People wander over the bridge from time to time, but normally I send them right back. I have a feeling that might not work in your case. Not if you're anything like your daughter."

Camilla laughed, too loudly. Margaret gave her a look. *The* look. It normally worked, and it did this time.

"Come, sit over here. I'll get the tea things." He led them to the end of the loggia and left them in the morning sunshine. Margaret reached for her sunglasses and put them on, surveying the scene. It was a special place. Despite everything, she felt grateful that David had been surrounded by such beauty growing up.

"Am I going to start things off, or are you?" Camilla was pacing up and down, stopping every now and again to inspect a fishing rod or one of the brightly colored flies, as if she were interested in such things.

"Leave it to me," Margaret said, crossing her hands in her lap. They were shaking ever so slightly, and clasping them together seemed to help. "This was the head gillie's cottage until the family sold the rest of the estate to the hotel owners in 1998. They let him stay here until his death a few years later. The owners used to come down to the big house, and he would take them out fishing for salmon."

"John Digby," David said, reappearing, carrying the tea tray. "He worked for my family, but he was like a father to me. You're well versed in the history of the place." The wariness was back in his voice.

"I read the brochure this morning. Camilla here slept in." Margaret gestured at her older daughter, who stood frozen between two columns of the porch. "Oh! I haven't introduced you properly. David, this is my daughter Camilla. Camilla, this is David Rowe."

David bobbed his head but didn't bother with any of the usual pleasantries, a slight color rising on his cheeks. Margaret raised her eyebrows at Camilla.

"Hello . . ." Camilla trailed off immediately.

"It's hard to know where to start," Margaret interjected.

"Why you're here might be a good start." He sat back with his arms folded, his legs kicked out in front of him.

"Oh, yes. Right."

His face softened at Margaret's unease. "Sorry. It's just . . . things didn't end well between myself and Susie." He took a nervous sip of his tea. "Where is Susie? This sort of impromptu gathering strikes me as being totally up her alley."

The question took them by surprise. "Oh." Margaret put her hand to her throat. A long silence. "Susie passed away. Suddenly. A month or so ago."

"I'm sorry." He swallowed. "I'm sorry to hear that. How did she, ah, how . . ."

"She fell, preparing for her fortieth-birthday celebrations."

A muscle in David's jaw visibly relaxed.

"She asked us to come here, in her will. She wanted me to scatter some ashes for her at various places around the world. Places that were important to her. Places where she was happy."

David shifted in his seat. Then, when Camilla presented one of the little pouches, he visibly twitched.

"We've been to London, to the National Gallery."

At the mention of the gallery, David looked up. "Do you think . . . is it . . . was it because of me?"

Camilla nodded. She rifled through her bag again and passed him the first letter. He read it quickly. At one point, he smiled. Margaret hoped it was the part about him being special. Or maybe it was the bit about the paintings. It *was* hard to know with the English.

"I think she was really devastated by how things ended with you." She found the photo of them on the Île de Clair and passed it across. "This was with the letters."

He held it in his hands for a moment. A tender look flicked across his face. Margaret noticed the paint on his hands.

"We went to London, and then she directed us to the island. She told us to find Henri."

"Henri." David sighed. "It was the perfect summer. Until . . ." He stopped, eyes glazing over. We all got on so well. Henri. Me. Susie. Valerie. Isabel."

"Isabel?" Camilla's ears pricked up at the name.

David nodded. "Things ended badly." He looked up at the cottage and seemed to make a decision. "Wait here," he said. He stood up in a hurry, knocking the table slightly with his knee. The teacups clattered against each other. Margaret grabbed a napkin, mopping up what she could.

They heard voices inside. Raised. And then silence.

Finally, after what seemed like forever, David came back outside. He wasn't alone. A woman a little younger than Camilla followed, long blond hair flowing over her shoulders. She was barefoot and dressed in overalls. As she walked toward them, the bracelets along her arms jingled.

"Hello," she said, looking at her feet nervously. "I'm Isabel."

53

Susie, 1998

All the lights were off at the cottage when Susie got there. She banged on the door and hoped that Henri wouldn't answer the door. There was no answer. She stepped back, looked up the upstairs windows. They were dark, shutters closed against the night sky.

"Yvette!" she called out, softly at first and then, realizing there was no one around to hear, more loudly. "Yvette!"

Finally the shutters opened, and Yvette stuck her head out. For a second she looked confused, her eyes still focusing. When she worked out that it was Susie, she hissed, "You! Again! I told you he is not here!" She moved to close the shutters again, shaking her head.

"Please!" Susie shouted. "I'm not here for Henri. There's an emergency up at the cottage." Yvette paused mid-shutter. Something clouded her face. Resignation?

"What sort of emergency?"

"It's Isabel. She's not well. I think she's taken something." She waited a moment, not sure whether to continue. "Or she has been poisoned."

Yvette nodded and put a finger to her lips. "Wait there. I will be down in a minute."

The minutes passed excruciatingly slowly. Susie was about to bang on the door again when Yvette finally emerged, closely followed by

Philippe. They nodded at her and set off. Philippe said something to Yvette, and Yvette translated. "We are going to take the coastal path. It's a local secret, and it's quicker."

Susie nodded, glad someone was taking control.

"I am just a midwife, Susie," Yvette said. "I don't know if I can help."

They walked the rest of the way in silence. The path was lit only by the moonlight, and the ground along the coast was rocky and uneven. They walked in the darkness along a barely marked track. At some points they passed through other people's gardens, Philippe reaching to the top of fences to retrieve hidden keys. At others the path came right up to the sea, and nothing lay between them and the dark water. All the cottages were dark as they passed, people tucked away in bed. Only the Rowe cottage was lit up, lights glowing in every window.

Lucinda was waiting on the terrace. She rushed over to them. "Please, do what you can, Yvette." Her hands were clasped together at her breast. "They are just young girls." She cast a sympathetic look at Susie, as if she hadn't been blaming her earlier.

Yvette rushed to Isabel's side and knelt beside her. She spoke to her softly, holding her wrist and then checking her eyes. David watched, red-eyed and frantic. He wouldn't look at Susie.

"She's going to be okay, right?" Susie cried.

"Perhaps you should have thought about your friend being okay before you tried to poison her," Lucinda said. "Laburnum!"

Yvette looked at Lucinda, something passing between them. She shook her head slowly.

"What?" Susie asked, her voice rising. She couldn't work out what was going on.

"I think we need to call Gerard," Lucinda said.

"Gerard?" Susie asked. Fear pulsed through her body.

Gerard was the island's gendarme; most of the day he cycled around the island, checking on itinerant campers and giving directions. Susie knew him as Marie's kind husband, who helped in the crêperie at the end of the day, but she didn't know if even he would believe her in the face of all the evidence.

Yvette stood up and took Susie aside. She spoke quietly. "We can make this okay for you, but you need to go now. I can help you. We can help you." She looked to Philippe for confirmation. He looked out the window into the dark night, his eye trained on some point on the horizon across the inky sea. Something out there was favorable, and he nodded.

"There's time," Yvette said. "Go and get your things."

"What?"

"You need to leave." Yvette moved closer. "This family will stop at nothing," she whispered. "You must go. Philippe will explain."

"No. I won't leave. Isabel needs me." The voice was high-pitched, urgent. Susie didn't recognize it as her own. She looked around the room. Isabel, unconscious on the couch. David, eyes only for Isabel, refusing to even look at Susie. And in the middle of it all, Lucinda, shoulders back and a defiant look in her eye. It was her turf, her family. Susie had no choice.

Up in the green bedroom, she threw a few things in her rucksack. She didn't have much; her swimsuit was still drying on the line, and everything else reminded her of the island. She grabbed her camera from the back of the door on the way out.

"We must go now," Philippe said. "It's nearly dawn."

Isabel made another sound, and Lucinda, David, and Yvette crowded around her. They weren't looking at Susie. No one even turned to say goodbye as she walked through the room. She took one last long look around before she left, taking it all in, trying to remember each and every part of the cottage. Her eyes ended on the table; the sketchbook lay there, open, where Lucinda had tossed it aside. Making sure no one was watching—and they still weren't—she snatched it up, a desperate act of resistance. Philippe pulled her out of the cottage, pretending he hadn't seen. In the distance, across the water, a small finger of light crept across the horizon.

Philippe shook his head. "We must hurry. Come on." He led her down the terrace and through a gate at the bottom of the garden that Susie had not seen before. "You are better off to go. Why stay with these people?"

Susie fell silent, tears running endlessly down her face.

They covered the same track they had earlier. At one point, the path rose, and there was a view across the water. Within an hour or so the sun would be up, but in that moment, the ocean was vast and mysterious. They paused to catch their breath.

"They have done this before," Philippe said eventually. "The Rowe family. Yvette and I have fixed things for them another time."

Susie watched him carefully. She remembered David the night he drunkenly goaded Henri into telling old island stories.

"The stolen baby?"

Philippe nodded. "It was a young woman. She looked just like you. Marie thought you were a ghost when she first met you. They sent Henri to see if you were real."

Susie swallowed hard at the sound of his name. "Who was it? What was her name?" she whispered. It *was* tied up with Nellie—it had to be.

"Margaret," Philippe said. "I will never forget her. Rupert brought her to the boat, and she cried all the way back to the mainland. When she got off the boat, I gave her my handkerchief. It was all I had to offer."

"Margaret? My mother?" She didn't know, though. She didn't know anything of her mother's life before her. "My mother was here?"

"It was a woman called Margaret. You look like her. That is all I know."

"Did you tell Lucinda I was here?" She already knew the answer.

"Yvette," Philippe said, simply. He put his head down. "We must walk now."

Philippe took her hand and did not let go, either terrified she would run away or worried she would fall. Every now and then she tripped on the unstable ground and he caught her, his footsteps sure and steady as he traversed the track. She kept her eyes trained on the soft sneaking light of dawn and thought about her mother making the same journey, almost exactly thirty years before to the day.

Eventually they reached the rocks near Philippe and Yvette's house. His boat was tied to the dock, bouncing and ready to sail. There was no one else around.

"Thank God," Philippe muttered as they approached. "We made it."

It was hard to discern the colors of the boat in the dim light, but Susie remembered it. Red and green and blue. Henri told her he had helped to paint it at the beginning of the summer, and he would help to paint it again before he left the island for home. Henri. She hadn't given him a chance to explain. She hadn't had a chance to say goodbye.

For a heartbeat, she was tempted to turn around and run: to go back to the cottage and make sure Isabel was okay; to find Henri and let him explain about what she had seen; to force Lucinda to admit there was a connection between her family and the Rowes. There would be only trouble waiting for her, though; that much was clear. The Île de Clair cast its spell over many, but like the fairy tales Nellie had told her as a child, it wasn't always enchanting. There was poison in the apple; there were curses across generations.

Philippe climbed into the boat and held out his hand for her. The boat rocked and rolled in the changing of the tides. Susie took a deep breath and climbed aboard. She took one last look at the familiar terrain before Philippe motioned for her to sit inside the tiny cabin. In the few short minutes it took Philippe to prepare the vessel for sailing, she made a promise to herself. One day, when she knew what had happened to Isabel, she would tell her mother about what she had found on the island. She would make things right.

Phillipe smiled, a thin rope of a smile that asked for something Susie wasn't ready to give. Instead, she took the sketchbook out of her rucksack and felt its weight for the last time. With a heavy heart, she handed it over.

"Can you give this to Henri?" she asked. "It should be here on the island. Not with me. Ask him to keep it safe."

And then the little boat pitched forward and out past the waves. Within moments the tiny island of Île de Clair was fading into the distance.

54

Camilla

Isabel looked exactly the same as she had in the photo. "You're alive?" Camilla said. "I mean, you're alive." She didn't know what else to say. She didn't know if she was relieved or angry or confused or all three.

"Yes, I'm alive." Isabel looked a little confused. "Why wouldn't I be?"

"Susie thought you were dead." *Susie thought you were dead*. She felt a bolt of sympathy for her sister, carrying that guilt her whole life. Meanwhile, life appeared to carry on in bucolic bliss here for David and Isabel. Oh, anger. That's what she felt.

"The last night on the island," David explained, and Isabel's eyes opened a little wider. Then her expression clouded over.

"Henri tried to explain a little about what happened that night," Camilla said, "but he didn't know all of it."

Isabel flushed. "I can explain."

"I'd like that." Camilla sat back, crossed her arms. She felt her mother's eyes upon her.

"David said that Susie . . . that Susie . . ."

"Passed away." Camilla was losing patience with Isabel. The way she looked at David from under her lashes, constantly searching for reassurance. Encouragement. She didn't understand why Susie had been so fond of the girl.

"I can't believe it." A tear formed in the corner of her eye. "I always thought there was a chance I might see her again."

"Why didn't you?" Camilla asked, bitterly.

"David and I made an agreement, after that summer, that we would move on, leave everything behind us. Susie. Henri. Lucinda and Rupert. The cottage. It was too complicated." David took her hand and squeezed it, encouraging her to continue.

"Susie wanted to move on, too, but she couldn't."

Isabel shrugged. "We are very private people, but we haven't hidden away. We have always been here. She could have sent us a letter. If she knew."

"She was scared. Worried she would be somehow implicated in your death." Camilla took a deep breath and explained the letters from Susie. The task she had undertaken with the ashes. When she finished, Isabel looked moved.

"I wanted to make contact over the years. I really did. But we decided it was better for everyone if we didn't." She reached across and took David's teacup, bolted down the liquid. "We had an intense relationship, Susie and I. From the moment we met, there was an instant connection. She was good fun, opinionated. I admired her, traveling across the world on her own. She didn't answer to anyone. I wanted to be more like her."

Camilla glared at Margaret as she nodded in agreement.

"That night, though, the end." She blinked, remembering. "There was a fair in the village." She glanced in his direction. "I paid for us both to see a fortune-teller. It was meant to be a bit of fun."

Camilla shifted in her chair. Susie had always given too much credence to the mystical side of life. If anyone was going to let a fortune-teller influence her, it was Susie.

"I went first." Isabel looked nervously at David. "I'll give you some background. I was a student of David's, back when he was a teacher. I had just finished school that summer. David was twenty-nine?" She looked at David, who nodded. Margaret nodded as well. "We fell in love while I was still a student, and things moved along quite quickly. David invited me to the Île de Clair for the summer, so I went."

"What did your parents think of that?" Camilla asked.

"What did your parents think of Susie going to Europe on her own?" Isabel batted back. Camilla flinched. "Things between David and me were serious, but he encouraged me to take my time, maybe travel for a little while. Actually, Susie and I were planning to spend some time in Italy and Greece, before everything happened."

"The fortune-teller?" Camilla prompted her.

"The fortune-teller told me I was going to die young."

Camilla snorted. Margaret tapped her on the hand. A warning.

"I know, I know. I was eighteen! I'd had a few drinks. She told me I was going to die *very* young." She looked nervously at David.

"And you believed her?"

"Have you ever had your fortune told?" Isabel snapped.

Camilla looked at the ground. "No," she mumbled.

"It's really *convincing*. This woman, it was like she saw beyond my bravado and picked out all my insecurities. She knew what she was doing."

"Did you tell Susie?"

"Yes." A pause. "Maybe that's why she was so certain I was dead."

Margaret made a sympathetic noise. Isabel smiled weakly.

David coughed. "Isabel doesn't really remember anything after that." He looked apologetic. "We ate dinner at the cottage. Mother, Isabel, Lucinda, and me. I was exhausted, so I went to bed. Later that night I woke up to shouting, and came downstairs. It took me a while to work out what was happening. Isabel was unconscious on the sofa, and Susie was hysterical."

"Isabel was unconscious?" Margaret looked alarmed.

"Things moved quickly after that. Isabel wasn't well. She was feverish, vomiting. I got the impression that Susie had done something to her. That's what my mother was saying, and there was evidence of it, broken up seedpods on the table and scattered about." David shifted in his chair. "Susie went to fetch Yvette—there were no doctors on the island, and I suppose she thought Yvette might be able to help."

"Laburnum!" Margaret snorted. "That won't kill you. Susie should have known that. Might give you a little fright." She sat back. "Labur-num." She shook her head.

"But why would Susie poison Isabel? From what I can gather, and from what you've told me tonight, she loved Isabel." Camilla was try-ing to piece it all together.

For a moment David and Isabel looked uncomfortable. "We think, well, it seemed Susie was in love with David and was jealous of my relationship with him," Isabel started. "She followed him to the island, you know—he hadn't given any indication that he was available. For a little while she was distracted with Henri, but he lost interest in her, and she felt humiliated, I suppose. She took it out on me."

"David," Margaret interrupted. "This has gone on long enough."

"Mrs. Anderson, I know it's tough to hear." David turned his at-tention toward Margaret and gave her an apologetic smile. "We liked Susie. That's why we let it go."

"Has your mother never explained to you about the night you were born?" Margaret asked, her eyes trained on David.

"Oh yes, the story is deeply engrained in the Rowe family mythol-ogy," David started, his chest puffing a little.

"August tenth, 1998, at the cottage on the Île de Clair," Margaret interrupted, speaking softly. "Happy birthday, David."

David's mouth dropped open, his chest instantly deflating. "Fifty-one today," he said, when he regained his composure. "How did you know?"

"You see, David," Margaret said, leaning down and fiddling with her shoelace, "I was there that evening as well. I spent the summer on the island with your parents as we prepared for the birth of my child, a child that I had willingly agreed to let your parents adopt. We signed an agreement, which I assume was ferreted away by the family solic-itor who arranged it all. A Mr. Carter, I recall."

David swallowed, looked at Isabel.

"What does it mean, David?"

"I don't know, Iz, let me think a moment."

"Does any of that sound familiar, David?"

"There were rumblings before that summer," he said quietly. "Stories that my parents had stolen a baby. My mother said it was all gossip, rumors the island people started because they didn't want us there. But that summer, things started to turn. One, Susie arrived and shook things up a little. My mother swore she was deluded." He looked out across the meadow. "Then that autumn, they gave up the cottage on the island. Simply handed it over to Yvette and Philippe and wouldn't explain why."

Margaret nodded. "Yvette was there on the night you were born. She helped them to arrange it all."

"You never asked them about the cottage?" Camilla interjected. "I thought you were all obsessed with the place."

Margaret was doing something to her foot again. Camilla wanted to tell her to concentrate.

Both Isabel and David looked guilty. "We thought it was for the best. We came here instead, to Pond Cottage. And after that, we never left."

"Aha!" Margaret held her foot up in triumph.

"Mum, stop. What are you doing?"

"Let me see your feet, David," Margaret said.

Isabel gasped. "She's got them too, David—the toes."

Begrudgingly David looked down. His cheeks pulsed a little. "My mother said it was very common."

"*Common* was one of her favorite words." Margaret put her head on the side. "Wasn't it?"

David was very still. Down by the river, a fisherman called out. Then a big splash. A cheer.

"It's okay, David. It's a lot to take in. We'll leave you to think things over." Margaret stood to leave. "I'm going to stay up at the hotel for a few days, and if you want to talk to me, you can call on me up there. Come on, Camilla, let's leave these two in peace."

"No." Camilla felt the anger like a hot current through her body. Normally when she felt like this she would breathe, remind herself to stay calm, count to ten, but today she wanted to feel the anger and use it. She let it build up, and then she unleashed it on the two stunned strangers in front of her.

"Susie lived with the guilt of what happened to you for the rest of her life, Isabel—you know that, don't you?" She pointed at each of them in turn. "The least you could have done was let her know you were okay. She wanted me to apologize to you, Isabel, for abandoning you that night, but she's the one who deserves an apology. My sister wouldn't poison anyone! Anyone could work out that it was Lucinda, trying to cover her tracks!"

It was hard to shake the image of Susie leaving the island, alone and fearful. Not for the first time, Camilla wished she had pushed her more on what had happened on her trip. She doubted she would have believed all this, though; she would have dismissed it as another of her sister's fantastical concepts. She still hardly knew what to believe, even with the sketchbook and the stories.

Margaret took her hand and gave it a squeeze. "And yet she wanted us to find them. That says something, don't you think, Camilla? That she hadn't given up on them?"

Camilla opened her mouth, but nothing came out. Instead she took the sketchbook from her bag and handed it wordlessly to David before turning to leave.

55

Margaret

"Wait!" David shouted, and then for a moment he was struck dumb, holding the sketchbook in his trembling hands. The others held their breath as he turned it over and over again, as if trying to work out if it was real.

"Don't go," he added. "I always wondered where this went. It disappeared after, well, everything. With everything else that happened that night, I thought it must have been destroyed. Stolen. I was bereft. But I didn't want to make a fuss, not when . . ." His voice petered out. He flicked through some pages at random, and then he went back to the beginning and very carefully turned each page over again.

Without being invited, Margaret pulled her chair closer to David's and gestured for Camilla to do the same. Her children were together. Her children! She needed them to appreciate just how marvelous this was. Camilla was angry, yes. Margaret appreciated that. And she expected David would take some time to come around, as well.

"Where did you get this?" he asked, as he paused on a painting of his father coming out of the ocean. "This one I did from memory. Dad swimming down at Rupert's Regret."

"Rupert's what?" Margaret asked.

"The small beach closest to the cottage. Dad named it." A small smile danced across Margaret's lips. She remembered the night David was born, her midnight swim with Rupert. Maybe he was closer to changing his mind and coming away with her than she thought.

"Henri had it," Camilla said matter-of-factly, interrupting her reverie. Margaret could see that she was still fuming.

"Henri?" David looked puzzled. He turned a few pages, looking for something, and then came to the missing page. "Henri." He exhaled. Margaret moved closer again so she could look over his shoulder as he leafed through the book. David smelled of turpentine up close, and firewood, and something else. Perfume. It was dark, musky, incongruous with David and the surroundings. She leaned in, inhaled deeply. "That fragrance . . ." She knew it. Oh, did she know it.

David leaned back a little. Blushed. "You recognize the scent?"

"I could never forget it." He held her gaze for a moment, his eyes questioning, but Margaret was far away in a garden. The feeling of skin on skin. Twilight. Cold grass. She swallowed, returning to herself, to the present. Camilla was watching her.

"My mother wore it. It was my father's first, but my mother adopted it as her own. She was always ahead of her time."

"It's very strong. It's making me feel quite dizzy," Margaret said. She took a moment to swallow a maelstrom of emotions before turning her attention back to the book. "I can't imagine how it must feel to wear it."

David flicked past paintings of daily life on the Île de Clair. Pictures of Susie and more of Isabel. Close-ups of the island flowers; imagined shipwrecks. The sea in varying shades of blue, the shadows of the watercolors light and multitudinous against the deep grain of the thick paper.

"What do you think?" Camilla was losing patience.

"You say Henri had it?" David asked. He stopped on the picture of Susie and Isabel on the beach, one hand protectively placed on the page. He thought about it for a bit. "I wonder if Yvette was threatening my mother with it? And that's why she gave up the house?"

"To be honest, I think Yvette had more on your mother than the sketchbook," Margaret said. She told him the story of the history between Lucinda and Yvette.

David sat back and thought about it. "It makes sense." He nodded thoughtfully. "My mother—Lucinda—has always been very determined." He stopped for a moment and looked Margaret in the eye. "I'm sorry I believed what my mother told me about Susie."

Margaret waved a hand at him. "Oh, I would have believed her too. She could be very convincing. She persuaded me to give you up, after all."

"I appreciate your saying that," David said slowly, the words forming almost visibly. "But the thought of all this being true is deeply upsetting to me. This is my family. My mother, despite her faults, did her best for me when I was a child. My father and I are still very close. In fact, he is rather ill at the moment, and I plan to head to London to see him this week. I hate to think what all this would do to him."

Camilla stood up and gathered up the tea things. "Isabel and I will take these to the kitchen, if you like." She gave Margaret a pointed look as she passed.

Margaret waited until the door closed behind Camilla. "This part is hard for me to admit, David. I'm not proud of it. I was young. We all make mistakes."

"There's more?" His face went a shade of gray.

Margaret told him the story of meeting Rupert, and how she came to fall pregnant. When she finished, David stood up and walked over to the edge of the covered loggia.

"I must say, this is all a terrible shock."

"I know."

"And Susie set this in motion from beyond the grave? Did she want you to find me?"

Margaret registered the doubt in his voice. She went over to join him, standing as close as seemed permissible. "I wanted to find you over the years, but I was frightened. Lucinda was capable of anything to protect you—she loved you—and still does, I imagine, very much."

Something twitched in David's cheek. He wouldn't look at her.

"Why do you think Susie went to so much trouble to bring you here?" He nodded in the direction of the house.

"I'm not meant to be here. She wanted Camilla to come on her own.

I think she wanted to somehow check on Isabel, that she wanted you to have the sketchbook. She knew Camilla would sort things out, that Camilla needed this trip."

"Why did you come, then?"

"I knew it would lead her to you."

David sighed. He needed a moment.

"Does my father know about you? About me?"

"Yes. He does."

"What about my mother?"

"She does now. We visited her yesterday. She didn't phone you?"

"I don't have a phone here. One of the perks of the valley. I have a mobile, but it only works when I walk up near the hotel."

"Sounds heavenly."

"Yes." He was distracted, the phone the least of his concern. Margaret sat quietly and let him think, enjoying the sensation of being close—so close—to her son after all these years. It was enough to sit there.

The door slammed, interrupting the silence. Camilla reappeared on the patio, looking out of breath.

"Mum—there's something inside I think you should see." She looked at David, her face flushed. "Sorry. I wasn't snooping."

"Christ, you Anderson women are all the same." David shook his head. "Find something interesting in my sock drawer, did you?"

"Sorry! It's on the wall. It was just *there*."

Margaret followed Camilla and David into the cottage. It was dark after the brilliant sunshine. As Margaret's eyes adjusted, she noticed signs of life. A humming fridge, a television muted in the corner. Other than that, the cottage bore little signs of the twenty-first century.

"It was through here." Camilla looked guilty as they followed her into the next room.

The room looked out the other direction, over a small vegetable garden, and despite the humble outside of the cottage, the walls were lined with ornate wood paneling. Some of it was taken up by honor boards, the names etched in gold script and stopping abruptly in 1997. The rest of the walls were covered in photos, mostly of people holding their catches aloft. Black-and-white photos of men in traditional attire gave way to some color shots, the portraits faded by time but the joy still evident on the faces of the fishermen. Isabel was waiting, her eyes shining.

"This one," Camilla said, drawing them toward one photo in particular. Unlike the others, it was framed and placed on a sideboard. "I noticed it because it was on its own. It's so weird—the woman looks like Grandma Nellie."

Margaret felt her heart begin to race as she picked it up. There was no doubt it was her mother. Even though the photo was black and white, she was glowing, holding a large salmon triumphantly and smiling for whoever was holding the camera. She turned over the frame, and someone had written on the back: "Nellie, 1945."

Margaret gasped.

"It's her, isn't it?"

"Your grandmother?" David came closer. "That's John's writing."

"John Digby?"

"Yes."

A calm descended over Margaret. The sight of her mother beaming in the photograph solidified something inside, a sureness that Pond Cottage was somehow connected to her. She felt a great affinity with the place, and now, seeing the photo of her mother not just beaming but glowing from within, she knew why. Her mother had been happy here.

Margaret was quiet, looking at the photo of her mother. "She looks so happy. Radiant. I never saw her look like that. Not once."

They stood in silence for a moment.

"I have one question," David said after a little bit.

"Yes?" Camilla said, softening toward him.

"Just one?" Isabel asked. Camilla had forgotten she was there.

"Did Susie want her ashes scattered here as well?" He looked around at the acres of green and garden surrounding them. "I mean, it's lovely, but she's never been here."

Camilla looked at her mother. "Well, she did," she began, "but I tipped them all out on the beach on the Île de Clair. You can't always do what your sister wants."

56

Camilla

"Where's your ring?" Camilla had noticed her mother's bare finger when she first arrived at Matilda Downs but waited until the right moment to ask. The boys always liked to run around the garden as soon as they arrived, to stretch their legs after the long journey and to check on the hiding places and dens they'd created on their last visit. Ian was following them, ever diligent, checking for snakes, wombat holes, and all the other myriad hazards of the outback. With them occupied, her mother would be able to answer freely.

Margaret passed her a gin and tonic and sat down on the old wicker chair next to her, the soft cushion expanding under her weight. She took a sip of her drink and smiled, wiggling her fingers. "It feels strange to be without it, to be honest. It was mine for twenty years."

"You gave it to David?"

"And I assume he will give it to Isabel."

Camilla, being the eldest child, had always thought the ring would come to her. It was Nellie's and then Margaret's, and now it was David's. It felt strange to no longer be her mother's eldest child. With a jolt, she realized that she was also now her mother's youngest child. The family dynamic she had always relied on, nodding with recognition as she read about typical character traits of firstborns, had shifted and tipped under her feet. It was exactly how she suspected Susie would feel if someone had told her she was no longer a Cancerian.

Margaret had stayed on at the hotel in Devon for a few more days after Camilla left to fly home. It had been time for Camilla to return to her family, in the same way it was time for Margaret to be there for hers.

"We spoke to a woman who worked at the estate for years. She remembered Mum well."

"That must have been nice."

Margaret pursed her lips slightly, and Camilla realized that *nice* was too basic a word to describe the emotions Margaret would have experienced over the last few months, beginning with Susie's death and leading to now, sitting on her veranda with her grandchildren playing cricket in front of her, enjoying the sunny respite from the winter dragging out along the east coast of the country.

"How are things with Ian?" Margaret asked, as the man in question delivered a slow ball to his eldest son.

"How did you know?"

"I know what it's like to try and be strong." Margaret placed her hand on Camilla's back, kneading the tension gathered in the muscle. "There's no shame in being softer, Mills." There was a loosening, the slow exhale of the breath leaving her body. It felt like she had been holding it since Susie died. "If you're soft, you can bend. You can stretch. If you're too hard, you snap."

Camilla considered this. She always thought her mother's strength was what had gotten her through the tough years of raising a family with a distant husband and dried-up finances. The idea that it was softness shifted Camilla's view of her mother. It shifted her view of herself.

"It's too soon to tell," she said, honestly. Ian had agreed to accompany her on this trip, missing school and sports practices and piano lessons to come. When they returned home on Monday, their lives would start to become more normal again. Normal, apart from the fact that, for now, Camilla would be staying in a small serviced apartment near the school. Normal, apart from the fact that Camilla would need to rebuild her relationship with Ian.

The five letters—they had left Henri's with him on the Île—sat between them on the table for a moment while they watched the kids. Oliver was batting, and Timmy was bowling. Ian was fielding. Oliver blocked the shot, almost bowled out by his younger brother.

"That Timmy has a good arm," her mother finally said.

"What are you saying?" Camilla smiled.

"I'm just not sure who he gets that from. That's all."

"Not from me, that's for sure."

Camilla picked up the glass of gin from the table. "Whoa!" Margaret had made them in Nellie's old brandy glasses, like she always did, but the condensation was moving quickly in the heat, and the little glasses were slippery.

"The letters, Mum."

"All of them?"

"Yep."

"Do you want me to read them?"

Camilla nodded, and they sat quietly while her mother read the five letters in order. The view of the garden was lush from where they sat, but beyond the borders the land was hostile. Her mother had created a sanctuary, and Camilla was only starting to understand just how hard that must have been.

When Margaret was done, she folded up each letter and put them in a neat pile on the table.

"I always knew you girls did something to the screen door. It was never quite the same after your acrobatic period."

"After reading all five letters, that's all you have to say?"

"Oh, there's plenty more I want to say." Margaret raised her eyebrows. "The first being, don't take these letters to heart too much, Mills. We don't know if she ever wanted us to read them. Not for sure. Susie was one for grand gestures. She could have been just as likely to tear these all up a week later had she not . . ." Her voice trailed off.

A cheer went up among the boys. Bill had come in from his jobs and taken a catch coming through the gate. He looked older, the stress of the last few weeks having taken its toll on him. Camilla waved at him, and his face was transformed by a big smile. He came toward them and picked up one of the extra drinks from the table.

"I'll be right back, ladies," he said, clinking his glass against Margaret's and Camilla's in turn. "I'm needed on the field." He took up a position near the barbecue.

"So, Mum, Susie wanted me to tell you about the journey," Camilla joked, buoyed by her father's happiness.

Margaret chuckled. "Bit late for that." They both sipped their drinks, lost in their own thoughts for a moment.

"How did it all go with David, in the end?"

"It took a couple of days. I guess he needed to work through it on his own."

"What about Lucinda and Rupert? Did David talk to them?"

"He went to see them in London after he dropped me at the airport. Lucinda admitted everything. She even admitted to drugging both Susie and Isabel, but she asked David not to tell Rupert. Apparently, he's very frail."

"Hold on, drugging Susie and Isabel?"

Margaret's voice caught slightly. "She gave them both sleeping pills apparently, but told Susie that Isabel had ingested laburnum." They both looked at the innocuous but majestic plant in front of them.

"Laburnum?"

Margaret nodded sadly. The one at Matilda Downs wasn't as resplendent as the one on the terrace on the Île de Clair, but the yellow flowers were in bloom, the wilt in the leaves hard to see from a distance.

"She also told David that her brother Laurence died in 1944."

"So he couldn't be . . . ?"

"No." Margaret squeezed her hand. They watched the children for a moment.

"Did she say who it was?"

"No. But I have an idea." Margaret smiled to herself.

Camilla had one more question for her mother. "Did you love Rupert?"

Margaret checked that Bill was out of earshot.

"Yes, I think I did."

"What did Dad say when you told him about David?"

"He was okay. He was more upset that Susie had dealt with the whole thing on her own. He always had a soft spot for Susie." Margaret sensed a change in the atmosphere. "And I always had a soft spot for you." She reached over and put her arm around Camilla.

"Will you see David again?"

"I hope so. He said he may come to Australia to visit."

"Will you see Rupert again?"

"I might just remember Rupert as he was in 1968, I think." Her little Jack Russell wandered past, and she picked him up and put him in her lap, absentmindedly stroking him. "What are you going to do about the ashes?" she asked, watching Camilla carefully.

"Luckily I didn't take them all with me," Camilla said. "There were so many! I hadn't realized how many there would be." She pulled a small pouch out of her dress pocket. It was her yellow dress from the Île de Clair; it seemed just as well suited to outback life as it did the island.

"I was shocked too, when I collected Nellie's," Margaret agreed.

"I didn't realize Nellie was here," Camilla said, nodding at the laburnum.

Margaret looked over her shoulder, smiling a little.

"What?" Camilla asked, sensing her mother was holding something back.

"I never did it. Even though she asked me to scatter her ashes here, I couldn't help thinking she was just being kind. Asking to be near me. Something was holding me back."

"And?"

"I took a little of her with me on the trip. Just in case. Susie and Mum were always so close, and those letters made me think she knew something I didn't."

"Ha! So you didn't just come to help me. I knew it!" Camilla was smiling though. "And did you find somewhere to leave her?"

"The stream at Pond Cottage. I thought it was fitting."

Camilla squeezed her mother's hand and the dog whimpered in protest.

"I've got some left, though. I thought we could scatter them together."

There was a roar from the lawn. Timmy had knocked one up in the air, and Oliver caught him out. There was a brief scuffle over who was going to bat next.

"Do you think Susie would have been happy with us?" It was a thought that had plagued Camilla ever since she got home. Sure, she had visited all the places Susie had asked her to go, and she had delivered the ashes to the requested locations, but she had gone off-piste at some points, and she hadn't done it alone.

"Well, we'll never know," Margaret said. "We did our best." From the side, with the soft afternoon sun on her face, she looked more like Nellie than ever. The children were starting to tire of the cricket game. The sound of bickering floated across the lawn, interspersed with Bill's calm remonstrations.

"I wish she was here," Camilla said.

"Me too," Margaret agreed, "me too." Camilla reached over and squeezed her hand, not sure if her mother was thinking about Susie or someone else entirely.

"The sun's about to set." Margaret sat forward and drained her glass. "It's time."

"Sure." Camilla and Margaret stood up just as the children finished their game and flopped down in the cool grass.

"Are you ready?" Margaret asked.

"I'm ready." Ashes in hand, they walked down the steps and joined the rest of the family under the shade of the laburnum tree.

Letter Six

Lucky last and home sweet home.

Matilda Downs
You know the way from here

xox

Hello,

One last note from me. It's taken me a long time to write this last letter.

I've asked you to do a lot of things over the years, and you've always done them for me, even things I shouldn't have asked and you should probably never have done. This is the last thing, I promise. It's also the most important thing.

I want you to take the last of my ashes home to Matilda Downs. Nellie is there, waiting for me under the laburnum tree in the garden. Mum scattered her ashes under the tree in 1998, and I'd like to join her.

Wait until the afternoon sun slips into the gentle pink glow of twilight. It was always my favorite time of the day anywhere in the world, the ordinariness of daytime slipping into the glittering possibilities of evening. Have a gin and tonic with Mum and tell her about your journey. Tell her about David. I know you will do a better job of it than I ever could.

A letter from Nellie started me on this journey. Maybe she sent me to the gallery simply to broaden my horizons, or maybe she hoped seeing the painting would set this chain of events in motion. I'll never know. Sending me in search of the Rowe family secrets seems a long shot, and besides, you were always the historian, not me. You would have been a better foot soldier. But maybe Nellie thought that I was the Anderson woman for the job. These letters are my way of not letting her down.

Mills, we've had our issues over the years. I know I haven't been the sister you wanted me to be. It felt like our roles in life were set out early, you so capable and reliable and me, well, the opposite. As each year passes, it feels harder to step out of the molds we've made for ourselves, but one thing these last few months has told me is that a leopard can change its spots. I'm saving money and working hard. I've met someone, and it's going well. You don't have to always be the person that other people expect of you.

I've dreamed about you making this journey for years, wondering how I could make it happen. I imagine you in London, walking up and down the streets, stopping for every blue plaque, soaking up the history and the stories that you love so much. Then, stepping off the ferry on the Île de Clair in the bright summer sunshine. Tasting the sweet and sour of the crêpes, feeling the salty evening breezes as the island winds down for the night. Even if you didn't go, I've had the pleasure of imagining you there.

Perhaps I will never know what happened to Isabel. I've accepted that, and I've lived with the guilt of what might have happened all these years.

I ran away that night when things got hard. When I got home, no one asked any questions. Once I realized how easy it was to run away from things, I kept on doing it. The problem is, you leave a lot of people behind that way. I left Isabel behind, and Henri and David, and countless others in my life, but I could never leave you. You bore the brunt of it—the lucky recipient of my repeat offenses. For better or for worse, I could never run away from you.

You're probably wondering why I didn't ask Mum to do this. I wanted to send you ahead like a kind of emissary. You and Mum have always been so close, and I think it will be better if she hears about this from you. Like always! And yes, I'm thinking of the time we (I) broke the screen door/started the grass fire/ran up an enormous phone bill on the horoscope hotline. You always knew how to get me out of trouble.

The women in our family hold so many secrets, and our secrets hold so much power over us. You were always so clear, so clean—I didn't want to burden you with them. Now I see that these secrets don't have to be a burden. They may help you to understand me and why I came to rely so much on you over the years. You were my lightness, my reassurance that people didn't always mess up or make mistakes. That's too much to ask of a person.

I'm sharing this story with you, hoping that the journey changes your perspective a little and, more than anything, Mills, gives you permission to let go.

Your lightness has always been your gift to me. Now I'm giving you my darkness. I know you can handle it.

All my love,
Susie

Acknowledgments

Many thanks, as ever, to Sara Nelson at HarperCollins for her endless patience and insightful feedback on every single draft. And thank you to my agent Rob Weisbach for his tireless encouragement and ongoing support. It's always a pleasure—and such fun!—to work with you both.

Thank you to Miranda Ottewell for editing with such a keen eye.

In Australia, thank you to Jo McKay and the rest of the team at HQ and HarperCollins Australia. My special thanks to the sales team who got *The House of Brides* into bookstores as well as the booksellers who then helped get it into readers' hands.

Thank you to Kirsty Manning, Lisa Ireland, and Sally Hepworth, who remain the best author friends anyone could hope for, and are amazing for both writerly advice and funny, funny stories.

Around twenty years ago, on a family trip to Ireland, my aunt Helen O'Keefe suggested the idea of a grand tour for scattering ashes. Thank you for this nugget of inspiration, which burrowed its way into my subconscious and then on into this book.

And lastly and always, thank you to the extended Chisholm and Cockram clans and, of course, to the most special people in my life: Wally, Alice, and Edward.

About the Author

Jane Cockram was born and educated in Australia. After studying journalism at university, she worked in the publishing industry, fulfilling a childhood dream of reading for a living. Her first book, *The House of Brides*, was published in 2019. She lives in Melbourne with her husband, two children, and a frisky Labrador.